Praise for *Dating Dead Men*

"*Dating Dead Men*, Harley Jane Kozak's hilarious debut novel, proves that the search for love can be as funny as it is deadly, as it ricochets from one madcap misadventure after another with the speed of a bullet and the uproarious fun of a three-ring circus. An absolutely delightful tale, told with warmth and charm."

—KRIS NERI, author of the Agatha, Anthony and
Macavity Award–nominated Tracy Eaton mysteries

"*Dating Dead Men* is the funniest mystery I've read in ages. Any woman who has ever wondered how many more Mr. Wrongs she'll have to date to meet Mr. Right will love this book."

—JAN BURKE, author of *Nine*

"*Dating Dead Men* is a page-turning romp alive with fresh, quirky characters and inventive situations that left me anxious for another date with Wollie Shelley, provided author Harley Jane Kozak is amenable next time around to a man who's still breathing."

—ROBERT S. LEVINSON, author of *Hot Paint* and
The John Lennon Affair

"Harley Jane Kozak fashions a doozy of a debut, starring cars, cads, clothes, and an L.A. gone hilariously mad."

—MARY DAHEIM, author of *The Alpine Pursuit*

"Wollie Shelley, Kozak's entrepreneur extraordinaire, manages to deal with a murder, the Mafia, an appealing but mysterious love interest, and a killer who wants to see her dead, all with originality and humor."

—LEE HARRIS, author of *Murder in Hell's Kitchen*

"Lots of action, quirky characters, an engaging new sleuth who designs greeting cards, and a ferret named Margaret—what more could any reader want? *Dating Dead Men* is a superb debut."

—VALERIE WOLZIEN, author of *A Fashionable Murder*

dating dead men

dating dead men

Harley Jane Kozak

Broadway Books

New York

BROADWAY

A hardcover edition of this book was originally published in 2004 by Doubleday, a division of Random House, Inc. It is here reprinted by arrangement with Doubleday.

PRINTED IN THE UNITED STATES OF AMERICA

BROADWAY BOOKS and its logo, a letter B bisected on the diagonal, are trademarks of Random House, Inc.

Visit our website at www.broadwaybooks.com

First Broadway Books trade paperback edition published 2005

Book design by Chris Welch

The Library of Congress has cataloged the hardcover as:
Kozak, Harley Jane, 1957–
Dating dead men / Harley Jane Kozak.—1st ed.
p. cm.
1. Women artists—Fiction. 2. Commercial artists—Fiction. 3. Greeting cards industry—Fiction. I. Title.
PS3611.O75D37 2004
813'.6—dc21
2003046236

ISBN 0-7679-2123-2

1 3 5 7 9 10 8 6 4 2

To Greg Aldisert,
my last blind date

dating dead men

chapter one

I t was a cigarette burn.

I could scarcely have been more shocked if I'd discovered it on my own flesh, appearing out of nowhere, like stigmata. But it wasn't on me. It was on my grass green carpet, Aisle 3, Condolences/Get Well Soon, where I knelt, rooted in horror.

"Dear God," I said. "Dear God. Dear God."

"Girl, get a grip," Fredreeq called out, barging through the front door of my shop, Wollie's Welcome! Greetings. "I can hear those 'Dear Gods' all the way out to the parking lot. Did someone die? Is it Mr. Bundt? Please tell me Mr. Bundt died and I can take the day off and go to the beach."

"He's not dead. He's due here any minute. I was doing the final Dustbusting, and look, *look*—" I waved at the carpet. "At the last inspection, Mr. Bundt questioned the decor. I told him it was French Provincial. I can't pass this off as French Provincial."

"No." Fredreeq loomed over me. "Cigarette burns are strictly Trailer Park. White Trash, no offense." She leaned down, sending a wave of Shalimar my way. "That's one hell of a burn. That is the mother of all cigarette burns. That's a cigar burn."

I looked up at my friend and employee, took in her attire, and said it again. "Dear God."

Earrings the size of teacups dangled from delicate earlobes. Zebra-print stockings stretched from the hem of a very short, very tight skirt to a pair of velvet stiletto heels.

"Yeah, I know, I'm pushing the envelope here." Fredreeq straightened up and moved to the cash register counter. "Is it the stockings? You think bare legs are better?"

It was a tough call. I wasn't wearing panty hose myself, but I had on a long calico skirt and socks and red high-tops. Also a red sweater with a dalmatian appliqué. It had seemed like a good outfit an hour earlier, but now I wasn't so sure. I'm over five foot eleven. Next to Fredreeq, I could look like a piece of playground equipment.

"Maybe," I said, and turned to scratch at the cigarette burn with my fingernail. "You're black, which I always think makes the high heels–no stockings look—"

"Less slutlike?"

"No," I said, "just more—"

At that moment, Mr. Bundt walked through the door of Wollie's Welcome! Greetings, setting the Welcome! greeting bell to ringing. I jumped to my feet, planting a red high-top right on the cigarette burn. "Good morning, Mr. Bundt," I said. "Welcome."

A pink carnation graced the lapel of his beige Big and Tall suit. There was something incandescent about Mr. Bundt, his skull as shiny as his wing tips, the few strands of hair combed neatly, slightly damply over the top of his head, like one long eyebrow. He saw me and smiled, and for a minute I thought it was going to be all right, but then he saw Fredreeq. Well, he could hardly miss her. She was sitting on the counter, a bunched-up chunk of stocking hanging from one foot as she struggled to get a stiletto heel off the other.

Mr. Bundt stared for a moment and then—and here's what I admired about him—he turned and began inspecting the Welcome! Greetings racks, beginning with Birthdays, Juvenile. If there was a Welcome! way to handle every situation in life, this man, either from instinct or training, knew exactly what it was. Mr. Bundt was the field representative for the Welcome! Greetings Corporation, devoting his life to inspecting all Welcome! shops seeking an upgrade to Willkommen! status. Willkommen! status allowed Welcome! shop managers to buy their shops. This was what I longed for. This was the stuff my dreams were made of. This man held a piece of my life in his hands.

Mr. Bundt dropped out of sight behind the Condolences/Get Well Soon rack, checking stock in the bottom drawer. I motioned to Fredreeq to hurry up with her changing routine.

"Wollie," his disembodied voice said, "is this Frank Sinatra?"

For a minute I thought he meant in the drawer. Then I realized he meant on the stereo.

"Yes," I said. " 'That's Life.' The song, as well as the album."

Mr. Bundt rose, his skull appearing slowly from behind the card rack. "Wouldn't we be safer with easy listening? Here in Los Angeles, KXEZ." Mr. Bundt was based in Cincinnati, yet knew every major easy listening station in his territory, North America. It was a gift.

"Frank Sinatra isn't—safe?" I asked.

"No one is safe, Miss Shelley." His sudden use of my surname chilled me. "No album, no CD. Not for a manager who seeks to change her shop from a Welcome! to a Willkommen!"

Willkommen! The word acted upon me like a bell to Pavlov's dog. I stared at him, poised to respond appropriately.

"KXEZ radio can be trusted," he explained. "They have done their market research. Even their advertisements provide reassurance. Favorite albums, on the other hand, are expressions of personal taste that run the risk of—"

"Mr. Bundt, blame me," Fredreeq called out. "I keep changing the music on her. Easy listening is very difficult for my people."

Mr. Bundt pretended to just now notice Fredreeq. She'd moved behind the counter, where, from the waist up, she looked almost normal. "Yes, well," he said. "The music is not for you, Ms. Munson, but for the customer. Let's remember that key phrase in our company's Promise to the Public: 'We are here to soothe, not to offend.' "

"Is headquarters aware that there are people offended by banality?" Fredreeq asked.

He did not respond. I thought maybe he wasn't sure what "banality" meant but didn't want to ask. I was a little fuzzy on it myself. I gestured to Fredreeq, who hit the stop button on the music system, cutting off Frank mid-note. For a moment there was silence, except for the sound of a distant car alarm on Sunset Boulevard.

And so we were all able to hear, very clearly, when the phone machine clicked on—the ringer having been turned off—and a voice choked out the words, "Wollie? It's me. Murder, Wollie. *Murder.* Cold blood. He's talking, he doesn't know I'm here, I'm going to have to—no. No. *NO—*"

Within seconds I was across the selling floor, reaching over the counter for the phone that Fredreeq was handing me as though we'd choreographed it.

"Hello?" I said. "P.B.?"

My brother hung up.

I hung up too and clung to the counter for a second, telling myself everything was fine, we'd been through this dozens of times, P.B.

and I, whatever it was, and it would turn out okay. Then I turned and smiled at Mr. Bundt. "Heh," I said. It was the best I could come up with.

Mr. Bundt stared at me, his eyebrows so high it looked as if he'd had a face-lift in the last half minute. "Murder?" he said. "Murder?"

"Nothing to worry about," I said. "Family . . . thing."

"What is?"

"Whatever—that was referring to. You know. Just—family stuff."

Mr. Bundt looked doubtful. "That was a relative on the phone?"

"Yes."

"Shouldn't you . . . deal with it?"

"Oh, no," I said. "He'll call back."

"Hadn't you better call him?"

"No, he's—difficult to reach." Could I explain that this was because my brother was in the state mental hospital? No.

Mr. Bundt's eyebrows finally lowered. "I suggest you take care of this now, Miss Shelley, because we don't want this person calling back during the hours of operation and startling the customers the way he just startled us."

"Yes, of course." I picked up the phone and dialed the number from memory, long-distance, the 805 area code. "This hardly ever happens."

"I should hope not. Welcome! policy frowns upon family matters intruding upon business. Is this a close relative?"

There was a tug on my heart, but I shrugged in a manner that I hoped indicated a second or third cousin. There are people made uncomfortable by the notion of a paranoid schizophrenic in the immediate family.

My call was answered by a recording, which I also knew by heart, and I gave it half an ear. I watched Mr. Bundt head for the free-standing racks—the spinners—that display the small, independent card lines. Freelance cards made up 25 percent of our selection, and, as I myself was one of these freelancers, there was a lot at stake there.

Mr. Bundt picked a card and studied it so closely he appeared to be searching for drug residue. It was one of mine, a Good Gollie, Miss Wollie. After a moment, he handed it to Fredreeq. She pointed out the writing inside. They appeared to disagree. She shook her head. He nodded. They did it again. Nodding and shaking, they headed my way.

The hospital's outgoing message droned on in my ear, as the two of them went around me, to the cash register side of the counter. Fredreeq opened the file drawer, probably to show Mr. Bundt sales statistics on the card. And that's when his gaze fastened on the List.

I'd taped the List to the antiqued gold counter weeks ago, as a reminder of the Dating Project specifications. Fredreeq and I had become so accustomed to seeing it, we'd forgotten about it.

We remembered it now.

Slowly I hung up the phone, a trickle of sweat sliding south between my breasts. Please God, let him go blind, I prayed. Not forever, of course. For fifteen or twenty seconds.

Then I sprang into action, slapping my hand down on the counter right smack on top of the List. Mr. Bundt peered at it, trying to read between my splayed fingers, then said, "Miss Shelley, what on earth is written here that's not fit for public consumption?"

"Mr. Bundt," I said, "I promise you the public never sees that; come around to this side of the counter and you'll see how impossible it is to read it from here."

He stood his ground. "What *is* it, Miss Shelley?"

Fredreeq piped up. "Okay, I confess. These are soul mate qualifications. I'm looking for a soul mate."

"Fredreeq—" I said.

Mr. Bundt frowned. "I thought you were married."

"Divorcing," she said, fast dispensing with her long-suffering husband. "Working here at Welcome! Greetings showed me I had real high professional standards and real low personal ones. So I made a list. I'm finding my next man strictly by the book." She moved my hand aside, slapped a file on top of the List, and slid it down an inch. "You see, number one is A Good Name."

Mr. Bundt said, "A good reputation, you mean."

"Okay, yeah." Fredreeq smiled.

Mr. Bundt reached beyond her and moved the file down an inch. "Number two: Not a Convicted Felon. Surely that's not a recurring problem, Ms. Munson?"

I reached over the counter and slid the file over the List again. Fredreeq picked up a receipt book, and began to stamp pages with the Have A Nice Day stamp we used to spruce up our receipts. It seemed an odd thing to do.

Mr. Bundt reached over and moved the file. "Three: No STDs. What are ST—"

Fredreeq stamped him on the hand. Hard. I mean, it must have hurt. I gasped.

Mr. Bundt jumped backward, and I moved in on him, solicitous, but also wedging my body in front of the List. I offered turpentine to remove the ink, but he waved me away. As he waved, his right hand showed the word "Nice."

"Let's lose this." I turned to the List and ripped it off the counter. "There. Gone."

The rest of the inspection tour went better, but then, it could hardly have gone worse. I managed to keep him away from the cigarette burn, which, I realized, must have occurred during Uncle Theo's Wednesday Night Poetry Reading, and somehow escaped my notice for thirty-two hours. Mr. Bundt found no fault with my Passover/Easter decorations, although he did raise an eyebrow at my small selection of seasonal books, *Baby's First Easter Story, A Child's Haggadah,* and *Sri Ramanavami, Hindu Holiday.* He then went so far as to call my peripherals beyond reproach: wrapping paper, sealing wax, snow globes, crystal balls, astrological calendars, collectible watches, bookends, bookplates, bookmarks, sterling silver yo-yos, and dollhouse furniture. The other forty-one Good Gollie, Miss Wollie cards on their own spinner passed muster, then Mr. Bundt checked the books and asked if I had additional resources, in the happy event that I won my Willkommen! upgrade.

"Because I must tell you, most of our franchise candidates are more fiscally stable."

"Mr. Bundt, you don't have to worry. I've been approved for four small business loans and I have a—a nest egg—earmarked for the down payment. I'm stable. I'm fiscal."

"Yes, well. Don't count your nest egg before you're hatched. You have two more inspections prior to Decision Day." He nodded toward the wall calendar, where the Monday after Easter was highlighted. "These next inspections, however, will be conducted by plainclothespeople."

"Plain, uh, clothes people?"

"To observe the shop in action," he said, "through the eyes of 'a customer.' Should you achieve Willkommen! status, supervision will cease, so we must determine now your level of fitness." Mr. Bundt leaned in, smelling of breath mints. "No more morbid family phone calls, Wollie. You will not wish to remind anyone of the error made with your predecessor."

My predecessor, Aldwyn Allen, two weeks after Aldwyn's Welcome! Greetings had been upgraded to Aldwyn's Willkommen! Greetings, had hanged himself. In the shop. Nobody knew why, nor had I been able to find out exactly where it had happened. I liked to think it was the utility closet, the only piece of the premises I had no emotional attachment to.

I walked Mr. Bundt out to his Lincoln Continental, chatting to divert his attention from his surroundings. The shop was on Sunset Boulevard, east of Highland, smack in the middle of a small strip mall comprised of a twenty-one-hour locksmith, a mini-market called Bodega Bob, Loo Fong's Chinese Fast Food, Neat Nails Plus, and a Colonel Sanders knockoff, Plucky Chicken. The good thing about the location was, there were no other greeting card shops for 2.7 miles. The bad news was, this little piece of Hollywood was not optimum in terms of sales.

"Seedy," an old boyfriend once called it. Fredreeq put it another way: "It's like your shop was headed for the suburbs and got off at the wrong bus stop."

It wasn't the prettiest corner of the world, but I couldn't afford the franchise if it were. And my philosophy was, hookers need greeting cards too.

There were no hookers this morning, just a man sleeping in a wrecked red Fiero in front of Loo Fong's, whom Mr. Bundt, by the grace of God, seemed not to notice. Corporate policy stated my jurisdiction included the shop and all public areas connected to it, but you can't really dust and vacuum people.

Back inside moments later, I hugged Fredreeq, dodging her earrings and absorbing her Shalimar.

She patted my back. "Yeah, I know, I'm a saint. Saint Bullshit. What was I gonna do, watch you tell him whose List that really is, Miss Compulsive Honesty? Okay, I'm gonna go put myself back together." She pulled her panty hose out of her pocket and headed toward the back room, then stopped with her hand on the doorknob. It was my *pièce de résistance*, that doorknob, a ceramic lemon attached to a door that was painted as a tree, set in a wall-length mural of a lemon grove. "Wollie, is P.B. all right?"

"Yes. I mean—" With a sense of unease, I picked up the phone and pressed redial. "He's been off his ziprasidone because of his foot thing, which is why he's talking murder. He's delusional again." The hospital's after-hours recording greeted me once more. I hung up and looked at my watch. "Still too early. The thing is, I don't want to leave a bunch of messages. Once he's back on his meds, these episodes just embarrass him."

"Well, you're the boss, Wollie." Fredreeq disappeared into the back room, her voice trailing off as she said, "But to quote somebody famous, just 'cause your brother is paranoid, doesn't mean that somebody isn't dead."

DESPITE REPEATED ATTEMPTS, by early evening I still hadn't talked to my brother. The psych tech on P.B.'s ward told me he seemed fine, but refused to take incoming calls.

I was dressing for a date in my apartment, a one-room-plus-kitchenette that barely contained the old grand piano I lived with. The apartment's main appeal was its price and its proximity to my shop—sixty-nine steps if you used all back entrances. On the radio, the closing music of the talk show *Love Junkies* swelled.

"Chemistry shmemistry," said Dr. Cookie Lahven, the host. Her magnolia-blossom voice took on a slightly manic edge as she raced against her own closing music. "You wanna get laid, go for chemistry. You want the long haul, the ring on your finger, go for character. The whole trick to keeping the guy is finding the right guy in the first place. How? Honey, I could write a book. I *am* writing a book. *How to Avoid Getting Dumped All the Time,* hitting the stands next Valentine's Day, and—"

My phone rang. I turned off the radio, feeling the thrill I always get when I hear a reference to myself on the air. I was the research for *How to Avoid Getting Dumped All the Time.* Well, me and fourteen other women across the United States. We were the Dating Project.

"Hello?" I said, but there was silence on the other end of the phone. "P.B.?"

A guttural noise answered me. It could have been the growl of an animal. It could have been phlegm.

I felt a sudden, inexplicable chill. As though a flame had been extinguished.

"P.B.?"

Click. Silence. Dial tone.

chapter two

"That outfit is hot, hot, hot. Guys go for leather. Guys go for blondes in leather." Fredreeq aimed a Polaroid at me. "Wollie, you gotta put down the phone."

I was now pressing redial every few minutes, and getting a busy signal. It was after 6 P.M., shift change hour at the hospital, when a chatty patient could monopolize the phone unnoticed or an overworked staff member might take it off the hook. I hung up, sucked in my stomach, and summoned a smile. Fredreeq snapped the picture, and a flash illuminated the back room.

Dark and cavernous, the store's back room was bigger than the selling floor, with a maze of storage units, shelves, and old gym lockers, all of which I'd painted, wallpapered, or decoupaged. There was a drafting table where I designed my greeting cards, and some rococo furnishings inherited from my friend Joey when she'd married a minimalist. Her giant Persian rug covered half the concrete floor, making the space more appealing than my apartment. Had it been zoned for residential living, I'd have brought over my toaster oven and moved in.

"I'm going out front to file this Polaroid," Fredreeq said, making notes on it. "We're making progress—tonight is Number Nineteen. Dave. Those shoes don't go with that outfit, by the way. They're too flat."

The shoes *were* flat, in deference to Dave. There was a height requirement on the List, number seven, 5' 9" or Above, suggested by Dr. Cookie herself. She felt my date need not be as tall as me, just tall enough to escape Short Man's Complex. Dave barely squeaked through.

Fredreeq stuck her head in the doorway. "Phone. For you. I think."

"Hello?" I said, and heard loud breathing. "P.B.?"

"No names."

Thank God, I thought. "Honey, I've been so worried about—"

"I need aluminum foil."

"Okay," I said. "I can't bring it right now, but tomorrow—"

"There's a dead body."

"A what?"

"Dead body. Cadaver. Corpse. They said there'd be a murder and now there's a body. Can you come right now?"

"I wish I could but I can't. I have a date now and visiting hours are over. Tomorrow—"

"No, *now*, they're here *now*, I need it *now*."

His anxiety always got to me. Born of delusions, it was nevertheless real. "I'll come by later tonight, okay? After my date. I'll leave the foil with the night staff and it'll be waiting for you when you wake up and—" A click. "P.B.?" Silence. Dial tone.

Fredreeq's head appeared in the doorway. "Number Nineteen is here."

DAVE HONKED THE horn of the oversized turquoise convertible as a city bus lumbered into our lane. "Touch this paint job and I'll sue, you ignorant clod!" He looked over at me in the passenger seat. "Yeah, it was the tall blond part of your ad that caught my eye. Oh, and the title, 'Where Were You in 1968?' That got me thinking. Where I was was in nursery school, having wet dreams about tall blondes."

"Ah."

"So what are we dressed as there, 1980?"

I looked down at my outfit. Leather skirt, black bodysuit, opaque stockings. Was that eighties? Was that bad? Concern for P.B.'s problems gave way to concern for my own.

Dave himself wore black jeans, a brown sports jacket, and a rayon floral shirt. And loafers, without tassels, pennies, or snakeskin. Acceptable, as per number eight on the List, Good Shoes. A Fredreeq contribution.

The premise of the List was simple. For every woman in America who's chronically lovelorn, Dr. Cookie maintained, there are people in her life—a mother, a co-worker, a best friend—who know what the problem is, who could literally make a list of what characteristics she should demand, based on what was lacking in the losers from her past. Not that I thought of the guys I'd dated as losers, but the doctor was one tough cookie. "If they didn't step up to the plate with a marriage proposal, they're losers," she said. "So recruit those friends. Make that list. And for now, forget big-ticket items like 'integrity' or 'intelligence.' You're teaching yourself discernment, so start with what's verifiable. Even shallow."

Hence, Good Shoes. My own feet, I now realized, were numb with cold. "Dave, I'm sorry, I should've grabbed a sweater," I said. "Any chance we could put the top up?"

"This is a classic car," he said. "There is no top."

"Oh. I guess that's why there's no seat belt. But what about the seat belt law?"

He glanced at me. "Well, aren't you the goody two-shoes?"

I was, but also, a seat belt would've been a two-inch layer of warmth. Rush hour traffic kept our pace slow, so there wasn't a big wind factor, just standard California mid-March frigidity. Twenty minutes on the road and we'd just reached the Fairfax district, a world away from the Hollywood of my shop, or that of the tourists. Resistant to change and chain stores, this stretch of Fairfax was mostly mom-and-pop operations squeezed into narrow storefronts. Black-clad pedestrians hurried toward synagogues, making better progress than the cars. If only I were an Orthodox Jew, I thought, I'd be dressed warmly. Of course, if I were an Orthodox Jew, I wouldn't be in a convertible after sundown on a Friday. I wished I were back at the shop, lighting Shabbat candles. I focused on the taillights of the bus ahead and recited to myself the Hebrew prayer I knew from childhood, then added in English, Bless this Sabbath, let me be dressed right, and help me get through this date, amen.

We neared Canter's Deli, the neighborhood's emotional core, and a stream of pedestrians crossed Fairfax, stopping our progress. I gazed at a thrift store, then Eat A Pita, a fast-food joint, and my mind drifted off into greeting cards, envisioning little falafel wearing second-hand mittens, wrapped snugly in their pita overcoats—

Dave's horn startled me once more. A trio of Chassidim hurried into the crosswalk, oblivious to their red light. "Freaks," Dave muttered.

I stared at him. "What?" he said, gunning the engine.

"Well, good heavens, Dave. Freaks? Why, the clothes? The payes?"

"Payes?" He looked at me. "Jesus, a Zionist in a shiksa suit. Listen, babe, just because my name is Fischgarten, doesn't mean I feel some tribal solidarity. You're not Jewish, are you?" His eyes narrowed, as though to assess my gene pool.

I'm not Jewish, but I wasn't about to tell this guy about Ruta, who had taken care of my brother and me when we were little; Ruta, who had taught us about challah and matzoh and love; Ruta, who spent World War II in Poland, hiding under the floorboards of a general store. "No," I said. "But religion interests me. My friend Joey, for instance, studies Buddhism—"

Dave snapped on the radio. A male voice said, "Sex. Sex with children. Child molestation. Pedophilia. Think about it, think about that word, 'pedophile.' "

I thought about it. What I thought was that I didn't want to be thinking about it. I wondered what Dave thought about it.

"A guy who does it with little kids now lives on your block," the talk show host continued. "Does it bug you? Hank from Tarzana, you're on the line."

"Yeah, hi. Thanks. Okay, what ticks me off is how, okay, they let some child molester out of jail and everyone's upset, okay, but then Ron 'the Weasel' gets out on a technicality—"

"Who's Ron 'the Weasel'?"

"It was in the *L.A. Times,* he's that guy, last year he got sent up on conspiracy—"

"Is he a pedophile?" asked the host.

"Naw, he's a guy from my neighborhood. See, first he cops a plea—"

"Hank? Wake up. The topic is pedophiles. Arnie from Glendale, go ahead, you're—"

Dave changed the station.

"Have you ever heard of Dr. Cookie Lahven?" I asked. "A show called *Love Junkies*? She wrote a book called *How to Avoid Killing Yourself* and now she's—"

"Huh." Dave switched to FM. Fifties music blared, sounding the way the car looked. "Sheb Wooley," he said. "My man!" He drummed on the steering wheel and threw me a smile. I stared, marveling that my perpetual shivering didn't seem to register with him. Well, what did I expect? Single, on the shady side of thirty, finding men through classified ads—he probably figured I should be grateful for a free meal and a ride in a great car. Dates Four and Thirteen had practically told me as much. And so what? It wasn't as if Dave was my type. Of course, it had been so long since I'd been attracted to anyone, I was no longer sure I had a type. I'd once had a type, in the olden days, but Dr. Cookie maintained it was a type known as the commit-o-phobe. Fighting an urge to climb out of the convertible, I reminded myself that I wasn't here for fun, I was here for science. And, of course, money.

The Dating Project consisted of fifteen women around the country dating six hundred men over a period of six months, in an organized and documented manner. Each subject enlisted one or more discriminating friends to create her List and compose an ad to run in the Personals section of local newspapers, and/or the Internet. The friends fielded responses, interrogated the men, and scheduled a preliminary meeting—what Fredreeq called the Drive-by—to determine, for instance, whether a prospect who claimed to be five nine was indeed five nine, and to allow the prospect to get a look at the woman in question. It sounded like a lot of work, but as Dr. Cookie pointed out, most people have a matchmaking instinct, and in fact, finding the Discriminating Friends was the easy part. Even so, I insisted on giving Fredreeq 10 percent of my research fee, just for the time she put in. My other discriminating friend, Joey, wouldn't take any money—bad enough, she said, that she was currently sponging off her husband. Fredreeq said that was the kind of marriage she aspired to, but as her own husband was more sponge than spongee, she was happy to get a piece of my research fee.

The tricky part was getting men to agree to the Drive-by and interrogation process, and a certain number of prospects dropped out at this point. But Joey and Fredreeq were persuasive talkers, noting that the Drive-by worked both ways, and many men, being visually oriented, came to see the value of setting eyes on a woman before committing themselves to dinner and a movie. An unexpected side effect was that a fair number of them hit on Joey and Fredreeq.

For us research subjects, the entire process was designed to wipe out those three unscientific elements so dear to the hearts of romantics: chance, subjectivity, and "chemistry."

"I have a degree in science," Dr. Cookie liked to say, "and I'm here to tell you that what y'all call chemistry is nothing but plain ol' lust, with a half-life of about twelve minutes."

No danger of that tonight. I'd be lucky to end the night with all my teeth, they were chattering so violently. I pulled down the sun visor but there was no mirror attached. My eyes watered from exposure, which meant there were mascara tears grafted onto my face. I wiped my nose with my hand, wishing I had a Kleenex or even a coat sleeve. "Dave," I said, "I'm feeling a little self-conscious. I think the wind has blown off all my makeup."

"That's okay," Dave said cheerfully. "You were wearing too much anyway."

THE PEOPLE AT the Malibu Bat Cave hadn't heard of Dave. That pretty much killed his cheerfulness. After an extended discussion with a maître d' named Klaus and an exchange of twenty dollars, we were seated on the veranda, overlooking a Dumpster.

It was cold on the veranda. I drank a lot of hot tea, before, during, and after my angel hair pasta. Dave had multiple extra dry Beefeater martinis and sweetbreads in carmelized citrus sauce.

I learned all about Dave's last girlfriend, who left him to follow the Dalai Lama, and the girlfriend before that one, who joined Alcoholics Anonymous and was no fun anymore. I learned about the sexual preferences of people I'd never heard of. As Dave talked, I took a discreet glance at my watch, a Patek Philippe from the thirties, inherited from Ruta when she died. My only real piece of jewelry, the watch had a tiny face and required some squinting, but I was delighted to see we were approaching the two-hour mark, that magic point that made a date official, by Dr. Cookie's rules. Number Nineteen was the first date I'd considered bailing out on. That I hadn't done so was due to Ruta's voice in my head, urging me on. Telling me I could do this, that I was tough.

I had to be. Thirteen of the Dating Project subjects had been at it since Halloween. Pittsburgh was replaced at Christmas when she eloped with Date Number Five, and the original Los Angeles had dropped out to act in a production of *The Fantasticks*. I was her successor, brought in on Groundhog Day—so late in the game that my forty dates had to be squeezed into the space of two months for Dr. Cookie to keep to her writing schedule. If I averaged two nights off each week, it worked out to be forty dates in forty nights. There were those who said it couldn't be done, but there were those who didn't know what it was to truly need five thousand dollars.

". . . guy inside the sliding glass door?" Dave was saying, as he stabbed a pearl onion. "Big Eddie Minardi. Mafia don. East Coast, but when he's in town, does all the hot places."

I looked over, wondering how a research scientist from UCLA knew a mob boss on sight. Beyond the Mafia table I saw the rest room/telephone sign. I excused myself to call P.B. Not only was he a better conversationalist than Dave, I was desperate to stop worrying about him, and talking was the only way to do that.

"Hello, you have reached the after-hours switchboard at Rio Pescado . . ." the indefatigable message voice said. A woman behind me in the narrow hallway gave a lame cough, reminding me there were other people who hadn't brought their cell phone to dinner, or perhaps, like me, didn't have one.

Excuse me, I wanted to say, I'm dealing with phantom corpses, so you just wait your turn. But I didn't. I hung up, stuck with the creepy feeling I'd had all day. Walking back to the veranda, I snuck a look at the alleged Mr. Mafia, a sixty-something man in a gorgeous suit, smoking a pipe. He returned my look openly. I know, his eyes seemed to say, murder is hell.

Back at my table, Dave picked up where he'd left off on his travelogue with chaos, a mathematical theory explaining behavior that seems to be random but turns out not to be.

This was my favorite part, hearing what the Dating Project guys did for a living. On previous dates I'd learned about: perchloroethylene, a cancer-causing chemical used by dry cleaners; the air-conditioning system at L.A. Community College; weightlifting; divorce settlements; zoning laws; the Talmud; how copper conducts heat; and how Pizarro conquered Peru. Now I learned that randomness and chaos are not the same thing: while random is random, chaos is not. If you can find the pattern in chaos you can change it. I loved that.

I was mentally composing my journal entry on Dave—"not a people person"—when he reached across the table and stroked my wrist. His fingernails were buffed.

"You have really soft skin," he said. "Goose bumps, though. Are you cold?"

Seven minutes to go, I thought. Four hundred twenty seconds. "I'm fine."

"My apartment is warm." He smiled as if he were trying out a new set of teeth.

This was the worst part of dating, maybe for everyone, but certainly for me. In addition to the two-hour minimum, Dr. Cookie had spelled out official standards of behavior: no crying jags or sitting in stony silence or running screaming into the night. No assault, no bringing a book. Mindful of all this, I mustered up a simple "No, thank you, Dave."

"Come on, Woollie. Your place is far away, it'll be so late by the time we get there."

"It's 'Wollie,'" I said. "And it'll be later if we go to your house first." I began to calculate how much driving I had ahead of me, to Rio Pescado, then saw he was still smiling, waiting for an answer. But what was the question? Oh, yes.

"I can't stay over," I said. "I can't sleep with you."

His smile faded. "Why not?"

"I don't want to."

Dave looked around impatiently and snapped his fingers. "Check."

"He's not our waiter," I said. "That's Christian. Ours is Jonathan."

"Who cares?"

I ended up taking a cab home. Dave paid half.

MY VW RABBIT zoomed up the 101 north, past the Denny's, McDonald's, and International House of Pancakes of Woodland Hills, Westlake Village, Thousand Oaks. I drove without the radio, a habit left over from the days when a trip to Rio Pescado made me nervous to the point of nausea. I thought about how it was now more fun to go to the mental hospital than it was to go on a date, and I wondered if that was progress.

I'd dressed haphazardly, in the interest of speed and warmth: my long calico skirt from earlier in the day, heavy wool socks over my tights, red high-top Converse All Stars, gray hooded sweatshirt, jean jacket. Nothing matched and it didn't matter. It's hard to dress wrong for the hospital. On the seat next to me were seventy-five square feet of Reynolds Wrap quality aluminum foil. In my jacket pocket was a Regency romance, *Sylvester, or The Wicked Uncle.* A useful thing to know about mental illness, which you won't find in pamphlets or medical textbooks like the *DSM-IV,* is how much time is spent, by everyone involved, waiting at hospitals, pharmacies, police stations, or on hold, which is why it's important to carry reading material at all times, or a portable hobby, like needlepoint or whittling.

After forty minutes the terrain changed dramatically. Flat, complaisant communities gave way to a sweeping vista as the freeway snaked around canyon curves high above the valley floor. I took the Pleasant Valley exit.

Entering the little town at midnight was disorienting, like spotting the cleaning lady at an after-hours club. But I made the drive to the hospital most Thursdays at noon, so it didn't take long for my internal compass to kick in. My Rabbit bounced along past the corn and onion fields till the Deer Crossing sign reminded me to slow down.

And so, when the shape loomed in the road ahead, there was plenty of time to imagine what else it might be, must be, other than the thing it was, until I'd come to a gradual, disbelieving stop.

I kept the motor running and covered my wide-open eyes with my hands like that would make it go away. I reached over to lock the doors in the Rabbit, even though they were already locked. And I told myself that the thing in front of the car wasn't what it appeared to be. Finally, reason rolled in like the tide. With all the things that existed only in my brother's head, this one also existed in the real world.

Dead body. Cadaver. Corpse.

chapter three

P.B., I thought, and stopped breathing.

My eyes focused. My headlights showed a head of dark hair on the body in the road. P.B. is as blond as I am. Relief hit, then fear—I could not leave my car to make sure that body was dead, or save its life if it wasn't. I'm not a brave person.

"Brave shmave," said a voice inside me. Ruta's. "How do you know that's a corpse? What if it's a person trying to get to a hospital, taking a rest along the way, maybe having a small coma? You find out. You, who used to be a Girl Scout."

A conscience is a dreadful thing. I tried to recall ways to tell if people are dead, short of feeling around for a pulse, something I find tricky even on myself. There was the sticking-someone-with-a-pin method. I looked around. On the sun visor was a No on Proposition 29 button, but it seemed like adding insult to injury, stabbing someone who was already clearly unwell, and with an old political button. And if a person was unconscious, would he respond to jabs? Oh! Mirrors. You held a mirror to someone's lips, right?—or nose— and if it fogged, he was breathing. Of course, that would mean looking at a face, which might be okay if the face was alive, but not okay if it was dead.

"Enough wasting time. Go save a life maybe," Ruta's voice said.

Armed with a cigar-sized flashlight and a Cover Girl mirror compact, I made a sign of the cross and got out of the car, leaving the door open and the headlights on.

He was faceup, wasn't moving, and didn't look comfortable. Ten feet separated us, and I focused on his clothes as I advanced. Dark shoes, gray sweatpants, an ancient-looking sweatshirt the color of, well, blood. With letters on it. MIT.

"Buddy," I said, to get his attention, but it came out a whisper. I couldn't look at his face. I sniffed the air; I'm not sure what I was sniffing for, but there was a courtroom set up in my head, and I was rehearsing the possibility of "Your honor, he smelled dead, I didn't need to go any further." But the air smelled like night in the countryside, and whatever death smelled like, it probably wasn't this.

I focused my little flashlight on the body part closest to me, a leg. Exposed between dark socks and the gray fleece of sweatpants was some four inches of hairy male flesh. That's what I touched, the fleshy part of the calf. With my index finger.

It was as cold and firm as a naked turkey sitting in the refrigerator Thanksgiving morning. Waiting to be stuffed.

I pulled back. The imprint of my finger stayed on the leg, white against the surrounding skin. I stared at it, transfixed, then stood, stumbled back to the car, got in, slammed the door, put it in reverse, backed up twenty yards, and stopped.

I was shaking. The body wasn't P.B., but it was somebody, somebody most likely loved by other people, people whose world was now about to change. I was glad it wasn't my world, my brother, and I felt guilty about feeling that way, and I felt sad for the man in the road and people who loved him. I was at a loss about what to do next.

I could drive to a gas station, call the hospital, and say there was a body in their driveway. But that would be leaving the scene of a crime. If it was a crime. What if the man had simply dropped dead on the road to Rio Pescado? That was no crime. But my driving away from it might be. Unless I was driving away to report it to the police.

Police.

Police would want to know what I was doing there in the middle of the night and that would lead to P.B. And his arrest record. And—

P.B.

How had my brother known there was a corpse in the road? P.B. was stuck on the old surgical ward, recovering from a broken foot. Wasn't he?

I had to find out, make sure he was safe, and talk to him before I talked to the police, if I talked to the police at all, which, now that I thought about it, was a terrible idea. And I shouldn't have touched the dead man. What if they found my fingerprint on his calf muscle? I put the car in gear and inched ahead, scared now of veering into the ditch in my effort not to drive over the poor man.

I headed for the Administration Building in slow motion, hands at ten and two o'clock, concentrating as though taking a driving test. I heard myself talking, saying, "You're okay, you're okay, you're okay."

The empty parking lot was well lit, but some instinct made me drive around the corner of the building and park in the dark.

I walked into Administration, and over to the glass-enclosed security office. Nobody there. Through the window I could see signs of a Carl's Jr. dinner in progress. I glanced toward a door leading to the hallway. When people aren't where they're supposed to be, I assume they're in the bathroom. A glass door led to a courtyard, and beyond that I could see my destination, the building known as RT, for Rehab/Treatment. I tried the door. Locked.

I went to the hallway and tried that door. Unlocked. I hesitated. In the past, I'd been buzzed through, so clearly I wasn't supposed to be wandering down there. Not that I wanted to. It was pitch-black. A jangle of keys behind me scared me into a decision. I stepped forward, closed the door, and faced darkness.

Dr. Charlie's office was here somewhere, and if memory served, some back way we'd taken to visit P.B. in RT, where they'd brought him after his foot surgery at a local hospital. I walked toward a red exit sign, hands in front of me, heart thumping, certain that every dark office I passed harbored someone who would jump out and do some nameless, dreadful thing to me. Mercifully, the exit was unlocked and suddenly I was in a garden of night-blooming jasmine, with the sound of crickets and a three-quarter moon above. Ahead was the RT building.

Open.

A single light pointed the way to the elevator, but they weren't frittering away funds on extra watts. No need to worry about surveillance cameras, either, in the hallways or elevators—Rio Pescado, Dr. Charlie once told me, had a smaller security budget than the average 7-Eleven. I pressed the up button. The rest of the building was older than the elevator, brown linoleum and green walls, bringing to mind my old elementary school. The stillness unnerved me.

I remembered Dr. Charlie telling me that back when the hospital had been a full-service operation the basement had been a morgue.

The elevator went *ping!* and I jumped.

The elevator interior was huge, big enough for a gurney, a gruesome image somehow, but at this point, what wasn't? On the second floor I crept past an empty nurses' station to P.B.'s room.

Moonlight illuminated two beds. P.B.'s was by the window, and a curtain separated him from his roommate. The roommate didn't seem murderous, hooked up to an IV tube, pushing ninety, and wearing a hospital gown. P.B., in seersucker pajamas, slept soundly. His blond baby-fine hair, identical to mine, was damp. Night sweats. The clean-shaven face looked closer to sixteen than thirty-three. I could see the altar boy he'd been at ten. Whatever demons had tormented him all day had the night off.

I considered waking him. The odds of getting coherent information without rousing his roommate, the rest of the ward, and whatever staff was nearby were not good, and a midnight visit, irregular at best, would be construed as suspicious once that body on the road was discovered. Knowing P.B. was safe would have to do for now.

I set the aluminum foil on the nightstand, moving aside his Chap Stick and an action-adventure comic book. I kissed my brother on the forehead, touched his pajama collar, and crept out.

The hallway was empty, but the elevator was not. Inside was a gurney. Empty.

Next to the gurney stood a man.

I froze.

In addition to a white lab coat he wore a green scrub suit, complete with paper hair cover and shoe covers. Only his face was exposed, a Mediterranean-looking face, with dark eyes and darker eyebrows and the beginning of a beard. Just my type, I thought, surprising myself, and felt a wave of desire so inappropriate I chalked it up to post-traumatic stress syndrome.

He didn't ask what I was doing there at that hour. He didn't say a word. I stayed frozen until the elevator began to close, then I snapped out of it and came aboard. He held the door-open button.

I started to say thank you, then stopped. Opening my mouth could activate my honesty compulsion, especially potent around authority figures such as doctors. Already I had an impulse to grab him and say, "I've just seen a dead body." Instead, I pressed 1, and lowered my head so he wouldn't get a good look at my face. His paper slippers had no shoes in them, only socks.

That struck me as strange.

The elevator went past the first floor and continued to descend; we were headed for the former morgue. I stepped closer to the man. His body heat was palpable.

His head was bent, looking at the paperback in my jacket pocket: *Sylvester, or The Wicked Uncle,* for heaven's sake—why couldn't I be reading something hip? Jack Kerouac or somebody. Nietzsche.

We hit bottom with a thud, but the elevator doors remained shut. This beautiful doctor could be a serial killer, I realized, luring victims to the old morgue in order to—

With a creaking that cried out for an application of WD-40, the doors opened.

Two men stood waiting.

One was dressed like a security guard. The other was a near giant, a foot taller, in a suit. I guessed he was a guard too, and there were no uniforms his size. Clearly, they'd come to haul me away for entering the RT building without permission, for finding a corpse without reporting it. I backed up to the rear wall of the elevator.

The guards looked at us, and then at each other. As the elevator doors rumbled shut, they hurried through. The doctor did not hold the door-open button for them.

I was now practically stapled to the back wall, slightly behind the doctor—*my* doctor, as I was beginning to think of him. Not a serial killer, I decided, but an ally. I was close enough to see the perspiration on his neck curling a lock of hair that had escaped the scrub suit cap. I could smell his smell. The top of his head was level with my eyes, which put his height at about five six or seven. Short. Sweaty. I wanted him.

We waited for the elevator to move.

The guards, it seemed to me, were staring at the doctor's feet—perhaps noticing, as I had, his strange footwear.

A subtle clicking, like tiny Morse code, drew my attention to the doctor's lab coat. He had one hand in its pocket, holding a lump the size of a blow-dryer. The lump was in motion. The doctor must have sensed my scrutiny because he turned. His eyes looked up into mine and stayed there.

Read my mind, they seemed to say. Then he winked.

Perhaps because I have no aptitude for winking, I'm a sucker for winks. This man could have a hand grenade in his pocket now and I'd give him the benefit of the doubt.

The elevator still did not move. The clicking grew louder. The two men in front of us turned just as I happened to sneeze.

"Gesundheit," said the uniform.

"Thank you," I said, and sneezed again.

The two men took turns pushing the 1 button, the way you do when you want to make things happen faster, and the uniformed one threw a look back at us. A hand—*his* hand—wrapped around my wrist. And readjusted to grasp my fingers. What a shocking thing to do, I thought. How thrilling.

With a clang and a hum, the elevator ascended. From the pocket of the lab coat, where the doctor's hand had been, the hand that now held mine, there emerged the snout, then the face of a small white animal. I stared at the animal. It stared back.

The doctor squeezed my hand, and now I was absolutely sure he was telling me something, only I had no idea what. I squeezed back, in an "I don't know what you're saying, but I like you" manner. He squeezed again. "I like you too," I decided it meant.

When the elevator doors opened, the security guards stepped out and turned, clearing a space for us to exit. Then they stood there. Waiting. Waiting for me.

I didn't move.

The doctor let go of my hand and said, "After you." He had the voice of a more macho man, the voice Mike Tyson should have gotten. I liked it. I wanted to hold his hand some more.

I said, "No, that's all right."

"Go," he said, more forcefully.

It showed good manners, but there are situations that override standard etiquette.

"Gurneys first," I said courteously.

"Fine." He pushed the gurney out, then stepped back, reached around, and grabbed onto my—well, I think he was going for my arm, but he found my breast instead and fumbled around and I stumbled against him and then his arm was around my waist and I was being held tight against him and I thought, Wow, and then he spoke again.

"Nobody moves or she gets it."

chapter four

What went through my head was, People really say that? The security guys froze. The gurney came to a rattling halt just past them. The elevator began to close and the doctor stuck his foot out to stop it. I felt the muscles of his inner thigh when his leg stretched out and something stirred inside me, and I thought of something my friend Joey always said, that the thigh muscle is a highly underrated body part. I looked at the doctor's face.

He smiled.

He had dimples.

The elevator doors reopened, revealing two confused guards. We moved toward them. The doctor's right arm was around me but his left hand was back in his pocket, and if you didn't know about the animal, you might think there was a gun there.

Was there?

As if reading my mind, the doctor said, "Now give me your guns."

The guards looked at each other. "We don't carry guns," the giant said.

"What do you mean, you don't carry guns?"

"There's one in the guard booth, but we don't carry them around in general."

After a pause, the doctor said, "All right. Where's your car?"

"Me?" I asked. I couldn't see who he was talking to.

He squeezed my waist. "Not you."

The giant answered. "We drove Phil's car, north side of Administration."

The doctor said, "All right, let's go. Phil, you lead the way."

Phil said, "Why don't we all just keep calm, and—"

"Shut up," the doctor said. Phil nodded and we moved out.

It's awkward to walk with someone's arm tight around your waist; I found it both erotic and embarrassing. Also not very efficient. Progress was slow, and we stayed so close to the guards that occasionally I'd step on the heels of the big one. The first two times, I said "Sorry" just out of habit, and then decided that being a hostage means never having to say you're sorry.

Except that I wasn't really a hostage, because this guy wasn't a kidnapper. For one thing, there were those dimples. Then, the way he held on to me: more salsa dancer than desperate criminal. This doctor—if he was a doctor—was not a danger to me and the reason I knew this was that I wasn't afraid. Of course, it could be that my day's supply of fear had been sucked out of me, by Mr. Bundt and P.B. and the dead body.

This part of Rio Pescado wasn't as familiar to me as the South Complex, P.B.'s regular unit, and in the dark I lost track of everything except basic motor skills. I found there's nothing like walking with another body Velcroed to your own to make you realize how limbs work. Eventually we reached pavement and a brown Mazda.

The doctor said, "Open it," and then, "Get in, both of you. Fast."

They got in. The giant had to fold himself to fit into the passenger seat.

"You got radios?" the doctor asked him.

"It's busted. Phil listens to tapes."

The doctor said, "No, I mean walkie-talkies."

"Oh. Yeah, we have those."

"Hand them over. Cell phones too."

They passed them through the window. The doctor told me to take them, his voice pulsating through my back. "Hey, Phil," he said, "that thing on your key ring, is that a security system for the car?"

"Yeah."

"Okay. Start the ignition and roll the window halfway down." He waited, then said, "Now turn off the car and hand her the keys." It was done. "Now lock the doors. Activate the system." After a beep, a red light came on in the console between the men.

The doctor said, "I want you to sit in the car for twenty minutes. Got a watch?"

"Yes," the giant said. "It's twelve-oh-two A.M. In the morning."

I felt a chuckle from the doctor. "Okay, pal," he said. "We're walking away. At twelve-thirty A.M.—in the morning—you can get out of your car. If you get out any earlier than twelve-thirty, I will hear your car alarm go off and I will shoot the girl."

I liked that he called me a girl. Fredreeq likes to be called a woman, but I prefer girl; not always, but often. Now, for instance. I think it has to do with being very tall.

"I will shoot the girl," the doctor said again. "You got that?"

"You will shoot the girl," Phil repeated.

"You do what you're supposed to, she'll walk away from this. I promise. You screw up, she dies. It's all up to you and your partner."

"You can count on us." Phil looked at me. "You'll be okay, lady."

"Oh, I know," I said. "Don't worry about me."

"Worry about her," said the doctor.

"Oh, yes, that's what I meant," I said quickly. "Worry about me."

The doctor pulled me back from the Mazda and told me to take him to my car. When we were some distance from the guards, he said, "You okay?"

"Yes, fine, thank you."

He had me leave the radio, phones, and keys on the ground, then changed his grip so that he was no longer holding me around the waist, but around the arm. It was a lot easier to walk now, but I missed being welded to him. It was okay that he had my arm; holding hands would be even nicer. Shock, I realized, was affecting my judgment.

We reached my car. "Would you mind unlocking it?" he said, letting go of me to pay attention to his pocket. The thing that wasn't a gun was getting restless.

"Well, for Pete's sake," I said.

"What?" He reached in and with one hand pulled it out, a lanky white animal the size of a small cat. It was too dark to identify a species.

"You're leaving yourself wide open right now, 'Doc.' Anyone could just . . ."

With both hands, he lifted the animal to eye level and clucked to it. "Just what?"

I hesitated. "Well, kick you in the . . . or punch you."

He turned, presenting me with his torso. "Want to?"

"No."

"Then let's get out of here." He smiled. "Please."

My heart began to pack an overnight bag.

I opened the door and cleared off the passenger seat, throwing my purse into the back. When we were settled in, I fired up the VW Rabbit and started off down the road.

I wore my seat belt. He did not.

chapter five

"You're somewhat unusual, aren't you, Ms.—?"

"Shelley," I said. "Wollie. Wollie Shelley. Call me Wollie. And you are—?"

"Call me Doc. Would you mind driving without lights, Wollie?"

Talk about unusual. I'd never in my life—purposely, that is—driven without lights. I said, "Can we get past the body first?"

"What body?" Doc, scrunched down in the passenger seat, now raised himself until he saw what body. "Jesus Christ." He seemed as shocked as I'd been.

"Shall I stop?"

He looked behind us. So did I. There was nothing, not human or vehicle, visible. "Yeah," he said. "Wait. Are we sure he's dead?"

"Pretty sure. I sort of checked him on my way in."

He stared at me. "Yeah, stop."

I braked a couple of yards in front of the body and announced I was staying in the car, if it was all the same to him.

Doc got out. He squatted next to the body and studied it, then took the lanky white animal out of his pocket and stroked it as he did so. It was a strange thing to do, I thought, but then my own behavior was—as he'd pointed out—unusual. For instance, was there a good reason I didn't at this moment drive around Doc and the corpse and speed away, a reason that didn't involve dimples and winking? While I tried to think of one, he came over and got back into the car.

"You're right. He's dead."

I'd thought the man unflappable, but he was now clearly disturbed. He held the animal in his lap, slunk down into the seat, and put a hand over his eyes like he needed an aspirin. Apparently there was some comment from the animal. "Not now," he said.

I navigated the VW around the dead man. "Did you know him?"

"No." He sat up straighter and turned to me. "Did you?"

"Me? No."

He kept staring at me. I looked back. "What?"

He shook his head. "Nothing. Can you drive faster?"

"Sure. Just trying to show a little respect for the dead."

"And can you kill the lights now?"

What the heck. I killed the lights. The three-quarter moon fought its way through treetops to help me, but it wasn't enough. I slowed down again.

"Look, let me take the wheel," he said.

"No. You've got your hands full with that—what is that animal?"

"Ever been told you drive like someone's grandmother?"

"Whose grandmother drives without lights? On dirt roads full of potholes?" I heard my voice go unattractively shrill. No doubt I looked like someone's grandmother too, hunched over the steering wheel, all my nerve endings exposed. I took a breath. "At least let me use parking lights."

"No. You're doing fine. Sorry I insulted you."

I nodded. "So what killed that poor man? Heart attack, maybe? Aneurysm?"

"Bullet," he said. Then, to the animal, "All right, all right."

The creature, some sort of elongated hamster, started a climb toward the doctor's green paper head covering, which had managed to inflate in the night air. It reminded me of an old-fashioned bonnet hair dryer with a dangling air hose, a welcome image, undercutting the man's blatant virility.

"Stop!"

I hit the brakes. We'd come to the end of the hospital's private drive. Doc opened his door and aimed my tiny flashlight into the ditch, motioning me forward. He leaned way out, then came back up with a black vinyl gym bag. Then he turned to look out the back window.

I glanced in the rearview mirror. Nothing there but the Welcome to Rio Pescado sign warning against bringing in firearms, and stating, in English and Spanish, that it's a crime to help a patient escape. It was too dark to read, but I knew it by heart.

"What I'd planned," Doc said, "was to have you get out here and walk back—"

"What?!"

"—to the hospital. You don't have to yell, I'm right next to you. That body changes things. We don't know who's out there, and I'm not going to risk your life. So when we get to town, you can jump out at a gas station and call the police and say—"

"What are you talking about?"

"I'm trying to tell you. Can you listen and use the accelerator at the same time?"

"Faster? Fine." I switched on the lights. "I'll even go the speed limit, but I'm through roaming in the dark. Shoot me if you must."

"Would it improve your driving?"

He looked behind us again, then turned back to me. "Wollie, I need your car. I won't pretend I'll hurt you if you say no, but I'm desperate. You'll get it back tomorrow, I'll even fix that defective CV joint—"

"That what?"

"The click click click noise that sounds like horses' hooves. Meanwhile, if you could give the cops a slightly modified—"

"Whoa, whoa, whoa. No cops. No dropping me off at gas stations. I'll drive you anywhere you want to go, within reason, within the continental United States—"

"No. I want to keep you out of this."

"Well, you should've thought of that when you took me hostage and—what *is* that animal and why is it staring at me?"

"Ferret. Listen to me. That guy in the road, I don't know who killed him, but I think I know why, and the sooner you and I split up, the safer you'll be."

"What's a ferret? Not a member of the rat family, is it?" I asked. It was smaller than a cat and very oddly shaped. I don't know how he'd kept it still in the elevator, because now it was a real live wire, climbing over his shoulder and onto the headrest of the seat with considerable energy, even with some sort of leash attached to it.

"She's a member of the family Mustelidae. Not a rodent. She kills rodents. Her name's Margaret." He turned around. "I'm letting her crawl around in the back. You okay with that?"

I wished I could say I was okay with that, but I didn't say anything.

"What? Are you scared of her?" he asked. "She's domesticated. She won't bite. Some do, but not her."

Unless you're a rodent, I thought. We were coming into town:

lights, traffic, civilization. "I don't have a lot of experience with animals. I'm more of an indoor person."

"You never had a pet?"

"I'm allergic to things with fur." Number nine on the List, I thought automatically, No Pets.

"Says who? You're not breaking out in hives, are you?"

I wasn't. Except for the sneezes in the elevator, I had no symptoms. "My mother always told my brother and me we were allergic to things with fur."

"Smart mother."

I looked over and caught the tail end of a smile. The dimple again. And a good profile. Strong nose. He pointed out the window to a gas station just short of the freeway entrance. "There. Pull in."

"No need," I said, and stepped on the gas. "We have half a tank."

WOULD THINGS HAVE gone differently if I hadn't had to pee?

North of Thousand Oaks sat a good-sized mall, dark except for a corner facing the freeway, featuring the Donut Stop ("Fresh—All Day, All Nite!"). I parked in front of a blue neon doughnut and practically leaped from the car.

Doc got out too. "Throw me the keys, I'll lock up and meet you inside."

I stopped. "What do you take me for?"

"Look, I won't drive off. Margaret's gotta pee, then I'll put her back in the car."

"So leave it unlocked. She can't open doors, can she?"

"Leave your car unlocked?" He sounded shocked.

"It's a sixteen-year-old Rabbit with a defective CD joint," I said and ran inside.

The bathroom at the Donut Stop doubled as the supply closet for industrial doughnut making. From the toilet I stared at multi-gallon-sized cans marked "blueberry filling" and wondered what the chances were that Doc was actually waiting for me, as opposed to hot-wiring the car. Just in case, I squandered a full minute in front of the mirror to see if my appearance could be improved. It couldn't. I looked tall, tired, and tense.

When I emerged from the bathroom, Doc was at a window table, reading the paper. A warm holiday feeling engulfed me, at being in a well-lit, well-heated place redolent of brewing coffee and rising dough. Where a man like that sat waiting for me.

The scrub cap was gone. I'd hoped for a little baldness, something to reduce him to mere mortal status, but he had a full head of hair, black and wavy. Whole wigs could be made from its excess. I sat opposite him.

Without looking up from the *L.A. Times*, he tapped a well-stocked plastic plate. "Crullers. Chocolate éclairs. Glazed." He handed me a napkin.

"You're awfully well brought up for a kidnapper," I said.

He acknowledged that with a smile, but kept reading. He'd already put away a doughnut or two, judging from the powdered sugar dotting his five o'clock shadow. One of those men who has a five o'clock shadow six minutes after shaving, I decided. He looked like he'd been up since the seventies. He looked ravaged. He looked good.

He took the paper and ripped out a piece of the page he was reading, then tossed the rest onto a pile on the adjoining table. "Okay, Wollie, plan B: I borrow your car, give you money for a cab, and later, you tell the police—"

"Shh." I nodded toward the counter, where a husky red-faced trucker type fortified himself for the return to the convoy. "We'll talk in the car."

"You're not listening."

"I've already taken a cab tonight; one's my limit." I broke off a piece of cruller and put it on my napkin. "My best offer: you drop me in Hollywood, you can have the Rabbit." There were four coffees in front of him. I opened one and added a drop of half-and-half from a tiny plastic container.

He opened a second coffee, threw in five packets of sugar, and stirred violently. His black hair and unshaven face brought to mind the Middle East: one of the Apostles, on a coffee break. He looked out the window. I did too. The Rabbit was the only vehicle in sight. Margaret stretched out on the dashboard, looking back at us.

He spoke quietly. "Look, I'm trying to limit your involvement here. Why are you making it so hard?"

"Stockholm syndrome."

He stopped stirring. "I'm serious."

"You think I'm not? There are dead bodies in the road and killers out wandering around, and you keep looking over your shoulder to see who's following you, but you want to strand me in the middle of Ventura County at whatever time it is, hailing a cab? It's like a horror movie. I won't do it. You want my car, you take me too."

"How do you know I'm not the killer? A killer doctor."

"You may be a killer; you're not a doctor, 'Doc.' Those paper slippers are supposed to be worn over the shoes, not instead of—you'd have learned that in surgery school. The guards noticed it too. And nobody at Rio Pescado dresses like you're dressed, it's a mental hospital. They only do simple stuff, like stitches, and they don't dress up for it. Anything complicated, they go to a regular hospital."

"Then what were these scrubs doing in a supply closet?"

I shrugged. A thought occurred to me. "You're not a patient, are you?"

"Yes. I'm a patient. A dangerous one, with whom you do not want to—"

"Yeah? What meds are you on?" I took a bite of cruller and watched his mind working. "Meds," I repeated. "Haldol, Thorazine, lithium. You're not on anything, and except for this obsession to drop me off places, you don't seem symptomatic."

"Symptomatic." He looked out the window again. "Tell me something. Do you think every patient at Rio Pescado is crazy?"

"It's not a word I'd use. But it's a state hospital, so there's not enough money to keep them if they're not."

The bell-rigged door—not as musical as my shop's—made us turn. A man in a madras shirt and a name tag held the door for the departing trucker, then surveyed the crowd, which was us. "Hey, Douglas," he said to the proprietor. "Coffee fresh?"

"Also—" I said, but Doc reached over and put a hand on my arm to silence me.

"—show biz!" we heard, then laughter. Douglas, behind the counter, talked a little louder than was strictly necessary, the way you do when you like being overheard.

I was still transfixed by the hand on my arm, when Doc stood and leaned over the table. "Occupy them. The guy who walked in— don't let him leave till I get back."

"Wha—"

"You can do it. You're very distracting." He left me with my mouth open.

This was the moment to walk outside, evict the ferret from my car, and drive home. That would be the act of a rational person. Grab a few hours of sleep before another day of blind dates and shop inspections.

"If you hurry," Ruta piped up, "you could even get some vac- uuming in before dawn." I did a mental double take. Was that sar- casm?

She had a point, though. I couldn't sneak off and leave him

stranded, because I didn't believe he would do that to me. Plus, he'd just called me distracting. I got up, put my cruller down, and moved toward the counter. Create a diversion, I thought. You read espionage novels, you'll think of something.

I sneezed. It sounded phony to me, but the two men turned and I fixed the madras shirt man with my best smile. "Allergies. Pollen. Powdered sugar." I perched on a stool next to him, my heart palpitating over this lie.

Douglas said, "What can I get for you?"

"I'll have whatever he's having." Then I remembered I'd spent my last dime on the cab. "No, I mean a napkin. Just a napkin for me." I turned back to my quarry. The name tag was on his far pocket, and I couldn't make it out. Pumping seductivity into my voice, I said, "Working late?"

"Yeah. Dry cleaners. Two doors down."

"Really? Dry cleaning? I love dry cleaning—" I stretched across the counter until I could read the name tag. "—Raymond. Do you work all night long, Raymond?"

He leaned back but his eyes stayed on me or, actually, on my breasts, draped over the counter. He was leaning so drastically I thought he might fall off his stool.

"He's working on the movie," Douglas said. "The Civil War thing."

"No! Really? A Civil War movie?"

"You didn't hear about it? It's got Whatsername in it. Elizabeth Montgomery."

"Elizabeth McGovern, maybe?" I was pretty sure Elizabeth Montgomery was dead.

"Last night," Douglas added, "he did two hundred uniforms with caked-on blood."

"Caked-on blood," I said. "What a challenge, Raymond."

"And he can't even get himself an autograph." Douglas's voice leaked contempt.

Raymond stood and reached into the pocket of his chinos. Was he leaving?

I spoke fast. "Raymond's an awfully nice name. What is it, Spanish?"

"Norwegian." He plunked down some change and turned to leave.

I looked out the window. The green scrub suit was nowhere in sight. *"Wait!"*

Raymond stopped.

"Let me buy you a doughnut," I said. Maybe they took credit cards.

Raymond shook his head. "Sugar, white flour, it's all poison."

"Okay, but let me just ask you something. In your dry cleaning, do you use . . . poly . . . Poly-something. That stuff that eats up the ozone?"

Raymond frowned, and reached for the door handle.

I slid off my stool. "Poly . . . urethane. No. Some chemical. Poly—"

"I don't know what you're talking about."

"No, listen, this is important." I was losing him. My assignment was out the door. "Perchloroethylene! That's it. Raymond! Do you guys use perchloroethylene?" I followed him outside. "Because it's dangerous, Raymond, dangerous for *you*."

He headed to the left, not trying to ditch me, but not slowing down.

"Not just for the consumer," I said, "or the planet, but you, you're the one who works with it, day in and day out. If you don't care about the ozone, care about your lungs. Cancer." I was alongside him. "Sterility. Chernobyl. Doughnuts? Doughnuts are *vitamins* in comparison."

He moved faster. I didn't know what to do so I leapt in front of him and grabbed at his shoulders. We lost our balance and thudded against the glass window of A-1 Travel Agency, Raymond's startled face framed by a poster of Cabo San Lucas.

I let go of him. "Sorry. I'm really sorry, Raymond, but it's my life's work."

He straightened himself. "Weirdo," he muttered. Eyes fixed on me, he moved backward toward Lotus Blossom 24-Hour Martinizing. I figured that Doc was in there and I wanted to alert him so I yelled, "Agent Orange."

It worked. As Raymond reached the dry cleaner's, Doc emerged. He looked so different, though, I had to look twice. Gone were the green scrubs; the erstwhile doctor now wore a tuxedo.

"Are you open for business?" he said, as Raymond literally backed into him. "Because the door was open—"

"No. Eight A.M." Raymond righted himself and went inside.

Doc came my way but didn't look at me. The suit was small for him, tight in the shoulders and short in the sleeves. As he moved past me he touched my elbow in a "follow me" gesture. Pant cuffs dangled a full four inches above his paper slippers.

I turned and followed, pulling at a piece of plastic that emerged from the suit jacket. A receipt clung to it.

"Good work," he said in a low voice, taking the plastic. "Let's go."

"Car keys," I said, and ran into the doughnut shop. I grabbed the keys and then, for good measure, the half page of the *Times* Doc had been reading, the one he'd torn apart.

When I reached the car, he was in the driver's seat.

I got in and handed him the keys.

chapter six

We hurtled out of the parking lot so fast that the ferret was thrown against Doc. He tossed her gently into the back, which didn't seem to bother her.

"You stole that suit," I said.

"I did. It was this or a Confederate soldier. The soldier might have been less conspicuous." He looked down at the ruffled tuxedo shirt, bright yellow and open to the waist, lacking the little studs they use instead of buttons.

"Do you plan to return it? Because it could be someone's wedding suit."

"A dwarf's?"

"I'm not sure they call themselves dwarfs anymore. I've heard—"

"I'll return it. If it makes you feel better."

"Dry-cleaned?"

He smiled. "Don't push it."

In the gym bag, a phone rang. Doc frowned. "That can't be mine, it's new—no one has the number."

"Well, it can't be mine; I don't have one." I was about to add that I couldn't afford one, but I didn't want to appear judgmental about his spending choices. I unzipped the gym bag and found the phone amid shaving gear, books, and underwear, and handed it over. His bag looked like my junk drawer.

"Hello . . . Yeah?" His voice dropped an octave. "What do you want?"

I itched to explore the gym bag. A pack of cigarettes nestled against some sort of calculator. Marlboro Reds, not even low tar. Number ten, I thought, No Smoking. And what books was he reading? I moved aside a sock to see the spine of a paperback. *Mortal Splendor.* Oh, dear. Romance? Religion? Pornography?

"I don't have your stash." There was an edge to his voice, an animosity that startled me. I zipped up the gym bag and folded my hands in my lap.

"No," he said. "I'm saying I didn't want the information, not then, not now." Violence played across his face, and was gone. "That's bullshit. I've been in a lot of places this week, that's the point of life on the outside. Just so you *capisce,* the body count goes higher, I go to the cops."

That ended the call. He gripped the phone like a soda can he was about to crush. I felt queasy. Doc knew something about the murder, and I should find out what. If the investigation came around to P.B., I could use information to bargain with the cops.

"Close friend?" I said.

He looked straight ahead. "Never met the guy. Long story."

"It's a long drive."

His expression softened, but he shook his head. This wasn't going to be easy. "Tell me one thing," I said. "Tell me you weren't involved in that man's death."

He looked at me, then back to the road. "I didn't shoot him, I've never shot anyone, I'm sorry he's dead."

"Okay, fine, relax. No need to get defensive. Have a cigarette."

He almost smiled, but said nothing. I stayed quiet too, for about thirty seconds, then said, "So you were in jail?"

His head snapped toward me. "Why do you say that?"

"You talked about 'life on the outside.' Which implies an inside. Like jail. Or, I suppose, the CIA, FBI, cults, monasteries, the military, higher education—"

"But prison sounds the most likely?" The dry-cleaning receipt was stuck to his sleeve; he gave it a glance, then crumpled it and tossed it back to Margaret.

"No offense, Doc," I said.

"No problem, Wollie. Wollie, as in Wally Cleaver?"

"Pronounced that way, but spelled with an 'o.' As in Wollstone-craft."

"As in Mary Wollstonecraft? *Vindication of the Rights of Woman*?"

I stared. "Pretty esoteric stuff for a criminal. Okay, then, you're CIA. Or some monastic order—"

"I don't think monks concern themselves with eighteenth-century feminism. I'm fairly sure spies don't. So, Mary Wollstone-craft—"

"Actually, Mary Wollstonecraft Shelley. That's my full name."

He smiled. "Quite a handle. This, from the mother who claimed you were allergic to fur? Or is your father to blame?"

"My mother. She's always been . . . whimsical. My brother had it even worse, since—" The mention of P.B. put me on dangerous ground. I said quickly, "How about you, what's your name?"

He glanced at me, then away. "I'd rather not say."

"After I just bared my soul? Come on, how bad can it be?"

After a long pause, he said, "You tell me. What do you think of Gomez?"

"As a last name?" I said hopefully.

"Both."

I gaped at him. "Gomez Gomez?"

He met my look. "You got a problem with that?"

Seven miles later, I was still fixated on it. Back during the Persian Gulf War, when CNN was always quoting Boutros Boutros-Ghali, Fredreeq had said, "Double names are never correct." You could see her point. Try coming up with a double name that has real dignity. Marky Mark. Circus Circus. Rin Tin Tin.

Sirhan Sirhan.

"If you don't mind," I said, "I think I'll keep calling you Doc."

"Call me whatever you like." He crossed six traffic lanes in five seconds.

When horns stopped honking and my stomach returned to its rightful position, I asked, "Are you trying to lose whoever might be following us?"

"That's the idea." The Rabbit slowed and the exit ramp's centrifugal force sucked us into the darkness of Coldwater Canyon.

"What are they driving?" I asked.

"Not a clue."

"Who are they?"

"Not sure," he said.

"Why are they after you?"

He charged a yellow light and turned right. My body was thrown toward his, and I let it linger there for a little longer than was strictly necessary. He made a left, and leaned my way. "Half the trouble I'm in, it's because someone felt compelled to spill his guts to me."

"And the other half?" I said softly. "What accounts for that?"

He straightened up. "Bad attitude. Bad judgment. Bad luck."

"What were you in jail for?"

He fished around under his seat and brought Margaret onto his lap, to pet her. I imagined him locked in a place of concrete and metal, hard surfaces, with nothing soft or furry to touch. Margaret stood on her back legs to look out his window, a big white tube sock with paws. "Prison, not jail," Doc said. "Sentenced to a year and a day, served half. Minor felony."

"Contempt of court? A journalist protecting a source, something like that?"

"Nothing like that," he said. "What do you do for a living?"

"I'm sorry, is it bad etiquette to ask about a person's crime?"

"Yeah, let's move on," he said. "What do you do?"

"I'm in business."

He looked at me. "You're not a businesswoman. You're not the type."

I blinked. "I better be the type, I have small business loans from four—"

"All right, that's your day job. What else do you do?"

"As it happens, I also design greeting cards, but—"

"There you go," he said. "What were you doing at the hospital tonight?"

"Long story. What do you do for a living?"

He smiled, a flash of white teeth in the dark. "Unemployed."

Of course. Number five, Has Job. "Just tell me one thing," I said. "Your minor felony wasn't of a sexual nature, was it?" I had pedophilia on the brain.

He gave me a look so long I thought we'd drive off the road. "Ms. Shelley," he said, "I haven't been this close to a woman in six months. Do you really want to bring sex into the conversation right now?"

. . .

HE PARKED AT Vons, a twenty-four-hour grocery chain that es-
chewed apostrophes in its title, in a strip mall on the corner of Lau-
rel Canyon and Ventura Boulevard. The other stores were dark and
gated except for Kinko's, the all-night copy shop. Neither Vons nor
Kinko's appeared to be doing a thriving after-midnight business,
judging from the paucity of parked cars. A lone woman wobbled on
high heels, weaving her cheerful way around lampposts, clutching a
plastic bag like a trophy.

Doc reached across me for the gym bag and stopped, an inch from
my face.

"What?" I said. The buttonless shirt was open. He had a lot of
chest hair.

"God. You're really pretty, aren't you?"

"I—no, no, no, that's an exit line. You can't dump me, not yet, not
in front of Vons, I have things to ask you—"

"I'm not dumping you." He reached for the ferret. "You're
dumping me."

I caught his dangling French cuff. "Wait. I've got my own stake
in this. I need to know what you know about that dead body, I need
to—"

"You need to remain blissfully ignorant." He put his hand on mine
and squeezed it before extricating his cuff. Then he was out of the
car.

I climbed over the console to the driver's seat. "Look, I won't go
to the cops, I promise, and if the cops come to me—"

"Hey." He leaned down, his face framed in the open window, eyes
so dark I couldn't see the pupils. "Tell them the truth. I had a gun,
you were scared, you found out I was a criminal, you did what you
did to stay alive."

"You had a *gun*?"

The eyes half closed and for one wild moment I thought he was going to kiss me. Then he reached through the window, locked my door, and slapped the side of the car like it was a horse he was sending on its way.

"Doc!" I said, as he headed toward Kinko's.

"Doc!" cried the weaving woman, like a backup singer.

Pulse racing, I put the Rabbit in drive and took off after him. An inner voice screeched, "Don't let him get away," drowning out years of cultural conditioning and weeks of actual training in how to be a girl, lady, woman, date. Dr. Cookie's face popped up like a greeting card, appalled by my naked pursuit of a man. "Number eleven," she reminded me. "No Guns."

I'm doing this for my brother, I told her. I passed Doc, pulled around, and hit the brakes, blocking his progress. "At least give me your number."

"You go, girl!" the woman called out, toasting me with her plastic bag.

Doc threw a look her way and then changed directions, walking toward the back of the car. I shifted into reverse, but I gave it too much gas.

The Rabbit backed up with a lurch and hit him.

"Jesus," he yelled, "you've run over me!"

I jumped out of the car and grabbed Margaret's leash, as he held his thigh in his hands, massaging it through the tuxedo pants. The edge of his paper slipper was caught under the Rabbit's rear tire. It was true. I'd run over him.

He eased his foot out of the slipper and took a slow step forward. "One dead body wasn't enough for you?"

"I'm so sorry. You know how, when you're in reverse, you confuse the brake and the accelator, because you're facing backward? What—does it hurt?"

He was staring off, over my shoulder. "How long has that car been there?"

I followed his gaze. A middle-of-the-night mist had settled in, making things hazy in the floodlights. It took a moment to see head-lights at the other end of the two-block-long parking lot.

Doc grabbed Margaret and his gym bag. "Lock up your car. Fast."

I did it, then followed him up concrete steps. We passed Kinko's and Baskin-Robbins, and moved into the shadows in front of a movie poster store.

"Is it whoever's after you?" My heart was pounding.

"We're about to find out. With luck, they haven't spotted us yet. Get down."

"Can't we go inside Kinko's and—"

"No. Get down."

I squatted. The building jutted out, blocking our view of the car, and its view of us. Doc leaned forward to sneak a look and I had to restrain myself from pulling him back. I felt exposed here and hoped anyone looking our way would take us for a couple smoking crack, or whatever it is people do in doorways at two in the morning. My new best friend, the inebriated woman, had disappeared.

I said, "Where are you parked? I vote we go into Kinko's and sneak out the front entrance, get to your car, and worry about the Rabbit later."

"I don't have a car."

"What do you mean—what are we doing here?"

He nodded across the street. "The bus stop."

"You take the bus?" Number four, I thought, Has Car.

"I have to get back to the hospital; I'm trying to spring someone." He set Margaret on the ground. She reached the end of her leash, and he reeled her back.

"You're saying you got to Rio Pescado today by *bus*?" I asked.

"You think buses exist just to annoy cars?" He looked across the lot again.

"No, listen—you're right, you do need my car. I'll give you a ride, I have to go back to the hospital tomorrow—today, actually."

He turned. "You can't go there. You'll be a police flyer by tomorrow, as a kidnap victim."

I stared at him. "My God. But I have to—I mean, how am I going to—?"

He held up a hand.

The car came into view.

It traveled with the speed of a funeral cortege. It passed under a floodlight, revealing itself as a sporty little thing with a canvas top. It reached the smattering of cars in front of Vons and slowed further, as though taking down license plates.

"What is that, an Alfa Romeo?" Doc asked. The car made a forty-five-degree turn, and headed toward us like a heat-seeking missile.

I flattened myself against the brick. "I don't know. I'm not a car person."

"There's a surprise." He put a reassuring hand on my knee. "It's dark; they won't see us."

The slow, inexorable approach was excruciating. I was reminded of tanks in World War II movies. My legs shook and I abandoned my squatting position to sit, feeling the cold cement seep through my cotton flannel skirt. "Look," I said, "if I can't go back to the hospital, you can't either."

"I'm in different clothes." He kept his attention on the car. "I'll shave, I'll speak Spanish, they won't know it's me."

"Well, I can change too, disguise my—"

"No, you can't. There's only one of you. How many six-foot blondes—"

"Five eleven and seven-eighths," I said. If I slouched. He had a point, though. Already he was a far cry, visually, from the doctor in the scrub suit. It wasn't just the tuxedo; he had a chameleon quality that I lacked.

The Alfa Romeo passed under lights again, showing two passengers, of indeterminate age and gender. "Good," Doc said. "Come on, come on . . . Let's see your license number."

Let's not, I thought. I did not enjoy hide-and-seek with sinister sports cars. My intrepid friend Joey would consider this a good time, but not me. And what would we do with a license? Call the police, report slow driving?

The Alfa Romeo made a sharp right and I let out a breath. The thought of police led me back to my brother. P.B. would be okay without me; he had his aluminum foil, more vital to his peace of mind than my presence. I just had to figure out how to keep him away from the murder investigation. Maybe I could arrange for him to visit Uncle Theo for a few days and—

The Alfa Romeo stopped. Five parking spaces away from the Rabbit.

"What are they doing?" I whispered.

"Wondering where we are. My guess is, they were too far away to see you run me over, but they recognize your car. I lost them for a minute on the exit ramp, then they got lucky."

My poor, defenseless Rabbit. "For the record," I said, "rather than 'spring' someone from Rio Pescado, you might try going through channels; the staff is surprisingly human. But say you do it your way: What then? Wait for the getaway bus? Hide in the woods, live on leaves? If you're determined to break the law, you really will need my car."

"You're right," he said, surprising me. "But that will require some doing."

"Like most things in life." A dark suspicion crossed my mind. "Only it's not my turn to create a diversion."

He turned the full force of his dimples on me. "But you do it so well."

chapter seven

Eight minutes later, I walked to the Rabbit with as much natural-
ness as I could muster, sensing the scrutiny of three men. That
one of them was Doc did not help. I felt I was on a high wire without a net, a sensation furthered by the fact I was shoeless; I'd given
Doc my Converse All Stars.

What would Ruta do, in my socks? "Pretend it's wartime," she
said. "Only they don't know what side you're on yet, so they're not
going to shoot you." I wasn't sure about the analogy, but it didn't
seem that my death was in anyone's best interest.

Careful not to look at the Alfa Romeo, I got into my car and
reparked it properly, despite shaking limbs. From the hatchback
I grabbed a large piece of cardboard in the shape of sunglasses, which
I positioned on the Rabbit's dashboard, as though the sun were
overhead rather than across the world, shining down on Europe.
I made a show of checking door handles, and prayed the Alfa

Romeo was too far away to see that the driver's side was in fact left open.

My key was under the front seat.

I clutched my purse and turned toward Kinko's. A voice stopped me.

"Who's sorry now?" sang a gravelly soprano. The high-heeled woman wobbled out from behind a set of blue Dumpsters. I speeded up, but she wobbled faster, serenading me. Catching up, she offered her Vons bag. I waved her off.

This could mess things up. The Alfa men were supposed to think I would lead them to Doc—they'd seen us, presumably, in the Donut Stop, they knew we were a team. If it looked like I was hanging with this woman, would it confuse things? Would any of this work? How fast could a heart beat before it exploded?

I reached the steps to Kinko's, the singer right with me, continuing her way through "Who's Sorry Now," a version of the song that contained just those three words. I climbed a step. Then another. Behind us, a car door slammed.

The Alfa Romeo.

I hesitated, waiting for the sound of the other door. It didn't come. Was only one man getting out of the car? This complicated everything.

"Corn chips?" The singer held out the Vons bag again. It must have been an instrumental break in her song. I shook my head and plunged into Kinko's.

The copy shop was warm and blindingly bright and blessed with human beings, one at a computer terminal, two working the printing machines. They looked up at our traveling lounge act. I strode down the aisle toward the front of the store, picking up speed until I reached the glass door, then turned to the chanteuse. "Stay. Do not follow. Sing to these people, they need a song."

She turned to check them out. At the back of the shop, someone opened the door we'd just come through—one or both of the Alfa Romeo men. I didn't wait around for a good look; I hurried outside, onto Ventura Boulevard.

A gym bag sat against the brick building, inconspicuous unless you were right on top of it, at which point you might notice it bulge and move, as if it were about to give birth. I grabbed it and ran into the street, to the taxi summoned by Doc with his cell phone.

I PAID WITH a credit card and, as Doc suggested, had the taxi drop me off a block early. I'd spent the entire ride staring out the back window, so this was probably unnecessary, but I wasn't taking chances. There was always the possibility my pursuer had cleverly attached himself to the taxi's trunk and ridden there undetected.

Activity on Sunset was minimal. Even street people had retired into doorways with their blankets or furniture pads or newspapers as defense against the cold March air. I knelt down and unzipped the gym bag.

Margaret regarded me with a dubious expression. She had little button eyes that looked like she'd rimmed them with eyeliner, and pink ears, a pink nose, and pink toenails. A real girl. I offered her my hand, in case she was trained to shake, the way dogs are. She took my finger in her tiny teeth and shook it like she was bringing down big game. Doc had said she didn't bite; I guess that didn't count as biting. "Be nice," I said, and set her on the sidewalk. "I'm new at this."

She was intriguing to look at, I had to admit. Her movements were sensuous, like a belly dancer's, with a back-and-forth sway. The torso was long, relative to her legs, a dachshund's body. With a fluffy tail. Her head sloped into her back like a sports car, and the lack of neck dictated the need for the harness that attached to the leash; a collar alone wouldn't have anything to hold on to. It was impossible to look at her without wanting to draw her, and a greeting card began to unfold in my head: Margaret in combat fatigues, holding a machine gun, saying, "Don't call me rodent."

I let her walk, since she'd been cooped up all night in pockets, cars, and gym bags. We made our slow way east, the sidewalk tough and pebbly under my wool socks. I didn't regret giving my shoes to Doc—he'd need them more than I did—but it was depressing to know his feet were smaller than mine.

I kept looking behind me.

When I reached my block and a patch of grass in front of Loo Fong's, I stopped. Doc had said Margaret was housebroken but I wasn't sure how that worked. I needed to pee again, so she might too, but how to communicate this?

"Pee, Margaret," I said. She looked at me and yawned.

I explained that this was the best bathroom for her on the block, the block that was her new, temporary home. "See," I pointed, "we live at Wildwood Arms Deluxe Apartments two doors down that way, and we work at the mini-mall right here, and there's a courtyard in between, I'll show you that tomorrow, but right now this is the optimum stretch of grass for bodily functions. Truly. Please."

Incredibly, Margaret started sniffing the grass, perhaps hearing the call of nature. She turned her back on me and I looked away, to give her privacy.

I stretched to see around Loo Fong's neon CHINESE! Good! Fast! Cheap! sign, and almost lost my balance. There, nestled in the corner position between Plucky Chicken and Neat Nails Plus was Wollie's Welcome! Greetings.

Visible through the curtains, there was light.

When I'd left for Rio Pescado the shop had been dark.

. . . .

DID I HAVE to check it out? "Yes," said the voice in my head. Ruta again. "But not in socks."

Inside my apartment, I turned on all the lights, cranked up the heat, and tried to focus. The shop was locked when I'd left for the hospital; I might be nonchalant about the Rabbit, but I would no more leave my shop unsecured than a mother would send her child to school naked. The mini-mall parking lot was empty now, which meant that whoever was in the shop was on foot or didn't want their car seen. Something stirred in me, some primal homesteader-on-the-frontier impulse that gets people to load up their shotguns. Not that I had a shotgun.

The ferret crawled into the cupboard under the kitchen sink to commune with Mr. Clean. I fished her out and tied her leash to the refrigerator handle. The apartment grew warmer, but it would be hours before my extremities thawed. I donned a dry pair of socks, then hiking boots, sitting on the black-and-white checkerboard kitchen floor to lace feverishly. "Margaret, I've got to go out," I said. "Believe me, I don't want to, but I've pumped my life's blood, not to mention my life savings, into that shop."

Margaret crept under the oven. I pulled her out and shortened the leash.

"I don't expect you to understand feeling this way about a store, you're not a small business owner, but maybe you feel strongly about something—ferreting, say. If you take ferreting, and imagine four walls around it, that's my store. Maybe you find it gimmicky, the whole Welcome! Willkommen! Tyrolean village thing, but it works, these stores sell cards. Well, not my branch, not in record numbers, but that's changing. Too many people need me to stay in business. Fredreeq. My brother. Vendors."

Margaret wrinkled her nose, then turned her back on me. I stood.

"I can't call the cops in case there's one of those APB things out on me, so I'm on my own." I paused. Doc hadn't said what she ate. I poured Wheat Chex into a ceramic bowl, and showed it to her. She couldn't have cared less. I added milk. "Okay, here's food. And a paper slipper, to remind you of Doc. Gomez. Your human."

Margaret studied the cottage cheese ceiling.

"All right, I'm leaving. Good luck to both of us." I stashed the gym bag on top of the refrigerator and started scouting around for a blunt instrument.

MY HIKING BOOTS squeaked on the linoleum stairs outside my apartment. I was armed with a marble bust of Dante and a can of Raid. In my jacket pocket was a cordless phone. All the better household items—police flashlight, hammer, carving knife—were in the shop. I didn't own a gun (number eleven, No Guns), nor did my life include ice picks, tire irons, hatchets, shovels, pitchforks, electric drills, or bowling balls.

Was I overreacting? Several people had keys to the shop. Of course, all those people had cars, too, except for Uncle Theo, who didn't drive. In any case, it was hard to imagine circumstances that would lure Uncle Theo here from Glendale at 4 A.M.

But if it was intruders, it would be my second criminal episode tonight—me, who'd never before seen anything worse than illegal U-turns. Still, vandalism ran rampant in L.A. I thought of the Hummels, tiny porcelain Bavarian children, so fragile . . . the shop was insured, but Welcome! policy required managers to pay the deductible, which—

In apartment 1A, a dog barked. I hurried out the back exit, into the courtyard that connected the Wildwood Arms Deluxe Apartments to the rear of the mini-mall.

The cold hit me anew. The courtyard was too dark to make out anything but the scraggly citrus trees. I moved slowly and stepped on something squishy, probably a rotten lemon. I stopped.

My plan had been to go through the courtyard to sneak into the back room of my shop. But then what? Hit the intruders? I couldn't hit a golf ball with conviction. My best bet was to scare them off, but I'm not visually intimidating, despite being tall. I backed up into the shadows of the Wildwood Arms, as close as possible to my own apartment, one story up, so my cordless phone would still get reception, then dialed the shop. I waited through my outgoing message, then put on the most vicious voice I could muster. "I know you're in there, whoever you—"

There was a wail from apartment 1B. I'd managed to scare the Tomlinson baby. Next it would be Mrs. Albertini in 2B, who called the police as a hobby—yes, there was her light popping on. In a minute her curlered head would appear in the second-story window, a truly scary prospect. I whispered into the phone, "I'm coming with *cops.* So you better *get out,*" then raced back through the apartment building and out to the alley.

Gravel crunched underfoot as I stumbled ahead. My new plan was to sneak to the front of the mini-mall and see if I'd flushed out someone, without actually confronting them. The alley was dark and gave me the creeps, and I fervently hoped the dead cat carcass from earlier in the week was gone. I remembered how Ruta felt about alleys: the urban equivalent of dark forests, a place little girls should never go into at night. Of course, I was no longer a little girl. After tonight I'd be lucky to pass for middle-aged.

Near the shop's freight entrance I encountered a car. Joey's.

At least, it looked like her car, an old silver Saab. I moved in for a closer look. The map light was on, illuminating a copy of *Vanity Fair* and an empty frozen yogurt container on the front seat. Yes, Joey's car.

That light shouldn't stay on, or she'd run down her battery. I tried the door.

The car alarm blared. Behind me, the freight door opened. Someone grabbed me. I screamed.

. . .

BEING HUGGED BY my friend Joey was like being hugged by an ironing board, Joey being five foot ten, all angles. I let myself be fussed over as I shivered in the alley, relieved yet enraged, probably headed for a breakdown, now that the crisis was over.

"You're freezing," Joey said. She was pale and lovely, with wild hair the color of an Irish setter. "You're shaking like you have palsy. What are you doing?"

"What am I doing? What are you doing? Why didn't you park out front like a normal person?"

Joey herded me into the back room, illuminated by candles. "I brought over the chaise longue," she said, "so I had to use the freight entrance."

The back room was Joey's home away from home, in part because it housed so much of her furniture. She spent the night often when her husband was out of town, occasionally when he was in town, or whenever she felt the need to, as she put it, run away and join the circus.

"How come you didn't pick up the phone a minute ago?" I asked.

Joey led me to the red velvet sofa that had once been hers, now folded out into a bed and made up with sheets and pillows. "I un-plugged it back here," she said, covering me with a quilt. "Someone's been calling every half hour."

"What? Who?" I shot up, shedding the quilt.

"I don't know who, they hang up when I answer. God, you're jumpy. Look, I've got the space heater going and tea, so why don't you just sit down and warm up?"

I sat, watching her cowboy boots clomp across the room to my drafting table, where steam rose from an electric teakettle. She wore paisley pajamas with her boots, a look I found oddly comforting. She made tea, the steam distorting her profile, fogging up her John Lennon glasses. Joey had a nearly flawless face, made interesting by a scar in the shape of a crescent moon running from cheekbone to jaw line, dead white against her ivory skin. Sometimes she covered it with makeup. Mostly, she didn't bother.

"Do you think my brother is capable of killing someone?" I couldn't believe the words had come out of my mouth. I hadn't meant to talk about this. Forty seconds in front of the heater must've thawed it out of me.

Joey unplugged the teakettle, and came over to hand me a mug of tea. She stretched out on the brocade chaise longue, looking vamp-ish, her long red hair flowing over the side of the chaise, nearly to the floor.

"Anyone is capable of killing," she said, "if they're scared enough or mad enough. Even Quakers. But I don't think P.B.'s more likely to kill than, say, you are, which is a lot less likely than your average person. Did you have a particular method in mind?"

"Shooting."

"Really? Would P.B. have access to a gun, in the hospital?"

I wrapped the blanket tighter around myself. "Maybe. It turns out security at Rio Pescado isn't state-of-the-art. And Dr. Charlie says P.B.'s foot is healing well, so he may have some mobility—oh, heck." I fell back onto a pillow and gazed up at Uncle Theo's circus trapeze suspended from the ceiling. Maybe I could just lie here until this was all over.

"Wollie, having introduced the topic of murder, you can't now fade out mid-sentence. You know, you look like a refugee from East-ern Europe."

I roused myself to glance at the full-length mirror on the bath-room door. The hood of my sweatshirt was bunched up under my jacket, giving a hunchback effect. My long skirt was torn. Hair hung around my face like limp straw. This was how Doc had seen me all night. "I can't talk about it," I said, "because I'm sworn to silence."

"You can't tell me why you're carrying bug spray and a bust of Lenin?"

"Dante, not Lenin. Alighieri. *The Divine Comedy*."

"Yes, I know who Dante is. I was wondering what you're doing with him."

"He was a gift from Date Number Three, the financial planner who liked to sculpt. We were discussing whether blind dates were hell or just purgatory, and—"

"All right, you don't have to tell me anything tonight. Drink your tea."

I focused on the tea, pale yellow. I took a sip and choked. It had a shot of alcohol in it. "No, I want to tell you, I have a profound need to tell you," I said. "I just have to figure out which parts are okay and which . . ." I leaned back and closed my eyes. I should be getting back to Margaret. But that would require standing up, and anyway, Margaret was safe, living in a circus tent, with good psychiatric care, and I would turn her into a Get Well Soon card in Spanish and English, right after Doc and I started dating, but first Joey was taking the mug of yellow tea out of my hands as I heard myself snore.

I'm asleep, I realized. I'm dreaming.

And I'm in love.

chapter eight

"Ventura County Sheriff." Her voice was crisp as cornflakes. Sunset Boulevard, on the other hand, was like a hangover on this foggy Saturday morning. From the pay phone, I glanced at an abandoned shopping cart and two sleeping people, and fought down queasiness at what I was doing.

"Hi. I need to ask someone a question about a possible body?" I strove for a casual tone, as if calling Bloomingdale's and asking for Accessories.

"What is it you need to know?"

"Whether you've found one in the last—recently."

"Found a body?" she asked. "Is this about a missing person?"

"No, it's about a found corpse. I was wondering, do you give out information like that to regular citizens? About corpses?"

"Ma'am, we have no information on bodies unless a crime's involved."

"Okay, say a crime's involved."

"What's your name, ma'am?"

I hung up.

Darn. I'd wasted the call. I couldn't now phone back without arousing suspicion, if the same woman answered, and I was dying for information.

The pay phone rang. I jumped, then reached out tentatively, as if the graffiti-covered box were alive. "Hello?"

"Ma'am, did you want to—"

"She's not here." I hung up and hightailed it back to the shop. I should've said something clever, like "I'm from Iowa," so they wouldn't connect me to that phone, this neighborhood. But telling one lie was hard enough, and you can't think of everything on three hours of sleep.

I glanced around the parking lot. Too early for customers, including Mr. Bundt's spies. I went in and switched the radio from easy listening to news.

The police would be swarming the hospital by now, maybe even armed with a sketch of me, the "kidnap victim," based on the description furnished by the security guards. I imagined them showing it around, the artist's rendering of my limp blond hair and jean jacket, with the caption *Have You Seen This Woman?* Someone would say, "Hey! It's the sister of the guy on Unit 18—what's her name? Wollie. She's missing, huh?"

I would try a preemptive strike. I dialed Rio Pescado and left a breezy message on Dr. Charlie's voice mail, saying it was Saturday morning, I was fine, and just wondering when P.B. might get to leave RT and go back to Unit 18, his regular ward, and ziprasidone, his regular meds.

I redialed and this time got through to a psych tech named Jacob on Unit 18. We were interrupted twice by call-waiting. I had trouble clicking through to the other call, which I blamed on my new—cheap—telephone, but it gave me a moment to make up questions about the upcoming Easter potluck. This gave Jacob an opportunity to bring up dead bodies and police investigations, if he were so inclined, but Jacob was worked up about the plethora of cakes and pies coming to the potluck and the paucity of vegetables, and I had to promise a three-bean salad just to get off the phone. At least I'd established myself as being alive and well.

It was time to call P.B. I got through to the floor supervisor in the RT building, who told me my brother had gone to breakfast in the dining hall.

"Dining hall?" I said. "That's acres away. I thought he ate in his room."

"Oh, not since he's off the crutches. I think he's missed his friends."

"Wh—when did he get off his crutches?"

"Oh, just a day or two ago. We can't hardly keep up with him."

I hung up, stunned. Just because someone can walk doesn't mean he's a killer, I reminded myself. Most people walk. Until I talked to P.B., it was useless to speculate, but it was now imperative to find out who Doc suspected of this murder. When he showed up, I intended to squeeze it out of him. Somehow. Drugs, maybe.

A large yellow something danced past the window and then danced back. I turned and recognized it as Fredreeq, in lemon yellow toreador pants and matching sweater set, waving her arms in excitement. "Robert Quarter," she yelled through the glass. I gave her a "huh?" kind of shrug and she shrieked. With a beckoning gesture, she danced off once more, to Neat Nails Plus, the business adjoining mine.

In addition to her hours at my shop, Fredreeq was a part-time facialist at Neat Nails Plus. On Saturdays she opened and closed as well, for the Seventh-Day Adventist owners. Curious, I locked up my place and went next door to find Fredreeq plugging in hot wax machines and other sinister appliances in cubicles surrounding a fruit-laden altar. The salon staff was mostly Vietnamese, and the decor, with its red walls, shrouded lamps, and posters of Southeast Asia, was a combination Buddhist temple, travel agency, and opium den. "Don't tell me you've never heard of Robert Quarter," Fredreeq said and disappeared through a bead curtain doorway into the salon's back room.

"I've never heard of Robert Quarter," I called. "But if it's about a date—"

"Girl, don't you read the trades?" she yelled. L.A.'s two show business newpapers, *Daily Variety* and the *Hollywood Reporter*, were read by everyone from pool cleaners to migrant farm workers.

"Tell me later. I have to go open up," I said, then stopped. Near the door was a coffee table buried in strata of periodicals a full foot deep. I pushed aside beauty magazines and grabbed up every newspaper in sight. "Fredreeq, I'm borrowing a paper," I called out, my arms full, and ran back to the shop.

"MAY I HELP you?"

My first customer of the day looked up, startled, then dropped his head, like someone caught in a criminal act. He was about sixteen, with dismal posture and bad skin, and he stood at the LoveLetters, Ltd. spinner, spinning it slowly. He would take twenty minutes to choose a card, six days to write in it, and if the object of his desire did not respond, he would consider suicide. Sometimes my heart so ached for my customers, I wondered if I was cut out for this business.

I returned to the table in the northeast corner, covered with newspapers and the crumpled half page of the *L.A. Times* I'd grabbed from the Donut Stop the night before. The other half was with Doc—the more interesting half, presumably, as mine had Ralph's grocery store coupons on one side and lottery results and auction notices on the other. Mine also had no date or page number, so I was going through the pilfered papers a page at a time, looking for a match.

"Morning." Joey, in blue jeans, emerged from the back room. The teenage customer followed her long, thin legs with his eyes. She was morning pale and her red hair shot out in all directions, follicles energized from a night in bed. "There it is," she said, unearthing her cell phone from my mound of newspapers. "I'm hanging here today, if you don't mind; Elliot's out of town and his evil sister's visiting. She was going on last night about my chaise longue, how it violates the aesthetic integrity of the house, until I finally just hauled it out of there."

Joey had married into an architecturally important house, which is why her former furniture kept migrating to my back room. I flipped through a Friday Calendar section. "Are you allowed to abandon a houseguest like that?" I asked. "Doesn't it violate some in-law hospitality rule?"

"No, because my sister-in-law likes the housekeeper more than she likes me. What are you doing?"

I showed her the page I was trying to match and she started to look through the papers with me. I should borrow her house-keeper for Margaret, I thought. At 7 A.M., I'd taken the ferret for a courtyard stroll, replaced her glutinous Wheat Chex with tuna fish, a rice cake, lettuce, and grapes, apologized for leaving her alone, and told her I'd return as soon as I could. Margaret had been un-moved.

I felt Joey's look as I furiously turned pages. It was a big mistake, this vow of silence I'd taken. Bad enough that I couldn't talk about Doc or the corpse, but he'd been really adamant about Margaret, as if she were in some witness protection program. The fact was, I was bursting to discuss it all; I wasn't programmed for discretion. Maybe it would be okay to just ask questions, the kind that come up in general conversation. That wasn't "talking," exactly. "Joey," I said, "how do you find out about the progress of a murder investigation, beyond what's reported in the paper?"

Joey perked right up at this. She came from a family of law enforcement professionals and had worked herself, briefly, in a morgue. "The best way is to be a close relative of the victim, or know someone on the force. We don't have you dating any homicide cops, do we?"

A woman with a walker struggled through the front door, causing the Welcome! bell to ring incessantly until I rescued her. She cut off my hello with a toss of her steel gray spit curls and said, "Just looking," in the tone of voice that means "Don't bug me." I went to the register to ring up my teenage customer, then turned to find Joey exiting to the back room, phone to her ear. Prominently placed on the table for me was the Friday California section, folded open to page B9.

"Plea Bargain of Mob Figure Reversed on Appeal" said the headline. The word "Mob" seemed to pulsate. Mob. Mob. Mob.

"Shit!" cried the woman in the walker.

You're telling me, I thought, and hurried over to Birthdays, Humorous. The woman stood with an open purse, cursing. On my grass green carpet was a compact of pressed powder, broken and crushed. When I knelt to pick it up, the customer snapped shut the purse and exited, her walker thumping across the floor.

I was desperate to get back to my clue, but the woman could be a spy, lying in wait outside. This was the sort of thing Mr. Bundt would test me on, the Immediate Cleanup Response that was drilled into us on a cellular level. But there are times a person has to live dangerously. I returned to my paper.

Next to the mob article was an ad for Ernest Bovee, M.D., who specialized in cosmetic body surgery, and provided a smiling photo of himself with before and after shots of a woman's thighs. It was possible Doc saved liposuction ads. It was also possible he'd felt compelled, last night at the Donut Stop, to collect coupons. But it wasn't likely. With a sigh, I read the article.

Plea Bargain of Mob Figure Reversed on Appeal

LOS ANGELES—In a unanimous decision, the California Court of Appeals for the 2nd District ordered a guilty plea to be vacated in a conspiracy case against Ronald "the Weasel" Ronzare.

The appellate court acknowledged that overturning a plea bargain was unusual, but determined that trial judge Anna Whitestorm erred by failing to follow established procedures for ensuring that the defendant understood his plea before it was entered.

According to Ronzare's attorney Calvin Walsh, "It's all in the transcripts. [Judge Whitestorm] was in such a hurry to get to Palm Springs before rush hour, she would have accepted a guilty plea from a poodle. My client's former counsel was inexperienced, the D.A. was lazy and the judge—with all due respect—sloppy."

Ronzare, an alleged operative for the East Coast crime family headed by Eddie "Digits" Minardi, was sentenced to 10-20 years for conspiracy to commit battery on two LAPD officers early last year. A second, more serious charge of conspiracy to commit murder was dropped. Ronzare is to be released on bail from Corcoran State Prison pending a new trial.

Conspiracy charges were dropped last year against two other suspects, Tor Ulvskog and Olof Froderberg, alleged operatives for Las Vegas's Terranova crime family.

I glanced regretfully at Dr. Ernest Bovee's smiling face, then returned to the mob story and read it again. I was still mulling over its significance five minutes later, as I collected jagged bits of tortoise-shell plastic and sucked up pressed powder with my Dustbuster.

A shadow stepped in front of me.

A hand reached down and switched off my Dustbuster.

chapter nine

He wasn't a customer. This was not a person who went card shopping.

I was backed up against the Birthday rack, Dustbuster pointed at him like a gun.

He had several inches on me, a big man, and not a young one—sixty, at least. His hair was white and the rest of him was tan, and not just a living-in-southern-California-without-sunscreen tan. His tan was like a vocation.

"Can't stand those." He nodded at the Dustbuster. "Remind me of a former—"

I waited, but he seemed to forget he had a sentence in progress. I lowered the Dustbuster. He raised his hands, big brown paws, and with a flash of metal—massive Rolex, heavy gold chain-link bracelet—reached into the pocket of his suit and withdrew a slip of paper. It was a nice enough suit, but one that had been around awhile, judging from the smells emanating from it. Mothballs, for instance. "Is your name . . . Welleslington Shelley?"

"Wollstonecraft."

He hacked a pretty serious smoker's hack and stared. "That's a first name?"

"In this case. And you are—?"

He wheezed. "The authorities."

Dear God, I thought, they've come for me. A vision of Ruta appeared, aproned, hands on hips. "What authorities call themselves the authorities?" she asked. "But you play along with him. That's how you play it safe."

I said, "What is it you want, Officer—?"

He pondered the piece of paper again, as if waiting for reading glasses to materialize. Then, "Do you drive a Volkswagen vehicle, license 1NJC, uh—"

"Close enough." If he was a cop, I was the attorney general.

"Could you tell me where your vehicle is now located?"

My heart rate speeded up. "Could you tell me why you want to know?"

"It was involved with an accident, so we're checking the whereabouts."

Doc. My throat tightened. "What sort of accident?"

"We're not at liberty to diverge, uh, divert—"

"Divulge?" I asked.

"Yeah. That type of information. Look, just tell me where the goddamn car is."

"Are cops supposed to swear?" He was clearly not a cop, but I thought he should do a better job of impersonating one.

Before he could respond, a customer came in, distracting us. I said, "Would you excuse me for just one moment?" and went to greet him.

The customer wore a blue crewneck cashmere sweater that matched his eyes. He gave me a long look and said no, he didn't need help finding anything.

Spy?

I went behind the counter, set down the Dustbuster, and took a deep breath. If Mr. Sweater was one of Mr. Bundt's plainclothespeople, all I had to do was act normal and professional. Of course, I'd have a better shot at this minus the wheezing man. Who was the wheezing man, anyway? At the moment, he frowned at one of the birthday card spinners, his eyebrows merging. They were thick and black—

"Girlie! I don't got all day," he called out.

With a glance at the sweatered man, I hurried to Aisle 2. "Please don't bark—"

"Just tell me where's your car and I'm outta here."

"I lent my car to a friend."

"What's the name of this friend?" he asked. Behind him, in the mural-painted wall, the lemon tree opened a crack.

"Well, he's not really a friend," I said. "I just met him."

"You gave your car to someone you don't know?"

"Okay, could we not—raise our voices?"

The lemon tree opened all the way. Joey emerged, lowering sunglasses to scrutinize him. The sweatered man was staring at us too.

"Tell me where I can reach you," I whispered, "and I'll give you a call the second my car's back."

He took a deep, labored breath and nodded. "I'll write down my numbers."

He followed me to the counter, accepted a pen and a Kitten Cuddles notepad, and wrote painstakingly. The little hairs on the back of his knuckles were white, like the hair on his head. He said, "That's my cellular, and that's voice mail, I live on a boat, I don't have a real phone. And here's my name: Carmine." He wrote it in capital letters, then leaned on the counter, sending an odor of old wool and Old Spice my way. "We're looking for a piece of merchandise in connection with this. Your friend mention that?"

"What kind of merchandise?"

"Something he shouldn't mess with, that's what kind. He knows what kind." Carmine leaned in closer and removed a cigar from his pocket. His eyes, bulbous and bloodshot, bored into mine. "Tell him this: If the merchandise isn't returned, he's in some very big trouble. Very big." He hacked again, hard enough to rearrange his lungs. Then he stuck the cigar between his teeth and was gone.

I wanted to disinfect the counter.

On Aisle 5, my other customer stared at the front door, watching his exit. Joey joined me at the register. We looked out the window to see Carmine approach his car, a Cadillac Eldorado. It was white, setting off his tan. "Creepy," she said.

"Joey," I said, "is there a chance that man could be a cop?"

"Yes," she said, nodding slowly. "On reruns of *Hawaii Five-O*."

IT HAD RAINED raisin bran. My kitchen was covered in it. The empty box lay overturned on the floor.

There was no other sign of Margaret.

Half the nylon leash dangled from the refrigerator handle, chewed and frayed. I got on my knees and searched, consumed with visions of the ferret drowned in the toilet, ground in the disposal, browned in the toaster oven. Darn it, I'd *told* Doc I was all wrong for this. There was a reason I had no pets: I couldn't even keep houseplants.

I combed the tiny apartment and was back in the kitchen, starting over, when I saw her. A cupboard door, opened a crack, revealed a pair of eyes. Margaret was deep in the recesses of the shelf, amid Tupperware. Her leash fragment had caught on a cast-iron kettle, but she seemed reasonably calm. "I'll give you this," I said, liberating her. "You're a good sport."

I tied a string to her and we went outside. We waited for Mrs. Albertini to round the corner on her daily Lenten pilgrimage to Mass, then grabbed a few minutes of grass time. Back inside, I put Margaret in the shower, hoping the sliding door would contain her and that she wouldn't figure out how to turn on the water. I gave her a washcloth for company.

I swept up bran and listened to news of fires in Florida and the condition of the yen, but no local murders. I turned off the radio and noticed my answering machine blinking.

"Margaret, pick up," said the message. "Margaret? M. Ferret: Are you there?"

Doc. I caught my breath.

"Kidding, Wollie. Ferrets are actually not capable of answering phones. Hey, I'm springing the patient legally. Happy? The problem is, the administrative type who signs off on these things is gone today. I'll call you tonight and we'll talk about it."

I replayed the message, trying to detect some hidden sentiment, a sign Doc was pining away for me. I didn't find one, but just to be sure, I played it four more times.

NEVER HAVING BEEN in a pet store before, I couldn't say whether they all smelled like Pet Planet, the air heavy and somehow unhygienic, even with no real animals in the place but fish. Aquariums lined the windows, luring Joey to their blue-green depths.

Only a true friend would come through during a pet emergency without pointing out that I had no pets, but Joey was that kind of friend, letting me borrow her Saab. Since I couldn't drive a stick shift, I had to borrow Joey too.

I made my way through aisles of toys, spinners full of flavored bones, and bins of pig ears—pig ears?—to the small-animal habitats. The best of them was the Pet Palace, a green carpeted split-level with entertainment center and gym. But the price was prohibitive, so I chose a plain metal job, a new leash, and looked around for food.

There was nothing for ferrets in the food aisle, so I took my crate to the counter and asked. I spoke quietly, mindful of Joey's proximity and my vow of secrecy.

"No ferret food," the clerk whispered. "Did you see the hammocks, though?"

"Ham hocks?" Why was *she* whispering, I wondered.

"Hammocks. For ferrets. They're made of plush, they come in turtles and lobsters, and attach to all the habitats. Fourteen ninety-nine."

I wasn't clear on why a ferret would want to recline on a swinging lobster, but there was no time to ask. Joey appeared at my side.

"Wollie," she asked, "is there any reason someone might be following you?"

chapter ten

Hancock Park was a world away from Pet Planet, aesthetically speaking, and we arrived there after a series of circuitous turns. The houses were ancient by L.A. standards, some stone, some ivy-covered, all with front lawns and real sidewalks where children rode tricycles. It was as if one of the better neighborhoods of Cleveland or Philadelphia had come west for the weather.

I loved these streets. Pieces of my childhood were lived here, as Ruta and her husband had occupied the guest house of an honest-to-goodness mansion, the husband a sort of butler to the family, and Ruta the nanny to the children, all grown by the time we came to her. My brother and I spent long summer days there, afternoons during the school months, and most Saturdays, for three years. I preferred the cramped guest house to the cavernous main house, but it was in the main house that P.B. discovered the Steinway grand piano and everyone else discovered P.B.'s almost frightening ability to reproduce any music he heard, his stubby fingers racing across the keyboard in complicated arrangements that flowed out of him like water from a faucet. In the beginning he was so small, his feet didn't reach the pedals. But as he grew and his talent grew, so did his effect on people. He was an engaging child, funny and introspective and outgoing all at once, right at home in the ballroom-sized living room, not burdened, as I was, by the knowledge that we didn't belong there. I was eleven the summer Ruta died, deemed old enough to look after P.B. and myself from then on. We were watching cartoons the stifling August morning a van pulled up to our Burbank apartment to deliver the old Steinway. The memory of that day made up for a lot of other days in my life, the knowledge that people, even far-off people, people living in the mansions of Hancock Park, were capable of such acts.

"Okay, if this guy's still following, we'll see him now," Joey said, interrupting my reverie. She turned north onto Arden Boulevard. "I first noticed him turn down La Brea behind us, and then from the pet store window I could see him circling the block."

"You're sure it was the same car?" I said.

"How many blue Humvees do you know?"

Joey was right; everything behind us was visible. The streets were flat, straight, and empty. Speed bumps and four-way stop signs slowed our pace. My nerves were shredded. Joey's were not.

"Back to last night," she said. "P.B. was safe, and you left the body in the road and drove off. I'm still not clear what happened to your car."

I'd been filling Joey in on the previous night's proceedings all the way from Pet Planet. It was a highly edited version, leaving out all mention of Margaret and her enigmatic owner, Gomez Gomez.

"That's what I can't talk about," I said. "I shouldn't have mentioned the murder either, but since they're following you too now, it's the least I can do." I turned to look out the back window. Joey turned too, hair flowing behind her like a Clairol Nice 'n Easy commercial. Joey had enough hair for a family of four, in dramatic contrast to her stick-figure body. It was a combination prized by fashion photographers and coveted by women across America, and would have made her the object of envy, were it not for the scar on her cheek and her habit of dressing, as Fredreeq put it, like she raided yard sales.

"I know you're worried about P.B.," she said, "but any cop smarter than Barney Fife will see he doesn't have a mean bone in his body. And without evidence, nobody's going to—" She honked her horn at a weimaraner napping in the street.

"But what if there is evidence?" I asked. "We don't know what happened on that road, and anyway, P.B. has a thing about cops. It's like an allergy; he gets very worked up. If they even just question him, he's going to act suspiciously."

"He's in a mental hospital. It's appropriate for him to act suspiciously."

"But if they find out he was arrested, that he used to hear directives from the Symbionese Liberation Army—"

"But what's his motive to go limping down the road picking off people? That's what a cop's looking for." Joey glanced in the rearview mirror. "Does he have enemies?"

"Marie Osmond," I said. "George Bush, senior. Mary Baker Eddy. Those are the ones I know about. They're not enemies, precisely— he believes they're walk-ins, who monitor his activities and transmit their findings to the Milky Way."

"What's a walk-in?"

"An extraterrestrial who walks in and takes up residence in someone's body for the duration of their life. Look, even if P.B.'s innocent, the cops will bring up his record. That's the problem. Dr. Charlie had to 'misplace' that part of his file to qualify him for the ziprasidone studies. They won't use even nonviolent offenders in the drug trials, and if he gets kicked out of the program, Dr. Charlie won't be able to keep him at the hospital. And he likes the hospital. He feels safe there."

Joey glanced at me. "Could he try living with you again, or Uncle Theo? Or even—your mother?"

I stared at her. "Live with my mother? At the ashram? It's not the kind of place to send someone who's mentally ill. At least, not that kind of mentally ill."

"Yeah, but if this new medication is working—"

"Oh, they all work, to some extent, until he starts to feel better and decides he doesn't need pills, and stops taking them, at which point the delusions start again, and the wanderlust, and it's a nightmare for Uncle Theo and me, losing him for months—"

"Yeah, okay. Don't think about it now, not until you talk to him and see what the story is. Tell me more about these walk-ins."

WITHIN THE HOUR, I was talking to P.B. Which was not the same as P.B. talking to me.

"Incoming information only," he said. "No outgoing. You speak."

"Why can't you speak?" I spoke softly, mindful of the family of customers walking into the shop. "Didn't you get the aluminum foil?"

"I did my ears, not my teeth. We're going to lunch." Applying foil to teeth was a tedious process, not worth doing before meals.

"Okay. Remember what you said last night, about what was in the driveway there? The body," I whispered. "How did you know about the body? Is it something you witnessed, or—" I paused, hesitant to ask my brother if he'd murdered someone yesterday.

"What's that?" he said sharply, in response to a short beep.

"Call-waiting. Hold on." I tried to click in to the other call, but kept returning to P.B. Call-waiting was annoying when it worked, and worse when it didn't; either way, it upset him.

"Okay, they must've hung up," I said, clicking back to him a third time. The family of customers trooped out of the shop. I raised my voice to a normal level. "I need to know everything you know about this murder, not that I think you had a hand in it, but if you did, I'm sure you had your reasons and I'm sorry I was so distracted yesterday when you tried to tell me about it, and—" I stopped, getting a funny feeling in my stomach. "P.B.?" I asked.

Silence. Then a voice nothing like my brother's said, "And who is P.B.?" I hung up and backed away from the phone. What had I just said?

And who had I said it to?

chapter eleven

The horror of that phone call remained, killing my appetite for shrimp fried rice.

Joey, Fredreeq, and I had a standing Saturday lunch date at the table in front of the shop, going over the classified-ad guys for the upcoming week in between bites of Loo Fong's takeout. My journal was in front of me, open, awaiting my entries for the previous week's men, but I couldn't even look at it. Fredreeq was describing a new date she cryptically referred to as Rex Stetson, her chopsticks waving in the air to illustrate her points. I nodded as though paying attention, dying to blurt out that someone had just heard me invite my brother to confess to murder. But Fredreeq was not Joey. If she heard any part of the story, she'd demand to know all of it, and wouldn't like any of it. Her personal attire notwithstanding, Fredreeq was straitlaced about a lot of things. Felons, for instance. Dead people.

Who had been on the other end of the phone?

The cops, Mr. Bundt, or Mr. Bundt's industrial spy: these were the worst-case scenarios. The fact that I hadn't recognized the voice meant little. Four words weren't much to go on. I'd considered pressing *69, but what would that accomplish? So I'd stood there waiting for him to call again, at which point I would have answered in Spanish. He didn't call.

"Morgue," Joey said.

Fredreeq and I turned to her. A gust of wind sent Joey's red hair swirling around her, Medusa-like. Her green eyes had a faraway look.

"Morgue?" Fredreeq said. "What do morgues have to do with anything?"

Joey's eyes snapped into focus. "Pork. I said pork."

Fredreeq looked suspicious. "What about pork?"

"Didn't I order pork?"

"What are you talking about? You just plowed through a carton of spicy broccoli. Here, get out of the direct sunlight, you're too white, it's frying your brain." Fredreeq made Joey switch seats with her, then pulled up her own yellow midriff top to expose her dark brown abdomen to noonday rays. "Oh, good, here's UPS." Fredreeq waved at the truck pulling into the lot. "It's that driver with the bad weave. Let's see what Wollie's wearing for Rex."

Each Dating Project subject was outfitted by Tiffanie's Trousseau. The national clothing chain sponsored Dr. Cookie's research, paying us five thousand dollars apiece upon the completion of forty dates, with an additional ten dollars per date for incidentals. In return, we wore the clothes they sent us, documented each outfit via Polaroid, and pasted it into journals, along with the vital statistics and our editorial comments on the men, which Tiffanie's Trousseau used for market research purposes. But the main benefit for Tiffanie's was its proposed advertising gimmick: when Dr. Cookie launched *How to Avoid Getting Dumped All the Time,* Tiffanie's would launch Hot Date fashions. The ad campaign would feature our journal entries superimposed over professional models wearing the corresponding outfit. Dr. Cookie, who couldn't possibly afford to pay the research subjects out of her own pocket, or even her publisher's pocket, called this a beautifully arranged marriage between science and commerce. Joey called it another sleazy example of corporate-infected media and Madison Avenue infiltrating our lives. Fredreeq called it a damn shame that the research subjects did not get to keep the clothes. Given the style of Tiffanie's Trousseau, I called that a blessing.

"I hope they sent something black for tonight," Fredreeq said. "Black and bare."

"Tonight?" I said. "Did you say tonight?"

"L'Orangerie with Rex Stetson, honey. Where've you been?"

This was bad news. I couldn't do two hours of labored chitchat at L'Orangerie, not tonight, not until I'd talked to both P.B. and Doc. I signed the UPS invoice while Fredreeq tore into the Tiffanie's Trousseau box. She held up a dress the boutique considered suitable for sipping Pouilly-Fuissé on Saturday night, black spandex with a sweetheart neckline.

"Gorgeous," she said. Joey gestured with a napkin, signifying assent and a mouthful of broccoli.

"I can't wear that," I said. "I'm having a big breast day."

Fredreeq snorted. "Like that's a negative? If Rex Stetson has his own list, you can bet that Big Breasts are headlining it."

"PMS." The words caught in my throat. This was agony, lying to a friend.

Fredreeq returned the dress to its box. "Did Golda Meir cancel the Six-Day War because it was the wrong six days? She did not. She took Motrin and laid off the sodium." Moving the soy sauce out of my reach, Fredreeq squinted at me. "Although I have to say—girl, you're wrecked. Are you getting any sleep?"

"I—" I turned to Joey for help.

"She had a rough night," Joey said. "Go ahead, Wollie. Tell her about Dave."

It worked. Fredreeq had strong feelings about transportation (number four, Has Car) and the idea of Dave sending me home in a taxi so appalled her, she gave me the night off. "And you *have* had seven dates in the last eight days," she said, reaching for her cell phone. "We don't want you burning out. Rex will just have to do brunch."

I LEFT OUR alfresco lunch to wait on a customer, and was restocking Easter cards when Joey joined me. "What was that about morgues?" I said. "You think I should call them?"

"No, I think I should. I'm a really good liar. You're really not."

I couldn't argue that, although in her case, what she called lying I like to think of as improvisation; Joey had worked a lot as an actress before she'd acquired the scar on her face.

I went to greet new customers, members of the oldest profession, judging from their dress—micro-miniskirts, one paired with torn black stockings, one with thigh-high boots, both with bustiers. Not an easy look to pull off, but you have to give people credit for trying. One of them asked me to change a hundred-dollar bill.

When we got to the register, Joey was already on the phone, apparently to the morgue. "I'm on hold," she said, and covered the mouthpiece. "Wollie, what city's *ER* set in?"

"Chicago," the streetwalkers said, in unison.

"Thanks." Joey moved down the counter and talked into the phone. "No problem. And what's your name?" Her voice really carried. I should have asked her to make the call from the back room, but too late now. "I'm a former staff writer for *ER,*" she told the morgue. "Ever watch it?"

The streetwalkers were riveted to Joey's conversation. I counted out twenties, tens, and ones for them and rang up two packs of gum, trying in vain to regain their attention.

"Sid, I couldn't agree more," Joey said, her voice exuding an unusual degree of charm. She explained that she was surveying small to midsize morgues all over the country in the interest of getting an insider's view for an upcoming series called *Morgue.* "It's gotta be frustrating when you see your profession on TV and we get it all wrong—right?"

I turned up the easy listening music and the ladies of the evening left, with reluctance. I turned down the music and heard Joey ask how many bodies had been brought in lately and if this number was normal for a non-holiday weekend. She asked questions related to traffic accidents and heart attacks and talked so long about AIDS that I got interested myself and forgot what she was really calling about.

The shop's bell announced a woman of Wagnerian proportions, in heavy tweed. I turned up the music again and hurried over to ask if she needed help. She headed to the back wall with the air of someone who's done her reconnaissance work.

"These," she said, holding up a set of wooden Winnie-the-Pooh bookends. "Too masculine for a newborn girl?"

"Oh, no," I said. "Winnie transcends gender. Even the name is ambiguous."

She sniffed, leading me back to the register. "I don't care for ambiguous names. This gift is for an unfortunate child named Brie, like the cheese. Plus Ann. Brie Ann."

Something about her disapproval brought to mind Mr. Bundt. She could have been his elder sister. Or, more alarmingly, his undercover agent. I moved around the counter, glancing at Joey, whose back was to us. Joey's outfit was innocuous enough, but her hair had matted itself into something approaching dreadlocks, giving her the appearance of an Irish Rastafarian.

"There's no accounting for taste, is there?" I said, turning back to my customer.

"No, there is not," she agreed. "Gift wrap those, please. I was hoping to find some Engelbreit, but you don't seem to carry her."

Joey was six feet away, the phone cord stretched its full length, but she was on a roll and her voice carried, winning out over easy listening. "If you're a fan, you know the kind of thing we love: choking on chicken bones, suicides, homicides, sudden infant death syndrome."

My customer swiveled her head sharply to the left.

"We do carry Mary Engelbreit," I said, willing her gray helmet of a hairdo to swivel back. "But T-shirts and mugs, primarily. Nothing appropriate for a baby."

"Mary Engelbreit is a marvelous talent," she said, returning her attention to me.

"With an unambiguous name," I added.

Joey's voice came through again. "Let's move on to blood. Anyone dismembered or disemboweled this week?"

"Mary Engelbreit," I said loudly, "does a beautiful boxed notecard. Let me just show you. For my money, her paper products are groundbreaking." I came around the counter, indicating the back wall, and by sheer force of will got my Wagnerian lady to move toward it.

Unfortunately, Joey's healthy laugh carried across the shop. "Great, Sid," she said. "Now give me your best gunshot."

"WOLLIE, WHY WOULD Mr. Bundt send a spy who *looks* like the Gestapo? It defeats the purpose. She's gone, forget her." Joey handed me the Kitten Cuddles notepad covered in notes. "Our man was brought into the Ventura County morgue this morning. A dead-on shot, from a nine millimeter. The bullet had an eggbeater effect: it ricocheted off the clavicle, went through a lung, and ended up in the abdomen. Not very distinctive, I'm afraid."

"It sounds distinctive to me," I said, unnerved.

"Yes, the *wounds*. I meant the bullet. I was hoping for something more conclusive."

"Like what?"

"Oh, a .222 slug from four hundred yards. Or a Teflon bullet. Or a Black Talon, the exploding round, which—okay, never mind. The idea being, something that says 'professional' rather than 'patient who got hold of a gun.' A hollow point, for instance, could indicate an assassin. Of course, it could also indicate a cop—my brothers both use them—so they're not exactly rare, but at least they're interesting. A nine-millimeter, half the customers who walk in here—the Gestapo lady included—could be packing them in their purses."

I put on a smile for an incoming customer. "Hi," I called. "Let me know if I can help you." The woman, in unseasonal shorts and halter top, smiled back and nodded.

Joey lowered her voice. "Time of death was put at between five and seven last night. We got lucky. It was a trainee on the phone, and a very talkative one."

"The shooting must have come after the six P.M. shift change," I said, "or else someone would've seen the body in the road. But if nobody heard the shot, does that mean a silencer was used? Because they're not common, are they?"

"Not common, because not legal. Good point." Joey ran a finger down her face, tracing the faint line of her scar, an unconscious habit. "Theoretically, if P.B. could get hold of a gun, he could get hold of a silencer, or even make one, but it doesn't sound like him. It sounds like a hit man after all, doesn't it?"

I nodded, happy. Who'd have thought the words "hit man" could sound so lovely? Not that I'd ever heard of hit men outside of TV. Did they really exist in everyday life? Then I remembered the *L.A. Times* article.

Yes. They did.

I GOT FREDREEQ to finish out the day and close up shop, and went back to my apartment to liberate Margaret from her new metal house. Then I picked up the phone.

P.B. was over in physical therapy, but due back any minute, according to his roommate, the elderly gentleman I'd seen sleeping the night before. The roommate had not noticed anything unusual at the hospital—a murder investigation, for instance—being too preoccupied with the condition of his prostate and his recent eighty-ninth-birthday party, the details of which he was eager to share with me. I managed to get a word in edgewise and impress upon him how vital it was that P.B. call me the moment he came in.

I'd wait ten minutes and try again. Tuning the radio to news, I grabbed a sketch pad and settled on the floor near Margaret, who terrorized the legs on my daybed.

I stashed sketchbooks and pens in my apartment, car, and shop, with different greeting card projects in each sketchbook. This one was a line of Good Luck cards: Good luck on coming out, both gay and lesbian versions; Good luck with your lawsuit, your in vitro fertilization, your plastic surgery. I now had another, inspired by recent events: Good luck with your parole hearing. The Good Luck line, in black and white, was too avant-garde for Welcome! stores, but my first set had sold so well in local independent shops, I knew I could turn a profit, if I got my marketing act together and went national. Once I won the Willkommen! upgrade, I'd have time for all the things I'd been putting off: Life. Art. Maybe even love, I decided, and let my thoughts drift toward Doc. His dark eyes. His deep voice.

I was sketching a penitentiary when the phone rang. Finally, I thought, and turned down the radio so it wouldn't scare P.B. If only I could turn off call-waiting.

It wasn't P.B.

"There's something I've been dying to do all day," Doc said, his voice husky.

My God, I thought, we're about to have phone sex. "What?" I whispered.

"Replace your wire connectors. They're rotted away."

"Was I supposed to—polish them?" What the heck were wire connectors?

A beeping sound came over the line, then, "Cell phone losing battery—I'm surprised to get any reception at all out—" His words began to randomly disappear. "—phone, this—happening."

"Wait, Doc!" I said. "Doc?"

"—here."

"What's Margaret eat? What do I feed her?"

"Well," he said, "the thing is—needs—but—tricky, so box of—"

And that was it. Loud static, then silence.

I looked at the phone in disbelief. I hadn't told him about Carmine or the Humvee, hadn't learned his cell phone number, or found out anything at all, really, except that I possessed rotten wire connectors. Wait—*69. This was what that little device was for. My thumb reached for the star key, but the phone rang. Too late.

"Hello," I said, not very graciously.

"It's me," my brother said.

I took a deep breath. "Good. You're alone, you can talk? Teeth all wrapped?"

"Yes."

"Okay. Tell me everything you know about that murder."

"Why?"

"So I can figure out what we do next. The police are probably going to show up at the hospital, if they haven't already and—"

His voice lowered, into his paranoia range. "Special forces?"

"No, the regular local police. Sheriff's department, I think. I'm not sure."

"Not the Sssssss—?"

I looked at Margaret, puzzled. "Sssecret Service?"

"No. The other ones. The ones looking for me."

"Someone's looking for you? Since the murder?" I hesitated, then said, "Earthlings?"

"It was an execution," he said. "Point-blank range. His soul was not able to ascend. I couldn't see his face. Ssss . . . Swedes, that's the word. I'm going now." He hung up.

Execution? My brother had witnessed an execution?

Or carried one out?

This time I did press *69, but the phone, somewhere at the mental hospital, just rang and rang.

chapter twelve

The Korean-operated Bodega Bob was often devoid of basic items; in this case, boxed cat food.

"Wet! Wet!" insisted the clerk-manager. "Just as good! Better!"

"No. It has to come in a box." The word "box" was the only actual clue I had about Margaret's diet, and cat food was my best guess.

"But. Wet food, they like so very, very much, the cats." The manager's voice took on a piteous quality. "I'm telling you. Tasty white fish."

"No fish," I said. "She rejected tuna." But I accepted a tiny can of Fancy Feast turkey and giblets, even though I had doubts about a ferret eating a turkey.

My doubts were well-founded. Back in the apartment, Margaret continued not to eat. Doc and P.B. continued not to call. I was searching the yellow pages for a pet store to give me food advice when Dr. Cookie's radio call-in show, *Love Junkies,* made me look up.

"Who is this guy? That's my question," Dr. Cookie was saying to her caller. "You answer with how cute his baby blues are and, because this is L.A., what kind of car he drives. Well, darlin', any yahoo can rent a car. I repeat: Who *is* this guy? Forget the bedroom eyes. Where does he stand with the IRS, what's under his bed, does he call when he says he's gonna call?"

I looked to the top of the refrigerator, and Doc's gym bag. "Margaret," I said, "what if that bag contains vital information—or food for you? That would be a reason to look inside."

Margaret, tasting a yellow page, appeared to consider the possibility.

"Or an address book," I said, standing. "With his phone number, so we could call him."

Dr. Cookie was now yelling at her caller. "You know the saying 'Ignorance of the law is no excuse'? Well, the same applies to romance, honey. It's your responsibility to find out about this man you're dating, and your reluctance to do it means you're afraid."

Not me, I thought. I'd faced down a corpse. Gym bags didn't scare me.

"Afraid," Dr. Cookie persisted, "that it's gonna be bad news."

"Margaret," I said, "you're his next of kin. If you tell me not to look in there, I won't."

Margaret said nothing.

I pulled the bag down from the refrigerator. "It's not as though he told me not to. This isn't a Bluebeard situation, with the wife and the locked room. Actually, if Doc didn't want people in here, he *would* have locked it. Unconsciously, he must want me to look."

I unzipped the zipper.

The first thing I pulled out was the paperback I'd seen the night before. *Mortal Splendor* was neither romantic nor religious, and certainly not pornographic; it had no cover art. As far as I could tell, it was something to do with economic theory, its author described as a post-Toynbee historian. Hmm.

There was the pack of Marlboros and the pocket calculator and a silver lighter, with July 12, 1948 engraved on it. There was an *L.A. Times,* two days old, a key ring from Yellowstone National Park with two keys on it, a pack of disposable razors and some shaving cream. There were black cotton socks and black Calvin Klein low-rise briefs, new looking. There was a toothbrush and toothpaste and dental floss.

And there was a gun.

It was wrapped in a man's white handkerchief embroidered with the letter "F." The gun itself was dark gray. "Gunmetal gray," I realized, thinking of the words as I'd seen them on tubes of paint. The gun lay heavy and serious in my hand, its coldness piercing the thin white cotton. The handle of the gun was scored, and the rest was smooth. The words "UNCETA y COMPANIA" were engraved on the upper part of it. I placed it on the floor and stared at it, scared it might go off, scared it had absorbed my fingerprints through the handkerchief. Number eleven, I thought, No Guns. After a time, I rewrapped the handkerchief around it, and set it carefully back in the gym bag, cushioned amid socks and underwear. I zipped the bag and carried it like a sleeping puppy back to its place on top of the refrigerator.

"Let's get out of here, Margaret," I said, closing the yellow pages. "Let's buy cat food."

We went through the shop to ensure that it was locked up, then out the front door. In the parking lot a limousine the size of a city bus sat idling, as if waiting for valet parking. You'll be waiting a long time, I thought, setting Margaret on the sidewalk. She was delighted to be outdoors. I clutched her leash and steered her onto Sunset.

I'd never considered my neighborhood from a ferret's point of view. It wasn't pleasant. Within a block we'd encountered a syringe, a tampon, and a partial, mustard-encrusted hot dog. Margaret seemed charmed by it, but when the next street yielded a shopping cart full of dirty pillows, driven by a man with few sexual inhibitions and a desire to know me better, I'd had enough. I picked her up and hurried on, until the sound of yelling made me turn around.

Behind us, the extraordinarily long limousine was making its left turn out of the mini-mall parking lot onto Sunset, closing down three lanes of Saturday night traffic in the process. Engines gunned and horns honked. Margaret wanted to get down and join in the fun, but I held her tight, watching as traffic waited and the limo crept toward us.

There's something sinister about a slow-moving limousine.

I wanted to run.

But where? Straight ahead, and the limo could overtake us. Behind us, Mr. Shopping Cart stood with open arms and open raincoat. Crossing Sunset amid all that traffic was suicide. I skidded down a side street, assuring Margaret that this was almost certainly an unnecessary detour, because people don't get stalked by luxury vehicles.

Halfway down the block, I glanced back to see the limousine make a labored left turn onto our side street. Heart pounding, I made myself wait until it was almost upon us, then did an about-face and headed back to Sunset. Don't run, I told myself. Don't panic. Don't let him know you're on to him.

I heard the limo stop, then go into reverse. Fast.

Could I, carrying a ferret, outrun a car driving backward? If I reached Sunset, would anyone stop to help? I sped up.

The vehicle reached us, kept going, and screeched to a halt. It was even with me now, and for reasons I couldn't quite explain, I stopped. It was brown, I noticed irrelevantly, a color as not-quite-right on a limousine as it is on a tuxedo. One darkened window descended.

A uniformed driver looked me right in the eye and I looked back, mesmerized, waiting for whatever diabolical thing was going to come out of his mouth.

"Do you know where I could find an all-night hardware store?"

Hardware. Power tools. Chain saws. "No," I said and resumed walking, cradling Margaret against my chest.

"Really?" He coasted backward in perfect time with me, without even glancing in the rearview mirror. He was maybe ten feet away. I moved to the inside edge of the sidewalk.

"Come on, it's L.A., you got twenty-four-hour everything." He took off his cap to reveal a military haircut. His arm rested on the window, and I caught the glint of a silver watch. He smiled. "Help me out here."

Should I break into a run or keep him off guard? I kept walking, but I didn't speak.

"You need a ride somewhere? I'll drop you."

Are you serious? I thought, and glanced at him just as he looked into the rearview mirror. Was he checking where he was going, or was there someone in the back of his limo?

His profile was chiseled and his face craggy, like he'd done hard time somewhere. He turned to me and smiled again. "What's the matter? Your hamster doesn't like limos?"

"She's not a hamster." Mob, I thought. That's who rides in cars like this. Organized crime. Gangland executions. No, not execution—if he wanted to kill me, I'd already be dead. Kidnapping, then. He wants me in his car. Quietly, without a scene.

"What is it, one of those Chia Pets?" he asked, and when I didn't answer, said, "Not very welcoming, are you? For someone in the greeting card business."

I gasped. I stopped. The limo kept going, backing steadily toward Sunset, as he turned to look behind him, out the window. His chauffeur's jacket slipped open to reveal a leather harness-type thing, a little like the one Margaret was wearing, and the glint of a gun.

"*Run,*" said Ruta's voice in my head. I ran.

As I passed him, he speeded up. With Margaret clamped to my chest, I ran faster, praying for intervention, divine or human, because I knew he was going to catch me.

Ahead, on Sunset Boulevard, a westbound shopping cart came into view, piled high with pillows, pushed by the homeless man who'd suggested sex to me ten minutes earlier.

"Darling!" I called out. "Honey! It's me!"

I NOT ONLY locked the apartment, I actually pushed my daybed in front of the door, one of those horror-movie tactics that seems overwrought when you're watching it on TV, but now occured to me as the only sane thing to do. The fact that the limo had shifted gear and driven off the moment I'd hailed the bewildered Mr. Shopping Cart didn't matter. He was out there somewhere. I was in here. I was scared.

Margaret promptly climbed onto the sweatshirt I'd peeled off, and fell asleep, abandoning me to my fear. She was probably weak from hunger, along with everything else. There had to be a solution to this: she lived with Doc, so maybe she'd picked up his food habits. Doughnuts, for instance. I didn't stock doughnuts, but I did have frozen waffles. I stuck one in the toaster oven.

My phone machine was blinking.

The first message was a hang-up. The second message was from Fredreeq, saying that Dr. Cookie had moved up her research deadline for *How to Avoid Getting Dumped All the Time.*

"Because," Fredreeq said, "all the other cities are finished, so Dr. Cookie's just waiting on L.A. That means you gotta meet 'em as fast as we can screen 'em. And no second dates with anyone till after the deadline, because there's no time. I wish you'd let me advertise in the *Jewish Journal* again. We could score a lot of first dates before they have to know you're not Jewish. Think about it." Fredreeq took the

Dating Project very seriously, even aside from the five hundred dollars I was paying her. Joey, doing it strictly for my sake, considered Dr. Cookie a quack. I, who'd begun with romantic expectations, now just wanted to survive it all.

I rubbed my eyes. How many dates had I had now? Nineteen? That meant twenty-one to go. It exhausted me to think about it. From hysteria to fatigue, just like that. Danger plus sleep deprivation. This must be how soldiers did it, I decided, how they managed to sleep in foxholes between battles. I threw sheets and blankets onto the daybed and set a hot waffle near the nose of the sleeping ferret. I began changing into my signs of the zodiac flannel pajamas, got as far as the top button of the shirt part, and collapsed.

When I came to, the phone was ringing and Margaret was nestled in my armpit.

"I FIXED YOUR cigarette lighter," he said.

"Shut up, Doc," I said, instantly awake. "Don't say a word till I'm finished. I was accosted tonight by a large brown limousine. A man named Carmine wants his merchandise back. I have no idea what Margaret eats. A Humvee followed me to the pet store. And I need to know who it is you suspect of this murder."

"How did—"

"No, I'm not finished. Give me your cell phone number, for when we get cut off again, which seems to be a recurring thing with you." When he didn't reply, I snapped, "Don't worry, I won't sell it to telemarketers."

Doc gave me the number, which I wrote on a nearby Kleenex box, which woke Margaret. The ferret had crumbs on her whiskers.

"Can I talk now?" Doc asked.

"Yes," I said. "You can start by telling me what kind of bullets your gun shoots."

"My gun? Oh, the one in my bag."

"Are there others?"

"I'm surprised at you, Wollie, going through other people's stuff." I could hear the smile in his voice. "It's called an Astra 400. I don't know what kind of bullets it uses."

"Oh, please. You expect me to believe—"

"It was my grandfather's gun, from the Spanish Civil War, it's a relic. I don't even know if it works, it's been in a safe-deposit box for years. Tell me about being followed."

"Would you like the limousine story or the Humvee?" I asked.

"Hummer, not Humvee," he said. "The Humvee is the military version, and I doubt they're doing maneuvers in Hollywood. You sure this isn't just guys hitting on you?"

"No one's hitting on me. It's the merchandise they want, not me. I assume. The merchandise Carmine talked about." I started to tell him about Carmine.

He interrupted. "Did he smoke a cigar?"

"Yes."

There was silence, then, "Okay. Tell me about the merchandise."

"No," I said. "You tell *me* about the merchandise. Something big, Carmine said, not size-wise, but value-wise, and he seems to think you have it."

"I don't."

"Are you sure?" I asked. "Because you did help yourself to that scrub suit and you obviously consider dry cleaning to be community prop—"

"A lot of people are laboring under a misconception, because of something that was told to me in prison. That's all I'm going to say right now. Quit thinking about that, and listen to what I've found out here. The dead man was a patient, and the hospital isn't eager to release that, because they don't want to start a panic. The cops think it was done by someone outside the hospital."

"An outside job? That's good," I said, thinking of P.B. "That's great."

"Maybe. They're still interviewing everyone. They started with the staff, and they'll get to the patients sometime tomorrow. That's one of the things holding up this release I'm working on."

This was not good. P.B. and police in the same room was never good, even if he wasn't a suspect. "How'd you find out all this?" I asked.

"People tend to talk. And they tend to talk to me."

"Yes, we do, don't we?" I could just see him, wandering around the hospital in that too small suit, winning friends and influencing people.

"The main suspect," he said, "is, of course, me—or, rather, the man the guards saw last night. They wouldn't recognize me today, but I'm staying out of their way in any case. Nobody else saw me yesterday, nobody who's likely to remember."

"Except me," I said.

There was a pause. "Except you. You worry me. Are you falling apart?"

"No."

"Yes, you are. I can hear it. You're all tense."

I looked down and saw I was shredding Kleenex. Margaret too. Between us, we'd gone through a whole box. The daybed was covered in what appeared to be large, clumpy snowflakes. "I have reason to be tense," I said.

"Reasons beyond what we've talked about?"

"Yes. I'm afraid of the dark."

"Leave a light on," he said. "Are your doors locked?"

The door was right behind me, now that I'd moved the daybed. I reached up and touched it, not that there was any doubt in my mind. "Yes," I said.

"Good. Do you drink?"

"Do I what?"

"Pour yourself a shot of something. Unless you're an alcoholic, in which case, heat up some milk. Then turn off the phone. Then go to sleep."

Hot milk. I could see Ruta nodding with approval, but I shoved the image aside. What good was hot milk when I had a brain full of questions about prisons and merchandise and whether people still carried around guns from the Spanish Civil War, and whether those guns still worked, and if so, whether they shoot nine-milllimeter bullets?

"You're going to be all right," he said. "I can hear that brain working, but it's time to shut it down. Don't worry anymore tonight, I'll take over. You can start in again tomorrow."

He hung up and I realized I was still clueless about what to feed Margaret. I held on to the phone, both hands wrapped around it as if it were his wrist. I held it against my face and pretended it was him and that he was lying there next to me and that I trusted him. I kept it there until the computerized operator voice came over the line and told me to hang up.

chapter thirteen

It was still dark when Margaret woke me, around 6 A.M. Maybe she'd been restless all night and I'd slept through it, but now I was startled enough to jerk upright, disoriented to find myself in bed with a furred being, disoriented to be viewing the apartment from a different angle, my back against the door.

It took everything I had to return the heavy daybed to its place at the end of the apartment's long, skinny room. My adrenaline must've been working when I moved it the night before. Pieces of Margaret's previous meals littered the floor, along with, disturbingly, a chewed rubber glove. I grabbed the ferret, her leash, old socks, a cardigan sweater, and went outside.

There is a purity about early morning darkness, and I experienced something akin to serenity, watching the ferret stumble around in the grass. I sat down to put on my socks. Finishing her biological errands, Margaret lifted her nose, sniffed the air, then ambled past me to the length of her leash, into the shadows of a eucalyptus tree. A man stepped forward.

"Hey." He stood there, hands in pockets. Short black hair. Clean-shaven, tanned face. White T-shirt. Black jeans.

My red sneakers.

I sat on the ground, transfixed, looking up at him. He was a different man altogether from the guy in the scrub suit, or the one in the tuxedo, and likely to be more trouble than either, judging from the effect on my pulse rate. "Hey, Doc," I said.

He smiled. "Nice pj's." He bent down to pick up Margaret. "New leash."

I stood, aware of my pink cardigan and how it didn't go with the earth tones of my signs of the zodiac pajamas. I didn't even want to know what my hair was doing.

"I can't stay," he said. He was petting Margaret, who closed her eyes, and would've, if she could've, purred. "You'll be okay now, it's daylight. If you need your car, I can—"

"Keep the car. Just tell me what's going on, who these people are, populating my life, why they're—have you been here all night?"

"Since two A.M."

"Why didn't you come up? Why didn't you ring the doorbell and—"

"—give you a panic attack?" He looked at Margaret. "Hey, you—" He reached into the back pocket of his jeans and withdrew a large box of raisins. The ferret reacted like he'd produced the winning lottery ticket. Doc fed her a handful, then handed me the box. "This should tide her over until I come back. She also eats Cheerios. Okay, here's the story. Last week I was in Tehachapi State Prison, working the infirmary, waiting for my release. A kid came in, bad shape, stabbed with a shank, and—"

"A what?"

"Shank. Homemade knife. Prison art. Don't interrupt, I don't have much time. This kid gave me some information on his deathbed, information I didn't want and didn't use, but now I'm having trouble convincing people of that."

"What was his name?"

He blinked. "Whose?"

"The kid on his deathbed. It seems cold, to think of him as 'the dead kid.' "

"You don't need to think about him at all." He held up a hand. "Okay, his name was Shebby, he had a Cupid tattoo and a speech impediment. Happy? What he told me about was a hiding place."

"Having to do with this merchandise?"

He looked over his shoulder. "Leave it at that for now. If I thought it would help you to know more, I'd tell you more."

"You haven't told me anything! What, you drove all this way and now you're driving all the way back, just to drop off raisins?"

One eyebrow went up. The corners of his mouth twitched. He handed Margaret to me, then reached out and buttoned a button on my pajama top. "Yeah," he said, smiling. "Raisins."

IVY AT THE Shore was a cheerful restaurant, a kitschy-chic beach shack. If there was an official uniform for the Sunday-brunch crowd, it was baseball hats and flip-flops, but I was attired appropriately enough, in a Tiffanie's Trousseau floral sundress delivered that morning by a messenger who took back with him the unworn Saturday night spandex number. Tiffanie's prided itself on coordinating date attire with date location, whenever location could be determined in advance. My dress almost matched the high chintz-covered stools at the bamboo bar.

Rex Stetson wore a white polo shirt and khakis. He was six four or five, with a rangy build, thick brown hair, and startlingly green eyes. He lived in Houston, he told me, waiting at the bar for our table, but was moving to L.A. to take over a division of CBS.

"Grab the eighteen-to-twenty-four demographic," he said. "Kids like you."

"Ha," I said. It was hard not to like him. Everyone seemed to, from his CBS driver to other women at the bar. He was as approachable as a bowl of peanuts, which emboldened me to admit, halfway through my mimosa, "I've forgotten your actual name. My friends have been calling you Rex Stetson."

"Why?" he asked.

"You remind them of the character Rock Hudson played in *Pillow Talk*, the guy who pretends to be a Texan, to seduce Doris Day."

"Then I guess that makes you Doris Day." He smiled.

I smiled back. "So what's your real name, Rex?"

"Not so fast, this is turning me on. Would you put your hair in a French twist?" He tried to leer, but he was too clean-cut to pull it off.

I laughed. "It takes a big man to admit to liking Doris Day."

"Oh, hell," he said, "I'll even admit to liking Rock Hudson."

I found this so engaging, I asked the question that had been on my mind all morning. "What's a catch like you doing finding dates out of the classified ads?"

He looked blank for a moment, then smiled once more. "Just a fetish, I guess. Will you excuse me, darlin'? Gotta make a phone call."

John, the Romanian bartender, brought me a second mimosa without being asked. A song from the forties wafted through the air, and I realized, looking around, how attractive everyone was, and why people dated even when they weren't getting paid for it. I decided I loved this restaurant, with its pink walls, seashell-studded furniture, and woven straw ceiling, decided that nothing dangerous could happen to me in such a charming place. I started thinking about Doc, which made me smile, even as I considered how maddeningly enigmatic he was. I smiled at a passing plate of huevos rancheros, smiled at Robin, the hostess, smiled at the woman next to me who waited for her date to return, a messed-up Sunday *Times* spread out next to her. "Help yourself," she said, seeing me eye the paper.

We'd made the California section, front page. "Pleasant Valley Murder."

The victim remained unidentified. Investigators were seeking a man, medium height, in his thirties or forties, armed and considered dangerous. A female Caucasian, a possible kidnap victim, was also being sought. She was described as tall and blond.

ABDUL, THE CBS driver, steered the limo toward Hollywood and the two thousand stars in the Hollywood Walk of Fame he thought Rex should see. We took Sunset, the scenic route, wild and green near the ocean. We wound our way through middle-class neighborhoods that gave way to streets where a million dollars wouldn't buy you the garage. Rex took in every little thing. I tried to keep up my end of conversation, as I'd done all the way through crab Benedict, but inside I'd gone from Doris Day to Bonnie Parker, and was feeling pretty frayed around the edges.

Around UCLA, Rex drew my attention to the back window. "We get some interesting vehicles in Houston," he said, "but we don't see a lot of those. What would you call the color on that Hummer? Turquoise?"

I froze, then turned. I had trouble finding my voice. "Robin's-egg blue."

"Remember the ad campaign on those? 'SUV on steroids.' " Rex chuckled.

The Hummer was several cars behind us, too far back to see its driver. It was a sinister-looking thing, like an insect from a grade B horror movie. What did this mean? I'd been followed two days in a row by this overgrown Jeep, while in different cars, different company. Clearly, he—or she—knew where I worked and, probably, lived. What did he/she want? What did any of them want—the Alfa Romeo of Friday night, the limo on Saturday? They must be connected, part of an organized surveillance job, but why were their methods so sloppy? Wasn't the point of surveillance invisibility? Maybe not. Maybe the point was harassment. Or worse. Maybe it was terror.

It took some discipline to keep from turning around to watch the Hummer, but I limited myself to one glance, in Beverly Hills. Later, as we neared the Chinese Theater formerly known as Grauman's, Abdul said, "Look at that, boss. I think this guy's following us." He turned right on Hollywood Boulevard.

Rex laughed. "Maybe it's NBC, looking to squeeze me for the fall schedule. Or maybe it's the INS after you, Abdul." He turned to me. "How about you, Doris Day? Got any angry ex-husbands?"

I gave what I hoped was a carefree sort of chortle.

"Want me to lose him, boss?"

"Abdul," Rex said, "I'm from Texas. I want you to catch him."

Abdul nodded. Before I could register a vote, not that anyone was asking, the car turned north on Nichols Canyon. After a few miles on the winding road, Abdul swerved left toward a small side street and turned it into a tire-screeching U-turn, endangering the digestion of my crab Benedict. Rex put a hand on my arm to steady me, not knowing how close he was to being thrown up on. We drove slowly back down the canyon road.

Opposing traffic was heavy, and when we rounded a corner, there was the Hummer, facing us, at a dead stop. I stared at the man behind the wheel. Sun glinted off mirrored sunglasses. A baseball cap covered half his head. He could have been Mickey Rooney, for all I knew. He could've been Mickey Mouse. Whoever it was, he took a look at us, then dropped out of sight, coming back up with a gun. A big gun. A shotgun or a rifle, one of those guns.

I think I screamed. I did hear Rex shout to Abdul, who was rolling up windows before Rex pushed me unceremoniously down until I was face to face with the very clean gray carpeted floor of the car. When I came back up, we were on Hollywood Boulevard once more, heading east.

Abdul spoke rapidly, mostly in Arabic, with occasional lapses into English, variations on "Holy Almighty God in His Heaven," with accompanying hand gestures. He recounted the incident again and again, like some crazed sports announcer, as though Rex and I hadn't been there and seen it along with him.

I concentrated on slowing down my breath and keeping down my brunch. Rex checked the back window, the current favorite gesture of everyone I knew.

"You want I should call the cops, boss?" Abdul asked, his eyes wide and agitated in the rearview mirror.

"No! No cops," I said, too loudly. I could feel Rex's stare. Abdul's eyes in the mirror shifted from his boss to me. "I mean, why?" I said. "This is L.A., people have guns, it happens. I'm sure cops have bigger things to investigate. Murders and such."

Abdul took issue with this. "It is L.A., yes, but it is not Beirut— for this reason I left Beirut. Boss, I tell you, whatever you see on TV, for L.A. this is not normal, for a man to simply—"

"Yes, Abdul, but you've got to calm down. Do you want me to fix you a drink from the bar back here?" Rex had an almost eerie control. "If the lady doesn't want cops, it would be bad manners to insist. Let's get her home." He took some bottled water from the bar setup, poured it into a glass, added ice, and handed it to me. He did the same for Abdul. His hands were as steady as a surgeon's.

When we reached the shop, he said, "What kind of security system do you have?"

"I don't."

"You what?"

"I can't afford one," I said. "And I can't use a metal gate at night, because the Welcome! corporation doesn't like the look of bars covering their logo; they find it unwelcoming. But I'm meticulous about locking up."

"What about your place?"

"My place?" I was momentarily confused. "Oh, my apartment. No, I'm very vigilant about that. Not that there's anything worth stealing."

"Well, lady, there's you, isn't there?" He studied me, no longer the affable cowboy. There was also Margaret, I realized, probably up there stuffing herself with raisins, waffles, and Cheerios. I made a move to get out of the car, but he stopped me. "Look, I don't know who the hell that was back there and maybe you don't either. But it doesn't take a native to see this neighborhood is not Bel Air, and since you don't want cops, I'll feel a whole lot better if I take a look at your locks."

Rex had worked his way through college as a locksmith, he explained as he inspected my apartment building. This, he determined, could be picked by a tree toad. The shop's three entrances were somewhat better protected. Apparently Aldwyn, my predecessor, had sprung for brand-new locks—although not dead bolts—prior to hanging himself.

Next, he checked the shop windows in a businesslike silence, to Fredreeq's delight. On her way to assist a customer in Easter baskets, she slipped me a Post-it. The customer, I noticed, was the man who'd been in yesterday, in the beautiful blue cashmere sweater. To-day he wore a blue leather jacket. I looked down at Fredreeq's note. "Rex: VGL, huh?" VGL was the standard Personals ad abbreviation for "very good looking."

"Well, you're a puzzle," Rex said, strolling over to me. "You have your friends check out your dates down to their socks, but mean-while, you got yourself a store and an apartment that's open house to any crack fiend with a credit card." He took a business card from the bronze frog holder near the register and pocketed it. "You make a man want to watch out for you."

I said nothing. His security assessment alarmed me, and his con-cern evoked a kind of confusion. It was the second time today some-one had displayed protectiveness, and I didn't know how to respond.

"Hey, Fredreeq," Rex called across the shop. "Tell Joey I'll be back in two weeks with my Lamborghini and I owe her a ride." He kissed me on the cheek. His eyes, the color of sage, looked into mine. "Thank you for brunch."

He didn't mention a second date. I watched through the shop window as Abdul opened the car door for him. A sense of melan-choly, tinged with fear, came over me.

IF REX HAD been unexpectedly charismatic, Cliff, my second Sun-day date, was merely inoffensive. Not that that was cause for com-plaint, in these trying times. Cliff owned a picture framing shop, so we spoke about small business concerns while driving downtown to a museum exhibit on the Jain religion of pre-Christian India.

"When Fredreeq told me you had an interest in spiritual tradi-tions," Cliff said, "I knew you'd go wild for this. Can't believe you didn't see the Jain show at LACMA; I'll never forget it. I only hope this one measures up."

The Museum of Crafts and Culture, in downtown L.A., was the

size of my shop. After a twenty-minute black-and-white introductory film strip, itself somewhat ancient, Cliff steered us eagerly toward the exhibit. This consisted of photographs of artifacts of the long-gone Jains, with accompanying text. Cliff could not restrain himself from reading aloud the entire section on the Digambara group, a Jain subset that practiced asceticism by going nude. "What's your feeling on that?" he said, when he'd finished.

"To be honest," I said, "I was thinking about a guy who pleaded guilty to a conspiracy charge last year, and whether there are court transcripts of things like that, and if so, how I'd get access to them."

Cliff nodded, as though this were a normal response to nudism in the sixth century B.C. "Doing an employee check? U.S. District Court. Blue pages of the phone book."

It was late when we got back from dinner at Marie Callender's, a restaurant best known for its pies. I gave Cliff a tour of my shop, grabbing the opportunity to check the premises for lurkers while I had a nice-sized male in tow. Cliff was impressed with the decor, especially the lemon grove mural, and asked me for a second date in front of Engagements/Weddings, Aisle 5. Recalling Dr. Cookie's new research deadline, I told him to call back in a month, which he agreed to without questions. "Curiously incurious," I wrote in my Dating Project journal, "about events of the last 2,600 years."

There was no sign of Doc or my car around the apartment building when I took Margaret out for her nighttime ablutions. Nor had I been able to reach him on his phone all day. Would he show up tonight? The thought made me tingle with anticipation, that he might be here in the dark while I slept. That I might see him when I woke.

Back upstairs, Margaret watched me move the daybed in front of the door again. I threw my flannel pajamas into the laundry basket and went to bed in a black silk negligee.

. . .

MARGARET AND I slept in Monday morning. If Doc had spent the night on the street, he was gone by the time we got there.

As the morning wore on, I was in the shop growing annoyed, then worried about the fact that he didn't call and he didn't answer when I called him. By noon, I had all the early warning signs of an obsessive-compulsive disorder, the one where you pick up the phone several times each hour to make sure there's a dial tone. Was this someone who wasn't calling because he was dead, or just a guy I liked too much who said he'd call and then didn't? And if it was the latter, did that make him a car thief as well?

At one o'clock, I called my apartment. There was a message on the machine.

"Meet me tonight," he said. "Corner of Cherokee and Fountain. I'll be there at eight and wait as long as I can, and I'll keep my phone on. I've got good news."

chapter fourteen

I t took eight minutes to walk to Cherokee and Fountain. I did it with zigs and zags, and a lot of looks behind me. I wasn't followed. Of course, it was possible that I wasn't recognized. For my date following the rendezvous, I was dressed in faux snakeskin pants and matching high-heeled ankle boots, along with a Tiffanie's Trousseau trademark off-the-shoulder sweater. There was a recurring scent of early orange blossoms along the way, and despite, or maybe in addition to the sense of danger, I was dizzy with romantic possibilities. Not that much could happen in the twelve minutes I had with Doc before I needed to hotfoot it back to meet one Benjamin Woo.

Fredreeq had tried to delay my date, to no avail. "Benjamin's a personal manager," she said, "so everything's an Issue. He's taking you to House of Blues to hear this band he represents and he's all uptight about getting there on time."

I went ten minutes early to meet Doc, and spent those minutes alternating between excitement and anxiety, a longing to burst into song, something from *South Pacific,* and a desire to hide in the shrubbery.

Doc was on time. He appeared across the street, and waited for a break in the traffic. He hadn't spotted me. Dressed as he'd been the day before, in black jeans and T-shirt, there was more animation to him now. He glowed. I was probably glowing myself, my face smiling so hard it hurt, the orchestra in my head reaching fever pitch.

He caught sight of me and waved as he jogged across Fountain. "Hey," he said, reaching me. "Where's Margaret?"

"Back in the apartment," I said. "And she's fine. If you'd like to see her—"

"I guess I wasn't clear. I assumed we'd make our trade tonight." He handed me my car key and gestured over his shoulder. "Car's over there, behind that minivan."

"Is the, uh, patient with you?"

"Waiting across the street. Let's walk back and get Margaret and I can check out the parking situation and see what we can come up with that'll make you feel safe—"

"We can't," I said. "There's no time, I have a—an appointment in a few minutes. Can you keep the car and come back around midnight? Or tomorrow," I said, when he looked at me in surprise. "Anytime."

"It'll have to be tomorrow," he said. "We'll be in bed long before midnight. She's been through a lot."

She? I felt blood drain out of my face.

He looked across the street. "I told her about you, but she's not ready to meet anyone, particularly—" He smiled. "Well, you know how women are."

I couldn't speak. I couldn't move.

"So you don't need your car till tomorrow?" he said.

This was the moment to look him in the eye and say "She who?" and in a perfect world I would have; in a world where I had supreme self-esteem, I would say, "Who are we talking about here, your mother, your cousin Beth, or your one true love?" Dr. Cookie would do that. Fredreeq would. But I'd been down this road so many times I could find my way in the dark and I couldn't bear to hear the words spoken aloud, each one like a slap, *Yes, there's someone else. I thought you knew.* To see his brown eyes lose their sparkle, replaced by comprehension, then embarrassment for me. He would be kind. It would be horrible.

I managed to shake my head.

"You okay?" he looked at me searchingly. "Nothing bad happened today?"

I shook my head again, unable to trust my voice.

He smiled. "She'll be disappointed not to see Margaret—that animal's her baby—but another day won't kill her. You okay walking home from here?"

I squeezed out a "Yup, fine, thanks." Then I turned and took off toward Sunset, as fast as my faux snakeskin high-heeled ankle boots allowed.

TUESDAY DAWNED AS bright and blue-skied as an orange juice commercial, compounding my depression. I was dragging myself to the bank to make the morning deposit when Fredreeq caught up with me, carrying her own deposit envelope, from Neat Nails Plus. "How was Sorry About Your Sister?" she asked.

"Who?"

"The band you saw last night, with Benjamin Woo."

I pressed my fingers to my temple. " 'Metallica without the sentiment,' according to *Rolling Stone.*"

"And how about Benjamin?" she asked. "Was he a hottie, or what?"

"Very hot. Very nice. Loved my look—says snakeskin is this year's black. But he won't be calling for a second date since he can't get involved with anyone making under eighty thousand a year without doing long-term damage to his standard of living."

"Okay, screw him," Fredreeq said. "We have a Drive-by scheduled today with the Frog, and then tonight you're seeing—"

"Fredreeq, quit it. The nicknaming. I know it's your way of keeping them straight, but then I'm halfway through dinner and I try to think of their name and all I come up with is Elvis or Boris Yeltsin. It's disconcerting."

"Fine. His name is Jean-Luc Something and he sounds very ooh-la-la on the phone, and what's wrong, sister? You're about as chirpy as a box of hair."

"I'm just a little glum." I sped up my pace, zooming past Sacred Heart Church. "By the way, where did Benjamin get the idea I made anywhere close to eighty grand?"

"Who knows? Oh, I suppose there's an outside chance that something Joey or I said could've been construed by the casual listener as—"

"Hey." I stopped. "We *are* doing things by the book, aren't we? These are all guys who respond to my ad, right, and get checked against the List to—"

"Will you lighten up, please?" Fredreeq grabbed my arm and forced me across the street despite a blinking Don't Walk sign. "You just stick to your part of the job, missy, and let Joey and me do ours. Straight men do not grow on trees in L.A., not in multiples of ten, but somehow we keep dredging them up, so you just keep your eye on the prize and your body squeezed into those clothes."

She had a point. The one man I'd found lacked something so basic it wasn't even on the List: availability. So who was I to complain? What mattered, aside from my contribution to science, was the five grand the Dating Project paid. Money to buy my shop. Wollie's Willkommen! Greetings would mean financial independence for me, security for P.B. Once I had that, I'd join the nunhood, some nice order that still wore habits and didn't require dating.

BROWSERS FILLED THE shop. Spies, I thought darkly, or just garden-variety cheapskates, unwilling to spring for more than a pack of gum. They seemed to be working in shifts, exiting and entering as if choreographed, so that just as I picked up the phone, they'd ask a question, or ask for change, or ask to use the bathroom. I had my sketchbook out, experimenting with vampire fangs for Halloween cards, so it wasn't a total waste of time, but what I really wanted was to research Ron "the Weasel" Ronzare. The man in Doc's newspaper article. Whatever Doc knew I now had to discover for myself, since I didn't intend to spend another minute in his company, picking his uncooperative brain.

I figured the Weasel could be found somewhere on the Internet, but all I knew how to do on my computer was inventory, accounting, and graphics. For everything else I depended on Fredreeq, who was always threatening to send me to a twelve-step program for un-wired people. But I couldn't ask Fredreeq to research this.

Finally I was alone in the shop.

In the blue pages that preceded the white pages and the yellow pages was, as Cliff had suggested, a number for the U.S. District Court. This was answered by a bilingual computer offering a menu of options so exhaustive it could only have been devised by a government agency. The possibility of talking to a human being was not on the menu.

I'd spent four full minutes communing with the computer voice via touch-tone when Fredreeq came in, a strange man in tow. This, I realized, was today's Drive-by.

"Wollie," Fredreeq said, "meet Jean-Luc."

Jean-Luc was lanky and pale in that French, vitamin-deficient way that spoke of baguettes and Gauloises. Fredreeq had presumably asked the cigarette question already (number ten, No Smoking) but I'd noticed that Europeans often don't consider it smoking if it's under a pack a day.

I was about to hang up the phone when Jean-Luc grasped my hands so that the phone stayed wedged between my ear and shoulder. My head to one side, I saw him take in my plaid kilt and Peter Pan–collared shirt with loving approval. "Thanks you, thanks you," he said, almost making sense, in an accent as thick as Camembert.

In my left ear, the computer voice explained that with a written request, a case number, a twenty-dollar processing fee, a fifty-cents-per-page photocopy charge, and seven dollars per document—

Fredreeq said, "Jean-Luc, Wollie's an entrepreneur. Entrepreneuse. And an artiste. Check out these"—she grabbed my sketchbook—"teeth."

"Fangs," I said, and wrested my right hand from him to shut the sketchbook.

"For Halloween," Fredreeq explained to him. "Greeting card artists are five seasons ahead of the public, just like fashion designers."

"And farmers," I said. I hung up the phone.

This was enough small talk for Fredreeq. "Wollie, Jean-Luc is a fan of poetry, so I invited him to Uncle Theo's Poetry Reading."

Jean-Luc smiled. It was hard to tell if he was smiling about poetry or smiling in that way people do when they don't understand something.

"Come along, Jean-Luc," Fredreeq said, and led him away, holding the door open for an enormous roll of wallpaper, propelled by my Uncle Theo.

"What is it, what's going on?" I asked, hurrying over to help him. My uncle never showed up on Tuesdays. He rarely left Glendale, since he didn't own a car, coming in for the Wednesday Night Poetry Readings with his friend Gordon. "Is it about P.B., have you heard something?"

"No, no, dear, I had this leftover chinoiserie pattern that I thought would go nicely with the existing—" The rest of his words were lost behind the wallpaper. I was glad to see him, what was visible of him, anyway—hair, sticking out in thick white tufts, and feet, shod in old Earth Shoe clogs held together by electrician's tape.

I gave him a kiss on the cheek and took the wallpaper from him, leading him to the back room. "Well, it's a nice surprise, Uncle Theo. Could you watch the floor for a minute? I need to change into my date clothes."

In the bathroom, I tore the plastic from a pink angora sweater and pastel blue jeans with just a touch of spandex, Tiffanie's idea of what to wear to the movies. My date this evening was a special effects artist named Sterling, who was taking me to his current film, *High School of Blood*. I looked forward to sitting in the dark for two hours, eating popcorn. Subject matter was irrelevant. So was the company. As long as I didn't have to smile or talk or learn any more about guns, I'd be happy.

The minute I returned to the shop floor I knew I'd left Uncle Theo alone too long. He was a socialist, and tended to cut prices, if not give things away outright. Who knew what merchandise had been traded for the four dollars and sixty-two cents piled neatly near the register? My uncle was also compulsively chatty, currently in deep conversation with four men in soccer outfits. Plainclothespeople?

A quarter of spies would be too pricey for Mr. Bundt, I hoped. I prayed. Because Uncle Theo, as an employee, was not up to Welcome! standards. His crocheted vest had once been an afghan and his drawstring pants, made of hemp, were sold in bulk at the co-op where he bought his grains and lentils. I could smell his patchouli across the room.

"Oh, Wollie," he said and strolled over, "a nice young man just phoned, by the name of Dylan, regarding some sort of interview."

"Yes, Dylan Ellison, I think his name is. A Drive-by—part of this Dating Project I've told you about. Fredreeq will take care of it."

"Well, that's the thing," Uncle Theo said. "The young man is running late, detained on the 405 freeway. But not to worry, I invited him to the poetry reading."

"You what?" I gasped. "Oh, Uncle Theo, you can't just invite— I mean, there's a system here we're supposed to be following and— oh, heck." I took a deep breath.

"I simply thought," Uncle Theo explained, "that as long as he's driving all the way from Tarzana to meet you, he may as well be rewarded with poetry."

"Well, he'll hardly want to stay overnight for it," I pointed out.

"Oh, the reading's not tomorrow," Uncle Theo said. "It's tonight. At eight."

"What do you mean?" I said, growing cold. "Today's Tuesday."

My uncle patted my angora shoulder. "Dear, didn't I mention? There's a strong possibility that Thom Gunn, who's flying in tonight from Paris on his way back to San Francisco, will stop by, so instead of Wednesday—no, perhaps it was P.B. with whom I had this conversation."

"Well, that's too darn bad," I said. "Because we can't—Thom Gunn?"

"Yes, isn't it amazing?" Uncle Theo radiated happiness. "The flyers have been circulating, the sign is up, we're expecting a full house."

"The sign?" I heard myself squawk. "Who put up the sign?" I ran outside, my uncle at my heels, and saw it, the POETRY TONIGHT!

sandwich board, facing Sunset. "Who did this? And when?" I asked, hoisting the big easel and collapsing it.

"Fredreeq. This afternoon," Uncle Theo said. "Is there a problem? I called yesterday, and she answered and said she'd take care of it. You seem grumpy, dear."

"I'm darn grumpy." I struggled with the sandwich board, nearly pinning my uncle against the side of the building with it. "If Mr. Bundt's spies have seen this sign, they could show up tonight and—"

"Spies?" His white eyebrows shot up.

"Industrial investigators. Secret shoppers." I stopped to let a Plucky Chicken customer get around us. "The point is, having fifty people in the shop after hours is completely unauthorized, it always has been. I was going to cancel it this week, I tried to call you, but—"

"Cancel poetry?!" Uncle Theo laughed merrily, falling in with me. "Oh, my dear, what an extraordinary idea. Like canceling oxygen."

"Just until the upgrade decision is made." I maneuvered the sandwich board through the doorway, banging it and chipping off a bit of paint in the process.

"Careful, that's my prized possession," Uncle Theo said, holding the door open for me. "My favorite Girl Scout painted it for her uncle, three decades ago."

"She'll paint you a new one," I snapped, walking backward toward the utility closet. I shoved the sandwich board inside, causing an avalanche of cleaning supplies. Customers glanced our way. I gave a general smile and squatted to the floor.

"Wollstonecraft," said my uncle, squatting too and gathering up broom and mop. "I want you to consider whether anything that makes you talk of canceling poetry and discarding art is worthy of you."

"Uncle Theo," I said through gritted teeth, glancing at a soccer player on Aisle 1, "this is my job. This week is critical. What happens if I don't get the franchise, if I have to keep working at minimum wage? Who's gonna take care of P.B. if—" I stopped. Better not to go down that road. "Sorry. I just can't have a bunch of poets whooping it up in the shop if I'm not here to supervise, and I can't be here, because I have to be at a horror movie." I took a bottle of Liquid-Plumr from him.

Uncle Theo said nothing, just sat with slumped shoulders, biting his lip. I noticed he was wearing his special Middle Eastern cap, the one he'd worn the Wednesday night in 1995 when Allen Ginsberg had dropped in and had us all write haiku.

I reached over and tucked a tuft of white hair behind his ear. "On the other hand, there's only one Thom Gunn, isn't there?"

He looked up, smitten with hope.

"All right," I said. "But Dylan Ellison, the guy on the 405 that you invited? You've gotta head him off at the pass. I'll cancel my movie, but I don't think I can cancel my date, so I'll have to bring Sterling to the poetry reading, and believe me, one man is all I can handle tonight."

How I underestimated myself.

chapter fifteen

"What do you mean he approved Dylan Ellison?" Fredreeq yelled over her cell phone. I'd found her in her car, heading home for the day. "When did Uncle Theo join the support team? Does he even know about the List?"

"He has his own list," I said. "Here's his list: no serial killers."

"But to invite the guy to the poetry reading? Jean-Luc's coming to the reading."

"Not tonight!" I said.

"What do you mean, not tonight? You were there, you said, 'Great, yes, come!' "

"But I was talking about tomorrow."

"Well," Fredeeq said, "we were talking tonight. The sign's outside for tonight."

"But I *have* a date," I said. "Sterling, the special effects guy Joey scheduled—"

"—without writing it down? That girl has feathers for brains. Okay, don't panic." Fredreeq switched to mothering mode. "I'm turning the car around. Meanwhile, you're at the register? In front of you is the Dating Project file with phone numbers. Start calling and see which guys can reschedule."

BY 7:35 THE shop was ready for the reading, with card racks 5 and 6 moved against the back wall, and folding chairs set up in their place. Uncle Theo stood next to me at the register, napkin tucked into shirt, eating his ritual Plucky Chicken.

None of the dates answered their phones, so I'd left identical messages on three machines, asking them to call the minute they got in. At 7:40 Joey showed up.

"Fredreeq's stuck on the Santa Monica Freeway. I'm here to lend moral support until she comes."

"Here's the plan," I said. "We have no idea what Dylan Ellison looks like, but if you can somehow figure it out, intercept him and keep him occupied. I'll deal with the other two as best I can. Uncle Theo will help."

Uncle Theo nodded and smiled, displaying more chicken than we cared to see.

"Piece of cake," Joey said. "Think of this as a social triathlon. You'll make Fredreeq proud."

At 7:45, Uncle Theo was at the front door handing out photocopied programs.

At 7:48 Jean-Luc bounded in. One of his buttons caught in Uncle Theo's crocheted vest; unaware, he walked on, until Uncle Theo's knees buckled and Jean-Luc was bungeed backward. They disengaged and shook hands.

Jean-Luc continued over to me and kissed me on both cheeks, smelling mildly, though not unpleasantly, of garlic. He took my hand and was reluctant to let go, so I led him to a chair in the back row, hoping to plant him there. I got him to sit by sitting myself momentarily, but then had to climb over him to exit the row. His hand slid from my waist to my derriere as I did so. He certainly was tactile.

Sterling showed three minutes later. Sterling was of African-American descent, not as tall as the Frenchman—or me—but more substantial, with an intelligent face and wire-rim glasses. I met him at the door and told him about the poetry snafu.

"Great," he said. "I see movies all the time, but I've never watched poetry."

Before I could suggest that tonight was no time to start, Uncle Theo took Sterling off to meet the evening's opening act.

Chairs filled up fast, due to the prospect of Thom Gunn, and only half the crowd were Wednesday night regulars. Some were neighborhood people—I recognized a Loo Fong delivery girl, and one of the hookers I'd made change for days before. This would please Uncle Theo, who liked to say that everyone was a poet, and poetry was for everyone. My stomach, though, was in knots as I scrutinized faces for signs of Dylan, and also for Mr. Bundt's secret shoppers. I'd had low-level anxiety about the poetry readings since the first Wednesday I'd lent the shop to the poets, after their previous meeting place, a church basement, had succumbed to earthquake damage. One Wednesday turned into several years, because who could evict poets? Also, the chance of getting caught had seemed remote. Until now.

Joey sidled up to me. "Three possible Dylans. From his phone interview we know he's writing his dissertation in sports medicine and voted for Ralph Nader. Now, there are three guys, each one alone, with shoes that suggest orthopedic awareness or third-party politics. A guy over by the snow globes cabinet has on Birkenstocks—with a suit—and then there's a serious pair of running shoes on—whoa, baby." She pointed to a man in sweat clothes standing amid the Easter baskets display, joined by a man who kissed him lingeringly on the mouth. "Cross him off the list."

"Ladies and gentlemen," Uncle Theo called out, "it is now after eight and while Thom Gunn is not yet here, we have other poets to enjoy, so we're going to begin. Please take your seats." Sterling joined me as Joey went to investigate the Dylans.

From the back row, Jean-Luc yelled, "Wolleeee!" There was one seat next to him, obviously saved for me. I grabbed a hand-painted $29.95 milking stool, and headed over, Sterling in tow.

"Jean-Luc, Sterling. Sterling, Jean-Luc." I propelled Sterling into the chair meant for me and squeezed the milking stool between them. "Bad back," I explained.

The poet, a grandmotherly woman, brought to the podium a cactus in a terra-cotta pot painted with the word "Woody." She barked out a single word: "Breasts."

Someone laughed.

"Breasts" again filled the room, a command, compelling silence.

"Breasts, breasts, breasts
Boobs, knockers, kachungas . . ."

Jean-Luc sat up straight. Sterling shifted his position. I kept very still.

"Love muffins." The poet read like a schoolmarm, with equal emphasis on every word. "Lung mittens."

My clasped hands were suddenly surrounded by Jean-Luc's hand, which felt like a damp sponge. I saw Sterling glance down. Whether he was looking at Jean-Luc's hand or my breasts straining against the pink angora sweater, I couldn't tell.

". . . pert little melons,
big blushing apples . . ."

A tap on my shoulder sent me nearly to the ceiling. It was Fred-reeq, behind me, crouching. She beckoned me closer. "I'm here, Joey took off. She says none of the guys are Dylan, but I just found out, the guy in Birkenstocks is a Welcome! spy."

My insides turned to ice. I whispered back, "How do you know?"

She leaned in closer. "He said to me, and I quote: 'I have a message for the woman of your shop. She has stuff here that do not belong.' "

"My God, I've got a roomful of poets that 'do not belong.' What else matters?"

Jean-Luc, on my left, leaned toward us, wanting in on the conversation. He massaged my hands. I pulled them away.

Like a train picking up speed, the poetess cried out, "Hot cakes, hot cakes, hot cakes, hot cakes. Flapjacks! Pancakes! Little balls of dough!"

Jean-Luc asked loudly, "What are flapjacks, please?" Heads swiveled toward us.

"NIPPLES, BOOBIES, TITS, PO-POS"

Heads swiveled back. My bra felt tight and nausea swept over me. I stood. Maybe the spy had been in the back room, seen Uncle Theo's hookah on the shelf, and mistaken it for drug paraphernalia.

". . . wizened mammary love missiles
sinking down . . ."

Yes, there he was. Planted amid the snow globes, arms folded, the man in the suit had the look of an industrial spy. Beefy and stern.

Early twenties. Too young to date me, I now saw. I sat, and turned to Fredreeq. "We're dead."

"... ancient milk bottles"

Fredreeq gave my arm a supportive squeeze and scurried back to her seat.

"... seeking teeth."

Yawning silence filled the room. Then came tentative applause. As the clapping continued, I turned to look at the Minnie Mouse clock, thinking, How much longer can this nightmare continue?

Which is when I saw Doc outside the window of my shop, looking in.

MY FIRST INSTINCT was to hurl myself through the glass window to get to him, and in that moment I saw how far I'd sunk, that I could get so excited over an unavailable chain-smoking ex-con I'd been mentally trashing for the past twenty-four hours. I did not give in to my first instinct. I mumbled an excuse to my dates, ran into the back room, through the freight entrance, and outside.

Jogging through the alley, I came around the outside of Bodega Bob to find a full parking lot and no sign of Doc. I paused at a Land Rover parked on the sidewalk, and wondered if he'd gone inside or maybe into hiding, crouched among the cars.

"Doc!" I called out softly, and then heard a noise over by Neat Nails Plus. Irrationally, I panicked and ducked behind the Land Rover.

And came face to face with a child.

She sat cross-legged on the sidewalk, apparently hiding too. She held a round pink suitcase, a piece of Barbie merchandise that was ancient—as old as I.

"Hello," I whispered.

The child said nothing, although she looked straight at me. She was maybe ten or eleven, with a wide face and serious eyes. Too big for Barbie, I thought. She had frizzy hair and pale skin, and a vaguely doughy look to her.

"Hey." Doc appeared out of the shadows of Plucky Chicken.

I looked up at him, then back to her. Dots connected in my brain. I said, "Is this your little girl?"

He smiled and stepped closer. The child stood, hugging her suitcase, and took his hand. She was close to five feet tall, I estimated, and maybe older than she seemed at first glance. Twelve? Thirteen? I had little knowledge of children.

Doc spoke to her. "Ruby, this is Wollie. Miss Shelley."

"Wollie's fine," I said.

He nodded. "This is Ruby."

"Hello, Ruby."

Doc said, "I've been telling her a lot about you." There was an awkward silence. I noticed the red Converse All Stars on his feet, my own shoes. I noticed how the white of his T-shirt matched the white of his eyes. He was missing something he'd had the night we met and it took me a moment to figure out what it was.

Invulnerability.

I smiled, recognizing a home court advantage. I rose slowly, and spoke the word that was practically my middle name.

"Welcome."

chapter sixteen

Two minutes later I was leading Doc and Ruby through the alley.

"We shouldn't have come," Doc said. "I don't think we were followed, but—good God."

"What?" I held open the freight door as they stepped into the back room.

"This place," he said. "This is some—place."

He and Ruby stared, taking it all in, the off-season displays and oversized decorations hanging from the ceiling and climbing the walls. There were posterboard evergreen trees and Santa Clauses, a Fourth of July Revolutionary War marching band and an entire pumpkin patch. There were Styrofoam pilgrims, a six-foot menorah, and a papier-mâché heart the size of a small hot air balloon suspended over my drafting table. "It's the back of my shop," I said.

"It's like walking into an album cover from the sixties," Doc said.

Ruby nodded, big-eyed. I couldn't recall a child ever being in the back room before.

"It's the overflow of my life," I said, suddenly needing them to like it.

Ruby turned to me. Although quiet, she didn't seem shy. I returned her look, my own shyness around children overcome by curiosity. She resembled Doc, but it was an overexposed resemblance, her coloring lighter. What features they shared, a strong nose and thick eyebrows, didn't work as well on a girl. Maybe she'd grow into them.

She looked beyond me, and tugged at her father's sleeve, pointing to the north wall. High on the concrete hung a bicycle built for two and a pair of stilts.

"My uncle's," I said. "I store things for people, stuff that has no place else to go."

A burst of applause from the shop floor brought me back to reality. "I have to get in there," I said, and explained the poetry reading. "But no one will bother you here. At intermission, people come looking for the bathroom, so stay around the corner here, by the sofa. As soon as I can I'll come and take you up to the apartment. That's where Margaret is."

At the mention of Margaret, Ruby snapped her head around with an expression of such radiance, she was almost pretty. She plopped down on Joey's red sofa, hands folded on top of her suitcase, as though the sooner she started waiting, the sooner the waiting would be over.

And all this time, she hadn't said a word.

INTERMISSION WAS UNDER way. Sterling was eager to discuss the poetry, so I parked him with Uncle Theo, who was on the phone tracking down his featured artist, Thom Gunn.

Jean-Luc joined the audience stampede to Bodega Bob for second-act provisions. I nabbed Fredreeq as she headed toward the back room. "Where's the secret shopper?"

"Outside," she said. "Get this, he's having a cigarette. Must be part of his cover, because I can't see Bundt hiring a smoker. Especially one hardly old enough to shave."

Something occurred to me. "Fredreeq, when he talked to you, did he point me out? I mean, would he know me on sight as the Wollie of Wollie's Welcome! Greetings?"

Fredreeq frowned. "Let's see, I was giving someone change from the register, and that's when he asked me if I work here, and I said yes and he gave me the message 'for the woman of the shop.' He's foreign, did I mention?"

"Foreign? What kind of foreign?"

She shrugged. "Like one of those films Joey's always making us watch."

"Foreign films? *Seven Samurai? Fitzcarraldo? The Garden of the Finzi-Continis?*"

Fredreeq closed her eyes, then opened them. "No, none of those. I'll know it when I hear it. But go check it out yourself—I can see him from here." She nodded toward the window. "He's hanging with another kid who's got a really serious widow's peak."

WHEN I SAW him up close with his fellow smoker, I knew he wasn't Mr. Bundt's spy. He was definitely not Dylan Ellison. And the "stuff" he cryptically referred to, I suspected, had nothing to do with my shop. It was Carmine's merchandise he wanted.

The two guys, in dark suits, leaned against the window of Neat Nails Plus, at a right angle to the shop. A trio of older women, also smoking, partially blocked my view, as they huddled against the side of the building. I stood in the shop's doorway, studying the pair.

They weren't exactly kids—more like mid-twenties, I decided, but something about them made them appear younger. The hair, maybe: short, and just enough of it to qualify them as blonds. The Birkenstocker's fellow smoker was slight, with a pronounced widow's peak. He wore some sort of high-tech rubber sandals. The footwear certainly altered the effect of the suits, reminding me of little altar boys with Keds peeking out from under their robes. I can't say why I felt they were dangerous, but these two gave me a bad case of the creeps.

I wanted to know what they were saying.

Opportunity was at my elbow. A pack of Marlboros sat on the cement ledge of the building, along with a yellow plastic lighter. I looked around, withdrew a cigarette from the pack, lit it fast, and inhaled carefully. I didn't choke, but I went weak in the knees as that thing that gives cigarettes their zing coursed through my bloodstream. I wobbled past the trio of women and took my position in the de facto smoking section.

The guys, maybe six feet away, didn't see me. I inched closer.

It took some listening for their mumbles to give way to actual words. Unfortunately, the words were foreign. Fredreeq was right, we'd seen this movie. What was it?

I closed my eyes and concentrated, running through films Joey had exposed us to over the years. *Rules of the Game . . . The Spirit of the Beehive . . . Potemkin . . .* No. It wasn't Italian, German, French, Japanese, Russian, or Spanish. What else was there? The language was animated and singsong. Then I recognized, just barely, "La Cienega," "Sepulveda," and "LAX," and deduced they were engaged in the classic L.A. debate, Best Routes to the Airport.

I wanted a good look at their faces, to be able to describe them to Doc. A breeze wafted by, momentarily dimming the glow from my cigarette and bringing inspiration. Before my mind could reconsider,

I snuffed out the glowing ember against the side of the building, then moved forward, and said, "Excuse me. Do you have a light?"

The guys looked at me, then at each other, clearly taken aback. The heavy one, with the Birkenstocks, asked a question of the widow's-peaked one, who gave a short reply, all in their singsongy language. The Birkenstocker responded, then turned to me, showing crooked teeth. It took a full nine seconds for me to decipher his response to me as "Vee Double-You," during which time his focus slid downward and stopped, riveted to my pink angora breasts.

VW. He was talking about my car. He knew me.

Were these the guys from the Alfa Romeo?

I couldn't be sure; it had been too dark to see them, but the thought made me go wobbly again. I tried to turn away, but my body parts were slow in receiving my brain's signal. The Birkenstocker, still riveted to my angora, reached into his breast pocket. Presumably he was going for a lighter.

But what I saw was a gun.

Here we go again, I thought, unbelieving. The gun was in a shoulder holster, with only the handle visible, black and stark. I was close enough to see a black screw, a rough surface, something stamped into the steel.

I kept staring, in fascinated horror, until the jacket flapped shut and a plump, hairy hand reached toward my face with a silver lighter attached to it, bursting into flame.

I recoiled automatically, backing into the widow's-peaked man, who'd moved behind me. Ruta's face popped into my head, and her reassuring voice. Stay calm, it said. Act normal. Hand shaking, I brought the shortened cigarette to my mouth and managed a pitiful inhale, igniting nothing. The Birkenstocker's other hairy hand took mine, steadying it, as he stepped closer. There was a rancid intimacy about all this, but "normalcy" dictated playing it out, so I sucked hard, got the Marlboro going again, and went utterly dizzy. The drum section of a rock band had taken up residence in my head.

"You leave here? Work here?" the guy said, which puzzled me, until I realized that "leave" was "live" with an accent.

"No habla españ—uh, *inglés,"* I said instantly. *"No habla inglés."* Belatedly, I realized I'd already spoken to him in English.

His smile grew bigger, the crooked teeth now showing gaps. Quite unattractive. "Your man," he said. "He is here?"

"Hombre?" I said, feeling less calm and normal by the second. Was *hombre* the word for man, or the word for hat? What was the point of this, anyway? I looked around for the trio of smoking women, but they'd disappeared. The blond guys were moving in on both sides, so that I was sandwiched between them.

"Tell your man," said the Birkenstocker, "if he leaves, tell him—" he paused, for effect.

If he leaves? No—if he *lives.* Dear God, I wanted to scream, of course he lives. Do I look like a girl who consorts with dead men?

I wasn't destined to hear what words followed. From the direction of Bodega Bob came a shout of "Woll-eeee!" with much waving of hands and a moment later, the enthusiastic approach of Jean-Luc.

The blond men melted away into the night.

HOW I GOT through intermission and dealt with Sterling and Jean-Luc I'll never know. Half my mind was on the foreign guys, their inherent creepiness, and that gun. The gun in particular, and something about it that I couldn't quite remember kept fear stapled to my stomach.

My keys were not in their place at the register counter, which disturbed me, but there was no time to search. I took an extra set from a file drawer, and waited for people to take their seats for Act 2, then excused myself, slipped into the back room, and took Doc and Ruby out the freight door, through the alley, and up to my apartment. I didn't mention my encounter; I didn't know the procedure for discussing guns and death threats in front of children, and I knew there'd be time enough later. I told Doc to lock the door behind me, and not to open it to anyone for any reason.

THOM GUNN NEVER did arrive, nor did Dylan, and the foreigners never returned. Uncle Theo helped me store the chairs in the back room and then he was off to Glendale, catching a ride with a Vietnam vet poet who'd impressed him. "Although," he said, sotto voce, as he hugged me goodbye, "he's no Thom Gunn."

Fredreeq approached with a large yawn. "All through intermission Uncle Theo was asking people if they were Dylan Ellison, babbling away about the Dating Project. I shut him down. He doesn't have the common sense of a housefly, does he?" She yawned again. "You need help getting rid of these dates?"

"No, go home, you've got children to see to. And a husband." I kissed her cheek. Fredreeq's fuchsia lipstick was fading; it must be late indeed. "I really, really appreciate this."

Sterling shook my hand and thanked me for an interesting evening. He was cool to the point of distaste, I noted, a far cry from the upbeat man who'd walked in earlier.

"I'm sorry, Sterling," I said, flooded with remorse. "I wasn't very attentive—"

He held up a hand. "Don't bother. It's not going to happen for us. You misrepresented yourself, know what I'm saying?"

Remorse gave way to alarm. "No, what are you saying?"

"You're a smoker. I could smell it on you half the night." He turned and walked off.

Dealing with Jean-Luc was easier—there was a lot of hand kissing, of course, but his excitement about the poetry overshadowed his interest in me. "Luminous," he said. "Transcendent. Healing." Big words for a man who didn't know "flapjacks," I thought. His English must've improved over intermission.

I ran the vacuum around a few lingering poets, and decided I'd gotten off cheap in the date department, if you didn't count the considerable guilt of misleading two perfectly nice men. God willing, I'd gotten off easy in the industrial spy department too.

As I locked up the shop, I spotted my keys, right on the counter. I pocketed them, along with the spare set, which I'd give to Doc. I thought of him and Ruby up in my apartment, and began to palpitate with excitement. I looked out the picture window to see if any poets remained in the parking lot, but there was only my own happy face, reflected in the glass, staring back at me.

Wild Strawberries. The film title popped into my head. The guys with the gun had been speaking Swedish.

chapter seventeen

Doc was sound asleep in my living room, his body splayed across the striped armchair. He looked as if he'd lived there all his life. His face was lit by a floor lamp, and I stepped in close to study it, something I'd been dying to do since I'd known him. Except for at the Donut Stop, I'd never seen him in good light. Now I memorized details: pointlessly long eyelashes, sunburnt cheekbones. His new short haircut emphasized his bone structure, and while he'd been clean-shaven yesterday, now there was that stubble again, all the way down to the opening of his T-shirt.

Something on the floor beside him caught my eye. A Cheerio. I bent to retrieve it, which brought me to his level. The level of his mouth, six inches away.

I moved in slowly, making believe I was about to kiss him.

His body gave a jerk, his ear brushing my nose. I pulled back, horrified to be caught eavesdropping on his dreams. But he didn't wake, just repositioned himself on the chair and turned his face away.

Across the room, a shape on the daybed stirred. Ruby. The only place left for me to stretch out was under the piano. No matter; a mood like this was wasted on sleep.

TWENTY MINUTES LATER he loomed over me, dark and male in my white kitchen. I looked up at him for a long time.

A siren sounded somewhere on Sunset.

Doc cleared his throat. "What are you doing?"

"Scrubbing the kitchen floor." I shifted on the black-and-white linoleum, to achieve a more graceful pose. It wasn't easy, given the tightness of Tiffanie's jeans.

"Any particular reason?"

"I was raised to believe that cleanliness is next to godliness," I said. "Also, it's kind of a Zen thing."

He raised an eyebrow. "Raised Buddhist, were you?"

I laughed. "No. Catholic. But with a Polish-Jewish influence," I added, recalling Ruta and her aphorisms. "God in the image and likeness of Mr. Clean."

He held a plastic bag I'd noticed him carrying earlier, containing, from the looks of it, clothes. He set it down and leaned back, elbows on the counter. "Here's what's going on: We were staying with a cousin, who, it turns out, has a girlfriend, who—okay, it's complicated. Anyhow, Ruby and I are temporarily—"

"Not a problem." A sign saying Number Six, Not Homeless popped into mental view. I ran over it. "You can stay here. Plenty of room."

He blinked. "This is a studio apartment, Wollie."

"Whole families occupy them, in this building. The Farhadiehs downstairs—"

"—don't have a grand piano the size of a yacht in the living room. What are you, a concert pianist, along with everything else?" He rubbed his eyes. "We should go to a hotel, but I don't want to drag Ruby off at this hour. You sure about this?"

"It's not easy for you, is it?" I said. "Being in someone's debt?"

"You have no idea." He stretched one suntanned arm across the counter and reached into the plastic bag. "Your car keys," he said, tossing them to me.

"Just so you know, none of this has been a problem," I said. "I haven't needed the car till now. As long as I get to Rio Pescado to-morrow."

"Back to the hospital?" Doc gave me a sharp look. "Why?"

I looked down at my linoleum. "You had a daughter there. I have a brother."

He stopped what he was doing and settled onto the lemon-scented floor. He sat opposite me, his back against the Tupperware cupboard, his feet stretched out in front of him. Our jeans touched. "Tell me about him," he said.

I did. I talked about adult-onset schizophrenia, how, with the end of my brother's teenage years, came the illness, a preoccupation with the Secret Service, a conviction that musical instruments were conduits for interplanetary surveillance. I explained how P.B. had stopped playing the piano, first because of the extraterrestrials, later because the drugs that kept hallucinations at bay brought side effects, a slowing of muscle memory and motor skills. Playing, P.B. said, no longer felt like play.

Doc didn't ask why I kept the piano, all these years later. He didn't ask about my long-gone father or my eccentric mother, didn't ask why all of P.B.'s concerns fell on me. He listened. He listened so well I just kept talking, going on to describe P.B.'s strange fore-knowledge of the murder, and then his apparent witnessing of it. I stopped short of admitting I had even the smallest suspicion he'd done it.

"The problem is," I said, "I can't get him on the phone, because he hates using technology when he's in crisis mode. I have to see him face to face to find out what happened and how involved he is, and how he's dealing with the police. I've got to—"

"Do you always visit on Wednesdays?"

"No, I go on Thursdays. But Thursday will be too late. You said so yourself."

He shook his head. "You can't go. Place is crawling with cops, and hospital security is beefed up, including the two guards we ran into. If they spot you, it's over. And everyone's looking for clues: you show up on the wrong day, you become one."

He pulled off his shirt. His torso was wiry, several shades paler than his face and hands, with all that hair on his chest I'd noticed before. He stood, went to the kitchen sink, and doused his head with water. His back was nice too. No hair there.

I stood too, and tossed him a clean dish towel. "A lot of people are probably making extra visits," I said, "worried about the fact that a murder took place there."

"Wrong. According to the news reports, the murder happened on the outskirts of Pleasant Valley. No one's mentioned Rio Pescado. You, Ms. Shelley, have just set off bells and whistles with that answer." From his plastic bag he pulled a scrunched-up piece of cloth and shook it into a black cotton T-shirt.

"Well, anyhow," I said, "it's unlikely that anyone will remember what day I visit, especially up on the rehab ward where nobody really knows me and—"

"You underestimate your effect on people." He donned the T-shirt. It was not particularly clean. I was torn between pleasure at the compliment he'd just paid me and an urge to do his laundry. "In any case," he went on, "consider this: if you're being followed, you lead the criminals back to their own crime scene." He moved to my refrigerator and opened it. "They're gonna wonder what you're doing—"

"I can lose them, I can—"

"I've seen you drive. You couldn't lose a tractor." He seemed to be checking out my frozen foods. "And if they realize you have a brother there, then he'll be in danger."

I felt hot inside my pink angora. "Well, what am I supposed to do? Forget about him? How easy was it for you to walk away from your daughter?"

He shut the refrigerator hard, and turned. "I didn't walk away from her."

I held his look, and he held mine, heat in the space between us.

A sound from outside, a loud crack, broke the tension.

The main room of the apartment was a rectangle, with a window at one end and the daybed at the other. A glance at Ruby showed she'd slept through it, whatever it was. We went to the window.

Intermittent streetlights illuminated parked cars. By craning our necks, we could see a tiny piece of Sunset, better lit, with moving traffic.

"Car backfiring, maybe?" I whispered. Doc was so close, his bare bicep pressed against my angora arm.

"Gunshot, maybe."

I pulled him back from the window. "Really?"

He looked at my hand on his arm and then up at my face. The phone rang.

I went for it, checking my watch: 11:20 P.M. "Hello," I said, and when there was no answer, said it again. "Hello?"

"I'm serenading you," he said.

The words sounded . . . pornographic. "Dave?" I said softly. I don't know why I thought of Dave Fischgarten, Date Nineteen. Something about the voice.

The response was a laugh and a single word. "Whore." And then a click.

I stood, phone clamped to my ear, listening to a dial tone. Doc was staring. I felt myself turn red. "Okay," I told the phone. "Thanks. You too." I put it down, avoiding eye contact. "Nothing," I said, although Doc hadn't asked. "Never mind."

"Wollie. Who was it?"

The phone rang again. I got it halfway through the first ring. "What?" I said.

"Second verse, same as the first." And from outside came another shot.

"Jesus dammit Christ," I blurted, dropping the phone and covering my head. "Get down! Get away from—" I was stuttering and stumbling and reaching for him.

The next thing I knew, Doc was pulling me roughly to the floor. The shooting stopped and in the silence I had an impulse to burst into tears, which was strange, since I felt more mad than scared. But I must have been scared, too, because when I tried to move I found I was quivering too much. "It's them," I said, from under his shoulder.

"Who?"

"Whomever," I said. "The guns, the—*guys,* the—"

He was across the room in four steps, to Ruby on the daybed. He bent over her, then came back to the window and looked out, staying to one side. "Unbelievable," he said. "She's still sleeping." He retrieved the fallen phone and hit three buttons.

"Nine-one-one?" I asked.

"Star sixty-nine." He put the phone to his ear. "He's blocked it."

"Mrs. Albertini—neighbor—she'll call the police—"

"Then let's kill the lights." He went into the kitchen; the kitchen went dark. "No point in giving him a target, or encouraging the cops to visit us." He moved to the floor lamp and switched it off.

The apartment didn't go completely black, being too close to the street. Light from the window illuminated shapes: table, armchair, man. I found I was clinging to a piano leg like it was a lifeboat, and let go.

Doc knelt and put his arms around me. There was no rocking or back-patting or caressing, just containment. A comprehensive sort of hug. Standing, the top of his head barely reached my nose; on the floor, all that changed.

"Okay?" he said eventually, and when I nodded, he released me. "Who was it on the phone?"

"He said he was serenading us."

"Us?"

"Well, me." The word "whore" was, after all, fairly gender-specific.

"Who's Dave?"

"Oh, just someone I—wait," I said. "It was a New York accent, that's what made me think of Dave. It was more pronounced when he called back."

"What did he say then?"

"He said, 'Second verse, same as the first.' "

"What else did he say?"

I looked away. "N-nothing." Footsteps on the stairwell sounded through the building's thin walls. They reached our floor and continued down the hall, and ended in a faint knocking. Mrs. Albertini's apartment.

"What if they come here?" I asked. "The police."

"They won't."

"What if they do?"

"You heard a car backfiring." He left me and walked back to the window. "You see now why I don't want you visiting your brother tomorrow?"

I said nothing.

"Look, I'll get us through this, I'll go to the cops as soon as I've got something to show them. Now that I have Ruby, I can focus on it. This won't go on forever."

"Why don't you tell me what 'this' is? Tell me what you know."

Doc circled the room, pausing at a framed picture on the wall, standing very close to see it in the darkness. It was my first published greeting card. "I want to keep you out of it," he said, "at least until I can—"

"Out of it?" My voice rose and I rose with it. "I'm sleeping with furniture in front of my door. I saw a gun tonight, my third—no, fourth in two days. I smoked a *cigarette*. I'm in this already, as far in as a person can be short of—of—"

"Ssh." He nodded toward the door. Feet clomped down the stairway. He waited, then came closer to me and whispered, "What gun did you see tonight?"

"The one the Swedish kid was carrying. Wait—" I closed my eyes. "Swedish. Ssss . . . Swedes. Yes. P.B. mentioned Swedes. What was it? Something to do with—"

Something cracked inside me, the wall I'd built against the possibility that my brother was a killer. Relief and shame rushed through. I put my face in my hands. "The Swedes killed that man in the road. That's what he was telling me."

I was glad for the darkness.

"GUYS IN SUITS, armed and threatening you, and you're just now getting around to mentioning it?" Doc said when I told him about my *Wild Strawberries* encounter.

"It slipped my mind," I said, embarrassed that his presence could have that effect on me.

"Describe the gun."

"I don't know guns," I said. "I'm more of a people person. And paper person."

"What do you mean?"

"Greeting cards. Stationery. Linen, rag, recycled, card-stock—"

"Fine. If you encounter another gun, pay attention. Color, size, markings, materials. Take a mental photo; you're an artist, you can do that. It'll give you something to do besides panic."

"Have I panicked?" I said. "I think I've been remarkably calm, considering I have been terrorized by Scandinavians, Hummers, limousines, phone calls, and a man with a very scary suntan."

He just looked at me. It was too dark to read his face.

Across the room, a small crash startled us both. We went to investigate.

Ruby lay on the daybed, snoring softly. My best blanket covered her. I turned up the lamp's dimmer switch, revealing the source of the noise: the Barbie suitcase lay on the floor, overturned. Margaret scrambled up onto Ruby's chest, a "who, me?" look in her beady, buttonlike eyes. The ferret's body went up and down with the child's ragged breaths, as if white-water rafting. And Ruby slept on.

Doc bent down to pick up the small cache of preadolescent treasures. I wanted to help, but resisted; I could only imagine what indignities, what losses of property and privacy Ruby had suffered in the hospital. In the dim light I studied her.

Her feet stuck out from the other end of the blanket. She wore dirty sneakers, untied. I was glad to see Doc take them off. I wanted her to feel safe here, not poised for flight. She didn't look like someone who felt safe anywhere, though, her pale face tense and troubled, even in sleep. Around her neck she wore a ribbon. The ribbon had a plastic-covered picture on the end of it, the size of a sugar packet. A scapular, it was called, a sacred trinket I hadn't seen since the religion classes of my Catholic childhood. Ruby's hand rested against it, her fingernails ragged and showing the remnants of ruby-colored enamel.

The portrait on the scapular was Saint Anthony. I remembered him well. He was the patron saint of lost things.

chapter eighteen

"What is this, do you think?" I asked Fredreeq, handing her a prescription.

Wednesday morning was as sunny as Tuesday had been, but today, walking to the bank, I was ready for it. I wanted to polka down Sunset.

Fredreeq squinted at the prescription. "Vulcan cylinders," she guessed. "Alpine cyclist. Who knows? This handwriting is a pharmacist's nightmare. Why don't you fax it to Dr. Cookie?" Dr. Cookie, while not an actual physician, had a degree in pharmacology.

But would Dr. Cookie have an ethical problem deciphering a prescription that wasn't mine? I'd rescued it from the pocket of a dirty button-down shirt, along with a Swiss Army knife, engraved "To Daddy—Love, Ruby." When Doc passed out again in the armchair, I'd caught a few hours of sleep on a quilt-covered floor, then gone to the shop to shower. I took Doc's plastic bag of clothes with me. The back room had a lovely washer-dryer set and the Gomez family wardrobe was now in the spin cycle.

"So how'd it go with your cousin last night?" Fredreeq asked.

"My—?" I stopped in my tracks.

"The guy I met at intermission. What's his name again?"

"G—Gomez?" I had no cousins, as far as I knew. It could only be Doc, making up cover stories for my friends. And neglecting to tell me.

Fredreeq said, "Lord, you'd think I'd remember that. Is Ruby talking today?"

"You met Ruby too?" I resumed walking.

"Stumbled over them in the back room, and struck up a conversation. With your cousin—not with Ruby, of course. What's that thing she's got? Selective—? No. Elective muteness."

"Elective muteness?" I focused on Fredreeq's turquoise jumpsuit, avoiding her eyes. "He hasn't really told me about Ruby's condition. We're a—reserved—family."

"Reserved? You and Uncle Theo?" Fredreeq sounded skeptical. "Or this Mexican branch that's turned up?"

"People can be very sensitive about diseases, so I didn't like to ask."

"Well, I asked. You know that Catholic boarding school Ruby was in? A few weeks ago, she stopped talking. No warning. Boom! Verbal anorexia."

We reached the bank. I held open the heavy door as Fredreeq continued. "The nuns at the school couldn't find the next of kin, the phone was disconnected or something, so they called Child Protective Services. Not that the nuns cared about *her*, I suspect, but when the tuition check bounced . . . So, okay. Social Services sends her from one department to another, and last week there's a fire at one of the foster care facilities, and they're plopping kids all over the county, finding beds for them, and Ruby ends up at Rio Pescado. What's wrong?"

My jaw must've been hanging open. "He *told* you all this, at intermission?"

"He told me all this in three minutes," Fredreeq said, "after I told him about Franceen's ADD. It's a parent thing, one parent to another. He was dying for advice. They call Ruby's condition elective muteness and told him to get her into therapy. I told him to enjoy the peace and quiet. I'd pay my kids to go mute for a month."

I wanted to know all about Ruby, and more about Doc, but I had my own responsibilities, as the mention of Rio Pescado reminded me. I asked Fredreeq to open my shop once the manicurists showed up at Neat Nails Plus; it was a risk, opening an hour late, but mid-week mornings were slow at both establishments, and with luck, Mr. Bundt's spies wouldn't be on the job at 9 A.M. If I hurried, I'd be back by noon.

HOLLYWOOD BOULEVARD WAS a playground of orange construction cones. These were my tax dollars at work, a project sprung up like weeds over the weekend, for the apparent purpose of slowing traffic to the speed of "park." The only real movement was my journey through radio stations, in search of news, to see if I was in it.

". . . synagogue spokesperson said that the vandalism was minimal and there was no clear indication this was a hate crime. Moving on to sports, weekend NBA—"

Hate crimes.

Hate crimes were the first crimes I knew about, the reason Ruta had spent World War II hidden in the cellar of a general store. Years later I understood the broader context of Ruta's personal adventure story. At the time, I just wanted to be Jewish.

But there was no shame in being Catholic, Ruta said; yes, the

Polish soldiers were Catholic, but so were the owners of the general store. "Does a duck pray to be a horse? You just be the best duck you can be."

I didn't want to be a duck or a horse, I'd said. I just wanted to be like her.

Cars moved forward a foot. My thoughts moved to the top of my head, where the wig I'd purchased an hour earlier from Cinema Wigs was giving me a headache.

The salesman who'd taken it down from the pegboard called it the Ava Gardner. Possibly a professional stylist could achieve a passing resemblance, but in my inexperienced hands it was more like the Don King. Still, it covered up my blond hair and this, along with sunglasses and the Tiffanie's Trousseau off-the-shoulder top from my Benjamin Woo date, would, I believed, disguise me from the guards at Rio Pescado.

I glanced in the rearview mirror to push down on the top of the wig, trying to flatten its fluffiness. Then I saw it.

The blue Hummer. A block behind me.

Panic coursed through me, the seat belt suddenly tight against my tensed body. I had a mad impulse to abandon the car and run. Then I realized that if the Rabbit was stuck, so was the Hummer. Traffic was bumper to bumper. Nobody was moving anytime soon. You're safe, I told myself, safer in the car than on foot.

Unless he got tired of waiting.

I surveyed the cars around me. My fellow travelers were occupied with cell phones, makeup, or fast-food breakfasts, windows rolled up to keep out the world. I could imagine the Hummer man striding up to the Rabbit and hauling me from it. Other drivers might not even notice or, noticing, would figure it was one more wacked-out bewigged woman on Hollywood Boulevard in trouble with her pimp.

I searched my car for something with which to defend myself, if it came to it. Pens, quarters, a sketchbook. My paperback. A dry-cleaning receipt for Gomez.

I couldn't just sit here, awaiting my fate.

To my right was a bus lane. It was cordoned off by orange cones, placed every few feet in anticipation of construction work, but the work had not yet begun. The lane, therefore, was empty.

I'd never driven over orange cones. Could they get caught under the car? Cause damage? I didn't know, and didn't want to find out. I undid my seat belt and hopped out of the Rabbit, leaving the engine running.

The cones were lighter than I expected. They stacked as neatly as paper cups, and I cleared a path, fast, and set them on the sidewalk. Amazingly, nobody stopped me. Then I heard a cacophony of horns, a block back.

I couldn't believe my eyes. The Hummer appeared to be driving over the car in front of it, bound for the very lane I was clearing of cones. Like a tank, it rolled up onto the bumper of a white compact, whose driver jumped out, screaming. I jumped back in the Rabbit, and with forward and backward maneuvers extricated myself from my place in line and squeezed into the bus lane. I didn't dare look in the rearview mirror.

Everyone was honking now. A hard-hatted and no doubt hard-hearted man in thick work boots strode toward me, his arm stretched out, threatening and authoritative as a traffic cop. "Tell it to the Hummer," I yelled, as I turned the wheel to the right and stepped on the gas, plowing up over the curb and onto the sidewalk.

There was a streetlamp on the sidewalk, and a concrete bus bench to the right; the space in between didn't seem big enough for me to squeak through, but I kept going. I sucked in my breath, as if to make the car skinnier, and kept my eyes straight ahead.

I did it. I got through a space that big lug of a Hummer couldn't.

As my Rabbit went over the sidewalk and came down over the second curb, it emitted a sound so dreadful, I apologized out loud. "Floor it!" Ruta yelled in my head. I floored it.

Heading south on the side street, I went a full mile before I began to relax. I unclenched my teeth and loosened my death grip on the steering wheel. There was no longer any thought of driving to Rio Pescado; the stress alone would kill me, and Doc was right, I couldn't risk P.B.'s safety. Maybe there was some sort of homing device on the Rabbit—or me, for that matter—that made us easy to follow; I didn't know beans about surveillance gadgets. I drove five blocks southeast of the shop and parked on a street called La Mirada, blessed my car for cooperating, locked it, and started homeward.

A pair of pedestrians walked toward me on La Mirada. As I got closer, they turned into Doc and Ruby, the latter carrying Margaret's metal crate. By the time I realized why I might not want to run into them just now, it was too late.

Ruby seemed not to recognize me, but Doc's face went through surprise and disbelief before settling on amusement. He came to a stop six inches from me.

"Please tell me that's a wig," he said.

"Of course it's a wig."

"Is it supposed to look like that? And what are you doing in it?"

I looked at Ruby's upturned face, her eyes fixated on my head. "It's personal."

Doc smiled. "I'm sorry to be the one to tell you, it's not very attractive."

"It couldn't be helped. I had some—business to attend to this morning."

"I thought you said it was personal." He was enjoying this.

"Personal business," I said. "But enough about me." In half a minute he'd figure out why I was disguised. "Did you get my note this morning, about your laundry? Find everything? Towels, coffee—?" I noticed they had wet hair. "Great," I said, not giving him time to reply. "Where are you off to, and mind if I join you? Because it's a good time for you to tell me what's going on."

BY TACIT AGREEMENT, we saved the real talk for our destination. Walking, we discussed the sketchbooks Ruby had found in my apartment, greeting cards in various stages of gestation. Doc was kind enough to compliment my rendering of crustaceans, saying I humanized without sentimentalizing them. I felt myself blush.

The park and recreation center at the corner of Cole and Santa Monica was on the grubby side. Watching Ruby prance ahead of us, with Margaret on her leash, I wished I lived in a better neighborhood, one where parks had flowers instead of potential. Ruby wore an unappetizing mustard-colored fleece shirt, the same one she'd shown up in last night. It looked right at home in the park, and that made me sad.

"She found Margaret last year, abandoned," Doc said, seeing me watch them. "She said Genghis Khan had a ferret, and Queen Elizabeth I, and that da Vinci painted them. Trying to win me over with the scholarly approach. But it was the look on her face that got me. It always is." He waited until they were out of earshot, then gestured to the patchy grass. We sat.

"Shebby," I said. "The kid with the speech impediment. What was it he told you?"

Doc looked down. "He was dying fast. He didn't know the guy who stabbed him, but he knew who was behind it: his cellmate in Corcoran, the last prison he was in. A guy he'd looked up to like a father."

"But this was—Tehachapi, you said? Can inmates arrange murders at other prisons?"

"There's not much you can't do on the inside, if you have the means, and this cellmate did. He was a regular cottage industry, the number of guys he had working for him. He'd hired Shebby to do a job on the outside, once he got out." Doc stopped, glancing up to my hair. "Think you could take that off?"

I touched my wig. The bangs felt puffy and stiff. Whatever my hair looked like underneath, it couldn't be worse than the Ava Gardner special. I pulled it off and began to pluck at my own blond strands. "This cottage industry—did he have a name?"

Doc hesitated. "Shebby called him Juan."

"What kind of job did Juan hire Shebby for?"

"Pickup and delivery. He'd pick up a package hidden somewhere in L.A.—"

"Why does everyone speak like they work at the post office? What 'package'? Are we talking drugs? Vital organs? Gutenberg Bibles?"

"Shebby didn't know. He was only told what it was hidden in: a box. We can assume it's not perishable, because it's been sitting for a year, since Juan went into Corcoran. Shebby was to hold on to the box for a decade or so, till Juan got out. He'd get five grand for the pickup, twenty-five more on delivery."

"Easy money," I said, thinking about what I was doing for five grand.

"The problem was, around the time Shebby got transferred to Tehachapi, Juan had a change of plans. He wanted out of the deal, but instead of just firing Shebby, he put out a contract on him. He had to figure the kid knew too much." Doc stood and stretched and looked to where Ruby and Margaret were playing in the dirt.

"But he didn't even know what he was picking up," I said.

"He knew its location, something worth thirty grand just in—postage."

"And Shebby felt compelled to share all this with you?" I asked.

Doc sat again, then leaned back on his elbows in the grass. He squinted up at the sun. "God, I love sky," he said. "I should be doing research, but I wanted Ruby to have some outside time before dragging her off to sit in an office."

"What kind of research?"

He shaded his eyes and looked at me. "I'll let you know when it's done. You ask why Shebby confided in me. His guts were coming out of him. Literally. The MTA—med tech assistant—wasn't equipped for that, so he was on the phone to the county hospital, and I was assigned to stand there with this kid who was scared and mad and desperate to screw the guy who'd done this thing to him. Shebby thought I'd jump at the chance to steal a fortune. I was happy to let him think what he wanted, but then they brought in his assailant, for twelve stitches and a tetanus shot."

I stared. "Into the same room? The guy who stabbed him?"

"This wasn't Cedars-Sinai. Actually, they kept the other guy in the hallway, but the door was open. Shebby saw him and started screaming that Juan had blown it, that the secret was out, that I—me, a guy he'd known a half hour—I was going to avenge him." He leaned all the way back, lying in the grass. "Not real smart, but he needed everyone to know he wouldn't go down without getting even. Twenty minutes later he was dead."

The sun felt hot now. High noon. There was no longer any breeze. A truck went by on Santa Monica, sending a wave of diesel smell our way.

"So word got back to Juan," I said, "who now figures you're out here helping yourself to his merchandise?"

"Pretty much." Doc surveyed the street, and I realized he'd been doing it all along. "Satisfied?"

I imagined, in a worst-case scenario, telling this story to the cops. How would they respond? "Thanks, Ms. Shelley, that certainly clears your brother of suspicion."

"No," I said. "Who are all these other people, Carmine and the limo and the Hummer? And why did the Swedes—Olof and Tor, I believe their names are—"

"Why do you say that?" He sat up.

"The article you tore out of the newspaper. How many Swedish hit men work L.A.? So if you'll just explain—"

"Ever hear the phrase 'need to know,' Wollie? It means—"

"I know what it means," I snapped. "But you're not the FBI, and I do need to know. I'm sharing the risk. At least tell me where this box is supposed to be."

"That's the last thing I'd tell you. Are you listening? People are getting killed for that information."

"But they think I have it already, so what's the difference? Don't you trust me?"

He leaned in, so close I could see the pores of his skin. "I know you. You're the sorriest liar I've ever met. I wouldn't let you in on a surprise party."

"I'm improving. Another two days with you, I could beat a polygraph test."

He shook his head, very deliberately. "You're out of your league here. I won't tell you what'll get you in trouble if someone questions you."

"Someone like who?"

"Someone not as nice as me." The sunlight was bright. His eyes were nearly black. Impenetrable.

"I'm not sure how nice you are," I said.

He reached out to touch a strand of my hair. "Nice enough. These are men who'd cut you up for knowing their names."

A chill went through me. "If I were tougher, you'd tell me more?"

Doc looked behind him, to Ruby. She was some distance away, trying to get Margaret to drink from a water fountain. He leaned over and whispered in my ear, "Maybe. But I wouldn't like you as much."

I turned my face back to his and focused on his lips, so close I could touch them just by puckering. "Like me less," I said. "Tell me more."

Instead, he kissed me.

chapter nineteen

The card read, "This is state-of-the-art and will keep you safe until you have a man around the house to fill that function. Regards, Rex."

"Rex, your brunch? The CBS guy?" Fredreeq closed the cash register and peered at the boxes accompanying the card. "Was he raised by wolves? You don't send hardware after a date."

The hardware was a complicated-looking security system, delivered in the early afternoon by UPS along with my Wednesday night date outfit. "No, it was thoughtful," I said, ripping open cardboard. "I can really use this."

The truth was, Rex could've sent an ant farm and I'd be smiling. Doc's kiss, brief as it was, had traveled the length of my body and altered my mind for the last hour, and possibly the rest of my life.

Fredreeq tore into the Tiffanie's package. "Network executives," she sniffed. "And he wonders why they have no demographics? This is worse than that head of Caesar sitting in the back room."

"Dante, not Caesar."

"Yeah, well, at least that had attitude. This has operating instructions, for God's sake. Whatever happened to long-stemmed roses?" Fredreeq pulled a scrap of silver material out of its tissue paper. "Oh, my. Now we're talking, sister."

I stared. "That's it? I've seen more fabric on a pair of socks. I can't wear that."

"You can. You will. We gotta do something with your hair, you've got a bad case of bed head, but if this dress looks the way I think"—she held it up to her jumpsuited body—"this man is gonna be drooling on himself. In a good way, of course."

Two senior citizens, regular customers, entered the shop and headed to the back wall, engaged in a heated debate. I gave them a wave, and they waved back, still arguing. Electric guitars in the ceiling speakers penetrated my consciousness. It was not easy listening. "Fredreeq, what's this music?" I asked.

"Hendrix. Oh! Dylan Ellison called this morning and I rescheduled him for tomorrow. Wollie, have pity," she said, moving to block my path to the stereo. "It's not my regular day. I'm only wired for bad music Tuesdays, Thursdays, and—"

"Fredreeq," I hissed, moving around her. "Spies."

"Who, Mr. and Mrs. Retirement Village?" She nodded to the customers, who looked heavenward as electric guitar gave way to flutes. "You think Bundt has the brains to recruit our regulars? I'm thinking he gets rejects from the Wal-Mart security guard program. Anyhow, now that you're back, I'm outta here, I've got three facials coming and I need lunch."

When Fredreeq and the seniors were gone, I slipped into the back room, propped the door open to listen for customers, then moved Doc's laundry from washer to dryer, adding a fabric softener sheet. My pulse raced with the thrill of taboo behavior.

In addition to the List, each Dating Project subject had individualized Dos and Don'ts, compiled by her discriminating friends. Mine were all Don'ts: Don't Do His Laundry, Don't Let Him Move In, Don't Use the "L," "R," or "B/G" Words (Love, Relationship, Boyfriend/Girlfriend) Until He Does. We research subjects were to note all List and Dos and Don'ts violations, which would presumably decrease our chances of romantic success. Joey, a cynic, was of the opinion that Dr. Cookie had already written her book and the "research" would adapt itself to her conclusions. Fredreeq, concerned with getting me to the finish line, didn't concern herself with philosophical details. But I was trying to be conscientious about it all.

In this case, I told myself that laundry wasn't technically "done" until the clothes were dry and folded, but in my heart I knew this was rationalization, the kind of thinking common to compulsive gamblers and heroin addicts. I was on a slippery slope.

The shop remained quiet, so I went into the bathroom to try on the dress. I wanted to make my own assessment before Fredreeq bonded to it; if it was unwearable, I'd talk the boutique into sending an alternative, or at least a larger size. I fought with the fabric and found my way through the various straps that constituted the dress, then contorted myself to check out the back of it in the mirror, only to find it had no back.

The phone rang. I bounded around the room, then out onto the shop floor and found the cordless phone in a box of newly arrived Passover cards. I gave a breathless greeting. There was a pause, then, "Is this the lady I talked to the other day?"

I closed my eyes. Carmine. I opened them. "Yes. It is."

"Okay," he said, and coughed violently. "So I'm wondering, you hear anything from that friend we talked about? He still got your car?"

"Uh . . ." My heart was beating fast.

"What about the merchandise? He gonna cooperate?"

A woman wearing a baby in a backpack entered the shop and headed to stationery. I watched her until my own reflection, in a glass-framed poster, caught my attention. A low-cut little silver dress. Someone who'd wear this before lunch might do anything. The thought inspired me.

"Carmine," I said softly, "if it's cooperation you're looking for, you'll find that I'm very—cooperative. I'm a businesswoman. I understand supply and demand."

"What are you saying? That you and me can work something out?"

"Maybe," I said. "Describe this merchandise."

"Aw, don't waste my time. If you don't even know what I'm looking—"

"You're looking for something found very recently. Something hidden for a year, while a certain person's been doing time in Corcoran."

He was silent. I held my breath. I could not believe I was doing this. Had he been able to see my face, I'd never have tried it. Finally, he said, "You've seen it?"

He was buying it. The ground seemed to shift beneath me, and I leaned against the wall for support. The wallpaper was cold on my bare back. "I have access to my friend's, uh, collection," I said, envisioning Doc's gym bag. "But it's extensive. That's why I need you to describe the—item."

"You telling me he *deals* in these?" Carmine demanded.

"Why not?"

"He got a middleman, or he fences them himself?"

"Depends. Locally, he does it. In Europe, he'll go through a middleman."

"Europe?" Carmine sounded startled.

"Or South America. Central America," I said, bringing it closer to home.

Carmine snorted. "He got a deal set up already? Because he's gonna take a bath on it. He'll never get what it's worth. You got it there with you?"

"No, we'll have to meet somewhere. You need to tell me how to recognize it."

"What do you want, the three C's, or whatever? It's got the name inside."

Three C's? Name inside? Fenceable?

He said, "Or bring the whole collection, I'll know which one it is when I see it."

Portable. Small.

"So how 'bout today?" he said. "What time's your place close?"

"Oh, late, very late," I said. "And then there's stockwork. Today's bad."

"Tomorrow night. Nine o'clock."

"Midnight."

"Nine-thirty. Done." He hacked again. "Where?"

"Jerry's Famous Deli, on Beverly," I said, naming the biggest, brightest, most public place I could think of. "Listen, Carmine, what do you think it's worth?"

"I hear half a million."

I exhaled slowly. "For something that small?"

"Well, it ain't just size, it's whose it was. That's the whole point, isn't it?"

Hard to know what to make of that. "Well, I'm an artist, so I tend to think more in terms of . . . color?" I guessed.

"Color?" he said. "What? White? What the hell are you talking about?"

White. Drugs? Heroin?

"Never mind," I said. "Tell me this: what kind of deal were you thinking of? Because I have to tell you, other people have shown some interest in this item."

"People. What people?"

I hesitated. "Swedish people."

Carmine choked. "You outta your tree? You don't wanna be— Jesus, those guys are so connected, they're spitting spaghetti. You ever hear of the Terranovas? Or Eddie Digits? They're his—Christ, you deal with Olof and Tor, you're as good as dead the minute you hand it over." Carmine worked himself into a coughing fit. "Your boyfriend's a dead man already," he spat out.

"He's not my boyfriend," I whispered.

Although we were dating. Well, *one* date. It had lasted over two hours, anyway, and he'd bought—okay, not dinner, but doughnuts. It seemed important to be clear about this, absolutely accurate, if only in my own head, sticking to my Dos and Don'ts, in order to block out the second part of that sentence, the part where Carmine called Doc a dead man.

Carmine's coughing subsided. I swallowed, and spoke up. "So, what would your offer be?"

"Best offer there is, Blondie. You and him and the little girl don't get your balls shot off. Everybody walks away still breathing. How's that sound?"

Across the shop, the baby in the backpack uttered a cry, sending shivers up and down my naked spine. "That sounds good," I said.

chapter twenty

"Damn, you look hot," said Fredreeq. "Doesn't she look hot, Joey?"

I felt cold, actually. The back room, with its high ceilings, was perpetually drafty.

"Great, Fred, let's see how much more self-conscious we can make her." Joey was the only living person allowed to call Fredreeq "Fred," the result of a bet. She aimed a Polaroid at me. "Uncross your arms, Wollie."

It was 6 P.M. Normally we scheduled weeknight dates after eight, giving me time to close up the shop. The early hour was a concession to my date's mogul status. Joey would mind the store, with Fredreeq, working next door, as backup. In honor of the occasion, Joey wore ironed clothes.

I sighed. "I don't know how to talk to one of the Fifty Most Powerful Men in Media."

Fredreeq said, "Sugarplum, that dress will do the talking. Okay, I gotta go—big tipper next door in two minutes. Joey, bang on the wall if you need me."

When Fredreeq was gone, I turned to Joey. "Ever hear of the three C's?"

Joey made notes on the Polaroid and reached up to replace the camera on its shelf, next to an accordion. Her hair fell in a thick red braid down her back. "Yes. No—only the three B's. Bach, Beethoven, and Brahms."

"What do you know about the Mafia?"

"The usual—*Godfathers I, II,* and *III.*" Joey perched on the back of the sofa, her long legs dangling. "Why don't you ask Robert Quarter? He claims close personal relationships with several Kennedys, so ask him if the mob was behind JFK's murder. That'll get him going. Guys love talking about 'the Outfit,' especially if they have nothing whatsoever to do with it."

"You don't like Robert Quarter?" I asked, adjusting my garter belt.

"I don't know him. But I have friends who've dated him. Everyone's dated him. I'm not sure how Fredreeq found him, by the way, because he's not—never mind." Joey stood.

"What? We're not following protocol? Joey, we're on the honor system! Dr. Cookie trusts us, Tiffanie's trusts us. I know you think the Dating Project's a joke, that they don't care about research methods, but Dr. Cookie's a Ph.D., she's got standards—"

"Wollie, there're schools that give you Ph.D.s for frequent flier miles, they don't guarantee integrity. And Tiffanie's Trousseau would sponsor the Flat Earth Society if it would sell more bustiers. Uh-oh, the front door. I'll go. You relax."

"No, I'll go." I hurried out to the shop floor, wondering whether our playing fast and loose with the dating rules could affect the fate of lovelorn women everywhere. Joey was wrong. It wasn't her fault; she'd lived in New York for a long time. But her skepticism about the Dating Project was misplaced. It had to be. Dr. Cookie's method might not result in True Love for me, but I had to believe that others would benefit from my research, or else I myself was in it just for the money. This depressed me. "May I help you?" I asked the incoming customer.

He was the mysterious Blue Patron, he of the baby blue sweater and blue leather jacket. Today he wore a blue linen shirt. He smiled. "You look too lovely to be working tonight."

I felt myself blush. "I—thank you, I have a—" I stopped. Who was this man? Had he ever bought anything? Well dressed, middle-aged, why was he haunting my shop?

My suspicion must have showed. He stepped closer and lowered his voice. "I like your place. I like everything you've done with it." He looked around. "I was here when the previous owner—"

"Aldwyn Allen?"

"Yes. Aldwyn's Willkommen! Greetings. That didn't work out." He studied the lemon grove mural. "It'll work out for you, I think. You've made this your own. That's a gift." He turned back to me. "Well. That's all I wanted to say. I don't often tell people when I like their work, but we all need to hear it sometimes." He nodded, as though I'd responded, then shook my hand and walked away. He got to the door and turned. "Good luck."

I let out a breath I didn't know I was holding and floated into the back room. Could that really be Mr. Bundt's plainclothesperson? Had he really just implied what I thought he'd implied? I felt like drinking champagne. I said nothing to Joey, afraid to jinx things. She went onto the shop floor, and I hobbled over in my strappy high-heeled sandals to the dryer and began folding Doc's laundry, utterly giddy.

I'd managed to convince myself that Carmine calling Doc a dead man was just hyperbole, a figure of speech. Not that murders didn't happen; the corpse in the road was proof they did. But not to regular people, I decided, people I knew, people whose socks I mated, whose T-shirts I folded . . . There was a button-down shirt I longed to iron, but my silver dress, with its indeterminate fiber content, might explode if it got too close to an iron. I started in on Ruby's clothes, as intriguing as Doc's—one floral ankle sock, a puffed-sleeved blouse, a pea green velour shirt. Perhaps my laundry fetish was something platonic. Harmless. Not a romantic addiction after all, but simply—

I reached in the dryer for one last sock and felt something small and hard and circular. I didn't need to see it to know what it was.

A plain gold wedding band. Thick. The kind a man would wear.

I MADE MY way around the manicure stations of Neat Nails Plus, overwhelmed by nail lacquer and formaldehyde fumes. I tripped over a Crenshaw melon adorning the plastic Buddhist temple, and found Fredreeq behind a beaded curtain, doing a facial.

On a table lay a smock-wrapped, towel-turbaned woman, her face covered in broccoli green clay. A slice of cucumber rested upon each eye, creating a corpselike image, until a gentle snore animated the lips. Fredreeq, cell phone balanced on her shoulder, massaged the woman's ears. I waited for her to hang up, then showed her an invoice.

"You need to do this now?" she asked, deciphering her shorthand for me. "You're not taking paperwork on your date, are you?"

"No, but I'll need to work on the books late tonight. I'm behind on everything." It was true enough, I thought.

Fredreeq continued the massage, her thin black fingers strong on her client's fleshy neck. "What else? Something's taking up space in your head. What's bugging you?"

I took a deep breath. "Did Doc—my cousin—mention Ruby's mother?"

"The wife?" Fredreeq snorted. "What a piece of work. You ever meet her?"

I shook my head.

"She's either a knockout, or she's great in bed, or both, for him to make *excuses* for her. It's gotta be embarrassing to love someone like that."

"When did you guys talk about this?" I asked, trying to keep the petulance out of my voice.

"Hour ago. He and Ruby came into the shop looking for you, while you were off getting all dolled up. He didn't volunteer it, but I dragged it outta him. The wife's the one who dropped Ruby with the nuns and gave them a rubber check, and did he tell you what she did then? Flew to Japan. Hello? Sense of responsibility, anybody? He says she's impulsive." Fredreeq rolled her eyes. "Impulsive is buying shoes when the rent's due. Flying to Japan and not telling anyone, that's bullshit. Men. So blind about women sometimes, you wanna slap them upside the head." She was putting a little too much energy into her massage now, and the woman on the table stirred, mumbling something that sounded like "cigarette."

Fredreeq looked down. "A few less cigarettes, you wouldn't have to spend so much time in green clay."

Naturally, in the back of my mind I realized that Ruby had a mother, but I'd managed to avoid the kind of logical thinking that led to these questions. Dr. Cookie was right. I hadn't wanted to know this. I started to leave, then said, "Do 'the three C's' mean anything to you?"

But Fredreeq was back on her cell phone, giving dinner instructions to her husband. She paused long enough to wave me off. "Get outta here. Robert Quarter's probably waiting out front. Go out there and break some hearts tonight."

No problem, I thought, walking back to the shop. I was breaking my own heart without leaving the neighborhood. Never had I been less eager to go on a date.

I shuffled into the shop and slumped over to the counter. So I was on my own. Tomorrow I'd work on finding those court transcripts and—

"Wollie," Fredreeq said, running in behind me. "He's pulling into the lot, Robert Quarter, I saw him from the window. Go. Don't you even think about taking that sweater. Go. Go." She pried me from the counter, shoved an evening bag at me, and shepherded me out the door.

A woman stepped in front of us, plastic smock flapping in the wind. Fredreeq's client. Her green clay face moved in close as she exhaled a mouthful of smoke and said, "Wanted to tell you: cut, clarity, and carats." She pointed her cigarette at me. "Diamonds."

Before I could process that, she stepped aside, revealing a man standing in the parking lot, a man whose face and uniform were imprinted on my memory.

"Hello, Ms. Shelley." He smiled, and opened the door to a very large brown limousine.

HIS NAME WAS Kelvin and he was, he said, very sorry to have scared me Saturday night, in the course of checking me out. From the limo's front seat, a puppy yapped at us.

Confusion rooted me to the sidewalk. Did assassins introduce themselves? Apologize? Bring puppies?

One of the back windows descended with a hum, revealing half a head. I recognized the receding hairline and salt-and-pepper hair from the news photos. Robert Quarter. Kelvin, my erstwhile assailant, it seemed, was the mogul's chauffeur.

chapter twenty-one

Strung across a thirty-yard-long front porch, a banner proclaimed, "Saul and Elaine's 14th Annual Beverly Hills Hoedown!" I stepped out of the limousine and faced a lawn the size of a small golf course. Around me, Mercedeses and Jaguars disgorged cowboy-booted passengers onto the circular driveway. Robert joined me, liberated at last from the conference call that had occupied him the entire drive. In the limo, I'd had plenty of time to wonder about his red checkered shirt and well-pressed jeans, but here he looked right at home. I, however, was in couture hell.

Then I was attacked.

My assailant was Robert's dog, the half-grown boxer who'd been riding in the front seat of the limo. Oblivious to her owner's "Sweetie Pie! Sweetie Pie! Down," Sweetie Pie had to be physically separated from my silk stockings by Kelvin, materializing to haul her back into the limo. I began to sneeze.

"She's a juvenile delinquent," Robert said, leading me toward the mansion. My spike heels sank into grass with each step, which at least brought me closer to my date's height. He was solidly built and escorted me with the confidence of a man accustomed to tall, bobbing females. "I'm very sorry. You're all right?"

I nodded, wondering what had happened to number nine, No Pets. "The thing is," I said between sneezes, "I'm not really dressed for a hootenanny."

"I should have told you," he said. "I had a stock drop seven points this morning and I let it distract me until it went back up. What'll it take for you to forgive me?"

"A hundred shares of the stock would do it," I said, provoking a laugh. He thought I was kidding.

On the porch, a somber female employee handed out bandannas. Before I could twist mine into a noose and hang myself, Robert took it from me and knotted it around my neck, cowboy style. In the house, I excused myself and was shown to a black marble bathroom ample enough to store the contents of my apartment. I ripped off my shredded fourteen-dollars-apiece stockings, leaving my garters dangling, and when I couldn't find a wastebasket, I stuffed them into an urn. At least I hadn't paid for the dress. Fredreeq must've described tonight's original itinerary to Tiffanie's Trousseau as "five-star restaurant/nightclub" to have scored this number, which did not show to advantage with a bandanna. Well, it wasn't as if I was the only overdressed person on the premises, I said to the mirror. All the service personnel were in black tie.

The grounds—the term "backyard" didn't really apply—were lush enough to support a community of sculptors, farmers, and landscape architects. The evening was warm for early spring, but even so, heat lamps were set up every few feet along the trails, just in case there should be any shivering cowboys or cowgirls. The smell of night-blooming jasmine accompanied us on our journey across the plantation, and it was hard not to be seduced by the graciousness of it all. I began to relax.

Saul and Elaine's tennis courts had been covered over with a dance floor, parquet sprinkled with sawdust and the odd bale of hay. Some fifty guests swung their partners to and fro under Japanese lanterns. I was amazed to see so many people dancing.

"Saul insists on it," Robert said. "And few can afford to offend Saul. He's one of the top five lawyers in Hollywood, and seventy percent of everyone here is in law. The rest are Industry." He pointed out our host, a bespectacled man in a ten-gallon hat drinking a martini. Saul was talking to a guest who looked like John Travolta. On closer inspection, it turned out to be John Travolta.

"And even those willing to offend Saul," Robert continued, smiling, "are terrified of Elaine. She made up the hoedown rule: You can't get a drink without a name tag. And you can't get a name tag without showing up on the dance floor. Shall we?"

We followed the relentless instructions of the square dance caller to the twang of a banjo, reducing people to alligator boots to the east, suede fringe to the west, yoked shirt straight ahead. Cryptic pieces of conversation wafted past, as my quartet networked the neighboring squares.

". . . bastard rescheduled the deposition!"

". . . got you that TRO but we still . . ."

". . . reversed on appeal or we're screwed . . ."

A gal in an alarming petticoat hopped onto a hay bale and began to yodel. Perhaps I'd been Ma Kettle in a past life, because it came naturally to me, the do-si-dos and allemande lefts, even in heels. Limbs sashaying wildly, my mind was free to ponder . . . diamonds.

Cut, carats, and clarity, the three C's, sounded right the minute Fredreeq's client had said it. A diamond was portable, fenceable, more or less white . . . what else? Carmine mentioned a name inside. Engraving? Yes. Our item-in-a-box, I felt sure, was a piece of diamond jewelry, worth half a million dollars. Eureka. Wait till I told Doc.

Doc.

Married.

Depression reared its ugly head, but it was hard to focus on it, what with all the yodeling going on. Romantic angst would have to wait; I turned to my partner.

My partner was focused on his feet as if the NASDAQ itself depended on it. Robert had a face that stopped short of handsome, but he wore it well and smiled often. What he did not have was a gift for square dancing, a fact he acknowledged with lifted eyebrows, and I found that engaging. It began to matter less that I was dressed wrong and didn't know anyone. People seemed friendlier as the dancing continued. I could have promenaded all night, but when our yodeler hollered, "Git ready to POLKA!" Robert took my hand and bunny-hopped off the sawdust. A servant stood by with name tags. Mine said, "Howdy, I'm Wollie," and below, in fine print, "Welcome! Greetings Corporation." Robert's fine print was an understated "Quarter Enterprises." Number five, I thought automatically, Has Job.

We found the bar, adjacent to a rose garden. After procuring drinks, we claimed a heat lamp near a swan-filled pond, and I stepped out of my heels to revel in upper-class grass. Darkness had descended, Orion twinkled away at us, and I was beginning to give in to the charm of it all when I looked toward the mansion and saw Dave Fischgarten. Date Nineteen.

He strode down the path with an astonishingly built blonde in a pink calico dress. Had she rented the costume for the occasion? I wondered. Had Dave rented her? What was he doing here, anyway? He was not in law or show biz, nor, on a research scientists's salary, was he a client of Saul's. I doubted Ms. Pink Calico was either, judging by her openmouthed gawking.

Dave and Date were coming our way. Dave saw Robert, did a double take, then stopped, assuming an eager "Hi, remember me?" look, waiting for Robert to turn and see him. When Robert did not turn, Dave glanced at me. He may as well have worn subtitles: *Are you Somebody? No.* He moved off, with Ms. Calico, to the swan pond. Five days after our date and he didn't recognize me.

Wait. It wasn't lack of recognition, it was lack of surprise. Dave expected to see me here. With Robert. But how was that possible, with dates supposedly answering my Personals ad, randomly, and getting screened by Joey and Fredreeq—?

Memories of my Friday night date came stumbling back, the words "chaos theory" flashing in my brain like the clock on my VCR. What was it Dave had said?

Chaos was what appeared to be random, but had an underlying pattern to it.

"Robert, do you know that man?" I asked, pointing to the swan pond.

Robert looked at him, his face impassive. "Probably. I know everyone."

I shivered, convinced that Dave's presence tonight was no coincidence. Well, so what? So what if he gave my phone number to the entire Fortune 500, in exchange for party invitations or stock tips or whatever? You're paranoid, I told myself. The underlying pattern here is you, Wollie, dating so many men that eventually you'll meet them wherever you go.

"Irving and Lois Gorman-Goodman," Robert said, leading me up the hill. He was referring to a couple hailing us from the barbecue line, in matching overalls, straw hats, and fake freckles. "He's Sony, she's D.A.'s office."

A moment later, their name tags confirmed this and I made a

mental note for Fredreeq, who collected Who's Who stories. Robert made introductions and Irving asked, "Are you an actress, Holly, or an attorney?"

"Wollie's in retail," Robert answered for me, handing Irving a heavy china plate.

"I never got over Versace," Irving said cryptically, and went on to chat with Robert about mutual friends and mutual funds while I waited, and Lois drank. At the first opening, I squeezed into the conversation.

"Robert and I were just talking about JFK," I said. "And the Cuban Missile Crisis. And the Bay of Pigs," I added, as all three looked at me expectantly. It was a socially peculiar moment, but I plunged on. "And I was wondering if there were Cubans—or any Latinos—in the Mafia."

"There aren't Latinos at this *hoedown*," said Lois, "unless they're parking cars."

"There are Greeks here, though," Irving pointed out. "Tell me, does Arianna Huffington have a speech impediment, or is that just her accent?"

"But are there strategic alliances?" I persisted. "Like, in prison. For instance."

Lois snorted. "The mob's in bed with everyone. They can't afford to be picky anymore. These days it's all about the Russians, the Asians, the *Albanians,* for God's sake. The Serbs. This is not your grandmother's Mafia. Of course, you wouldn't want to say that to Eddie Minardi, it being a sensitive subject."

"Eddie Minardi?" I said, startled. I tried to recall Doc's newspaper article, and what exactly it had said about Eddie Minardi.

"Is he here?" Robert asked.

"Well, he's Saul's client. Haven't seen him yet," she said, "but it's the first night all week I haven't. The ubiquitous Eddie Digits. Morton's. Chinois. Laker game."

"NCAA's on in the screening room," Irving said, reaching for tortilla chips. "March Madness. Duke's going down." He addressed this last news to me, as if I had any idea what he was talking about. I turned to Lois and asked if she knew Eddie Minardi.

"In a manner of speaking." She helped herself to guacamole. "My boss just indicted him for jury tampering—that's why he's in town."

"Who are we talking about?" Irving asked, through a mouthful of chips.

"Eddie 'Digits' Minardi," said Robert, "also known as Big Eddie Minardi, as in the Minardi crime family. Pay attention, Irving."

I said, "Didn't I read that one of his soldiers is getting out of prison early?"

"Really?" Robert said. "Ratting out the boss?"

Lois sighed. "I wish. You're referring to Ron Ronzare, and believe me, we tried to turn him, but Minardi's his brother-in-law. And Ron was only doing a dime, meaning out in five. Five years is a sabbatical for these guys. He's a real piece of work."

"Who, Big Eddie?" I asked.

"Actually, *he's* a gentleman. Anglophile, very Savile Row, very 'tea with the Queen.' No, I'm talking about the Weasel. Aptly named, because he's an animal," she said, frowning at the pork ribs, "with a real facility for getting in and out of tight places. Weaseled out of a breaking and entering two years ago."

Irving laughed. " 'Weasel.' 'Digits.' Love that mob."

Ronald "the Weasel" Ronzare—the newspaper said he was at Corcoran. Which was where Shebby, the dead kid, met his cellmate Juan, who later had him killed. That's why I kept thinking there was a connection. Robert had his hand on the small of my back, steering me toward a table, but I turned once more to Lois. "Why is Eddie Digits called Eddie Digits?"

"He's kind of a dandy. Wears rings on several of his fingers. Toes too, for all I know. It's not gold chains, but it's a definite lapse in taste." She stuck a jalapeño in her mouth and made a face. "Diamonds all over his hands."

THE LIMO'S ROSE leather upholstery was cool, but Robert's body was close enough to give off heat. Also aftershave, something subtle and spicy. He talked on the phone to Tokyo and I was so physically relaxed from two margaritas, I'd have been dead asleep and snoring were it not for bells ringing in my head like a church at high noon. I collated information.

Juan, murderer and ex-cellmate of Shebby, had something stashed somewhere. Carmine implied that that something was a diamond. Diamonds were what Big Eddie wore on his digits. Big Eddie had a brother-in-law in Corcoran. Juan was in Corcoran.

But how was Coughing Carmine connected to Eddie Digits? And how was Ron, "the Weasel," connected to Juan, the cellmate, and Shebby, the deceased? Who was in the Hummer?

And what about the Swedes?

I rubbed my eyes, then stopped, remembering mascara. There were more names than people, and way too many people. Leaving out nicknames, unknown names, and dead people, there remained Eddie, Carmine, Ron, Juan, Olof and—

Ron. Juan.

I inhaled sharply, and sat up straight. Robert turned to me, curious, and I shook my head at him.

Speech impediment.

Shebby was a kid with a speech impediment. What were speech impediments but inabilities to reproduce certain sounds? The letter "r," for instance, the Wugged Wed Wabbit Syndwome.

Where Ron became Wan. *Juan.*

There was no Juan. There was only Ron, and Shebby's problem saying his name. Doc had quoted Shebby verbatim, to mislead me.

It was Ron "the Weasel" Ronzare, soldier in Big Eddie's crime family, who'd stashed a diamond. And killed Shebby. And wanted Doc.

And me.

chapter twenty-two

Robert kissed well. Parked in front of the shop, our faces were so close we looked at each other cross-eyed, practically mandating a kiss. I didn't resist. He smelled good. I liked him. I'd had enough of murder for one day. I closed my eyes, found his lips, let myself relax. I thought, Don't think about Doc.

The mouth was soft and the face too, making me wonder what kind of shaving cream he used. He had no discernible taste, probably because we'd shared food and margaritas all night. He took his time. This, I realized, was one of the 50 Most Powerful Men in Media, and as a businesswoman, I should pay attention to his deal-closing techniques. I felt strangely content, almost stupid, even when his strong hand found its way to my neck. Was this how stranglers do in their victims? I wondered, but then the strong hand slid south and ended up on my nearly bare breast, confident of its welcome. My breast, for reasons of its own, rose to the occasion. It had been a long time since I'd been touched like this.

The bark of a dog penetrated my consciousness, then the slam of a door and Kelvin yelling, "Sweetie Pie!" Something was going on outside, but my brain didn't really kick in until one of the limo's back doors opened and cold night air hit me. I stopped kissing and opened my eyes. There was Doc, looking as surprised as I was.

I froze. Across the long stretch of car, Doc's eyes went from my face to my breast, where Robert's hand stayed as if glued. I opened my mouth to say something—I have no idea what—when something outside drew Doc's attention. He wheeled around. There was a *whump!* sound. Kelvin was taking him down.

"Whoa!" I threw off Robert's limbs to scramble over the seat and across the plush carpet as fast as short spandex would allow. I lurched out of the car right into Doc and the two of us went down onto the asphalt. In a matter of seconds Sweetie Pie was on top of us and everyone seemed to be either yelping or swearing until Robert roared, "SHUT UP!" Amazingly, everyone did.

"It's okay, I'm okay," I said, hauled to my feet by various parties. "He's my cousin. Doc. Cousin of mine. Doc, this is Kelvin and Rob—"

"Yeah, hi. Excuse us. Family emergency." Doc put an arm around my waist and jerked me backward, veritably lifting me up onto the sidewalk. Kelvin was corralling Sweetie Pie, but Robert moved toward us, taking exception to my being manhandled.

"No, it's okay, Robert," I said, waving him off. "Family emergency. Happens all the time. Thanks for—you know. Everything. Call me." I watched them get back into the limo as I was pulled, not gently, into the shadows of Loo Fong's. "Doc," I hissed, breaking free, "you know who that was?"

He leaned against Loo Fong's red door, bent over as if he were going to be sick. After what seemed like a long time he said, "Which? The one with the—fist in my gut, or the one"—his breath came in spurts—"with his tongue down your throat?"

"Oh, God," I said, and put a hand on his back. "Are you hurt? Did Kelvin punch you? I'm so sorry. See, he's a bodyguard as well as a chauffeur, so . . ."

He didn't respond, apparently saving his breath. Finally, he straightened up. "Let's go. Stay in the shadow." He grabbed my arm and steered me toward Plucky Chicken.

I stalled, looking back at my shop. "But what are we—?"

"Sweetheart," he said, dragging me with him, "we're on the lam."

We picked up Ruby and Margaret in the alley behind Bodega Bob, and made our way through side streets, staying off Sunset. I was reminded of the von Trapp family, escaping through the Alps, except, of course, that none of us were singing. In this group, nobody was even talking, although I couldn't vouch for Margaret, in her crate. "Want to fill me in on what we're doing?" I asked, for the fourth or fifth time.

"Not in front of Ruby," Doc said.

"We're *not* in front of Ruby," I pointed out. "We're three yards behind."

The child bounced down the sidewalk, happy to be touring Hollywood after dark. She wore blue jeans, stiff with newness, which no doubt helped her high spirits. Doc wore new jeans too, but they weren't having the same cheerful effect on him. And I was in spike heels. "We gotta slow down," I said. "I'm not dressed for racewalking."

He didn't slow. He speeded up, caught Ruby, and steered her left, down yet another alley. "Doc?" I called. "Do we have a destination, or is this aerobics hour?"

"Try to keep up," he said, over his shoulder.

This was too much. I stopped and said the magic words. "Ron 'the Weasel' Ronzare."

Ahead of me, he came to a dead halt.

"Thank you," I said. "Now, you can tell me what new Mafia crisis has come up, or I can turn around and go home."

He called to Ruby to stop, then came to me. "What do you know about him?"

"That he's a soldier in the Minardi crime family. That he's the brother-in-law of Eddie Minardi, the big cheese. That he's getting out of prison early, which is why he no longer needed Shebby to rescue his thing-in-a-box, as he can presumably do it himself."

He studied me. "Ronzare was released Friday. He's the one in the Hummer."

"Oh, jeez," I said, recalling how close to him I'd been that morning.

"And he did the shooting we heard last night," Doc went on. "A half hour ago, he called your apartment. Ruby and I were eating pizza. We heard the message on your machine, but by the time I figured out it was him, he'd hung up. So we went down to the shop to wait for you, figuring you'd go there first."

I gulped. "What did the message say?"

He looked at me steadily. "I would have erased it, but I think you should keep it. As evidence."

Evidence. I waited in silence, my earlier bravado draining out of me.

"The gist of the message was that he was . . . waiting for you to come home."

"And—?" I asked. When he hesitated, I said, "I'd rather hear it from you first."

"He mentioned knives."

I noticed I was shivering violently. "I'm very cold."

"You're half naked," he said, and put an arm around me. "Let's go."

· · ·

THE BUDGETEER MOTOR Lodge lobby had a *Viva Las Vegas* look, screaming fluorescence featuring snappy casino-themed wallpaper. Waiting to check in, I slipped out of my torturous heels and limped toward the pay phone until Doc intercepted me. "I have to call my machine," I told him. "P.B. was going to leave a message."

"He didn't," Doc said. "Unless—he's not French, is he?"

"French? He's my brother. Do I look French?"

His eyes dropped briefly down my dress. "To be honest, I never know how to describe the way you look."

"What are you, a fashion consultant?" I heard the defensive note in my voice.

"No, a high school teacher. Physics and economics. You got six calls on your machine, as of ten-fifteen. Your brother wasn't one of them. Save the quarter."

A schoolteacher. I could see it. Probably taught at a military academy. What had become of the old Doc? Where was the good humor tonight, the insouciance?

He checked us in as the "Clark" family. I liked being his wife, if only in the glazed eyes of the Budgeteer night clerk, even with the foul mood Doc was in. It was a dangerous feeling to indulge in, but what the heck. Plus, he paid. Sixty-five dollars bought us a broom closet with a double bed and the promise of a rollaway, on plaid carpet so appalling I considered keeping my shoes on all night. Decades of cigarette smoke lingered in the air, despite a cardboard fragrance tree dangling from the bedside lamp. Ruby loved the room, jumping on the bed and freeing Margaret from her crate. After her stints in Social Services facilities and mental wards, this was probably her idea of the Four Seasons. At the window, Doc looked out on the courtyard.

"You don't think the Weasel could have followed us here?" I asked, joining him.

"In a Hummer? I think we would have noticed. But he's got a cousin working with him. Carmine, the guy who came into your shop the other day."

"No need to worry about Carmine. He and I had a nice long chat this morning."

Doc stared at me, then picked up a remote from the bedside table and turned on the TV. Tossing the remote to Ruby, he said, "One night only, you get to watch whatever you want. Keep it clean." He pulled me into a corner of the room. "Now, let's you and me have a nice long chat."

Hard to say which part of the story he liked least, the part where I made him the fence of stolen goods, or the part where I agreed to steal one of them back. Hard to say, because he listened in silence, arms crossed, sitting on the windowsill. Over on the bed, Ruby clicked through channels. "So it took some doing," I said, finishing, "but now we know what it is everyone's after. A diamond," I added, in case he wasn't clear on that point. I waited. Under his implacable stare, I began to twitch. "You know what?" I said, finally. "These John Wayne silences are getting on my nerves."

"In twenty-four hours," Doc said quietly, "Carmine is going to come after you, wondering why you stood him up, figuring you double-crossed him. Looking for a reason not to start cutting off your fingers to make you talk. I'm trying to come up with one."

"Carmine doesn't strike me as the knife type," I whispered, "and—"

"Don't be so goddamn naïve."

A knock on the door saved me from a reply. Our glassy-eyed desk clerk delivered the rollaway, and with help from Doc and much grunting and squeaking of old parts, managed to get it into the room. By the time he was gone, Ruby was gone too.

Alarmed, I ran outside, with Doc on my heels.

The motel rooms were built around a courtyard, eerily lit, with a cracked, kidney-shaped pool in the center. Ruby was circling the pool's perimeter, zigzagging erratically around bushes until Doc caught her and stopped her. "What's going on? What are you doing—hey!" He reached for her a second time as she pulled free and nearly fell over. "*Damn* it, Ruby, talk to me, can't you? Can't you?"

Nose to nose under the yellow floodlight, their profiles mirrored each other, his dark, hers pale and freckled. Abruptly, he broke eye contact, and pulled her into his arms. "Sorry," he said, and kissed the top of her head. "I'm sorry. For everything. All of it. Talk when you're ready." Ruby, her cheek pressed against his stomach, scanned the ground.

It was an intense moment to witness and I was struck by how much power the little girl had, how much strength there is in silence. Tyranny, even. Something occurred to me. I cleared my throat. "It's Margaret, isn't it? Is she lost, Ruby?"

Ruby looked up, her face clearing.

Doc said, "Is that it? You let her off the leash? Okay, go inside, I'll look for her. Go with Wollie; I don't want you wandering around out here."

Ruby went as far as the doorway and plopped herself on the concrete just outside the room, staring at her father as if watching a movie. I wedged the door open with my shoe, and stood behind her, looking down at her slumped and rounded back in a brand-new pink sweatshirt. Her brown hair managed to be both frizzy and oily. *And only eleven,* I thought. *You still have adolescence to get through.* Her hands were clasped as if she was praying, but then I saw a small photo clutched in her thumbs. I leaned down. It was a professional wallet-size photo, the kind they do at Sears. A much younger Ruby leaned against a seated woman, in front of a pastel cloud background. The woman was gorgeous.

I turned away. Naturally, she missed her mother. She probably wondered what I was doing here, usurping the mother's place in this moth-eaten hotel room. I wrestled with the rollaway, kicking the stubborn metal frame until, with one loud creak, it sprang open. Inside was a lumpy striped mattress.

Upon the mattress sat Margaret.

I drew in a breath, surprised to find her still three-dimensional. She blinked up at me, unperturbed, and gave a delicate yawn. "Ruby," I said.

Ruby turned, stood, and at the sight of Margaret, broke into a blinding smile. It was easily the best thing to happen to me all day.

I STOOD IN the doorway an hour later, breathing in takeout Indian food from an adjoining room. I'd wrapped the bedspread around me for warmth, a peach satin quilted number that had seen better days and worse nights. Doc lay just outside the room, in a rickety reclining lawn chair stolen from poolside, staring at Orion. I wondered if he'd always had a craving for night air, or if it was acquired during his half year in prison. Inside, Ruby and Margaret were riveted to Jerry Springer grilling guests on TV.

"Doc?" I said. "If these guys are cousins, if they're on the same team, why is the Weasel after me? Carmine thinks we have a deal, he thinks I'm showing up tomorrow with the diamond, so why didn't they both take the night off?"

He shrugged. "Failure to communicate."

"And the Swedes, Olof and Tor: aren't they with a different family altogether?"

"I'll know more about them tomorrow. A friend of a friend at the DMV is running a check on the Alfa Romeo license plate, and then I plan to—"

"Is that legal?"

He looked at me and raised an eyebrow. "Strange question, coming from you."

"What do you mean?"

"Forget it." He sat up and stretched. He didn't seem cold, even in a short-sleeved T-shirt. He looked awfully good—his marital status didn't change that, nor did his glacial attitude. This bothered me. What would it take to turn me off?

"Why don't you go to bed?" he said. "It's late."

"Okay. Think they'll give me a wake-up call? I need to be at the shop by—"

"Forget it."

I blinked. "Why?"

"What do you think 'on the lam' means? You're not going to work tomorrow. Or the next day, either; not till this is over."

"That's impossible." I felt a rising panic. "This is a critical week—"

"Too bad."

"—with so much at stake you have no idea. Four years of work have led to this, not to mention my night job, which you don't even know about, which is driving me—"

"I know about it."

I stopped. "You know? About the Dating Project? Who told you, Fredreeq?"

"Fredreeq's in on it?" he said sharply.

"In on it? She practically runs it. What?" I said, at his look of disgust. "You have a problem with this? You, of all people?"

"Why wouldn't I have a problem with it?" he said. "Because I'm an ex-con?"

"Because you're married! Yet you go around winking at people and kissing them and letting them think—look," I said, forcing my voice back down. "It's unorthodox, but it's a job; I'm not doing it for fun, or even for science, not altogether. I need money."

"Science?" He laughed. "Jesus. There are other ways to make money, Wollie."

"Like what, a paper route?" I snapped. "I already put in twelve-hour days at the shop, seven days a week."

Quite deliberately, he turned his back and resettled himself into the lawn chair, stretching out in the moonlight. "Well, congratulations, then. You're on vacation."

I LAY ON the rollaway, listening to sleep sounds emanating from Ruby in the double bed. Doc was next to her, lying on top of the covers, his jeans just visible as my eyes adjusted. What time had he come in? Out the window, the sky seemed lighter, and I judged it to be a little before six, my usual wake-up time. I'd thought I'd be too mad to sleep, but apparently not. I threw Doc a malevolent glance. I hoped I'd snored.

Reaching for the bedside phone, I called home to pick up my messages. There were six, according to the little computer voice. No new ones. None from P.B.

The first message was from Jean-Luc, a simple "Allô, I send you beeg kiss."

The second was Robert. "I'd like to pick up where we left off. Without your cousin. Maybe Saturday?"

The third was Rex. "Hey, Doris Day. Wish you were here. I'll try you again."

The fourth was Joey. "Hi, you got one, maybe two guys tomorrow and a box of clothes from UPS. I'll be around to do the Polaroids—the evil sister-in-law is back in town, so I'm spending the night. I'm going out now to get something to eat, but call if you get in and want to talk." I sat up. Joey had spent the night in the back room? Dear God. Was she safe? I got out of bed and began to search for my shoes.

The next message was almost as bad, in a very different way.

"Wollie?" said Dr. Cookie in her trademark radio voice. "Hope you're having fun with Man du Soir. Well, you must be, since you're not there. Now, this fax you sent me: looks like valacyclovir, which is a herpes remedy. Which I hope to God is not for you. Or, bless your heart, any of the eighteen or nineteen men you've been with the last month or two. Your moonlighting is going well, so don't screw it up with a sexual disease. Call me."

I could feel myself blushing in the dark, as if Doc, four feet away, could hear it all too. He hadn't learned about the Dating Project from Fredreeq; he'd listened to my messages last night and drawn his own conclusions.

He thought I was a hooker.

Anger returned, overriding embarrassment. I wanted to wake him up so I could knock him unconscious, but there was one more message coming through.

I listened just long enough to note the voice, playful and nasty, and then replaced the receiver. I was pretty sure I couldn't hear the Weasel's message right now and still do what I had to do.

chapter twenty-three

Hobbling homeward was no picnic. The perfect night had mutated into a dismal dawn, and while it was easy, even satisfying, to walk out on Doc, I hated doing it to Ruby, who'd seen enough disappearing acts lately. I wish I'd left a note. But my big concern was Joey.

I moved as fast as I could, which wasn't all that fast, given my heels, and within blocks I was frozen, which numbed my feet, which made me feel I was running on a pair of chopsticks. My braless breasts bounced violently and every thirty seconds or so I looked back to see if I was being followed. Sticking to side streets, my ten-minute trek turned into a half-hour marathon, the last of it in pouring rain.

Joey's Saab was in the parking lot, and she herself in the back room, stretched out on the red velvet sofa bed. I rushed over to make sure she was breathing, and her eyes popped open. Weak with relief, I threw my arms around her thin shoulders. "Thank God," I said. "You're okay, you're alone, he's not here?"

"Who?" She wiped water from her forehead. "You're wet. Is it raining?"

I stood, wringing out my hair. "Yes, I'm wet, I'm cold, I slept in these clothes. No, not with the mogul. Do you mind coming out front with me?"

I led her to the register desk, dialed my home machine, and put the phone on speaker. My messages started replaying. "I don't know how to fast-forward them," I said. "This'll take a minute."

Joey was pulling on a pair of skinny jeans. She'd slept in just a T-shirt and a pair of socks. The T-shirt was familiar—one of Doc's.

Joey saw me staring. "I found it on top of the dryer. I love this shirt. I used to go out with a guy who had this shirt. Where'd you get it?"

"Why? What is it?"

"It's MIT Press. The college newspaper. See?" She pushed aside her Lady Godiva hair and pointed to the logo, seven vertical white lines, with the fifth and sixth elongated. It looked like a bar code. "What's cool about this is that you have to know what it is, or you'd never know what it is." She traced over it with her finger to show how the lines represented the letters M-I-T-P.

Doc had gone to Massachusetts Institute of Technology? So had the dead man, if his sweatshirt was any indication. Doc had said he didn't know the man, but what were the chances of two unrelated former MIT students meeting on that road? Was there some abnormally large alumni population roaming Ventura County?

My phone machine reached the sixth message. I braced myself and pulled Joey closer.

"You there?" The voice was a whisper, low, gritty as sand. "All right. Anyway. I've been meaning to get together for a little gift exchange, so I'm coming over. Is tonight good? I'll leave my gun at home. I prefer a knife anyway. It's quiet. Ever think about that? I could go up into you, deep inside, scrape you out clean as a turkey and nobody would hear a thing except the sounds you make. It's messy, but I wear gloves. As for your gift to me, I think you know what I'd like. No need to wrap it. Just leave it in plain sight in case you're not going to be there."

Joey turned to me, her face doing what mine was doing. Like we'd just found ourselves with a mouthful of lemons. "Tell me that's not one of your dates," she said.

My voice shook. "We gotta get outta here."

"But he called you at home. Hours ago. This is your shop."

"It doesn't matter, he knows where I live, he's gotta know where I work, he follows me, he's the one in the Hummer, the pet store, the—bad, he's a bad man, come on." I threw her her shoes and pulled her outside, into the rain. With still-frozen fingers I searched my evening bag. "Do you have your key, I can't seem to—"

"Yes. Calm down." Joey pulled me back under the awning and locked up. "Think a minute. The guy on the phone: Why was he calling? What was his objective?"

"To scare me to death."

"Yes. To what end?"

I tried to concentrate. "I don't know. There's something he thinks I have or can get for him."

"Strange tactics, don't you think? To threaten you with—disembowelment."

"You're saying, in case I was home, he wanted me to panic and run?" I asked. "Okay, so what? Look, if I could call the cops I would, but I can't, so—"

"We don't need cops," Joey said, in a tone of voice I knew well. "Come on." She headed for her car. I followed.

She opened her trunk and handed me an umbrella, orange with a duck's head for a handle. She searched some more and pulled out something wrapped in a sock. "Does this guy know you can't go to the cops?" she asked, leading me toward the alley.

"I don't know."

"Okay, my guess is, he's not going to hang around if he thinks they'll show up. Assuming he was at your place, he's long gone now. If I'm wrong, we have an umbrella and"—she reached into the sock—"a Glock."

"Oh, my God," I said. "Does everyone but me own a gun?"

"Elliot bought it for me when he left for Europe. I just hope I remember how to use it—not that it will come to that," she added, seeing my face.

"You know how to use this—this Clock?" I followed her into the alley.

"Glock. Yeah. It's what Gun Girl carried."

In her acting days, Joey had starred in a TV series, *Gun Girl*. Seeing her eagerness to storm my apartment, I wondered if it had skewed her perspective, made her oblivious to real danger. Maybe she subconsciously assumed there was a camera crew in the shrubbery, filming our approach, ready to stop the scene if things got ugly.

Inside the building, that changed. I felt Joey's hesitation along with my own, a response to the dark. My landlord being too cheap to spring for anything stronger than Christmas tree lights, the entire Minardi crime family could be stuffed under the stairwell, unseen. Normally the darkness didn't bother me, not in the daytime, but nothing about this day was normal. For one thing, it was too quiet. There was rain pelting the roof and the beating of my heart, but where were the neighbor noises, the morning sounds, the Spanish radio, the colicky baby? Had the Weasel murdered my fellow tenants? I took Joey's hand and she gave mine a squeeze.

At the top of the stairs, a door opened.

The wizened face of Mrs. Albertini peered out at us. Her wizened terrier yapped. Mrs. Albertini's eyes went to our joined hands, to my umbrella, to Joey's gun, then back up to our faces. She slammed her door. We continued on our way, up the concrete steps to my apartment.

The door was open.

"Don't go in," I whispered.

"Why not?" Joey whispered back.

"They tell you not to go in if you come home to an unlocked door. I'm sure I've heard that."

"They tell you that because it's a sign there may be a burglar inside. In our case, we expect there *was* a burglar, and that he's gone. Going in is what we're here for." Joey pushed the door open with her foot.

It looked like I'd been evicted. My worldly possessions, plus a few of Doc's and Ruby's, covered every surface. Books were stacked next to bookshelves, pots and pans in front of cupboards. My wardrobe took up most of the living room floor, displayed as if at a yard sale. I felt laid bare. Only the knowledge that most of my photos and artwork and business records were stored in the back room of the shop kept me from coming unglued. I whispered, "It's all so neat."

Joey moved toward the bathroom, gun drawn. A flapping drew my attention to the kitchen, where the ceiling fan rotated at low speed, a spinning ball of color. I flipped the wall switch and watched the spinning ball slow and become bits of fabric. There was something familiar about the fragments. I reached out and touched a piece of stretchy blue silk shaped like a strand of fettuccine. Underwear. All my bikini panties, mutilated. "Yuck," I said aloud.

"Weird," I heard from the bathroom.

Joey stood looking at the closed toilet seat, upon which sat my own Hummel collection, the small porcelain Bavarian children forming a circle. They were headless. Each plump, decapitated body sported a jagged neckline, revealing hollow insides.

"What kind of man would behead a Hummel?" I asked, anger awakening in me.

"Not your average burglar. And not one interested in jewelry," Joey said, plucking something from the edge of the bathtub. "A perfectly good emerald. Oh, it's a class ring. From . . . 1948?"

"Uncle Theo's," I said numbly. "A present when I was ten."

"Guess our guy's not into emeralds."

"No. It's diamonds he wants," I said, and proceeded to tell her nearly everything about the events of the last five days.

BACK IN THE shop an hour later, I changed into the contents of a UPS box from Tiffanie's Trousseau. I couldn't bear to wear anything touched by the Weasel, not until it had been laundered or sterilized or blessed by the Pope. In any case, I had a lunch date later, as surrealistic as it seemed to go on a date under the circumstances. In the back room, I looked down at myself, all six feet of me, in cream-colored jodhpurs and a skin-tight white shirt, and called out, "They've got me dressed for a fox hunt."

"It's for some event at the Museum of Flying this afternoon," Joey said, coming from the shop floor to join me. "Dylan Ellison. Fredreeq's all happy because she can squeeze in a dinner with someone else afterward. No time to schedule the Drive-by, but we're going to let it slide. Come on, let's take the Polaroid."

"Joey, look, I'm not up to—"

"Yes, you are. Chores. Routine. Very therapeutic. You want this jerk bringing your life to a crashing halt? Come on."

Joey also agreed it was safe to open the shop. "After all," she pointed out, grabbing the camera, "why would the Weasel disguise his identity last night, only to show up in broad daylight? This guy's working to keep a low profile, otherwise he'd have confronted you days ago."

"I'm not so sure," I said. "Can we truly predict the actions of a sociopath?"

"Sure, why not? Smile."

I sighed, and struck my sex-kitten pose, feeling overgrown and unconvincing.

Doc walked in.

Behind him came Ruby, carrying Margaret's crate. Ruby looked interested, but Doc, taking in the scene, looked incredulous. A black look dropped over his brown eyes.

"Hi," Joey said. "I'm Joey and you must be the cousins Fredreeq mentioned."

Doc collected himself with an effort. He nodded to Joey, glanced at his shirt on her body, then turned to me. "You, I want to talk to. Alone. Excuse us, everyone."

He took me by the arm and steered me around shelves of merchandise. I put up a little resistance, which strengthened his grip, which annoyed me, so I jerked my arm away. Our eyes met, mine no doubt as angry as his. He said, "I'm not in the mood for this," and walked into the front of the shop. After a moment, I followed.

"You don't strike me as stupid," he said, then stopped, taking in my outfit. After a second, he continued. "Is it possible you don't understand how serious this is?"

"Look, this hasn't been my best morning, and it's not even eight o'clock. Can you just manage not yelling at me until I've had breakfast?"

He gestured toward the back room. "Your friend—how much does she know?"

"The whole story, except a few details about you. I thought I owed it to her, as she just spent the last hour with me trying to put my apartment back together."

"He broke in?"

"Yes. You don't seem surprised."

"I figured he might. How bad was it?"

"You figured he might? And it didn't occur to you to tell me? Or to do something about it?"

"Jesus. You really want it all, don't you?" He ran a hand over his dark-stubbled face. "I have my daughter to think about, Wollie, and you, for that matter. What did you have in mind, hand-to-hand combat? Me bringing him down with a dinner fork?"

"Or a gun. An Astra Falcon, maybe. If you had one, which you don't, because it's gone."

His eyebrows went up, then dropped, shadowing his face. "What else is gone?"

"Eighty dollars in cash. Fourteen bisque porcelain heads. That's all I could tell so far. I'd describe it as a violation, but his phone message gives new meaning to 'violation.' On the plus side, it was a very tidy break-in."

"On the plus side, you're alive," he said.

"Joey thinks the Weasel left the message on my machine to give me a chance to leave the diamond and run."

He leaned back against the muraled wall. "What else does Joey think?"

"That your T-shirt is from MIT," I said. "Which means you probably went to school there, yet you didn't know the dead man in the road, who also went to MIT. Interesting coincidence."

"So you suspect me of murdering a man because we shared an alma mater. Interesting motive."

"I don't suspect that. I give you the benefit of the doubt. There's always evidence that points to the worst in people, if you look for it. I don't."

"A real Mother Teresa, aren't you?" He plucked something from my shirt collar. It was a tender gesture, strange under the circumstances. "Do me a favor," he said, and took my hand. "Cultivate skepticism. You'll live longer." He returned the hand, and turned away. I looked at my palm, at a sticker saying "Inspected by number 3439."

I was about to ask him how he thought I could turn tricks, lacking skepticism, but the phone rang. I reached for it. Dr. Charlie, my brother's doctor, was on the other end.

"Wollie," he said, "P.B.'s eloped."

"Eloped?" I said, bewildered. "With whom?"

"No. Sorry. Hospital speak. It means he's gone. Disappeared, flew the coop."

Inside me, blood turned to ice water and I began to shake.

My first thought was of foul play, P.B. kidnapped by mobsters in Hummers. My next thought was relapse.

When his illness was dormant, my brother was a real indoor guy, devoted to routine. But gripped by obsession, he would hit the road without warning, without money, impervious to creature comforts, following some inner directive. These episodes were hell for me, not knowing if he was dead or alive, and it was all coming back now, like taking a fast drive through an old neighborhood.

". . . the bus," Dr. Charlie was saying, penetrating my mental trip. "Very embarrassing, but what with all the brouhaha, he apparently just boarded it and—"

"Bus? What bus?" I asked.

"The bus to the courthouse."

"Courtroom 95? The conservatorship hearings? San Fernando Road?"

"Yes. P.B. was distressed. We had a—a death here recently. Steven Stendaur, a patient in Unit 18, and a good friend of P.B.'s. When we told P.B. about it this morning, he must've—I tried the bus, but the driver seems to have left his pager at home and—"

But I was already out the door.

chapter twenty-four

"I don't understand how he could just walk out of his room and board a bus," Doc said, crossing three freeway lanes in twelve seconds, a rush-hour feat. "Even with the Mickey Mouse security they have there."

"P.B. has really good transportation karma. Once he got himself on a fishing boat in Alaska. Another time he boarded an Air Maroc flight and made it to Fez. We have no idea how." I glanced over my shoulder. No Hummer in sight, only hundreds of cars behind me on the 134 east. And, of course, Ruby and Margaret in the backseat, swaying with the swerving of the Rabbit. "Anyway, it's not a normal bus, it's a little one that shows up at the hospital every Thursday to take patients to the courthouse. The sort of opportunity that has 'P.B.' written all over it."

There was something I'd just said that rang a bell, but I was too distracted to pursue it. I was thinking of P.B. witnessing the murder, too far away to identify the victim, then later, finding out the victim was his friend. At this moment he would be playing the scene over and over in his head, torturing himself.

We drove in silence, picking up speed as we left L.A. behind and traffic eased. The rain had stopped and the fog was burning off fast.

After a time, Doc said, "P.B.'s not dangerous, is he?"

"Not remotely," I said, "except on very rare occasions when he's worked up about George Bush. Senior. And only then when he's off his medication."

"What kind of medication?"

"Ziprasidone," I said. "It's the best thing that ever happened to him and you don't know how lucky he is to be able to get it for free, not to mention live at the hospital."

"No, I don't know. I thought Ruby was damn lucky to get out."

"That's because you have no experience with good hospitals versus bad hospitals and bad hospitals versus the street."

"True enough."

"Okay then." I knew I was being petulant. It wasn't Doc's fault that my brother was schizophrenic, but I didn't feel like being emotionally mature at the moment. "It's not some snake pit, out of an old Joan Crawford movie, it's his home. Ordinarily, there aren't dead bodies in the driveway. If P.B.—"

It clicked into place, the image that had been eluding me for days. I saw Doc look at me. "The gun," I said. "The Swedish guy's gun— there was a marking on it, right in the metal, two letters: P.B. It flashed through my head that it had my brother's name written all over it."

"Pistol Beretta," he said. He glanced into the backseat and lowered his voice. "That's probably the murder weapon, the nine-millimeter. Gotta be a way to use all this. I spent two days at the hospital, waiting for Ruby's release, and I got friendly with a rookie in the Ventura County Sheriff's Department. Dambronski. Let me think a minute . . ."

"Think away," I said. "But that gun really does have P.B.'s name all over it because Olof and Tor are killers, and P.B.'s a witness, and if you have any ideas about finding him so he can identify them, think again. I won't let anyone do that to him."

Doc reached out and took my hand. It startled me and had the effect of shutting me up, which was something of a relief. I let him hold it, and when he finally let go, I left it sitting there where he placed it.

IT WASN'T AN imposing courthouse; it was actually kind of cozy. I hadn't been there for a few years, since Dr. Charlie had helped P.B. and me through the conservatorship process. There were a dozen people milling around the courtyard of the building, smoking or sitting or talking to themselves, and while some seemed a little odd, most you couldn't identify as anything in particular. They might have been patients or doctors or court personnel. The morning sun beamed down upon them all.

A security guard sat just inside the prewar building, at an ancient school desk functioning as a security checkpoint. He pointed through the doorway to the driver from Rio Pescado, identifying him as "Ned."

Ned sat under an oak tree, eating Cheetos, and listened with the air of someone prepared to not be responsible, whatever the problem was. "If he was on the bus, he's in one of the holding pens back there, behind 95," he said, pointing a Cheeto toward one of the courtrooms. "I drive 'em here and I drive 'em back, that's all I know."

At Courtroom 95, a bailiff barred our way, telling us to return in ten minutes. Nor would he let us into the holding area to see the patients. "No visitors," he said, in stentorian tones. "Counsel only."

Doc pulled me aside. "Let's split up for a few minutes. I'm going to have a look around. There's a phone over there; why don't you call home, see if there's any news from the hospital. By the way, what's your brother look like?"

"Tall and skinny with straight blond hair and brown eyes. He looks a lot like me, with messier hair, and his clothes always kind of hang on him like they're a size too big." *Unlike* me, I thought, realizing I was still dressed for the foxhunt.

Ruby, unexpectedly, chose to stay with me, plopping herself on the floor alongside the pay phone, and burrowing into the stash of comics she'd brought with her. I figured she was angry at her father for making her leave Margaret in the car, albeit in the shade, with windows cracked.

Joey answered at the shop, lowering the background music to report a twelve-dollar sale and four phone calls—Rex and Robert again, one from a new date, confirming dinner tonight, and one from Mr. Bundt, wanting to speak with me ASAP. I used my calling card and dialed Welcome! headquarters in Cincinnati from memory, and was put on hold, giving the butterflies in my stomach a chance to organize themselves into squadrons. Ruby tapped on my jodhpurs and pointed out a man outside Courtroom 93, zipping and unzipping his fly. I watched him until Mr. Bundt got on the line.

"Wollie," he said, without preamble. "Has your problem resolved itself?"

"I . . . believe so," I said carefully.

"Good," he said. "Because when I called earlier, the woman answering the phone did not do so in the approved manner. Moreover, the music in the shop, playing at full volume—Zylocaine, she called it?"

"Zydeco," I said hastily. "And I'm sure it—"

"It sounded like hogs singing. Good Lord, this, of all weeks, to leave a new, improperly trained employee—"

"It couldn't be helped, Mr. Bundt. I had a—family emergency." Outside Courtroom 93, the man with the zipper problem began to pee against the wall.

"We do not encourage family emergencies, Wollie. Now that you're back in the shop, I suggest you drill—Miss Rafferty, is it?—on Telephone Greeting Procedures and Easy Listening."

"Of course." If Mr. Bundt thought I was calling from the shop, I would not disillusion him. A woman in a fur coat rushed past me toward the peeing man, her arms waving. "Mr. Bundt, did you call for a reason? Is it about the secret inspections?"

"No. My reason for calling is that the Welcome! corporation has decided to divest itself of lower-profit shops. The Sunset Boulevard branch has underperformed for years, a moot point if you win franchise approval. As owner of a Willkommen! Greetings, the headache becomes yours. Should you not be approved"—he paused dramatically—"your shop will be liquidated. Excess inventory will go to the Beverly Hills and Westwood branches and your services as manager will no longer be needed."

This seemed to call for a response, but my brain had gotten stuck on the word "liquidated" and I could not formulate one, beyond a sort of choking noise.

He let the silence hang, then said, "In a worst-case scenario, Wollie, this phone call is your thirty days' notice."

I sank to the floor, still unable to speak. Ruby, perhaps sensing a soul mate, offered me a comic book, but I noticed Courtroom 95 had opened. I sprang up and reached for her hand and moved toward it.

Only half a dozen spectators had gathered in the courtroom, in what looked like church pews, so Ruby and I were able to grab a whole row for ourselves, moments before the entrance of the

Honorable Judge Randolph Milligan. P.B. was not among the par-
ticipants, nor was Doc anywhere to be seen, and I was debating going back out in the hall to look for them when the bailiff shut the
door decisively. I stayed where I was.

A doctor from Rio Pescado took the stand to testify, her Indian
accent so thick the court reporter had to interrupt several times, to
ask the judge for clarification. When the judge was stumped, a spec-
tator in the front row piped up with a translation. The bailiff shushed
him, but the patient, apparently understanding her own diagnosis for
the first time, stood and yelled, "That be total bullshit!" punctuating
each word with a shake of the head. The hair on the left side of her
head was in cornrows, but the right side stuck out horizontally, as if
the beauty parlor had closed up shop halfway through her appointment. Her lawyer, a very young man in a very bad suit, tried
valiantly to get her to sit back down, until the patient gave him a
good push, throwing him off balance.

Someone slid into the pew next to me and touched my sleeve. I
pulled away reflexively until I realized it was Doc, changed into a tie,
denim shirt, and glasses.

"Let's go," he said. "P.B.'s not here, he's headed for Venice."

THE FACT THAT we had no real idea where we were going did not
alter Doc's driving style. I grabbed the dashboard for balance, as the
Rabbit hurtled along San Fernando Road. Doc was wearing his own
clothes once more, having returned the glasses, shirt, and tie to Ned,
the bus driver.

"Ties work," he said. "I went back, told the bailiff I was counsel,
and he waved me in. Everyone in the holding area knew P.B., and
one woman swears he's headed to Venice. Venice, California, I
hope?"

I nodded. "P.B. doesn't believe in Europe."

We drove in silence for a while, scanning the road. I tried not to think about all the dire things that could happen to him, even without the murderous Swedes, but habit was strong, a vigilance born in childhood, the moment someone had clamped my hand around a squirmy fist and said, "This is your little brother and you're in charge of him."

"No messages at the shop?" Doc asked.

"Oh, there were messages," I said, and told him about Mr. Bundt.

"Screw him. You didn't hear that, Ruby," he said to the rearview mirror. "Seriously, Wollie. You don't need them."

"Seriously, I do need them."

"Come on, a low-paying job on a sinking ship? Design cards. That's what you do, isn't it?"

"Not lately," I said. "No time. And anyway, I can't make a living that way."

"Have you tried? Full-time?"

"There's not just me to consider," I said, exasperated. "There's P.B., and Uncle Theo—he's seventy, he can't hang wallpaper forever. And then there's Fredreeq, she's saving for her kids' college funds, and then the Wednesday night poets need—" I stopped, feeling myself start to hyperventilate. "I just want one place in the world we can count on, that's ours, that we can't be thrown out of."

"You won't find it in corporate America. You're not the type. And look what it's costing you, trying to fit in—this 'moonlighting,' as you so euphemistically put it. How long do you think you can pull that off?"

Now was the moment to enlighten Doc about the Dating Project, but I was oddly reluctant. Since childhood I'd been an A student, one of life's hall monitors, observing signs, avoiding cracks in the sidewalk, reading all instructions before starting the test. Only in art did I color outside the lines. Doc considered me capable of prostitution, and now that my shock had worn off, this intrigued me.

And I liked that it disturbed him. He disturbed me, with his black hair and deep eyes, his sinewy forearms and articulate hands on the wheel of my Volkswagen, steering us around the slow cars. Who was he to judge me, anyway, this—

Something on the side of the road caught my attention.

Doc saw it too. He slammed on the brakes. I was out of the car before it stopped.

P.B. lay on his stomach, in the ditch alongside San Fernando Road. The right side of his face was in the dirt. His eyes were closed.

I slowed my approach, aware of the morning traffic and birds singing and a second and third slam of car doors behind me. Most of all I was aware of dread. I moved slowly because if there was something terrible to be discovered, I wanted to prolong this moment, before darkness closed in.

I reached him. I stood over him. I saw the rise and fall of his back. Relief fell upon me like a warm spring shower, making my knees wobble as I sank down into the ditch. "P.B., it's Wollie," I said. "You can open your eyes."

He didn't respond, although his nose wrinkled. In the breeze, a lock of limp blond hair traveled across his forehead, stopping at his nose. I reached over and put it back. Then I rested my hand on his shirt, gingerly, as though my palm might leave an imprint. The shirt was hot from the sun, a pastel plaid button-down, fragile with wear, a Christmas present from a former decade. I marveled that he still had it.

"I'm glad I found you," I said. I settled next to him in the dirt, arranging myself on my side. A truck passed and I felt its vibrations in the earth beneath us.

P.B. moved again, turning his face away from me. He seemed engaged in some sort of ear-to-the-ground exercise, alternating ears. I leaned over and said, "I'd like you to come home with me. I'll make you a grilled cheese sandwich. You can watch TV. Uncle Theo can come over. I've really missed you."

There was no response to this.

After a time a shadow fell on us, and I looked up to see Doc. He was blocking the sun, and I couldn't tell what his face was doing. It occurred to me that this was as naked as he was likely to see me, lying in the dirt with my brother at 9:47 on a Thursday morning.

"P.B.," Doc said, "I'm a friend of your sister's, and I'll take you to Venice if you want. I'm sorry about your friend Steve."

P.B. sat up and scratched his scalp with both hands, vigorously, like there had been lice in the dirt. "Sand conducts sound," he said. "Without sand, I can't hear him."

I sat up too. "Hear who?"

"Stevie."

Nobody spoke for a minute. Ruby, who'd been behind her father, holding Margaret's crate, stepped in closer.

"Then let's go find sand," Doc said.

chapter twenty-five

"Sit down," Doc said, pulling me back to the sand without looking up from his reading. Margaret lay in his lap, shaded by newspaper. "You're at the beach. Relax."

The sand in Venice was the ordinary variety, suitable for beach volleyball, surfing, sun-worshiping. It was also the living room carpet of a certain percentage of southern California's homeless, more welcoming than the sand of Santa Monica and Malibu to the north, and this was important. The locals here were colorful enough that my brother, spread-eagle thirty feet from the shore, was not especially noteworthy.

But he was vulnerable. I felt this acutely, and glanced around from my own spot on the beach, some twenty feet inland. If someone had a mind to, someone on the boardwalk, for instance, they could hit him with one shot, probably. If they had a mind to. If they knew what he knew. It was driving me to drink, watching and waiting.

"I can't relax," I said. "He's out there receiving directives from his dead friend Stevie. I'm going for sunscreen. Look how white he and Ruby are."

Ruby sat near P.B., gazing at him as if he were TV. She'd taken a distinct liking to him, even holding his hand in the car the last miles to Venice.

"Look at this instead," Doc said, handing me the paper. "The synagogue story."

It was an article on a break-in at a Westside synagogue, the second in a week. The most recent one included acts of defilement. "Yes?" I said, scanning it.

"That's where the Weasel stashed the goods."

I looked at him, startled.

He nodded. "According to Shebby, when the Weasel was out on bail before starting his sentence, he hid his stuff in this synagogue."

"Tifereth Israel?" I said. "Where, exactly?"

"Shebby said a storeroom, in a box labeled 'Häagen-Dazs.' "

"The Weasel stuck his diamond in a carton of ice cream?"

"No," he said. "In a cardboard box with 'Häagen-Dazs' written on it."

"Is ice cream stored in boxes? Is Häagen-Dazs even kosher?" I stopped. "Why are you telling me this? Yesterday it was a big secret."

"Yesterday I was trying to keep you out of it. Today I'm just trying to keep you alive. It's time to go the police."

"What are you talking about? They'll arrest you. They'll arrest me. They'll—"

"Two reasons," he said, as if I hadn't spoken. "One, we can give them the guy who did this—" He indicated the newspaper article.

"Who, the Weasel? Do you have some kind of proof? Because it's not clear to me why he's crashing synagogues since he thinks the diamond's with us."

"The first break-in was the day he got out of prison. It was after that he decided I stole the diamond. As for evidence, if there is any— if he left fingerprints, for instance—the cops'll be all over it. They have their own reasons for wanting the Weasel off the street; if they can get him on breaking and entering, they'll do it."

"And what if he forgot to leave any evidence? And how does any of this keep you out of jail for Stevie's murder?"

"It doesn't." Doc gave me a steady look. "But P.B. can identify the Swedes as the ones who shot Stevie."

"No, he can't!" I yelled. "He was so far away he didn't even recognize Stevie."

"But from what he told us in the car—look. He saw them somewhere on the grounds, on his way back from breakfast. Olof and Tor. He heard them say on a cell phone they were prepared to shoot some guy if the guy didn't cooperate. Then, later, from his window, he sees a guy get shot. All he has to do is tell the cops what he told us, and—"

"He also told us that Olof and Tor are from an interplanetary alliance, posing as Swedish Secret Service. Do you see the cops running out to arrest extraterrestrials? And this assumes P.B. will even talk to the cops, which he won't, he'll get all hostile and then they'll—no. No, no, no." I was worked up to full volume, even though Doc was right in front of me. "And if by some chance he did talk, and they believed him and acted on the information, then what? He testifies in court against the mob? His life won't be worth a dime."

Doc squinted at me, then pulled his T-shirt up to wipe his face, giving me a glimpse of taut abdominal muscles. "We can't do this alone, Wollie. Until someone finds that diamond, none of our lives is worth a dime. What'll it do to your brother if something happens to you?"

"I'll risk it," I said.

"I won't."

We were in each other's faces now. His was turning tan right before my eyes. He'd be sunburnt, I decided, before I backed down. Abruptly, he pulled out his cell phone. "All right, we'll go at it from another angle. Let's see if my DMV connection came through with an address for Olof and Tor. Not that the sheriff in Ventura is going to race down with a search warrant, not for an anonymous phone tip." He looked out to the ocean. "Maybe there's a way to get the Swedes on the move. If the Beretta you saw is the murder weapon, and if they got pulled over while carrying a concealed—"

"Well, hey, why not just arrange to catch them in the act of shooting someone?"

"Why not?" he said dryly. "Any suggestions on how?"

"No. You're the convicted felon."

He gave me a speculative look, the kind that probably made his high school students quake. "I may have to drown you in a minute. What's making you so irascible? That I won't let you go home and sell greeting cards? Forget the shop. Your brother's safe. Count your blessings."

If there is anything more maddening than being told to count blessings, it's being told what someone won't let you do. I stood. "If it weren't for my brother out there communing with the dead, I'd be long gone. I don't like the beach. I'm an indoor person. I'm going to get sunscreen." I started off toward the boardwalk.

"Call Joey," he yelled. "Tell her to lock up that goddamn shop and go home."

Much as I hated the idea, that's exactly what I did, at a pay phone outside a sunglasses shop. The words were barely out of my mouth, however, when Joey interrupted. "You're in Venice? Perfect. Meet me at the Rose Café in forty minutes."

"But—"

"You won't regret it. And Wollie—come alone."

chapter twenty-six

The Rose Café & Market was a neighborhood landmark, pink on the outside, white cinder block on the inside, with enormous, erotic roses painted on the walls. Folk-rock music blared and preservative-free food abounded in one long display case, and for a moment, walking through, I remembered being twenty-three and carefree. My first published greeting card—a family of horses and ducks lighting Shabbat candles—had been carried in the Rose Café's gift shop. I still recalled the feeling of spotting it amid eye pillows, aprons, and blown-glass oil lamps.

It took two trips through the establishment before I found Joey, at an outdoor table obscured by shrubbery. Across from her was a man I'd never met.

He was dressed in a black suit and a plaid tie. His carrot-colored hairline was receding, but his face was that of an eternal juvenile, the kind that would be carded in bars until retirement age. For no reason, I was gripped with paranoia.

"Wollie!" Joey pushed aside a shrub to wave me over.

She'd unbraided her own red hair and put on makeup, rendering her scar invisible. Her lips were lined in plum, her eyes in charcoal, and on the table were eight-by-ten photos of herself. Autographed. "Wollie, meet Gerome," she said, gesturing to the man, who pulled up a third chair. "He's a friend of my cousin Stewart from Virginia. They went through their training together. Remember cousin Stewart?"

I cast my mind through Joey's enormous Irish family and came up blank.

"FBI," Joey said, and winked. "Anyhow, I called Stewart this morning with our question and he thought Gerome might help us with our research project."

"Ah," I said, only marginally less confused. I sat.

Gerome sat too, and cleared his throat. "I don't know how helpful it'll be, but I'll tell you what I can. This isn't classified. In fact, there's an article coming out in the *New Yorker* next month on the Minardi family, and I'm pretty sure Ronzare's mentioned in it, but Joey said you need information now." He turned to Joey with an enchanted smile. "And anything for Gun Girl."

"Gun Girl appreciates it, Gerome," Joey said. "We'll take anything you've got."

Gerome cleared his throat again, and downed a glass of water in a series of gulps. He pushed aside a turkey sandwich and leaned over the table. "Ron 'the Weasel' Ronzare came to our attention a couple years back, when his sister married Edoardo Minardi and he started doing work for the family out here on the coast. Nothing too strenuous, the kind of stuff you're given when your brother-in-law's the boss. Then last year, we were working a case, totally unrelated, infiltrating a neo-Nazi organization. Our guy on the inside got friendly with a couple of skinheads just off the boat, and he happened to be there one day when they got a call from the Weasel, wanting them to do a job for Big Eddie Minardi. Now, that was kind of intriguing, because these skinheads worked for the Terranova family out of Vegas. Minardis and Terranovas are like Letterman and Leno, you say yes to one, you piss off the other, and these two were friends with the Terranova kid, Luigi, went to boarding school with him in Europe. The deal was, Big Eddie planned to whack a couple of cops, and by using these boys, implicate the Terranovas. On a surveillance tape, we picked up a conversation where he arranged to deliver the fee, in full, in advance, to the skinheads. LAPD got wind of it, got to the meeting place first, and busted the Weasel."

"But not the skinheads?" I asked.

Gerome smiled. "They got away. LAPD wasn't happy about that, but it suited our purposes. The rest you may know. There was enough on the surveillance tapes to get a guilty plea out of the Weasel on a watered-down charge. I'm not convinced it would have held up in court, but—whatever. You still find these guys once in a while, old school, who see getting caught as the cost of doing business, and not wanting to bring attention to the family with a trial." He picked up his sandwich and took a healthy bite, leaving a dot of mustard on his upper lip. He chewed for a moment, then coughed.

Joey pushed her water glass across the table toward him, and then inched her plate toward me, an offering of fruit tart. "No thanks," I said. "So what happened to the payment, the fee that the Weasel was supposed to deliver?"

He held up a finger and drank Joey's water down to the ice, then said, "The Weasel claimed he gave it to the skinheads before the bust, but that's not likely. The hit never happened. If our boys had accepted payment, they would've done the job."

"So the Weasel kept it?" I asked.

Gerome shrugged. "He didn't have anything on him when they arrested him, no suitcase full of unmarked bills. Or at least," he said, smiling, "nothing that made it into the police report. Of course, it may not have been money. Maybe it was rare stamps. Lifetime tickets to the Vienna opera, something he dropped in a gutter and picked up later when he made bail. Or had a friend pick up. I always figured it was something more compelling than cash, to make our guys sell out Terranova. Excuse me." He stood, apparently in need of water.

"Wait," I said. "These guys, the neo-Nazis—"

"Uh-uh." Gerome shook his head. "Can't go there."

"Okay," I said. "But the *L.A. Times* mentioned two Swedish men, Olof and—"

"I really can't talk about that." He looked irritated and no longer boyish. Empty water glass in hand, he went in search of a waitress. I turned to Joey, wide-eyed.

Green eyes sparkled back. "You think Olof and Tor are the skinheads?"

"Yeah," I said. "But do they have skinheads in Sweden? Wasn't Sweden neutral in World War Two?"

"Maybe that's why they came to America, they were lonely." She picked at her pastry crust. "You know, we picture a nation of Ingrid Bergmans and Bjorn Borgs, but I'm remembering this guy I went to high school with, Todd Johnson, totally normal, math club guy; one day he changed his name to Gerhardt Knut, moved to Germany, and came back three years later totally Teutonic. Recruiter for something called Aryan America. My point is, you never know who's gonna hear the call and pick up the phone."

"Well, it sure doesn't sound like the FBI is going to rush in and arrest these guys."

"No," she said, "but that doesn't mean the local cops wouldn't, given a good reason. You think the diamond was the skinheads' fee?"

"Except you don't think of guys in their twenties getting excited about jewelry." I took her fork and captured a kiwi. "And it's hard to imagine the Weasel stealing from his own brother-in-law, a Mafia don, no less, and thinking he'll get away with it."

"Ego," Joey said. "And maybe he didn't get away with it. Trust me, it's not always possible to murder your spouse's family, just because it's your heart's desire. Maybe Mrs. Big Eddie wants proof before she lets her husband put cement shoes on her brother; maybe Olof and Tor were hired to get evidence. Or maybe they just want the diamond."

The words "brother" and "cement shoes" in the same sentence turned my bite of kiwi to sawdust. "Did you lock up the shop?" I asked.

"Nope," Joey said, picking up the fork. "Fredreeq says that no skinny-ass white-boy mob thug is gonna deprive her of her Thursday shift. I told her about the burglary and the yucko message and she said it sounds a lot less sinister than what she goes home to every day east of Normandie—says she's more worried about your next date being a Virgo."

"Joey, we have to get back there this minute, Fredreeq could be—"

"Wollie, relax." She stabbed pastry crust crumbs. "I left her my gun."

WE FOUND THE others eating corn dogs on the boardwalk at our rendezvous point. P.B. and Ruby were both less pale and more animated than I'd yet seen them. And Margaret sported an ID tag on her harness, an engraved red plastic heart. There was nothing you couldn't get on the Venice boardwalk.

P.B. handed me a corn dog, pleased with the results of his séance-in-the-sand. "Stevie's buried in Westwood," he said. "He's too close to Frank Zappa. He can't sleep. We're digging him up."

"Ashes," Doc said, as if that made all the difference. "And not until after dark. Listen—" he said, before I could interrupt. "I heard from my DMV friend. Olof and Tor live in Mar Vista, and I've got a plan. Joey, we need you—actually, we need your car."

"Sure."

"Why, what have you done with my car?" I asked.

He said. "Your car is bait. They follow me and the rest of you follow them."

"That's way too dangerous," I said. "These men are known by the FBI."

"It's not dangerous at all," Doc said. "They're not going to shoot me in a moving car, because number one, it attracts attention, and they're too professional for that, and number two, they need information from me. Now, you'll be driving with Joey in her car, with my cell phone. Once we're under way, you call the Ventura County Sheriff's and tell them you heard these guys bragging about the murder. Give them specifics, what the corpse was wearing, what kind of bullet was used, that'll get their attention. Then—"

"No," I said. "I'm terrible at that. If I'm questioned or treated like a crank call—uh-uh. If someone's gotta send in the cavalry for someone, it should be you. I can be bait; that sounds eaiser."

"Forget it," he said, in his implacable voice.

"If it's safe for you, it's safe for me. I'm not negotiating this," I said.

"I'm not either. So, Ruby, you'll ride with—what? What is it?" He looked down at his daughter, who'd wrapped her arms around his waist in a death grip. "Come on, Rube," he said. "Let go. There's nothing to be afraid of, we'll meet up in an hour." He tried to free himself from her pythonlike hug, but she was one strong eleven-year old.

"I'm with her," I said. "The world has enough fatherless children. We do it my way or not at all."

"And not that you asked, Doc," Joey chimed in, "but I'm with them. Being the bait's the easy part, and I've just figured out where Wollie's going to lead these guys."

GILMORE IS A small street off Centinela Avenue, near Washington, a residential block, but seedy enough that my own neighborhood's junkies would feel at home. The kind of setting you'd expect for a Mafia safe house.

In front of this particular safe house was the Alfa Romeo registered to Tor Ulvskog. In front of the Alfa Romeo, Doc and I squatted. With a last glance at the house, he turned to me and took my face in his hands. "Remember: at the first sign of them, go. Get out of here. Drive as fast as you can without crashing your car. With luck, they'll follow you, but we'll be right behind them. You can do this."

My face was smooshed, he was holding it so intently. I couldn't move my jaw to speak, so I said, "Mm-hmm."

Then he kissed me, right on the mouth, hard, which startled me, and let go. He moved to the driver's side of the car and within seconds the Alfa Romeo's alarm was screaming in my ear and Doc was sprinting back to the Saab, parked a block away.

I stayed where I was, in a squat, trying to look like I was involved in something dastardly, like planting a stick of dynamite under the car, but in fact, my focus was on the house and the Swedes that would surely be running out any second. I was shaking like a leaf and wishing I hadn't eaten that corn dog.

"Olof? OLOF! Kom snabbt! Någon håller på att stjäla bilen!"

I heard the yelling before I saw the screen door fly open, but I didn't wait for Tor and Olof to emerge. I hotfooted it to my car, already running, slammed it into gear, and peeled away from the curb.

I stayed on Centinela, heading north as fast as midday traffic would allow, my heart thumping and lips moving in my usual mantra of terror: "You're okay, you're okay, you're okay." When I reached Washington Boulevard, I spotted them.

Okay, the Swedes were behind me, but Doc and Joey were behind them, I told myself, and Doc and Joey wouldn't let anything bad happen to me. Being followed was the whole point.

"Just like a parade," said Ruta's voice in my head.

The Alfa Romeo was gaining on me.

I fought the impulse to swerve down a side street and busied myself instead with trying to guess if I'd reach my destination before Olof and Tor reached me.

By my calculations, I wouldn't.

chapter twenty-seven

The Santa Monica Airport wasn't for your basic guy bound for Newark, it was for people flying small planes, or dining in the trendy airport restaurants, or attending events at the Museum of Flying. There were several entrances, and mine was off a short street called, imaginatively, Airport, three blocks ahead. According to Joey, though, I should use this entrance only if I'd managed to keep distance between the Swedes and me.

"If they're right on top of you," she'd said, "go to plan B: drive to a main entrance and find your way to the museum, or anywhere you see people. The museum's good, because there'll be staff there. Make a scene. Yell. Say there's something suspicious about the guys behind you. It won't take much, it's an airport, they'll take that seriously. It may complicate things on our end, but it'll save you from physical assault."

My problem with plan B was that making a scene at an airport sounded as appealing as joining the Marines. With a glance behind me, I made a decision.

I signaled, then moved into Centinela's far right lane. My pursuers disappeared from my rearview mirror, but I hoped they changed lanes too. Two blocks later, I saw an opening and made my move, shooting across all lanes of traffic to turn left onto Airport, a feat that used up 40 percent of my nerve. Wincing at the angry honking in my wake, I raced down the near-empty avenue, past the Spitfire Grill restaurant, and swung right onto Donald Douglas Loop south. My mantra now was "Donald Duck south, six-eight-seven-four, tee-one-oh-four," a version of Joey's instructions, written on a Post-it stuck to the dashboard.

The entrance gate appeared and I swerved toward it, screeching to a stop next to a keypad on a standing black box. With shaking fingers I rolled down my window, whispering, "Six-eight-seven-four" as I punched in numbers. I begged the gate to open fast. I looked behind me.

The Alfa Romeo was passing the Spitfire Grill.

In front of me, the gate began its slow ascent.

Behind me, the Alfa Romeo made the turn onto Donald Douglas Loop south.

I faced forward and floored it, not caring whether I wrecked the gate or my car. I hoped the gate closed faster than it opened, but I didn't look back to check.

What I'd bet on was that the Swedes would not be as willing as I to damage their car. It seemed I was right: a full minute later they still hadn't appeared in my rearview mirror. I knew my luck wouldn't last. Most likely they'd gone to the airport's closest public entrance and would intercept me any moment.

Driving maniacally through the T-section hangars, I nearly plowed through a good-looking man waving his arms at me. This, no doubt, was my date, set up by Fredreeq that morning. Swerving around him, I drove until I found an empty hangar and pulled deep into it. A car cover would have been nice, or even a pile of leaves to camouflage the Rabbit, but my top priority was me. I ran to the edge of the hangar and peered out.

"Didn't you see me flag you down?" my date called, striding toward me down the wide driveway. "Where the hell did you park?"

"Oh, over there, in the shade, out of the way," I yelled back, with a vague gesture. Hugging the building's exterior, I started toward him. "Dylan, right? Where's your car?"

"What car?" he yelled, still some distance away. "We don't need a car, the Stearman's right back there—you nearly ran into it."

When I reached the opening between hangars, I stopped, scanning the area, reluctant to give up my cover. Visions of Olof and Tor, guns drawn, played in my head, and it wasn't until my date reached me that I even looked at him, registering prominent nose and good cheekbones, slightly sunburnt. He wore a brown leather bomber jacket, way too warm for the afternoon, and a Lakers cap.

"Wollie, right?" he said. "Nice to meet you. This way. Let's go."

"Great," I said. "Let's jog."

Dylan was game and handed me, on the run, a pair of goggles and a hat of sorts. "These are for you," he said. "You didn't bring a jacket?"

"For the Museum of Flying?" I panted. "Why, is there a dress code?"

"Museum? What, you think we're going to that fund-raiser?" He laughed. "Babe, we're going flying."

"Flying?" I stopped, mid-jog. "Like, in a plane? Right this minute?"

He turned around to face me. "Not scared, are you?"

"Scared of flying?" I took off again, grabbing his arm on the way. "Heck, no, I love it! Come on, come on, what are we waiting for?"

IT WAS THE tiniest airplane I'd ever seen, brightly colored with two sets of wings, one atop the other, and two compartments, each big enough to hold one not-fat person, not side by side, but one in front of the other, like on a bicycle built for two.

"Do I climb on like this?" I asked, trying to vault myself into the backseat.

Dylan caught me and redirected me to the front. "Really hot to fly this thing, aren't you?" He laughed.

"No, please, I'd rather you be the pilot." I struggled to remain pleasant as I scrutinized hangars, road, and runway for Swedes, Saabs, or cops.

"It drives from behind, Wollie," Dylan explained, then hoisted me into the seat, handing up his leather jacket after me.

Higher now, I had a better vantage point for my surveillance. After shrugging myself into the jacket, I was forced to sit still while my date trussed me in with a series of faded canvas straps and buckles, until I was as immobile as a child in a car seat. Wedged next to me, similarly secured, was the world's smallest picnic basket.

In the distance, I saw the Alfa Romeo, circling hangars.

"Goggles and helmet," Dylan reminded me, then tossed a third piece of paraphernalia into my lap. "Headset. Now, don't touch this pedal or this lever, and—"

"Yes, *fine*, I won't touch anything. Let's just *go*," I practically screamed, which brought him to a dead halt, frowning up at me. I forced a smile onto my face. "I'm sorry, it's just that I adore flying, and you've got me all excited, it's a . . . an instant gratification compulsion . . . a disorder, really, and we have to go *right this minute.*"

He shook his head, but moved to the rear of the plane, calling out, "No problem, babe. Your headset's patchy, okay? About half of what you say and hear gets garbled, but mine works, and that's what counts. If I tell you to lean right or left, do it. If I ask how you're doing, thumbs-up or thumbs-down—all right, all *right,* we're going."

My range of movement was limited now, due to the bondage just enacted on me, but I was squirming like mad, trying to scope things out. Turning in my seat, I nearly dislocated my shoulder, but what I saw behind me nearly dislocated my brain.

The Alfa Romeo was stopped outside the hangar where I'd parked the Rabbit.

"Dylan!" I rasped, then found my voice. "*Dylan!* Get this bird in the air!"

"Jesus Christ," I heard him mutter, but he climbed into the seat behind me, judging from the severe wobble that ensued. I was still contorting my spine to watch the Swedes, and as the plane's engine roared to life, I saw Olof and Tor spot us.

I turned to face forward, staring at the whirring propeller and fighting panic. Talk about a sitting duck—perched high like this, I was as inconspicuous as a parade float.

"Yo! *Helmet!*" Dylan yelled, and with a jolt I realized a disguise had been literally dropped in my lap. I crammed the canvas helmet onto my head and stuffed my telltale blond hair up into it, then donned the goggles. I had just enough time to smash the earphones on before turning to find the Swedes driving alongside us.

"Hurry up, hurry up, hurry up," I yelled into my headset, with no idea whether Dylan could hear, but seconds later the plane shuddered and rattled and inched forward with all the speed of my Rabbit with a cold engine.

I *walk* faster than this, I realized, and started to sweat profusely, seeing the Alfa Romeo immediately to my left, keeping perfect pace with us.

There was nothing for me to do *but* sweat. Olof and Tor looked up from their car, at me, Dylan, the plane, and each other, mouths and hands and even widow's peak moving vehemently. I assumed they were discussing the possibility of one of us being me. I couldn't turn sufficiently to see Dylan, but I figured he was in the same getup. With eyes, ears, and head covered, I assured myself, the two of us could just as easily be Siegfried and Roy as Wollie and Date Twenty-six. But I couldn't stop sweating.

The Alfa Romeo gained speed along with us, and static assaulted my ears, probably Dylan commenting on lunatics in foreign convertibles driving onto airfields. Seconds later the static cleared and a woman's voice came in, in fits and starts, discussing weather and flight paths. As we made our turn onto the runway, the Swedes did likewise, and seemed to escalate their argument until the driver, the Birkenstocker, pulled a gun from his shoulder holster. I stared, mesmerized, as he aimed it upward, and I wondered if Stevie had been as dumbstruck at Rio Pescado, moments before his death. How does a guy drive *and* shoot, I wondered, as if the question were purely academic, and then, abruptly, I began to scream.

But the engine screamed louder as the plane bolted like a horse, rattling as if every screw were loose. I rattled too, my teeth threatening to fly out of my mouth, until, all rattling notwithstanding, we lifted off.

I watched the Swedes on the ground grow smaller, and then Olof or Tor reached over and grabbed the gun from Tor or Olof.

Farther down the runway a police car started toward them, but the Alfa Romeo was already heading for an exit.

I was halfway through a huge sigh of relief when a new thought struck me.

This thing was in the air.

IF I'D NEVER experienced fear of flying before, clearly it was because I'd only ever flown in commercial airplanes, with plastic tray tables and seat cushions that doubled as flotation devices. As opposed to a winged kayak. Gripping the cheap plastic windshield, I looked longingly at grass and concrete falling away, wondering how I could ever have taken such nice surfaces for granted. The plane dropped altitude suddenly, leaving my stomach a few yards above my head, and I discovered a whole new realm of sensations to be scared of.

"Pretend you are in the French Resistance," Ruta said, giving me courage. I longed to give Dylan the thumbs-down signal, but there was opportunity here. I peered at the ground, determined to track the convertible as long as possible.

"Patchy" was too kind a word for my earphones, apparently salvaged from the Battle of Dunkirk. When I suggested going south, I was answered with a barrage of static, giving me no clue whether Dylan heard, understood, or cared about my navigational preferences. Chances were slim that I could explain things sufficiently to keep him hovering indefinitely over a couple of drive-by shooters.

We seemed to be headed west, and Olof and Tor had disappeared from view by the time words, such as they were, could be heard through the static. "...PT-17...fighter pilot...World War...commissioned..."

Good Lord, *surely* Dylan wasn't that old, I thought, then realized he was referring to our aircraft. I dragged my gaze from the streets of Santa Monica to study the flimsy aluminum, its Disneyesque red, white, blue, green, and yellow paint job now putting me in mind of a very new toupee on a very old man. Why was Dylan telling me the life story of an airplane, I wondered irritably, until I recalled I was supposed to be a fool for flying.

The open air did have an undeniable appeal, as did the low altitude, and under other circumstances I might have enjoyed myself. Now, though, the only view I cared to see was the Swedes, overtaken by police. I squinted at streets, straining for the sight of the convertible, or even a landmark, to get my bearings, when suddenly the plane nosed its way straight up, sending my equilibrium into outer space.

Terror hit me, purely physical and absolutely paralyzing. Looking into nothing but blue-white sky, unable even to scream, I wondered, Could I be going into a coma? Do people literally die of fright? Would this ever end?

It ended. We hung suspended, then did a vertical 180-degree turn and headed back to earth, and as bad as the preceding seconds had been, the sight of ground rushing to meet me was infinitely worse. I stopped breathing.

How long it went on I couldn't say; it's possible I blacked out momentarily, but at some point I realized we were level again and I was focused on my own hands, chalk white and gripping the sides of my plastic windshield. I was shuddering violently and wishing I'd let Olof and Tor shoot me dead while I had the chance. I started formulating the words to express to Dylan my willingness to be boiled in oil rather than play Evel Knievel again, when my mouth filled with saliva and my chest heaved convulsively. I leaned as far as my bonds would allow, and vomited over the side of the plane.

Some seconds later, my glazed eyes cleared and I even managed a shred of compassion for whomever had found themselves beneath me, catching the remains of my lunch. Which is how I happened to see, ahead of me and to the right, an Alfa Romeo.

I opened my mouth and screamed into my headset, "Follow that car!" I kept leaning to the right, stretching to keep the Swedes in sight, and this provoked a veritable assault of static in my earphones. ". . . quit! . . . up . . . damn it!"

I squirmed around enough to see Dylan's arm, pointing skyward, which I took to mean that leaning was not a good idea. This seemed highly ironic, given the death-defying flying maneuvers he'd just inflicted on me, but the plane was listing dangerously, so I straightened up. The car soon emerged on my other side, heading south. I pointed and yelled into my mouthpiece, "We gotta go left! Left! Thataway!"

There was no response to this and I had to assume Dylan couldn't hear. I gestured aerobically with both arms, pointing and yelling, "SOUTH!" but we kept flying west, until we were over the ocean and the Alfa Romeo was no longer in sight.

"Pacific!" Dylan squawked over the headset, in case I was in doubt about which coast we lived on.

"Who cares?!" I cried, nearly wild with communication frustration, but what could I do? For that matter, what were the Swedes doing, racing toward the coast on a diagonal that I guessed to be Lincoln Boulevard? Were the cops after them, or had the cops lost interest when Olof and Tor left the airport? And where were Doc and Joey?

These questions fell right out of my head when the left side of the plane tilted earthward and the right side skyward until we were completely upside down, another of my least favorite things in life. I was incapable of letting go of my windshield death grip long enough to make the thumbs-down gesture, or even work out whether thumbs-down still meant thumbs-down if one was upside down. Fortunately, this new nightmare was short-lived and I was right side up before I could lose consciousness.

I energetically pumped both thumbs down for a full thirty seconds, wishing I could turn around enough to make eye contact, or goggle contact, with Dylan. He seemed to have gotten the message, though, because we dropped altitude abruptly, until we were barely higher than the palm trees.

And once again, there was the convertible.

My spirits shot up and I could have kissed Dylan. It wasn't by chance after all that we'd found the convertible a second time—this man knew the way to my heart. Olof and Tor were pulling off Lincoln now, onto a tiny street that fed into the marina. They raced down a narrow alley, parked their car, and walked onto a slip, as we circled leisurely above them. What were they doing there?

It was unlikely they'd decided to go fishing. And then I remembered. Carmine. He'd said he lived on a boat.

But he'd also said the Swedes were dangerous, that they would kill for the diamond, that I didn't want to be dealing with them—

As if hearing my thoughts, a man came onto the deck of a boat, a man in shirtsleeves, with a dark tan and white hair. Carmine himself. I held my breath. Was I about to witness an execution, as my brother had? I waited for the gun, the shot—

But they didn't shoot him. Olof and Tor reached the big man, and kissed him, on both cheeks, exactly the way Jean-Luc had kissed me. The European way.

The Mafia way.

Was Carmine working for them, and not for his cousin the Weasel? Had he sold out the Weasel to the Weasel's own mob?

I was still struggling with the implications of this twenty minutes later, back on the ground at Santa Monica Airport.

"I owe you a picnic," Dylan said, helping me climb out of the plane. "Didn't like the look of those clouds."

"No problem," I started to say, then stopped. I checked my watch. We'd been together less than two hours, meaning that Dr. Cookie might not qualify it as a date. "I suppose we could picnic here in the hangar," I said, but without much enthusiasm. I was too worked up to sit around eating ham sandwiches.

Dylan must've picked up on this. "Rain check," he murmured, and sent me back to my car with a quick peck on the cheek.

Which freed me up to worry about a more important date. The one I had to keep with Carmine.

chapter twenty-eight

"You are *not*," Doc said, "meeting Carmine tonight. It's the transmission, by the way." He peered into the Rabbit's engine. "Hold that flashlight steady."

I held my temper in check and redirected my aim toward what I assumed to be a transmission. We were in the alley behind Plucky Chicken. Through the open doorway we could see Luis working his deep fat fryer and singing along with Cher on the radio. Beyond him were Ruby and P.B. at the counter, chowing down.

"Carmine is working with Olof and Tor," I said. "Don't you see the opportunity here?"

"Nope."

"Since Olof and Tor committed the murder," I said patiently, "Carmine is likely to know about it—details—how they did it and why. The kind of information cops listen to, the kind that produces search warrants and arrests, *un*like anonymous phone tips."

"The cops are already on it," he said, still tinkering. "While you were up in the air, Airport Authority was calling the sheriff's department to report a suspicious vehicle driving onto runways. I talked to my contact, Dambronski, the rookie up in Ventura County, and told him to check it out. He's driving down to L.A. tonight after his shift."

"Check what out?" I yelled. "We got nothing on these guys, no motive, no—"

"If you think," he said, straightening up to make eye contact, "that I'd let you walk into a meeting with a guy who thinks you've got a half-a-million-dollar diamond on you, when in fact you've got squat, you can just—"

"Let me?" I shined the flashlight in his eyes. "How are you going to stop me?"

Doc wrested the flashlight from me and pointed to my engine. "I don't have to. Your car's in for the night, and you," he said, "have a date." He aimed the light at the ground, into a shopping bag full of shoes, accessories, and something silky and red.

"Oh, for God's sake," I said. "A date? I'm not going on a date. I've got my brother in there obsessed with exhuming his friend Stevie, which I somehow have to talk him out of—he's probably scaring Ruby, by the way."

"She's not scared. Eleven's a bloodthirsty age. Listen, I told Fredreeq you'd had enough for one day, but she said you were a pro and wouldn't dream of missing a date. His name is Phig. He'll pick you up here in the alley, to be safe."

I was reminded that in Doc's mind, "date" was a euphemism for "john."

Keep it together, I told myself. Find a phone, cancel— "I'm sorry, did you say Phig?" I asked.

Doc smiled. "With a 'Ph.' By the way, what happened to Dylan?"

"Who knows? He landed the plane and took off. Look, I'm going to run over to the shop and—"

"Can't. It's locked up for the night. I installed the security system I found lying around in the back room, so one touch and you'll set off alarms."

I clenched my teeth. "My apartment, then."

"No time. He'll be here in ten minutes, you can change in the bathroom here."

The idea that ten minutes in the bathroom of Plucky Chicken was all I needed to prepare for a night of seduction was so ludicrous, I was bereft of speech.

"And don't worry about P.B.," Doc said. "We okayed it with his doctor to keep him overnight. I'm taking him to a late show at the Avco."

Knowing P.B.'s aversion to movie theaters, I could only stare.

"Ruby's spending the night at my lawyer's in Mandeville Canyon—he's my best friend, she's known him all her life. We would have gone there earlier, but he just got back from Rome." He paused. "She's not happy about it. Mostly because Margaret's not invited, but also, she likes it here."

The thought of Ruby leaving, of Doc having other friends and places to go, hit me in the stomach, momentarily knocking the fight out of me. But only momentarily.

"Whatever you did with that security system," I said, "undo it. It's my shop, I'll program the thing myself, since you obviously won't be around to—"

"Wollie," he began, but whatever else he had to say was lost, as a pair of headlights pulled into the alley. "Get down," he ordered, pulling me behind the Rabbit.

A car came to a stop, ten yards from where we crouched, the engine still running. My heart was pounding and Doc's breath was warm against my cheek.

"Wollie?" came a plaintive voice, calling into the night. "It's Phig, your date!"

PHIG SMITH, UNLIKE his moniker, was perfectly normal looking, except for a head of hair so yellow it seemed the result of food coloring. Studying him from the passenger seat of his BMW, I couldn't imagine how Fredreeq or Joey had approved him, unless he'd been wearing a large snood at his interview. And whatever happened to number one on the List, A Good Name? Clearly, our date standards were going to hell in a handbasket. But so were the couture rules. I'd traded Tiffanie's too tight, mile-high, suitable-for-a-drag-queen stilettos for the three-inch Miu Miu pumps I kept in the back of the Rabbit. Cheating, yes, but I had a long night ahead and didn't want to be crippled at the end of it.

When we pulled in line for the Regent Beverly Wilshire valet parking, I knew I was in for at least twenty minutes more of Phig, judging from the pack of vehicles crowded under the awning-covered walkway that separated the main hotel from its ballroom annex. And Phig was a talker, a yellow chickadee of a man, chirp-chirp-chirping, requiring of me only the occasional "uh-huh" and "wow." I spaced out momentarily, seeing my dates as animal greeting cards: Dave the hyena, Cliff the Clydesdale, Jean-Luc the Afghan hound . . . Then I snapped out of it, returning to the problem at hand: how to meet Carmine at Jerry's Deli in an hour.

Thirty-two minutes later, Phig and I joined the crowd headed down a black, white, and gold hallway toward the Grand Ballroom and the Friends of The Bill fund-raiser. Progress was slow, due to celebrities being interviewed every few feet. When things ground to a halt behind Sharon Stone expounding on the Bill of Rights, I'd had enough.

"Phig," I said, "I need a bathroom."

Phig sighed. "We're not connecting, are we? You haven't heard a word I've—"

"Basketball," I replied. "March Madness."

"Before that."

"Computer programming," I said. "Golf, rap, walks on the beach—look, I'm not kidding, I'm desperate to powder my nose. I'll meet you in the ballroom." Not waiting for a response, I turned and fought my way against the human flow of traffic, ostensibly toward the ladies' room, in fact toward the pay phones.

The mahogany alcoves were all occupied. Repressing a scream of impatience, I lined up behind the person I judged to be the fastest talker, edging out a man in a yarmulke. Smiling at him apologetically, I noticed his name tag. Rabbi Zev Rabinowitz. *Rabbi*. Hmm. "Excuse me, Rabbi," I said. "This may seem like an odd question, but do you ever serve Häagen-Dazs at your synagogue?"

He frowned. "Hamantaschen?"

"No, Häagen-Dazs."

His brow cleared. "Ah, the ice cream! Well, as far as the laws of kashrut—"

"Yes, thank you, sorry, must go," I said, suddenly catching sight of Phig, heading toward the ladies' room, clearly in search of me. I ducked behind a marble column, then doubled around, making my way back toward the exit.

It was slow going, my dress du soir being a Chinese red silk number, its skirt so narrow it had all the freedom of movement of a body cast. With mincing steps, my Miu Miu heels making little click click sounds on the marble floor. I trotted outside, past valet parkers, into the main hotel. Hearing a "Hey! Wait up!" behind me, I picked up the pace, racing across the marble floor of the Regent Beverly Wilshire like a terrier in heels.

Phig grabbed me outside the gift shop. "Whoa, Nellie. Where to?"

"I—have a problem with that bathroom," I said. "I prefer the one in here."

"That whole annex is an architectural afterthought," he said. "Nothing to compare to the Michael Pennington ceiling fresco in the—"

"Listen." I stopped and faced him. "I'm extremely sorry, but I have a family emergency and I have to leave, right this minute."

Phig stared, the remains of a smile sticking on his face. "You're ditching me?"

"No, not at all, it's just that I have to go do this—thing, and—"

"How are you getting there?" he asked, eyes narrowing. He still held my arm.

I looked away. "My grandmother's picking me up in front of the hotel," I said.

"When did all this happen?"

"Just now. I had a bad feeling and I used someone's cell phone to call home."

His voice hardened. "You're lying."

I looked at him, and sighed. "You're right, I'm lying. The truth is, I'm in trouble with the Mafia. I should never have come here tonight, I'm supposed to be meeting a man at Jerry's Famous Deli in half an hour, and if I don't show up, things could get ugly. Of course, if I do show up, things could get ugly. Still, I have to go."

Phig looked at me searchingly, eyes unexpectedly dark under those yellow eyebrows. "Well, then," he said. "I suppose I'll have to drive you."

JERRY'S FAMOUS DELI was so well lit, surgery could be performed there, and because of its close proximity to Cedars-Sinai, one could often find a couple of nurses and residents in a nearby booth qualified to do it. What I needed tonight, I thought, looking around, was a brain transplant, to turn me into someone who could lie credibly, talk tough, and squeeze information out of a big lug like Carmine.

My nerves were unraveling at the sheer thought of what I had to pull off, but what choice did I have? We needed the cops. With Olof and Tor on the streets, everyone I loved, including me, was in danger. And once those two were behind bars, the cops could stop investigating the hospital. They might never interview P.B., never find out he witnessed the murder. "You keep your mind on your brother," Ruta said, "and you'll be brave."

"Hey, Blondie." The big, white-haired man heaved himself into the booth opposite me, breathing heavily from the effort. "You got the goods?"

Here we go, I thought. "Yes, I do." I nodded. "You got a gun?"

"A what?"

"Gun," I repeated.

He looked confused. "Was I supposed to bring one?"

"No." I said. "That's why I'm asking. I need to know you're not armed. Do you mind just—taking off your jacket?"

Sighing, Carmine stood. He wore a worn tweed suit with a red tie and a pale lemon button-down shirt that showed off his suntan. He removed his jacket, did a lumbering pirouette, pulled his pant pockets inside out, and winked. "Wanna frisk me?"

If his body had private places that could harbor guns, I didn't want to know about them. I shook my head.

"Suit yourself. Where is it?"

"The merchandise? In the car. Perfectly, perfectly safe."

"Safe? In valet parking?" he said incredulously. "Nothing's safe with the spics."

Spics. I winced. "No, it's across the street with my girlfriend. Before I give it to you, though, I need to know what's in it for me. Not money—I want information."

Carmine glared at me, then snapped his fingers so loudly my whole body jerked. A waitress approached, and without a glance at the large, laminated menu, he rasped out, "Pastrami on a kaiser roll, mayo, lettuce, tomato. Shrimp cocktail to start, and a Pilsner."

For some reason, I realized it was Holy Thursday. The Last Supper.

"Coffee," I said.

The waitress gone, Carmine snapped, "What the hell you talking about, information?"

I cleared my throat. "I'm talking about what happened at Rio Pescado last Friday. Who shot that patient—you or your friends Olof and Tor?"

Carmine choked, a single, violent hack that turned his face red. "You wired?"

"I beg your pardon?"

"You wearing a wire? Stand up."

Hesitantly, I eased myself out of the booth and stood, smoothing down my dress. There was a slit down the front, beginning at the mandarin collar and ending at my solar plexus. The lower half of the dress was so tight, it showed the indentation of my belly button. "As you see," I said, "I'm not wearing much of anything."

Carmine made a twirling motion with his finger. "Turn around."

I turned, avoiding the appreciative gaze of four Sikhs at an adjoining booth. Then I sat. I did not invite Carmine to frisk me.

I must have passed muster. Nabbing a shrimp cocktail from the passing waitress, Carmine gave it his full attention: he plucked a shrimp with his big paw of a hand, coated it in sauce, popped it into his mouth whole, and after some oral machinations, spit the tail onto the saucer. It was the most frightening display of foodplay I'd seen since Date Six had knotted the stem of a maraschino cherry with his tongue.

Apparently, it was my move. "Look," I said, and leaned across the booth until his focus went from his shrimp to my chest. "Unless you can tell me what happened in the hospital driveway, I'll hold on to the merchandise until I find someone who knows."

His eyes met mine. Heavy bags underscored them, suggesting all sorts of things he did instead of sleeping. Unable to hold his look, I watched his mouth and the dab of cocktail sauce residing there like blood. Finally, I stood up.

"Okay, then, I guess I'll just have to—"

"*Sit.*"

I sat.

Carmine picked at the saucer of shrimp tails and proceeded to snap them casually, with tiny clicking sounds. "What do you want to know this for?"

"It's a Catholic thing," I said, silently apologizing to all practicing Catholics. "Stevie, the man who died, was a friend of the family. His priest thinks it might have been suicide, in which case Stevie couldn't be buried in hallowed ground. Which would bring great shame upon generations of—" I paused, unable to think of any surname except Jones or Smith, "—Stevie's family."

"Suicide? Guy was shot in the back."

"Just what I told the priest, and you know what he said?" I leaned in further. "Assisted suicide. Very trendy these days."

Carmine burped.

"But," I continued, "if I could tell the priest what really happened, under the seal of the confessional, then Stevie will get a proper burial. And here's the beauty part: the priest can't tell the cops. It's against Church law, he'd be disrobed. Uh, defrocked."

Carmine picked up his fork and frowned at the tines. He was wavering, I could see it. Probably an old altar boy. "I know you know what happened, Carmine," I said softly. "You just admitted he was shot in the back, and that's not common knowledge."

He tossed his fork onto the table and resettled his bulk into the corner of the vinyl booth. "It was no suicide. The guy was shot, but not by me. The Svenskis did it."

Svenskis. "Olof and Tor?" I asked. "What were they doing there?"

"I called them. I was following your boyfriend that morning, all the way up to Pleasant Valley, then I lost him on the hospital grounds. The Svenskis said to sit tight, they'd drive up and help me look."

"Those two hired you to do surveillance on my—boyfriend?" I asked.

He shook his head. "Not them. My cousin. Called me from the joint last week, tells me to follow your guy for a couple days. Next thing I know, the Svenski boys show up on my boat and tell me my cousin—the Weasel, that's what people call him—they say the Weasel's a dead man and if I plan to outlive him, I should keep them posted on everything he asks me to do. Tell you the truth, I didn't see the harm. Ronnie—that's my cousin, the Weasel—he didn't say *why* I was following your boyfriend, he just says watch where the guy goes, who he meets. It was the Svenskis filled me in on this merchandise Ronnie's ripped off from the boss. They told me more than I told them, so it's not like I ratted anyone out."

"So, the, uh, Swedish guys? They drove up to Rio Pescado and—"

"Yeah, it's hours later, I've spent the whole goddamn morning in that loony bin, scared to get outta the car practically, what with half the loonies having the run of the place—you'd think they'd keep them on a tighter leash. So anyway, the Svens call me on the cell phone to say they're there, what's our guy look like? Then a long time later they call back, say they got him, only he doesn't have the goods. I meet them down the road, come to find out that when they said 'they got him' what they meant was, they *whacked* him. Only it's the wrong guy. Right sweatshirt, wrong guy."

"MIT," I whispered, closing my eyes. The sweatshirt was Doc's. Stevie must have found it when Doc changed out of his clothes into the scrub suit. "Oh, God," I said. "Dead over a sweatshirt."

"No, dead because when the Svens found him wandering around and told him to stop and hand over the goods, he got in their face and yelled, 'I'm not giving it to you and you can't make me!' or some goddamn thing and then took off running, like a goddamn lunatic. Can't blame the Svenskis," Carmine said, shrugging. "What was he acting so crazy for?"

"For God's sake," I hissed. "It's a *mental* hospital."

"Well, what do you want, they're foreigners. Speaking of which—" He picked up his cell phone from beside his plate, punched in numbers. I began to shiver, struck by the knowledge, it was to have been Doc, dead on that dirt road.

"It's me," he said. "She's here, we're doing the deal." There was a pause while Carmine rolled his eyes, then did the universal "jerking off" motion with his free hand. "What'd you do, tap into his cell phone? All right, but you're barking up the wrong tree. Call me later."

"The 'Svenskis'?" I asked.

He chuckled. "You'll never guess where they're headed. Goddamn graveyard. Seems your boyfriend and some other bozo are about to dig something up."

chapter twenty-nine

In the movies, when people dash out of restaurants they either ignore the check or toss some loose bills on the table without a glance at the denomination. In the movies nobody stops these people.

Fortunately, this wasn't a movie. I was halfway out the front door when the waitress grabbed Carmine, hard on my heels. "Dude! Going somewhere?"

That slowed him, but it wouldn't be for long, I knew. I pushed past a group of incoming cross-dressers and out onto the sidewalk. Then I stopped.

There was little chance that Joey would be there. From Phig's car I'd called both her home and her cell phone begging her to meet me, but Joey could go days without checking messages. Now what? How to get to that cemetery before the Nordic Mafiosi? And how to lose Carmine? I could hear him behind me, yelling at someone to get out of his way.

The deli had pay phones inside. I'd run around the back, call a cab—

A white Porsche pulled up, brakes squealing. A red-jacketed valet parker jumped out and held open the door. "Angel" was embroidered on his lapel. A sign if I ever saw one. I hurried around the car and started to get in.

A female voice yelled, "HEY! What the hell—"

"Okay, okay." I jumped out. "Sorry, looks just like mine."

"Looks just like grand theft auto. Bitch." A caftaned woman barreled over and shoved me aside, throwing me off balance. I tottered and saw Carmine, on the sidewalk.

"What's the deal?" he yelled. "Is that your friend? She got the goods?"

"No! Yes!" I regained balance on my three-inch Miu Mius, and stumbled over to meet him. "The deal is, my friend's not here, I expect she's fallen asleep, she has occasional narcoleptic episodes—oh!"

Carmine had his beefy hands on me, squeezing the life out of my upper arms. He shook me in little bursts that punctuated his words. "*Look!* I've had *enough* of this shit. You fork it over this *minute,* or I'll ram your fucking *head* into—"

"DUDE. Your credit card." The waitress appeared alongside him, flanked by a burly busboy. "Sign the receipt. I wrapped your pastrami."

With a burst of profanity, Carmine relaxed his grip. I pulled away, to hobble somewhere, anywhere, when another car pulled up in front of me, brakes squealing.

It was an old silver Saab, with Joey inside.

I opened the passenger door and was pushed aside by Carmine. He proceeded to ransack the car. A takeout cup flew out onto the sidewalk, followed by a book and newpapers. A metal cage the size of a large mailbox came next, one I knew intimately. It bounced off the sidewalk and into the street, right in the path of traffic.

Inside, something moved. Something white. Furry.

Margaret.

Part of me stopped to wonder how Joey came to be baby-sitting the ferret, but the rest of me jumped into the street, hand raised like a traffic cop, and grabbed the cage as a honking car swerved to avoid it. Adrenaline pumping, I ran back to the curb and, without thinking twice, kicked Carmine in the back of the knee with my Miu Miu, as hard as I could. "You jerk!" I yelled.

Carmine turned. One look at his face, and I knew I'd acted rashly. I backed up fast. "Angel," I cried, and then in Spanish, *"An-hel,"* and then in English, "Assault! Help! Grand theft auto!"

Red-jacketed valet guys materialized. Carmine swore and turned back to the Saab, but now Joey was standing outside the driver's door, a gun in both hands, pointing at him over the hood.

"Stop right there," she said.

WE RACED WEST on Santa Monica Boulevard. Cell phone stuck to my ear I stroked Margaret, who lounged in my lap like Cleopatra, unfazed by her brush with death. "Ventura County Sheriff's Department, please hold," a voice said.

I glanced at Joey. Her pale skin was actually white with concentration, as she ruthlessly passed cars. "You were so professional, just like an episode of *Gun Girl.* Yes, hello," I said to the phone. "Officer Dambronski, please."

"Dambronski's gone for the night," the voice said. "You want Officer Skeel?"

"No, I have to talk to Dambronski; it's about the Rio Pescado shooting."

"Oh, for that you want Sergeant Hakie, try back tomorrow morn—"

"Dambronski!" I yelled. "I want Dambronski. Listen to me. His informant's about to be murdered by his suspect unless I reach Dambronski in the next five minutes."

The voice wouldn't give me a home phone, but agreed to take Joey's cellular number, and suggested I call 911 if this was a real emergency. I hung up and clutched Margaret.

Joey reached over and rubbed the back of my neck. "We'll be there in ten minutes. If Dambronski doesn't get back to us in five, we'll call 911."

"We can't. Cops will rush in and arrest P.B. for grave robbing, or trespassing, and he'll end up in jail, and that's if he's lucky, if he doesn't freak out and put up a fight. I know what can happen; I won't send in any cop I can't talk to first."

"All right, calm down," Joey said, and sped up. "Maybe we'll be the first ones at this rendezvous and we can intercept our guys."

Six minutes later we reached the graveyard.

I LEFT JOEY at the corner of Wilshire and Glendon, in the shadows of a huge office building, armed with her cell phone and her gun, and continued into the alley until I came to a sign. It was gray marble, like a headstone, with an arrow pointing the way to:

PIERCE BROTHERS
WESTWOOD VILLAGE
MEMORIAL PARK & MORTUARY

I followed the arrow. The lights of Wilshire faded with each click of my heels on the brick walkway, and my heart filled with dread, but I told myself this shouldn't be any scarier than the night at Rio Pescado. This was civilized Westwood, and with luck, all the dead bodies would be underground.

My tight dress dictated a short stride and slow pace. I moved past a guard station, dark and apparently empty, to the cemetery itself, a little jewel of a park protected by a heavy iron fence.

Now what? I wondered, and shivered as I stared through the gate. The thought of going into that near darkness appalled me, and seemed insane besides, even in a day filled with insane acts. I squinted. Nothing stirred but trees. Surely this was a wild-goose chase. Surely it made more sense to return to Joey in the alley, or to Margaret in the car, and wait for—something. It was so silent here. Silent as the grave, Ruta would say.

But then, how much noise did digging up ashes make?

If there was even a chance my brother was in there, I had to go in too. And fast. If the mob was in pursuit, every moment counted.

The wrought iron fence looked unassailable for anyone but a pole-vaulter. Vertical bars, eight feet high, were pointed at the top and joined by a horizontal bar well above my head. On the other hand, I'd done gymnastics. It had been in the eighth grade, it's true, but that had to count for something.

I slipped my high heels through the fence. Then I hiked my skirt up my thighs to give me freedom of movement. I jumped. I wrapped my hands around cold steel high up, above the horizontal bar. I didn't have the upper-body strength to just hoist, nor could I get any kind of real swing going to raise my legs by sheer momentum. In one attempt, my left foot kicked the concrete wall adjoining the fence, making contact with an electrical outlet box. I yelped in pain, then realized I'd found a foothold.

I got to within inches from the top of the fence, but getting to the other side required nerve I didn't seem to possess. I clung to the bars and considered the alternative: staying frozen in place until the sun came up and exposed me there, hanging like a monkey with my skirt bunched up around my waist.

I unclenched my right fist and reached for a spike.

A thin trickle of blood appeared on my forearm, but I felt no pain and kept going, another hand, a foot, another foot and with one hoist I was suspended over the fence like a Flying Wallenda, looking straight down. Then I was over. One hand lost its grip but the other held on to the spike until momentum and the weight of my body took over and then I was sliding down the rough wrought iron.

For a long moment I lay on the gravel inside the fence and stared at the sky, considerably shaken. An inventory of body parts showed a need for Band-Aids, but no broken bones, so I picked myself up, collected my shoes, and looked around.

As cemeteries go, this one was tiny. A gravel road circled a grassy section the approximate size of Saul and Elaine's tennis court. Beyond that was a mortuary. The lighting was subliminal, just enough to give a sense of the layout of the place and verify there was nobody on the lawn who didn't have a headstone on top of them. Still, I did not go bounding across the grass. Westwood Village Memorial could call itself a park all night long, but in fact it was a working burial ground, and I was raised not to step on graves. Besides, it was too exposed. I decided to search the perimeter.

I headed right, to the western edge, but I'd taken just two steps when I heard the crunch of gravel and the sound of a match being struck.

I froze.

Twenty feet ahead a cigarette was lit, illuminating a widow's peak, rapidly becoming a staple in my nightmares. He spoke, the words indistinct, but the cadence Swedish. The other voice uttered a single, harsh syllable, and there was silence.

I backed up, then headed the opposite way, no thought in my head but to get as far away as possible from Tor/Olof. Stones and twigs attacked my bare feet, and at the northern edge of the park, I stumbled into an alcove and crouched.

There was no sound but my own labored breathing. They weren't following me.

Where was I? Around me stretched an expanse of marble, more alcoves housing hundreds of engraved nameplates on metal rectangles: the cremated, spending eternity in safe-deposit boxes. I was about to move on when I heard a rustling ahead.

I held my breath and scanned the darkness. It couldn't be Olof and Tor, they were behind me. Carmine? He could hardly have reached the cemetery before me, let alone scaled that medieval fence. Security guard? P.B.? Squirrels?

Indecision tortured me. I rose slowly, and bumped into a profusion of flowers surrounding a particular metal rectangle. Someone newly shelved? I wondered, and glanced at the nameplate: Marilyn Monroe. Not much there in the way of inspiration. Bruce Lee, now, or Errol Flynn—*that* might give me the courage to—

Another sound, this time from behind, decided for me. I ran.

I raced past the vaults toward the southern edge of the park at a full sprint. I didn't even bother to stay low, just kept on the grass and tried not to hit any trees.

WHUMP.

I went down hard. Something heavy landed on top of me. A hand clamped itself over my mouth and most of my nose. I struggled and tried to scream.

"Wollie, stop it. It's me," a voice whispered in my ear. Doc.

My whole body sagged in relief. "Hey," I whispered back. "Where's P.B.?"

"Over there. He's okay."

Doc showed no signs of getting off me, which suited me fine. I lay under him, catching my breath, then said, "Olof and Tor are here, they—"

"Where?" Doc rose abruptly and pulled me into a sitting position.

"Over by the entrance gate a minute ago, but I think they're following me."

Doc looked toward the vaults. "Come on," he said, and led me deeper into the darkness. There was P.B., hunched over black earth.

I threw my arms around him. "Thank God," I breathed. "Let's get out of here."

My brother did not respond. I saw aluminum foil covering his ears, but this wasn't a hearing issue. He was going to be difficult.

"P.B.," Doc said, "there are men coming and if they see what you've got, they'll take it from you."

P.B. rose. He clutched something under his arm, football-style, and stood like a quarterback awaiting the hike. Doc pointed west, toward the mortuary. P.B. nodded and took off at a run. The two of us followed.

Halfway there, a cell phone rang.

Doc swore, stopped, and moved to the shelter of a tree. P.B. and I stopped and joined him. "Behind the Avco Cinema," Doc said. "Bring backup. You can arrest these guys, they just robbed a grave."

"Dambronski?" I asked, when he'd hung up. "Heck of a time to—"

A whirring sounded in my ear. Something snapped against the tree trunk to my left, splintering the wood. I stared at it and wondered what sort of natural phenomenon could account for that, when Doc pulled me so hard I thought a shoulder was being dislocated. "Run, dammit, it's a goddamn bullet." He shoved me in the direction P.B. was already heading.

Who'd shoot a tree? I wondered, but no sooner had the question formed than the answer occurred. I stumbled. Doc caught me around the rib cage and half dragged me past the mortuary. *Run, don't think; run, don't think,* I said to myself over and over, but a thought broke through anyway. How were we going to get over the fence?

We didn't reach the fence. The western edge of the cemetery turned out to be a wall, a small wall, cinder block, four feet tall, a wall a great-grandmother could negotiate. The three of us tumbled over, onto the rough surface of a Westwood parking lot.

chapter thirty

"Keep moving," Doc ordered. "Out to the street. Hurry."

I gasped as something imbedded itself in my foot. "I can't hurry, my feet are—"

"Jesus, where are your shoes? Never mind." Doc pointed to a vehicle parked against the wall. "Get behind that Jeep. Go."

With their help, I made it to the far side of the Jeep and collapsed, then pulled from the bottom of my foot a splinter the length of a golf tee. My hand shook badly.

Doc said, "I don't think they're following, but you can't stay here. Can you make it to the street? P.B. knows where the car is."

"Why, where will you be?"

"I'll wait for Dambronski. These guys aren't getting away again— it's attempted murder now, with a bullet in a tree as evidence, and if it's the gun they used on Stevie, we're home free."

Attempted murder. The term, stark and unequivocal, penetrated my brain in a way the bullet had not. I went cold and dizzy and wondered if I was about to faint, or whatever it is people do after near-death experiences. My breath came in pants, like a dog's, and I grabbed onto the Jeep's bumper. From far away I heard Doc say my name.

Then came the scream of a siren, jerking me out of wherever I was heading. I reached for P.B. My brother does not react well to sirens, and in fact was already rocking side to side, like a metronome. I covered his body with mine. It didn't stop him, but it steadied me and we rocked together.

More sirens joined the first, like dogs howling in the canyons.

Two minutes later, Olof and Tor bounded over the wall and headed our way. They came fast.

The big one had his gun; I caught a glimpse of it before we sank behind the Jeep. Doc put a hand on my back as I clutched P.B. and crouched tighter against the tire.

Olof and Tor passed two feet from the Jeep's rear bumper and kept going, one pair of rubber sandals, one pair of Birkenstocks pounding the pavement.

The three of us moved clockwise around the Jeep to stay hidden from their view, wedged between the front fender and the cemetery wall. "Shit." Doc peered around the tire. "There's the Alfa Romeo—they're outta here."

I grabbed his T-shirt. "Who cares? Let them go."

He resisted for a moment, then squeezed himself alongside me. Sandwiched between him and my brother, I waited to hear the Alfa Romeo drive off. It didn't. The engine tried to start, but wouldn't turn over. Doc and I peeked around to see the widow's peak exit the passenger side to check under the hood.

For the first time all night, P.B. spoke.

"I know them."

He stood and looked over my shoulder. Before I could react, he shouted, "I know you, I know who you are!" and stepped in front of me, out into the open, the object he carried held aloft like a talisman.

Doc and I came to our senses at the same moment, jumped up, and knocked into each other. I pushed my way around him, frantic to grab my brother.

"Assassins!" P.B. yelled, as I caught his shoulder. "I saw you shoot him—I saw!"

The Swede under the hood had straightened up. He called out a single word. The driver's door opened.

P.B.'s arms were raised like an avenging angel. I got him around the waist and did my best to pull him backward, when a bullet whizzed by my ear.

Doc grabbed me and I lost my hold on my brother. I saw the bigger Swede in front of the car, and the glint of his gun in the overhead light. There was a flash and a popping sound and P.B. fell to the ground. I heard yelling—it might have been me—as I threw myself onto my brother's body.

Doc pushed me aside and took P.B.'s shoulders. I got his lower body, and we hauled him to shelter around the front of the Jeep. Another pop was followed by a clink and then the slow shattering of glass from the Jeep's side window.

P.B. moved.

He shook his head, sat up, and reached behind him for a piece of aluminum foil, fallen from his ear.

Another pop hit the Jeep's front tire, and I knew we weren't going to make it, not all of us, maybe none of us, when from behind us came a shout, lovely as a poem.

"Police. Freeze!"

I froze.

Doc did not. He pulled me around to face him and said, "Get out of here, right now. You and P.B. Over the wall. Go."

I glanced at the wall, three feet behind us. We could do it. The Jeep would block us from view of the cops for thirty seconds, maybe more, depending on how fast they moved across the parking lot. If the Swedes didn't shoot us first, we could make it. But I couldn't move.

"Go." Doc gave me a shove. P.B., fully alert now, took my hand and with surprising strength pulled me toward the wall.

We tumbled over it, back into the cemetery, and hit the grass hard.

"Drop your weapon!" we heard from the parking lot. There was a long, dreadful silence, then a barrage of gunfire so endless it could only mean one thing. I curled into a ball, eyes squeezed shut, held on to my brother, and prayed for it to stop.

It stopped.

From above came blinding lights and the chop-chop sound of a helicopter. P.B. pulled me farther into the shadows, and we heard a megaphoned voice say, "You behind the Jeep. Come out with your hands up."

Oh God, *Doc,* I thought. Sirens sounded from another direction, came close, and cut off. Car doors slammed and more footsteps crunched across the gravel, accompanied by the static of radios. Red lights flashed, strobe-style, and voices barked out orders. "Fall to the ground!" and "Down on your knees!" and then "Cross your legs behind you."

Finally, through the cacophony of sounds I heard Doc. His words were muffled, and I pictured him on his stomach with someone's heavy shoe on his back. "Okay, okay," he called out. "Lemme just ask—is one of you guys Dambronski?"

Out of the chaos came a voice. "Yeah, I'm Dambronski."

"Thank God," Doc said. I could almost see him smile.

chapter thirty-one

I glanced out the back window of Joey's Saab every few minutes, until I was sure no one tailed us, not cops, not Carmine, not the Weasel. Finally I noticed Margaret, on the backseat with P.B. She was gnawing matter-of-factly on a clump of wires. I looked at Joey, driving fast, as usual, and asked what they were.

"Spark plug wires," she said. "From the Alfa Romeo. I figured I'd just—"

My brother screamed.

"What?" I gasped. "What is it, P.B.?"

He couldn't speak. He stared at the metal container he'd carried with him all night, then pressed it to him as if to stanch a wound. He rocked side to side, as he'd done earlier, moaning.

I unbuckled my seat belt and climbed into the back. "What's the problem—this urn? Can I look at it?"

Gently I pried it from him; he put up little resistance. The vessel was made of tin, useful yet artsy, a sort of pre-Columbian kitchen canister. It seemed a likely place to store human ashes, but was so lightweight it couldn't contain much of anything. Then I saw why.

Halfway up the base, nearly obscured by the design, was a hole the size of a bullet. A second hole went out the other side. Whoever had inhabited the canister—whether Stevie or some anonymous soul—was now pretty much gone with the wind.

Pretty much, but not entirely. When I shook it, I heard residue inside. "He's still here, P.B.," I said. "Maybe not all of him, but part of him. Maybe the best part. And wherever the rest of him landed, at least you did what he asked when he spoke to you through the sand. You liberated Stevie from . . . where he was. What's left in here, we'll scatter on the beach." How close the bullet had come to hitting P.B., I couldn't even think about. I touched his hair and dislodged a clump of dirt. "You did well," I said. "You were a good friend to him."

I handed him the canister. He clutched it to his chest, covering the holes. The rocking stopped, but his shoulders, pressing through his thin shirt, moved convulsively.

All the way to Zuma Beach, I watched him cry.

WHATEVER ROMANTIC IMAGE I might've had of scattering someone's ashes over the sea was soon squelched. There just wasn't enough of Stevie, and the wind blew the wrong way. We stopped some distance from the roaring surf. P.B. closed his eyes and lifted his face to the sky. He stayed that way long enough for me to realize how profoundly cold I was, then he knelt, uncorked the canister, and overturned it. A small amount of gray ash poured out and scuttled over the rocks and sand. I said a silent apology to Stevie's family, who might object to his relocation.

P.B. handed me the canister and got down on his stomach, ear pressed to the ground. His blond hair rippled in the wind, but his aluminum foil held firm. Finally he nodded, stood, and wiped his hands on his shirt.

He removed the aluminum foil first from one ear, then the other, then pried pieces out of his teeth. When that was done, he turned away and began walking back toward the highway. I followed. At the first trash can, he tossed the foil. He took the canister from me and threw it in too, as though it were no more interesting than an already-read *L.A. Times.*

Then he turned to me and stared, as though he just now figured out who I was. When he'd looked me over, head to foot, he sat down next to the trash can and pulled off his running shoes.

"Jeez, Wollie, you are so crazy." He handed me the shoes. "You can't go around barefoot. It's not safe."

DOC WAS SITTING on the front steps of my apartment building when Joey dropped me off. I stopped on the sidewalk and we looked at each other without speaking. I held Margaret's crate in my arms. The night air had a strange quality, calm, almost warm.

"The Swedes?" I asked, breaking the silence.

"Tor's headed for arraignment. The other one's dead. Olof. Cops shot him in the parking lot."

I nodded. It wasn't pleasant, to think of all those bullets I'd heard, landing in someone's body. But it was a relief.

"P.B.?" Doc asked.

"He wanted to go home. To the hospital, I mean. When I told him it was too early, he decided to visit Uncle Theo. Who was perfectly happy to be awakened at three A.M. He'll find P.B. a ride back to Rio Pescado tomorrow. Today," I amended.

"And you came here. The last place you should be. Tempting fate, aren't you?"

By "fate" I figured he meant Carmine or the Weasel, but I was too weary to get into it with him. At 9 A.M., one way or another, I was opening my shop, but I said only, "There is no fate worse than spending another hour in this dress."

"Speaking of which, your shoes are still at the cemetery. That's a problem."

"Actually," I said, "it's a tragedy. They're Miu Miu. Seventy-five percent off, which will never happen again in this lifetime. But I think I left them in front of Marilyn Monroe, so maybe the police will think they're an offering."

The mention of crime scenes reminded me what shape my apartment was in. "You know what?" I said. "Since I've got you here to disarm the alarm, I'd rather go to the shop. There's a bath-tub in the back room I want to soak in."

"Can't stay away from that place, can you?" he said, but he came down the steps and started toward the alley. "And you kept the date with Carmine, after swearing—"

"I didn't swear anything, and it's lucky for you I did keep that date, because that's how I found out that Olof and Tor were fol-lowing you. And what about you, telling me you were taking my brother to the movies, and taking him grave robbing instead?"

"I said we were going to the Avco. You knew it was a theater; you assumed the movie part."

"Pure rationalization," I said.

I expected some response, but we continued in silence, to the front door of the shop. There was something different between us, something missing, but I couldn't quite put my finger on it. Doc punched numbers into a keypad. The keypad flashed and beeped. "Give me a four-digit number," he said, and unlocked the front door.

"Nineteen sixty-eight," I said automatically. "One-nine-six-eight."

"Not your birthday, is it?"

"Nope," I said, and realized what was missing: the infatuation I'd felt for the last six days. The night's events had knocked it all out of me. I was crush-free. Liberated. "Hey, Doc," I said, "you know what I'd like? I'd like us to start over, with complete honesty. Straightforwardness. No lies of omission, no ambiguity, no—"

"Hold on." He handed me Margaret's cage, took out his Swiss Army knife, and tightened the keypad. "Punch in the code, one-nine-six-eight. Then hit this key to arm the system, or this one to disarm. If you press these two simultaneously, it's a panic button, and they'll sound an immediate alarm. Got it?"

"Yeah, I got it. Did you hear what I just said?"

He took back Margaret's cage. "Set the alarm and lock up. I want to see you do it."

I complied. When I finished, he set the cage on the counter and turned to me. "Yes. I heard what you said. You want honesty." He stepped in closer, put his hands on my waist, and pulled me to him. Then he kissed me.

It was straightforward and unambiguous. It was neither brief nor gentle, nothing like any previous kiss. I kissed him back like I'd been doing it my whole life.

A minute later, maybe two, we stopped. We drew apart a little, stared at each other without blinking, then went back to kissing.

Another minute passed, then Doc took me by the hand and led me to the back room. Once inside, he turned and pressed me against the wall, and kissed me again. I heard the sound of a dead bolt and turned my head to see him lock us in. "Where did *that* come from?" I asked, wondering how many other security measures he'd installed in my life that afternoon. By way of response, he led me across the room to the red velvet sofa. He lay down on it, looked up at me, and drew me toward him.

I got one knee on the sofa cushion, then stopped. This was it. This was what I'd wanted since the moment I saw him in the elevator at Rio Pescado. Several dozen thoughts zigzagged through my head, from *What about safe sex?* to *When did I last shower?* but what came out of my mouth was "You're married."

His expression changed. The moment was lost. I bit my lip and wished for some rewind button to hit that would put the words back in my mouth.

"It's over," he said.

My heart thumped. What was over, his marriage? Or us? His marriage, surely. I wanted clarification but I couldn't seem to formulate the words just at the moment.

It seemed he could read my thoughts, because a smile started at the corner of his mouth and worked its way to the corners of his eyes. I smiled back.

"God, I love looking at you," he said. His hand reached up and snaked around my neck and drew me down. My heart beat faster. I slid lower.

Some vague thought of herpes entered my consciousness and wafted away again. That's what that drug, valacyclovir, was for. Dr. Cookie had said so herself, and if I couldn't trust Dr. Cookie, what was the world coming to?

I got both elbows on the sofa before I stopped again.

"In the interest of honesty," I said, "I think I should explain something. I'm not a call girl."

"Good," he said. "Because I wasn't planning to pay you."

I CAN'T SAY what woke me. It was an hour later, maybe two.

Across the room, on my drafting table, the high-intensity lamp burned like a candle.

I glanced at Doc next to me. The sofa was unfolded now into a sofa bed and we shared the blanket. He breathed steadily, undisturbed by whatever woke me, his dark growth of beard in stark

contrast to his sleep expression, conferring on him a ravaged inno-
cence. Reluctantly, I extricated my leg from under his. I picked up
an afghan from the floor, wrapped it around myself, and tiptoed
out to the front of the shop.

Margaret was gone.

In her place, on the front counter, was my computer screen,
turned to face me.

I approached the screen slowly. It hit me that if Doc hadn't
dead-bolted the door to the back room, we'd have been as vulnerable as the shop floor had apparently been. But why hadn't the
alarm worked?

On the screen was a message. "Wanna see what I do to rats, look
in the alley. You know what I want. I'll be back for it tonight. Cute
hamster."

Oh, Margaret, Margaret, I thought, and my heart constricted with
fear for the little ferret. It occurred to me I was still asleep, actually
sleepwalking, because I had no desire to see any rats, in any condition, yet here were my feet propelling me to the front door of
their own volition.

The door was unlocked, and just the slightest bit ajar.

I pulled it open and looked around. Nothing.

I wrapped the afghan tightly around me and went through the
walkway into the alley. Then I stopped.

Carmine lay on the ground, his face unnaturally white. Something dark lay across his neck. The sky was just beginning to
lighten, and I stayed focused on his neck in strange fascination until my eyes adjusted and I saw exactly what it was.

Blood. His throat was cut.

chapter thirty-two

I did not scream, but sound may have come out of me, because at some point, there was Doc. He moved me aside and took a long look at the body in the alley. Then he led me back into the shop, and folded his arms around me.

"It's Carmine," I said. "The door was open, and there was a note and Margaret's gone and it was supposed to be a rat, but it was Carmine, with blood all—"

"Okay, it's okay," Doc said. "It'll be all right. We'll call 911 in a minute. You need to put on clothes."

I nodded, and started for the back room, still feeling like a sleep-walker. I stared, unseeing, into one of the metal lockers against the far wall, my afghan clutched around me. Doc joined me, pulled some sweats out of the locker, and led me to the sofa bed.

"Get dressed," he said, then picked up his wallet from the floor and extracted a business card. He was practically naked himself. He pulled the cell phone out of his unzipped jeans, then sat down next to me as I worked myself into a pair of gray sweatpants. "Did you touch anything out there? The doorknob, anything—?"

I shook my head. "I don't know. Maybe. The door was open, I—"

"It doesn't matter. Just tell the cops—"

"Cops?" I snapped to attention. "I can't talk to cops!"

"You have to. There's a dead body on your doorstep."

"But I can't—"

"Listen to me. Just tell them the truth. We slept in the shop because of the break-in at your apartment. Before that, while I was at the precinct answering questions, you were out with your best friend Joey. Leave P.B. out of it. And don't mention the graveyard. You with me?" He waited for my nod, then went on. "You went to the Beverly Wilshire for dinner with Whatsisname and then afterward—shit, did anyone see you meet Carmine last night, anyone who might remember?"

I pulled a sweatshirt over my head. "The entire night shift at Jerry's Deli."

"All right, you'll have to tell them about that. Tell it all, just leave out P.B., and don't volunteer that you were at Rio Pescado on Friday. Can you remember that?"

"What about the Weasel and the burglary and the diamond—"

"Everything; it'll match what I told them. You've got nothing to hide—you're mixed up with these guys because they're after me and I'm living here with you."

"What happens to Margaret?" I cringed to think of the ferret, left in her cage on the counter while we'd dead-bolted ourselves in the back room.

He tightened his lips. "I don't know. Put this away somewhere." He handed me my dirt-encrusted dress and scanned the room. Then he punched numbers into his phone and asked for a Lieutenant

Fondo. What happened to Dambronski? I wondered dully, then realized that this had all grown bigger than the murder of a mental patient in Ventura County. Fondo must be LAPD. Another of Doc's new best friends.

I stowed the red dress in the locker. Doc left a message on Fondo's voice mail, then dialed 911. He explained the situation calmly, his eyes on me. As I moved toward him, he zeroed in on my neck. "Is that dried blood?" he asked when he hung up.

We headed for the mirror in the bathroom. I wiped dirt from my forehead as Doc applied rubbing alcohol to a cut under my ear. It was not my best morning. Still, when I considered the cemetery, the fence I'd thrown myself over, gravel I'd hurled myself onto, splinters I'd impaled myself with, I wasn't doing so badly.

"Ouch." I glanced at him in the mirror. "It's worse under my clothes. I hope they don't strip-search me."

He lifted my sweatshirt up to my rib cage, revealing bruises and scrapes on my abdomen. His eyes met mine in the mirror. "I didn't notice this last night."

I blushed. "It was dark."

He pulled the sweatshirt back down and held me against him, my back against his front. His chest felt warm and I realized how cold I was. We breathed together. Then he said, "The cops will want to know how this guy broke in. I'd like to know myself. Even if he was familiar with this particular security system, he'd still have to guess the code."

"That would be a long shot, wouldn't it?" I asked.

"Would it? Is there any significance to—what was it?—one-nine-six-eight?"

I closed my eyes.

"What?" he asked.

"It's the title of my Personals ad," I said, "and the last four digits of my phone number, the one that's used for the Dating Project."

"What are you talking about, what kind of ad?"

"The Personals." I turned to face him. "We run an ad that says, 'Where Were You in 1968?' If you call, you get a machine that says, 'So, where *were* you in 1968?' It's a conversation starter." He stared, conspicuously silent. "It doesn't always work," I added.

"How many?" he said slowly. "How many men associate you with 1968?"

I looked away again. "Forty-two—"

"What?!"

"—guys called the number, but only thirty-six were on the level, thirty-two of whom showed up here for a preliminary interview. Of those, I've met and/or actually dated twenty-six. Twenty-seven," I amended, remembering Phig.

"Jesus." He walked out of the bathroom.

I followed. "It's still a long shot. Look: Carmine said Olof and Tor had you bugged, your cell phone or something. If they could do that, couldn't the Weasel? Isn't that a more likely scenario?"

He turned on me. "I was bugged? And you didn't mention it?"

"When did I have the chance? Between bodies? Between gunshots? And are you sure you installed the alarm correctly? I didn't see any instruction manual and—"

A stunned look came over his face. He turned and headed to the front of the shop.

"Now what?" I said, following.

"My Swiss Army knife." He searched the counter, then checked his pockets. "It was here, next to Margaret's cage." In a flash, he was out the front door.

"So what?" I followed him into the alley, the last place I wanted to be.

"It's got my prints on it." We reached the lump that was Carmine, and I averted my eyes. Doc said, "Look around for it, would you?"

My stomach lurched. "But—don't touch him, for heaven's sake!"

In spite of myself, I glanced at Doc as he squatted next to the beefy corpse.

He searched the ground. "It could be a setup. My knife could be in his back."

"His back? But it's his front that was stabbed, his throat." Did he expect me to help roll Carmine over? And remain conscious? I was about to set him straight on that point when the sound of a voice made us turn.

Two cops stood in the alley entrance.

Their guns were drawn and pointed at us.

BODIES SWARMED THE SHOP. If every cop, medical examiner, and fingerprint technician bought just one piece of merchandise, it would've been my best-selling morning since Valentine's Day. Of course, they weren't interested in greeting cards. They were interested in a few hundred other details, starting with what we'd been doing with the corpse.

After they frisked us, a fairly unpleasant experience, the first cops on the scene took us inside the shop to wait for the homicide team. I stayed with one of them at Condolences/Get Well Soon and tried to regain one or two of my wits, while the partner, a woman, led Doc to the corner table. She was absurdly young, a Girl Scout in a cop uniform. She flashed Doc a toothy and, under the circumstances, I thought, highly inappropriate smile. Funny how a detail like that could irritate me, even with a dead body in my alley, even with my shop being turned into a yellow-taped crime scene.

Eventually, guys in suits showed up. Mine was a Detective Pflug, gruff, rail thin, sporting a floral tie. He walked me through the actions I'd taken since waking, leading me around the forensic team dusting for prints. "Morbid curiosity" was the reason I gave for having gone out to look at Carmine a second time, which may have started Pflug and me off on the wrong foot. He made me look at the body yet again, to verify he was still in the position I'd discovered him in. Carmine looked worse in the full morning light, gray-skinned and huge, like a fallen elephant, and I hoped this was the last I'd see of him, or of any uncoffined corpse in this lifetime.

A woman in an LAPD windbreaker took Pflug aside and conferred with him. He returned with the news that they'd found a Swiss Army knife in the Dumpster, covered with what appeared to be dried blood. "Know anything about that?"

My insides turned to Popsicles. I shrugged. Smiled. "Unh-unh," I said brightly. "So, are we done? Is that it?"

"That's it for here," Pflug replied. "Now we head to the station."

chapter thirty-three

The Hollywood Division police station on North Wilcox, across the street from S.O.S. Bail Bonds and the Wilcox Arms apartments (furnished and unfurnished) was true Hollywood, with gold stars embedded in the sidewalk leading to the entrance. Instead of show biz celebrities, though, these stars commemorated fallen officers.

Pflug herded me through a small lobby with a homey, YMCA feel to it, into a large room humming with activity and an improbably mauve carpet. We marched toward the back, through a maze of desks and bodies, to an equally mauve series of doors.

The interrogation room was a nine-by-twelve-foot box that could have used wallpaper. By hour number three I'd mentally redecorated it in four different themes, complete with cost estimates. The frontrunner was Polynesian.

The good thing about long bureaucratic procedures is that they grind some of the fear out of you. I'd quaked through the first half hour, especially when I realized that there would be no contact with Doc, but then settled in as Pflug and a few others came to question me, offer me coffee, and leave. I was not under arrest, Pflug assured me, and while I did have a right to an attorney, he saw no reason for one. Did I?

No, I responded, particularly as (a) I didn't have an attorney, (b) I couldn't afford one, and (c) I was innocent of anything but getting mixed up with a bad crowd. Upon reflection, it occurred to me that sleeping with a still-married man might be some sort of crime, but I didn't ask for confirmation on that.

Just as Pflug seemed to warm up to me, the worm turned. I recounted how Carmine had more or less assaulted me in front of Jerry's valet parking, when Pflug gave me a ruminative look. "So Carmine was your pimp? Or your john?"

"No! I thought I explained, the Dating Project is not prostitution, it's—"

"True love?"

"Social science."

"So you admit you dated him."

"I didn't *date* him, I—"

Pflug leaned in. "Bullshit. What was your relationship with that dead body?"

I stared. "We had no relationship. Are you accusing me of necrophilia?"

At that, Pflug wrote down my name, went to the door, and handed it to someone outside. "Run a vice check," he said, loud enough so that all forty or so people in the outer office could hear. He shut the door and sat, this time on the table, towering over me. "Tell me something: your boyfriend had no problem with your 'dating'?"

The trick now was to guess how Doc would answer, much like *The Newlywed Game*. I spoke carefully. "He wasn't my boyfriend when the Dating Project started. Even now he's not—anyway, as I keep saying, it's not like there's sex with these guys. Dr. Cookie Lahven—surely you've heard of her, she's syndicated—will back me up on this. They're not even romantic, these dates, they're . . . exhausting. Doc knows that."

Pflug looked down at his notes and frowned. His pager went off. He glanced at it, took out his cell phone, and made a call. This gave me time to wonder if having sex with Doc while participating in scientific research compromised the data. If so, was I perpetrating fraud? Perhaps not, if I reported it promptly to Dr. Cookie, but then, was I kissing my five grand goodbye? The thought made me want to cry.

And what about Doc's theory that any of my dates could have guessed the alarm code? Had I inadvertently dated the Weasel? My mind raced through the last week's worth of men. Dave was my first choice for a murderer, but the timing was wrong—he'd preceded my discovery of the corpse. Who else? Rex, who'd sent the alarm system? Cliff, the Jain enthusiast? Phig? The whole idea was ridiculous.

Pflug snapped shut his cell phone and returned to his notes. "All right: this meeting last night with the victim—did Flynn know about that as well?"

"Who's Flynn?" I asked.

Pflug's well-worn face registered confusion. "Tommy Flynn? Your boyfriend?"

"You mean Doc? I mean—Gomez. Gomez Gomez."

"What are those, nicknames?"

The room grew very quiet. "I'm sorry," I said. "What do you mean?"

He read from his notepad. "Flynn, Thomas, paroled from Tehachapi last week; high school science and math teacher, married, one daughter—"

The room spun around me. "Yes, that's him, but—"

"But you didn't know his name?"

The question hung there, an embarrassment. I closed my eyes.

THE INTERROGATION CONTINUED, and as the hours drew on toward noon, my answers grew sloppier. I couldn't focus. My eyes alternated between the dirty white pegboard wall and the frightful saffron yellow floor, and all I could think about was that I'd fallen in love with someone who'd let me, in the heat of passion, call out, "Gomez Gomez!"

"So from the time you left Jerry's Deli," Pflug was saying, "until the time you got home, around three, four A.M., you were with this friend of yours, this—"

"Joey Rafferty."

"—whose married name and phone number you 'can't recall.' And these places you went—" He referred to his notes. "Brentwood, Zuma, Encino—you just drove around, no reason, the two of you, and no one saw you, not one single person? Because"—Pflug shook his head—"I gotta tell you, this is a goddamn sad excuse for an alibi."

If only you'd leave me alone to phone Joey, I thought, it wouldn't be so sad. I'd let her know what to corroborate and she'd doctor it up. Joey excelled at that.

"If you're covering for Flynn, don't bother," he said, "because he's implicated up to his eyeballs. The knife we found in the Dumpster? His. Maybe it's a jealousy thing, maybe he finds out about you and the deceased getting it on while he's in the joint doing his grand larceny gig. Maybe he gets out and loses his temper and—what?"

I must have jumped, just a little.

"What part of this is news to you? Grand larceny?" Pflug lifted an eyebrow. "Along with his name, did Flynn happen to not mention he ripped off his students to the tune of thousands of bucks? This is a guy who steals from children. This is not a nice guy."

Grand larceny. It seems I'd subconsciously constructed for him some morally defensible felony, like liberating zoo animals, because this truly shocked me. What a fool I was. Dr. Cookie was right: the List was the key to character, and I should have known Doc/Gomez/Flynn had none the minute I saw him in that elevator in those paper slippers and thought to myself, Number eight, Good Shoes.

Pflug watched me. I, in turn, watched the carnations on his tie, which seemed to expand and contract as he breathed. Finally he spoke. "Wollie. My impression of you is: good person, bad liar. Don't make me investigate what you're hiding. Busywork pisses me off. You don't have a vice record, you don't even have parking tickets, but if you don't come clean right now about where you were last night, I'll start a file on you that says perjury, hindering prosecution, and obstructing justice. Is he worth it? Take a minute and ponder that."

I didn't need a minute. I felt sick to my stomach at the thought of Doc/Flynn, but my main concern lay elsewhere. "It's not Flynn that I'm covering for," I said. "It's my brother. That's who Joey and I were with last night. I was hoping to keep him out of this, but if you investigate me, I guess you'll find out about him soon enough." Come clean, I thought, and maybe no one will look very hard at P.B., maybe they won't connect him to the Rio Pescado murder. It was my only shot at protecting him.

Pflug nodded for me to continue.

"He was on an overnight visit from the hospital," I said. "What he likes to do when he's out of the hospital is ride around L.A., so that's what Joey and I did, drove him around. We ended up at my Uncle Theo's for cinnamon toast at three this morning."

Pflug's eyes narrowed. "Why not just tell me this two hours ago?"

"My brother has schizophrenia. He's scared of cops, and not without reason. No offense, but you guys don't have the best track record with the mentally ill."

"Anyone who can verify this?"

I wrote down three numbers. Joey would be savvy enough not to mention the cemetery, and Dr. Charlie and Uncle Theo didn't know about it. "One more thing I want to confess," I said. "The Swiss Army knife? If it says 'To Daddy—Love, Ruby,' it might have my prints on it, because I rescued it the other day from the washing machine."

Pflug shook his head as if I'd disappointed him, as if he knew about Dos and Don'ts number one: Don't Do His Laundry. With a sigh, he left the room.

I thought about being indicted for murder, or accessorizing or grave robbing or some crime I didn't yet know was a crime. I thought about being fired from the Dating Project. I thought about how losing the five grand wouldn't matter anyway, if Mr. Bundt picked today for a shop inspection. I didn't need him to tell me that homicides on company premises violated Welcome! corporation policy. Even if the police let me go, in Mr. Bundt's eyes I would forever be, like the parents of JonBenet Ramsey, under an umbrella of suspicion.

I thought about everything but the man I'd slept with the night before.

Forty minutes later I signed a statement and, to my surprise, was escorted out of the interrogation room, with orders not to leave town. From Pflug's incredibly messy desk I called Fredreeq at Neat Nails Plus.

"Sister, have I been worried about you," she said. "Joey too. We've canceled your date for tonight, and I want you to sleep at my place, but meanwhile, come on over to the salon for a massage—on the house. I'm dying to know the skinny, and I bet you're a prime candidate for aromatherapy. Don't stop at the shop, it'll just upset you. They've reopened the mini-mall, but your place is surrounded by that yellow tape, all locked up."

I was still digesting that piece of unpalatable news as Pflug escorted me to the lobby. There, on a wooden bench, staring up at Wanted posters, sat the second-to-the-last person I wanted to see.

RUBY LOOKED AS miserable as only a badly dressed eleven-year-old can. She gave the impression of having been planted there and left without watering instructions. I couldn't believe that I ever thought she was half Mexican. Looking at her now, it was clear she was Irish as a potato. What was she doing here, anyway?

I considered sneaking out a back entrance, and was engulfed by shame. What would Ruta say? To blame Ruby for her father's sins was—fascism, or something. I pasted on a facsimile of a smile and called, "Ruby?"

She turned. The look she gave me was so pleased that my resentment dissolved. "How ya doing?" I asked. "Hungry?"

She nodded with enthusiasm. I nabbed Pflug before he disappeared back into the bowels of the building and asked him what the story was with Flynn, because I wanted to take his kid to lunch.

"Take her to lunch, dinner, and breakfast, is my suggestion," Pflug said. "I'll find you a ride home—Flynn's not leaving anytime soon. He's on parole, so he's going to answer any questions we have for him, lawyer or no lawyer. If he's arrested, he'll be here a lot longer. I'll let them know you got the kid." He looked over at her and added, "There's a Denny's on Sunset."

Doc's lawyer was here. That explained Ruby's presence; she'd stayed at the lawyer's house last night. I went back to her and mentioned Denny's. By way of response, she pantomimed an object the size of a bread box, which she then petted.

"Margaret?" I asked. I sank onto the bench beside her and fixed my gaze on the white painted wall, at a domestic violence poster. I felt Ruby waiting for an answer. Doubtless there were techniques for breaking bad news to children. They should have a poster in here for that, I thought. I turned to her. "Very early this morning, Margaret was kidnapped. It has to do with a missing diamond. The cops are looking for her. Well, looking for the guy that did it. That's part of why we're all here at the station, answering questions, and—"

I stopped. Ruby's hands pressed against her ears and her eyes scrunched shut. I watched her face go red with the effort not to cry, and I braced myself.

It took her nearly thirty seconds to lose the battle.

WE DROVE THE Rabbit around Hollywood in ever larger concentric circles, but nothing got a response from Ruby, not Denny's or McDonald's or International House of Pancakes. The painful, heaving sobs had given way to a glum silence. Food wasn't much consolation, I knew, but it was all I could think of; she *had* been hungry an hour ago.

"Frozen yogurt?"

She seemed to sit up a little straighter in the passenger seat, which I decided to take as a yes, since I was hungry myself and we were approaching Toppers on Beverly and La Brea.

Toppers had eight different kinds of yogurt. Ruby showed signs of life at cookies 'n cream and I went for peanut butter. As the clerk made change, four Orthodox Jewish schoolboys trooped in behind us. So frozen yogurt was kosher. Was Häagen-Dazs? I considered asking them. Obvious dessert connoisseurs, they also looked knowledgeable about the laws of kashrut, with their side curls and school uniforms and identical books. I listened to them discuss the upcoming school break for Passover.

Passover, I thought suddenly. *Books. Häagen-Dazs.*

No, not Häagen-Dazs at all.

I clutched Ruby's arm. "I know where the diamond is. At least, I know where it was last year at this time. And if we find it, maybe we could trade it for Margaret, maybe we—"

And Ruby was halfway to the door, dragging me with her.

chapter thirty-four

ifereth Israel Synagogue occupied a full block in a residential area south of Westwood, a neighborhood distinguished by lawns so perfect they might have been putting greens. The temple's landscaping was stark and sophisticated, a few sculptured trees in strategically placed pots amid severe shrubbery. No undignified daisies here.

Ruby and I approached the entrance, enormous double doors wrought in wood and metal. "I don't suppose you know what a Haggadah is?" I asked her. "In the Jewish religion, every year on Passover, they have these special dinners called seders. They eat special foods on special plates, and they read the Passover story, from a book called the Haggadah, and the dinner guests read along and—"

We entered a cavernous stone foyer, so massive and echo-filled I stopped talking. We were desperately underdressed for this building. My gray sweats had the advantage of being clean, even if I wasn't, but Ruby's pea green velour shirt was as grimy as her face. When, I wondered, had she last bathed?

The first person we encountered was a daunting man, mid-fifties, with steel wool hair and ice blue eyes and the posture of a five-star general. A yarmulked general. "May I help you?" he asked, in a tone of voice that made it sound unlikely.

"I left something in a Haggadah last Passover. I wonder if I could look for it."

"Are you a member here? I don't believe we've met."

I smiled. "Hard to meet everyone in a synagogue this size. Look, I realize it's an unorthodox—so to speak—request, but it's extremely important." At my side, Ruby nodded. "If you could just point us in the direction of someone who could show us—"

"No."

"Uh—no?"

He gave me a stern look. "In the last week, this synagogue has twice been broken into. I therefore lack the patience I might otherwise have for unorthodox-so-to-speak requests. Good day." He turned and walked away. Ruby nudged me.

"Hold on," I said. "Maybe I should talk to someone else, someone who—"

"I'm the rabbi," he said, without breaking stride.

I grabbed Ruby's arm, ran across the marble floor, and blocked his path. "I could possibly tell you something about those break-ins," I said.

He glared and moved to go around us. Ruby and I stepped closer. "I'm sorry, Rabbi, I lied to you, I've never been in this synagogue before, I'm not even Jewish, but I need to see those Haggadoth. Look, I'll get down on my knees, it may be a gentile kind of gesture, but I'm doing it because that's how desperate I am." I dropped to my knees, and stared at the crease in his pants. I called upon the spirit of Ruta to soften his heart.

When he spoke, there was a tinge of amusement in his voice. "A gentile who knows the plural of 'Haggadah.' Get up, please. We'll talk in my office."

WITH THE EXCEPTION of a few graphic details that Ruby didn't need to hear, I told the whole story, all that I knew, and all I surmised about the diamond. Rabbi Susser sat calmly amid the clutter of his office and listened. "So what this dead convict called 'a box of Häagen-Dazs,' " he summed up, "you believe to be 'a box of Haggadahs.' Or, more correctly, Haggadoth." He stood. "It's conceivable. Follow me, please."

He led us to the synagogue gift shop, empty except for a woman at the counter, writing in a ledger. I resisted the temptation to check out the inventory and focused on her. The rabbi introduced her as Mrs. Gold, which was interesting, as she favored silver. Silver glistened on her lapel, circled her neck, dangled from her earlobes, and bangled her wrist.

"Mrs. Gold," the rabbi explained, "supervised the cleanup after last year's Passover seder. Mrs. Gold, will you recount for us what happened that night?"

She puffed up with importance. "Well, it was unseasonably warm that week, if you remember, so we had the back door open to let some air into the kitchen, and suddenly, in pops a man from the alley, which nearly gives Rose Kaminsky a coronary—Rose had a bypass two years ago." Mrs. Gold smoothed the silver chains on her massive bosom. "Now, this fellow is nicely dressed, not one of our homeless, but quite smelly, which makes us think he's been in the Dumpster, which he tells us he *has* been. He says there are men after him and he asks us to call the police. And while we're waiting for the police to come, what does he do but insist on helping us move the Passover china back into the storeroom. Because it's no job for ladies, he says, which I found refreshing, as anyone would who's married to Abe Gold, who won't so much as take out the trash on garbage night—"

"Mrs. Gold—?"

"Well, Rabbi, you asked me to tell the story, didn't you? So. When the police come, who does our mensch turn out to be?" She paused for effect. "A convicted criminal, turning himself in to start serving his sentence."

"And the Haggadoth," I said, "were they put away with the china?"

Mine was not the hoped-for response. She looked put out. "The what? Well, I don't recall specifically, but—yes, if we'd already collected them from the dining hall at that point, we'd have put them into the storeroom."

"Where in the storeroom would we find them?" the rabbi asked.

"Those? You won't. The new ones we ordered arrived while you were in Israel, and Rabbi Lieberman gave the old ones to the poor."

SAMMY FELDMAN WAS maybe thirty years old. With his tie-dyed T-shirt and Afro hair, he looked more like a devotee of the Grateful Dead than the cantor of a temple, even a small one. He met the three of us—Rabbi Susser had insisted on coming along—at the door of his bungalow, off Barham Boulevard, in the Valley, and ushered us through an incense-scented living room into a fifties-style kitchen, where dried fruit lay on cutting boards around the countertop.

"Yemenite charoset," he said. "Let me just put it away, before the ants get at it. Fig, anyone? Yes, our congregation, Shalom Shalom, or 'Reform Reform,' as we're sometimes called, is the proverbial poor. We're so poor we hold services in an Episcopal preschool. I'm in charge of the communal seder this year, and your hand-me-down Haggadoth are a real score."

"You have the books here?" Rabbi Susser asked.

"Right there." He reached above the refrigerator for a Cutty Sark cardboard box.

Worn strapping tape gave way and the box flaps fell open to reveal a folded piece of the *L.A. Times*. Underneath were dozens of books, hardcover, slightly oversized, dark red. Old. Ruby, the rabbi, and I pulled them out one at a time and piled them on the pink Formica counter, until we got to the bottom of the box. Empty.

I fought back the urge to weep. "There was nothing else in here?"

Sammy grinned. "What, you mean the ring?"

SOTHEBY'S, BEVERLY HILLS, occupied a corner of prime real estate within shouting distance of Tiffany and Cartier. Out front was a large red steel sculpture. Inside was a Berber-carpeted showroom with an exhibit of art made from recycled material such as aluminum cans and plastic grocery bags. Upstairs was the office of J. Carper Field.

"I worked for Sammy's father in the diamond district back east, many years ago. It was my first job." J. Carper Field used a monogrammed handkerchief to polish a pair of tortoiseshell glasses. He replaced them on his nose and smiled at Sammy, Ruby, the rabbi, and me. "My passion began earlier. While my schoolfriends collected baseball cards and G.I. Joes, I collected semiprecious gems."

"Mr. Field," I said, "does Sotheby's have some sort of confidentiality—"

"*Suth*-eby's," he corrected. " 'Uh,' as in 'southern,' not 'ah' as in 'sloth.' I'm speaking to you today not as a representative of Sotheby's, but as an aficionado of historical jewelry. Sammy thought the piece he found might intrigue me."

J. Carper withdrew from his desk drawer a small red box and used his handkerchief to extract the contents, which he proceeded to polish, but not reveal. "Sammy was right. This is special. Not the diamond, which is good, but hardly superb. Not even the silver-work, although it is well done. What distinguishes the ring is its origin. Design, markings, and metal content place it in Germany in the thirties. Note the engraving." He placed the ring upon a square of black suede and slid it across the desk. I glanced at my companions. The rabbi nodded at me. I picked it up.

The ring was feminine in style, ornate, elaborately etched, with an oversized diamond set flatly into silver. I squinted inside. " 'To W, worthy of a crown,' " I read aloud, " 'October 1937.' There's a tiny symbol I can't quite make out—"

J. Carper cleared his throat. "A swastika."

I set the ring back on the desk and folded my hands in my lap.

"The silversmith who signed the piece did a lot of work for the Third Reich," he said. "For Hitler himself, on occasion."

Rabbi Susser indicated the ring. "And 'W'?"

"One hears rumors. History is fifty percent rumor, it's said. It would be unprofessional to repeat the unsubstantiated, so I'll just remind you of some historical facts. In 1937, Wallis Simpson visited Germany with her new husband, Edward, Duke of Windsor. They met with Adolf Hitler. Now, if among the gifts given during that visit there was something of, say, an expensive and personal nature, it's likely that the Duchess of Windsor had the good sense not to broadcast it. The American divorcée was unpopular enough with the British, and the entire visit had become a huge public relations faux pas." He leaned back. "As for the Nazis, while they were known for meticulous records, it takes time and effort to locate such records, those that still exist. Still, one might find it worthwhile. Even rumor can create a market for something like this."

"A market comprised of whom?" I asked.

"Fans of the British royal family, of Wallis Simpson, who had something of a cult following, and of course, devotees of the Third

Reich. With authentication, the price for this could be . . . considerable."

"That's nice," I said, "but we won't be selling it. We're trading it." I reached for the ring, but Rabbi Susser clamped his hand over mine.

"I think not."

"THE POLICE?" I yelled. "What will the police do, give it to charity?"

The argument had grown so heated that J. Carper Field asked us to take it out to the street—in this case, Rodeo Drive. Sammy had taken charge of the red ring box, and I longed to snatch it out of his hands.

The rabbi said, "The police will return it to its rightful owner."

"Its rightful owner," I said, "is a Mafia don, who's not going to care that it's a ransom payment for Ruby's ferret."

"I'm afraid that is not our concern."

I stepped in front of him. "It's my concern."

Rabbi Susser put a hand on Ruby's shoulder and another on mine, and shepherded us forward. "I'm sorry, that was awkwardly said. Ruby, I do not lack compassion for your pet, and I'm very sad for you, but there is a moral responsibility here."

"But is it your moral responsibility?" I said. "That ring just crossed your path, and not even *your* path, your synagogue's path, and—"

"And what is life, Wollie, but that which crosses our path?"

Sammy nodded his agreement. I had an urge to slap him. We came to a stop with a red light at Rodeo and Brighton Way. "Then with all due respect," I said, "it crossed my path first, and it crossed at a bigger intersection, and it ran over a couple of lives—"

Rabbi Susser held up a hand. "People have been harmed because of this and that's unfortunate. But our feelings about that or the provenance of the ring or the character of its current owner are beside the point. The Talmud tells us unequivocally that we may not submit to blackmail."

"What about where the Talmud says that to redeem one life is to redeem the world, because each life is a whole world?" I said.

Rabbi Susser looked surprised. "The Talmud did not refer to ferrets."

"And I do not live by Talmudic authority."

The light changed but I stood my ground. Around me, a camera-carrying tour group surged forward, chattering in a consonant-heavy language. I could hear Ruta clucking from the great beyond, proud of my knowledge of the Talmud, aghast at my effrontery. The rabbi glared, and it was Sammy who answered me. "Since the ring's in my possession, it's kind of a moot point, isn't it? Rabbi, my wife's cousin is a detective in the West L.A. Police Department. He'll know the procedure for returning stolen goods. Would you like me to take care of this?"

The rabbi paused. Perhaps he was reluctant to relinquish responsibility, but perhaps also reluctant to touch something that might have been touched by Adolf Hitler. "Yes," he said finally. "As it's nearly the Sabbath, I need to be on my way. I'll call a cab." He turned to me once more. "The message of Passover is freedom. What we're doing is the right thing to do and it will set you free."

I watched him walk away and wondered if I could, with Ruby's help, physically overpower Sammy Feldman. Or break into his house during the Sabbath, or—

"Tell me something, Ruby—" Sammy said.

I put a protective arm around her. "Ruby doesn't talk much."

"Gave it up for Lent, huh?" He gave her a loopy grin, as she backed away from him. "Sorry, old Hebrew school joke. What I was going to say is, I've got this hole in my pocket I'm always dropping things out of, and—well, would you look at that? Case in point."

The small red ring box hit the sidewalk with a plunk. Ruby pounced on it.

"Maybe you should carry it the rest of the way," Sammy said. "And if you forget to give it back to me, well, I'm sure you'll do the right thing with it."

"Sammy—" I said.

"Come on, girls, light's changing." He led us onto the pavement, swarming with pedestrians from all four corners. "Beverly Hills," he said, shaking his chaotic hair. "They'll ticket you for jaywalking, but you can cross intersections diagonally. Gotta love that. Hey, are you heading up Little Santa Monica? If you drop me at Avenue of the Stars, my wife works at City National, I'll catch a ride home with her."

"Sammy, you're a cantor," I said. "Can you defy Talmudic authority?"

"Well, I'm Reform. We sometimes have problems with authority."

chapter thirty-five

"Thank God," Joey said, when I called her on her cell phone. "I'm at Neat Nails Plus with Fredreeq—where are you calling from?"

"Century City. A bank. A guy named Sammy Feldman has a wife who—"

"Hold on—Fredreeq! It's Wollie!" Joey yelled, straining to be heard over the salon's Friday afternoon rush. Then to me, "Is Ruby with you?"

"Yes, and—"

"Hold on a second."

Phone to my ear, I smiled encouragingly at Ruby, who sat with Sammy and me at the New Accounts desk manned by Sammy's wife. Now that Ruby and I had the diamond, my plan was to return to the shop. I figured the Weasel would eventually turn up there, like a bad penny. Of course, waiting for a knife-wielding sociopath had its drawbacks, not the least of which was, what to do with Ruby? If this were a *Murder, She Wrote* rerun there would be a concerned cop in my utility closet, ready to jump out and make an arrest when the killer showed. This being my life, though, that cop would be Pflug, who seemed as likely to come and hide in my closet as he was to join a Colombian drug cartel. I'd have to provide my own backup. Fredreeq and Joey, naturally.

"Wollie?" the voice on the phone said. "It's me."

It was the last voice I wanted to hear. What was Doc doing at Neat Nails Plus? "How's Ruby?" he asked. "How are you? Tell me you're okay. God, I've worried about you."

How dare he sound so concerned? Nothing I cared to say to Thomas "Gomez Gomez" Flynn could be said in front of his daughter, sitting companionably close. "We're fine," I mumbled.

"Joey says you're in Century City. Let's meet at my lawyer's office—"

"You're not under arrest?"

"Nope. They've picked up the Weasel for Carmine's murder, and Tor's being charged with killing Stevie. This nightmare's just about over."

Except for me. Ms. Heartsick. Ms. Gullible. "And what about Margaret?"

There was a pause. "It doesn't look good for Margaret. I asked the cops to keep an eye out for her when they brought in Ronzare, but I'll have to prepare Ruby for the worst."

I looked at her upturned face, riveted to mine at the mention of her ferret. She showed signs of early-adolescent acne. God, I thought, can't you give this child a break? Into the phone, I said, "Where's your lawyer's office?"

WE WALKED OVER the pedestrian bridge that spanned Avenue of the Stars, toward the setting sun and Century City shopping mall and the high-rise office buildings that contained a quarter of all the lawyers in Los Angeles. Around us, the nine-to-fivers moved at a good clip, in a race with rush hour. Ruby, however, dragged her feet.

"Ruby," I begged, "don't be mad, I don't know what else to do. I didn't anticipate the Weasel's arrest. This changes things, but the good news is your dad's free now and he'll figure out something. I'm going to leave the ring with you, and write a note for him, because I have to go now, and—"

Ruby stopped. She shook her head with considerable force.

"Why not? There's no reason for me to stick around. You need to be with your dad, get him to take you out for a real meal. I have to get back to my shop and try to salvage what's left of my life."

She folded her arms and mashed her chin down onto her chest and moved away from me, not looking where she was headed. I caught her seconds before she plowed into a street vendor planted mid-bridge to sell Easter lilies. She looked up at him, startled, and opened her mouth as if to say "sorry," then stopped herself.

Something tugged at the knot of ignorance that had plagued me for days. The knot loosened and began to unravel.

"Ruby." I turned her to face me. "You probably don't know this, but I was raised Catholic. Not that I go to church now, but I still give up something for Lent every year. This year was Sweet 'N Low. I've never done anything big. Like—a vow of silence."

She gave me a look I couldn't read, and moved to the side of the bridge.

I followed. "I look at the whole give-up-something-for-Lent routine as a way to keep Jesus company for the forty days and forty nights he's in the desert. That's why I do it. But I know that some people do it to atone for their sins."

Ruby kept walking. Her hand skimmed the top of the railing, fingers splayed across the expanse of smooth black steel.

"Other people do it to get their prayers answered, like making a deal with God."

Ruby stopped. She gripped the railing and leaned over it and stared onto the street below. Her hair hung down and hid her face. I moved to her side. "I personally don't believe God works like that, demands payment up front. I believe prayers either get answered—or they don't." I touched her hair. It had the feel of a Brillo pad.

Ruby gave one convulsive sniff that wracked half her body. Something I'd said was hitting home.

"And sometimes," I said softly, "no matter what you do, how hard you pray—they just don't."

I LEFT HER in a plush-carpeted law office, reading *Daily Variety* and making her way through a box of Pepperidge Farm cookies provided by a motherly secretary who greeted her like an old friend. Ruby did not look up when I said goodbye.

In the elevator it occurred to me that the lawyer would be useful if I needed to contact Doc/Gomez/Flynn, who wasn't likely to contact me, not after the pithy note I'd written him. I'd already forgotten the law firm's name. C. Something and Someone, on the seventh floor. I stopped in the lobby to search the building directory, amazed at how many entries said "Attorneys at Law." Saul Meier & Associates, for instance, on the tenth floor. Why did I know that name? Oh, of course: Saul was the Saul of Saul and Elaine's 14th Annual Beverly Hills Hoedown.

My heart thumped. Saul was counsel to Eddie Minardi. Big Eddie. Eddie Digits.

I walked into an empty elevator and pressed 7. I needed to see Ruby again.

· · ·

IT TOOK THE executive secretary eighteen minutes to find Saul, and it took Saul forty-three to find his client, once I stated the exact nature of my business. I was shown to a conference room to wait.

I took out the ring. The facets of the diamond made mirrors, through which I could see the picture window, the long mahogany table, the outsize sunflower arrangement, the high ceiling with its recessed lighting. My pulse raced when I considered what I was doing. At least I'd have the rabbi's blessing. And Ruby's. This time when I'd left her in the offices of Capparelli, Miyazaki & Zeiss, she'd smiled.

"Ms. Shelley." The voice boomed behind me. I slid the ring onto my finger, and closed my fist over the diamond. Then I stood.

Saul Meier looked less genial in a gray suit than he'd looked in a ten-gallon hat. He shook my hand firmly and introduced me to the man alongside him.

Edoardo Minardi could not have been more than five foot four. He did not shake my hand. A cultural thing, maybe, like the scarlet silk handkerchief tip peeking from the breast pocket of his deep blue suit. The handkerchief matched his tie, held by a diamond tie clip. He measured me with a look, then moved to the other side of the huge table, followed by Saul. A wave of aftershave lingered in the air. Saul gestured to me to sit.

I sat.

The three of us maintained a churchlike silence and I realized, with something akin to terror, that I was expected to speak first. I could not.

The Mafia don turned to his lawyer and raised his eyebrows.

This was not helpful. My vocal cords seemed to have fossilized, and I could only stare. Big Eddie sitting, I noted, seemed bigger than Big Eddie standing—all torso and no legs, apparently. For some reason, this gave me courage. I put my fist on the conference table and opened it slowly, as if I were having blood drawn.

"This has been in a synagogue for a year, and in my pocket for an hour."

I had their attention. I twisted the ring off my finger and set it on the polished wood. "Four men have chased me since Saturday. Two are in jail now, and two are dead. I didn't kill them," I added hastily. "What I want is for the two that are left, Tor Ulvskog, and the Wease—uh, Ronald Ronzare—" I amended, remembering he was Big Eddie's relative, "—I want them to know I don't have the ring. They're in police custody, and I don't know how to contact them. Not that they'd believe me."

Big Eddie nodded, a single dip of the chin, and a return to its original position. It was a dignified gesture, the kind you'd expect from the Pope. I wasn't sure if it was a "You got it" kind of nod or a "Please continue" kind of nod. I continued.

"It's also important to me that these guys don't come around looking for retribution, sometime in the future, say after . . . twenty-five years to life." This time Big Eddie's nod was barely perceptible. I slid the ring halfway across the table, next to the sunflower arrangement. Saul glanced at it. Big Eddie did not.

"One last thing," I said. "Mr. Ronzare kidnapped a ferret this morning. Her name is Margaret. If she is alive, I want her back. If she's not—" I felt my bottom lip quiver. I willed it to stop, and then just bit it. "—I'd like to know that."

Saul said, "What is a ferret?"

"A small animal, related to the stoat, or . . . weasel." I pulled a business card from my purse and did a quick sketch on the back. I stood to hand it across the table.

Saul glanced at it and passed it to his client.

Big Eddie turned the card over and read the front before looking at the sketch. His voice, when he spoke, was lyrical. Soothing. "It looks like an anteater."

He put the card in the inner pocket of his beautiful blue suit. Then he stood and nodded once more, that enigmatic nod, and walked around the table.

"Thank you," he said. He stretched out his hand and when I took it, held mine to his lips and kissed it.

chapter thirty-six

I returned to find my shop sealed off with yellow crime scene tape. Ditto the parking lot. The other businesses were open, as Fredreeq had reported, but only to pedestrians. Since parking on Sunset required an act of God, I had no doubt they'd had a dismal sales day and I was in the mini-mall community doghouse.

There was a sign on the shop's front door, a huge smiley face with the words "Back in business in no time!" coming out of its mouth, comic-book-style. Joey's handiwork. This made me want to cry, for reasons I couldn't even identify.

I should be happy, grateful, relieved. The bad guys were in jail, my brother's well-being was restored, and I actually trusted Big Eddie to guarantee our safety. But the adrenaline rush brought on by the diamond had subsided and left me feeling as zippy as a bag of dirty laundry. I drove around the block to my apartment and realized that while life was not materially different from the way it had been a week earlier, there was a yawning emptiness that hadn't been there before.

I walked through my apartment building and out into the alley.

The spot where Carmine's corpse had lain was marked by more crime scene tape, and the freight door was padlocked, as the front door had been. But there was one more entrance. I went through the apartment building, to the courtyard. No yellow tape here. The cops either hadn't cared about this door or, more likely, had missed it altogether. People often did. From the inside, it was covered with chinoiserie wallpaper and blended into the surrounding wall. I let myself into the back room and switched on the lights.

There was the unmade bed.

It's what I'd come for. The man who'd slept there with me last night—okay, so he was a liar and a thief and he'd had sex under an assumed name. Nobody's perfect. I missed him. I also missed sleep. The bed beckoned, its white rumpled sheets and pillows willing to seduce me all over again. Fully clothed, I succumbed.

Under the covers, I inhaled his scent until it became hard to breathe. I pulled my head out and opened my eyes. Above me was the cornucopia of personal effects suspended from the ceiling, all the stuff of my life. My eyes drifted downward, over well-stocked shelves, along the Persian rug, and came to rest on something unfamiliar on the cement floor: a plastic barrette. Ruby's. Too flimsy to be of any practical use, given the quality of her hair, it lay there pink and hopeful, an expression of vanity that—

In the front room, someone pounded at the door.

My heart leaped. I jumped up out of the bed, flooded with guilt. Violating a crime scene must be a crime. But if it was cops, would they knock? It was their padlock on the door, wouldn't they just let themselves in?

The knocking came again. Fast. Peremptory. I tiptoed to the

doorway of the shop floor and peeked out. Through the Cards-o'-Bob rack I could just make out a shape, on the other side of the front entrance. A very large man.

Carmine, come back to haunt me.

I clutched my throat, to stop the guttural sound it was making. I reminded myself that with all the preternatural phenomena I believed in, I didn't believe in ghosts. The regular world had plenty of large men, it didn't need to recruit from the afterlife. This was simply a guy with a brisk knock, not a bad guy, the bad guys were all in jail, maybe even a good guy, someone with news of Margaret, and besides, it was only eight o'clock in the evening, hardly a witching hour. I pulled myself together, slithered over to the doorway, and turned on the outside light.

Mr. Bundt stood there.

THERE WAS ONLY one reason for him to come over at closing time on Good Friday. The annual New Franchise Owners decisions had been made and he was here to deliver the news in person before the formal announcement on Monday. I turned on the shop floor lights and wished for the sixth or seventh time that I was dressed in something other than a sweat suit and saddle shoes.

Mr. Bundt indicated through the thick glass that he wished to be let in. I pointed to the padlock and yelled that I'd come around and meet him. Then I ran through the back room, the courtyard, the apartment building, and around the block to Sunset.

"Miss Wollie Shelley?" The voice stopped me.

A man rested against a convertible, illegally parked in a loading zone in front of the mini-mall.

"Yes?" From the sidewalk I could see Mr. Bundt at the door of the shop, checking his watch.

"Sign, please." The man, a teenager, actually, with advanced facial hair, wore a Hawaiian shirt and flip-flops. He shoved a clipboard in front of me.

"What am I signing for?"

"This." It was a padded manila envelope with my name on a typed label. "And this." From the convertible he lifted an all-too-familiar object. Margaret's crate. Empty.

"Oh, God." With a sinking heart, I signed my name and handed back the clipboard. I peered into the crate as if the ferret might have left a note. A piece of calcified raisin clung to one of the steel rungs. I thought I'd prepared myself for this, but grief came over me in a wave; I had to sit down on the curb. The convertible drove off.

The envelope lay heavy in my lap until I set down the crate and opened it. Inside were half a dozen thick bundles of money. I pulled one out. The bills were hundreds, crisp and new, with rubber bands over the faces of a bored-looking Benjamin Franklin. A cream-colored piece of paper with a Saul Meier & Associates letterhead said, "Regret to inform you no other sign of your ferret found."

I sat amid the lights and traffic noises on Sunset, holding an empty crate and a wad of money until Mr. Bundt's voice pulled me out of my trance.

"Wollie? I think you'll be more comfortable inside."

WHEN YOU SPEND years dreaming of a particular moment, the moment never plays out quite like you imagined. Anyone over age seven realizes that. Still, as I led Mr. Bundt through the courtyard entrance, I marveled at just how odd it was, that I was about to get the best news of my career on what was a contender for the worst day of my life. This was a Good Friday kind of paradox.

Which is why, when we'd trooped into the back room and he'd helped himself to a glass of water and I waited for words like "pleased to inform you" and "excellent reports" I found it odder still that Mr.

Bundt would speak in tongues. Not that I didn't understand the words, only that they were not appropriate to this scene, phrases like "truly disappointed" and "deeply disturbed." Perhaps he'd walked into the wrong store.

"Wait. Stop," I said. "Your spy—the secret shopper doing the inspection—he definitely implied he loved our operation."

Mr. Bundt lifted an eyebrow. "The industrial agent assigned to you was in fact a team. Of females." He cleared his throat. "Posing as, how shall I say—?"

"Hookers," I whispered and sank onto the chaise longue.

"Precisely. Who reported lights and activities at all hours, a wild *animal* kept on the premises, whose cage you are holding, if I'm not mistaken, and"—here he shuddered slightly—"your sponsorship of some sort of escort service."

"I can explain that."

"Explanations are not results, however, and the result of all this unauthorized activity is—" He nodded toward the front room. " 'Police line, do not cross.' In English and Spanish. Hardly an acceptable greeting for our Welcome! patrons. This shop will never become a Willkommen! Greetings."

Inside me, something tore, right in the middle of my abdomen. I gripped the steel edges of Margaret's crate and held on tight. Mr. Bundt's voice softened, seemingly embarrassed by what came next.

"As your services are no longer required, do you think you could vacate the premises by the end of the week? This branch, with its dark fiscal history, is to be terminated. An automotive parts chain takes over the lease next month."

Terminated. Inventory shipped to rival Welcome! stores. The trompe l'oeil lemon grove mural painted over, my greeting cards replaced with spark plugs and fur-covered steering wheels . . .

The Welcome! greeting bell interrupted my mental funeral. I

followed Mr. Bundt onto the shop floor and wondered if he'd ever stop talking. "We'll take the spinners, of course"—he gestured to the Cards-o'-Bob rack—"but your main shelves are shoddy. They should have been replaced years ago, and—sir, excuse me, we're closed."

The man stood at the table in the northwest corner looking out the window. He was in shadow, but I recognized the army green pants and the brown bomber jacket he'd worn on our plane ride the previous afternoon. I set down Margaret's crate and moved to him, summoning his name from my mental dating files.

"Dylan. Ellison, right? What are you—?"

He turned and smiled. "Guess."

"Sir," Mr. Bundt said, "this establishment is permanently—"

"Shut up."

The voice was mild, even pleasant, and the smile didn't waver, but the effect was chilling. In the ensuing silence I noticed a padlock on the table next to Dylan, and when I looked back up at him, I wondered how I'd found him so good-looking yesterday. He wasn't, really, he was too sharp-featured, too much like a—

"Weasel," I said.

And then I saw he wore latex gloves.

chapter thirty-seven

I t was all so unfair, was my first thought. Aloud, I said, "You're supposed to be in jail. I was told the cops picked you up."

"I'm sure they tried. I was out." His gloved hand reached into the bomber jacket and produced a gun.

Random thoughts scrolled through my head. *I have no experience with this. That gun looks plastic. I actually dated this man.* The decision-making part of my brain seemed to have shut down.

"Let's move away from this window."

I backed up, toward the front door.

"Uh-uh." The Weasel gestured with his gun to the middle of the room and I switched directions accordingly, down Aisle 5, Engagements/Weddings. One thing was clear: Mr. Bundt was not going to be any help. Deathly pale, his breath came in pants, and he followed me like a spaniel.

Talk, I thought. Pretend it's a date. Talk, and get the Weasel talking. I turned to him. "What happened to the real Dylan Ellison?"

He seemed to read my strategy and find it amusing. The smile returned as he sauntered toward us down Aisle 5. "I came to your poetry thing and your big-mouth uncle told me about the guy that didn't show. You don't exactly check ID on your dates, do you?"

Keep talking. Open your mouth. Say words. "Speaking of dates: our plane ride yesterday? I guess you knew those guys in the Alfa Romeo."

His face shut down, and I realized that of course he did, and that's why he killed his cousin Carmine—he saw him consorting with the enemy. This might not be the best subject to pursue. I switched gears. "So what really happened to our picnic?"

He smiled. "The Angeles Crest Forest was a little out of my way, as it turned out."

Angeles Crest Forest—Body Dump, Joey called it. I saw it all with sudden clarity. He would've fed me a sandwich, picked my brain, taken my keys, bumped me off, dropped me from a cliff, left me for the coyotes, flown back to the airport, driven my car somewhere, and abandoned it. Instead, he'd decided to deal with Carmine and the Swedes, which bought me an extra twenty-four hours. "Well, that's a relief," I said. "I'd hate to think you just found me unattractive."

He looked me up and down like a peruser of pornography. "I'd do you. Not dressed like that, though. I've been looking at those sweatpants for twelve hours and, frankly, I'm sick of them. Also that wreck of a car you drive."

Behind me, the faintest *thunk!* sounded in the back room. Was it possible? Was someone—? I spoke quickly. "You followed me? Today? In your Hummer?"

"Rental. I lost you on Little Santa Monica, but I saw you at the synagogue and with our Hebrew friends, so don't bother telling me you don't have my diamond. The world isn't that small." He pointed the gun and wiggled it in a suggestive manner, as if I had the ring buried between my breasts. "Give."

"Okay. Just for the sake of argument, though, if I didn't have it—?"

"You know about it. So one way or another, I'd still have to do you."

Do me. He used the same figure of speech for sex and killing.

"But I can do you nice and quick"—he gestured with his gun to illustrate this—"or I can use my preferred method." From his jacket pocket he pulled out a knife; thin and silver, it looked like something you'd use to gut fish. "Up to you, baby. How well you behave. How well you answer questions. One way is more fun for you, the other's more fun for me." He put the knife back in his jacket.

"Sir?" The reedy voice was barely recognizable as Mr. Bundt's. "I know nothing at all about whatever you're discussing, so perhaps you could allow me to—"

"Oh, sorry. Rude of us. We're discussing my retirement income. Unless I have to use it to bargain for my life." He shook his head. "In-laws. By the way, Wollie." He came to me, took my neck in his hand, and moved me gently aside. "Not entertaining anyone else back there tonight, are you?" He walked toward the back room, as Mr. Bundt, next to me, tried to flatten himself against Anniversaries.

The Weasel stumbled.

React! I yelled to myself. Do something.

The Weasel recovered and looked down and saw what had tripped him.

Margaret's crate.

He stared at it, then spoke, his voice quiet. "Where did you get this?" He turned toward us and pointed the rectangular gun.

Mr. Bundt backed into me, stepping on my foot.

"Ow! It's a—spare." I addressed the gun. I couldn't look at the Weasel. My face would undo me.

"You're a liar. Bald man." The gun swerved toward Mr. Bundt. "Where'd the cage come from?"

"Corvette, convertible. Young driver. Goatee. She signed for it."

The gun turned back to me. The voice was like granite. "That's Big Eddie's nephew. How do you know Big Eddie?"

Behind him, in the lemon grove doorway, something appeared, then disappeared. Pea green velour.

Ruby.

She was two feet behind the Weasel. One glance toward the back room and he'd see her and—

"How do you know him?" he yelled. "Lie to me and you'll be look-ing at your body parts on this carpet."

Ruby's head popped into the doorway, and popped back out.

I felt rather than saw Mr. Bundt glance toward her. I kicked him in the ankle, then met the Weasel's eye, willing him to look at me and only me. "I contacted Big Eddie," I said. "I told him I had the ring, but I wanted Margaret—our ferret—back first. I knew if any-one could find her, he could. He said to meet tonight, ten-thirty in his lawyer's office, but now this crate shows up, so what I want to know is, where the hell is my ferret?"

It poured out of me so readily, I wondered if I was channeling someone. But it got his attention. He stared at me as if I'd sprouted fur.

"Tell you what," I said, "I'll show up at the meeting and give him some other ring. Here—" I grabbed Mr. Bundt's hand and held it up. "What's this, a class ring? That'll work. And Big Eddie will see I made a mistake. And he'll be upset, but he won't connect it to you. On the other hand, if you kill me, he'll figure out what happened, he already knows you kidnapped Margaret. If I'm dead, you're dead."

I had a feeling there were holes in my logic and he was finding them. He didn't move a muscle, but the air between us seemed to vibrate. He would blow at any moment. What would it take to—

"Want your ring?" I said. "Because I'm wearing it."

His eyes went to my hand.

"On my toe." I lifted a foot, displaying my saddle shoe. Instinct told me to get within reach of him, in case he turned and saw Ruby. Balanced on one leg, I started to untie my shoe. It was awkward and allowed me to plausibly hop. I hopped toward him. Maybe a plan would evolve en route. I thought of the kickboxing tapes I'd meant to send away for. I continued to advance, fast little staccato movements.

"Try sitting," Mr. Bundt suggested. I ignored him.

The Weasel was still eight feet away. Too far. I kept hopping and pretended to encounter a knot in my shoelaces. "I'll wear a wire," I said. "At the meeting. So you'll know I'm not ratting you out. I have a little tape recorder that fits in my purse. You could keep Mr. Bundt here hostage." A sputtering sound emanated from Mr. Bundt. "And Margaret," I added. "You've still got my ferret." I struggled with the imaginary knot. I could feel his impatience, but what could I do? The only thing under my sweat sock was last month's pedicure. My hands shook visibly.

"Need help?" The Weasel pulled out his knife, ready to cut my shoelace.

I pulled off the shoe. I left on my sock.

"You don't know who you're playing with, do you?" he said. "I don't care about your fat friend and I don't think you do either. The ferret's roadkill on the 405. She bit me, I threw her out the window. Now get that ring over here before I cut off your—"

"Hey, creep."

It was a little girl's voice.

It was Ruby.

The sound was so extraordinary that time stopped. Anything was possible. When the Weasel turned toward the voice, I jumped him. I landed on his back and got him around the neck and hit him on the head and face as hard as I could with my size eleven saddle shoe and just kept hitting, smashing the hard heel against his forehead, nose, eye.

And then I was on the carpet, on my back, with no idea how I got there. I smelled my own sweat and heard myself breathe and looked up at the brown jacket and the glinting knife looming over me. So this is it, I thought, as things became very quiet and clear. I can't save us. I didn't save anyone.

There was a very loud *thunk.*

The knife dropped. The Weasel stood suspended, for what seemed like an eternity, and his eyes met mine in a moment of utter disbelief. He stumbled to the side, and I saw Ruby behind him, the white marble bust of Dante in her hands. Her second blow glanced off his shoulder. Then he turned to her and swung his gun arm across his body, winding up to backhand her.

I grabbed his foot. It didn't bring him down, but it gave Ruby time to back up, and then I got both arms around his army-green-clad thigh and hugged tight, like some overwrought Madame Butterfly. A hard object met the side of my face with such force that the whole world stopped and I thought, This is about to hurt very badly. I actually considered passing out, but as I slid down his leg, my hand came in contact with something sharp on the carpet and I knew that if ever there was a moment to stay awake, this was it.

I was on all fours, with the knife in my hand. I aimed upward, for the biggest target I could reach, the fleshy outer part of his thigh, and with the last bit of strength left to me, threw my body into it. At that second, he turned.

The knife went through his trousers at a more significant point.

The scream and the shot came simultaneously. The gun fell and bounced. The Weasel grabbed his crotch and fell into Engagements/Weddings and the whole rack went down with a crash.

I was still on all fours and there was blood on my grass green carpet. I looked for Ruby. She was standing, thank God, but I couldn't tell quite where. The geography of my store was growing murky. Plaster rained down. Had someone shot my ceiling? I lowered myself down onto my elbows and tried to collect my wits. My head hurt.

Mr. Bundt retrieved the gun from the carpet near me and moved with uncharacteristic speed to the overturned Engagements/Weddings rack. The Weasel's screams had transmogrified into an animal-like yowling that was disturbing to hear.

Ruby appeared at my side and I was simultaneously hugging her and trying to get up. She was either hugging me back or trying to push me down.

I saw Mr. Bundt stand guard over the Weasel in what had once been Aisle 5. In one hand was the gun, in the other his cell phone, which he spoke into with the old authoritative tones I knew so well and, suddenly, loved.

"It's okay, we're okay," I heard myself tell Ruby. "You're good. I'm good. We didn't die."

"I know," she said, after I'd stopped. They were the third and fourth words I'd ever heard her say and she sounded brilliant.

chapter thirty-eight

"Do you know what my dad did? Why he got sent to jail and stuff?"

I adjusted the phone and sealed up another cardboard box. "Yes."

"No, but I mean, the whole story. The really, really true one."

Now that Ruby was talking, there was no stopping her. Two days later, this was our seventh phone call. "Do you?" she said. "Know about the stock market part? And my mom?"

I pushed the heavy cardboard box across the back room to join eighteen others. "Ruby, I'm not sure I should be hearing—"

"My Grandma Vandenvieck told me the whole deal. Okay, my dad's economics class? He was teaching about the stock market, so his students, they gave him a bunch of money, like their allowance and stuff, because they wanted him to invest it, so first he put it in the bank, okay? But my mom went to the bank that same day and she saw it in the checking account, so she took it out and bought a new car."

I sat down on my box. "That's why he went to prison?"

"Yeah, because you're not supposed to take money from your students. Especially if it's a lot of money. Doesn't that suck?"

Could this be true? It was hard to reconcile the father she talked about with the man I was working to forget. "And then," she said, "my dad went to prison, and my mom went to Japan. So anyway. Wanna know how I'm going to invest my college fund money?"

I'd given Big Eddie's wad of bills—thirty-nine thousand, five hundred of it—to Ruby. I sent another ten thousand to Sammy's synagogue. The last five hundred went to Fredreeq, for her work on the Dating Project. This was my attempt at moral money laundering. "Blood money" was how I thought of it, although it probably wasn't, strictly speaking. Still, it was a good bet that somewhere in the making of Big Eddie's fortune, blood had been shed. I said to Ruby, "Not in a checking account, I hope."

"You mean 'cause of my mom?" Ruby said. "Don't worry, she lives in Japan now, with her boyfriend. I might get to go visit her. When school's out. So anyway, the money? I'm gonna invest it in your next shop."

"Ruby, there is no next shop."

"Yeah, but there can be. My dad did the math. Okay, I gotta go."

There were few taboo subjects with Ruby. She told me about her parents, her maternal grandmother, the school she was kicked out of, and the one she was going back to. The statement she'd made to the cops on Friday night. And how she'd sat in the lawyer's office that afternoon long enough to study the bus route in the phone book and get herself from Century City to Hollywood. In time to save my life. She even talked about her vow of silence. I'd guessed right, that she'd given up talking for Lent, hoping that God would restore to her the three beings she most loved, her family. In the end, she'd had to make do with her dad.

There was one thing she didn't talk about.

Margaret's crate sat on the chaise longue, haunting me. I took it out front and buried it in the giveaway pile.

With curtains gone and the racks stripped of their cards like so many leafless trees, the shop floor looked clinically depressed, made worse by a late afternoon fog. Whole sections of paisley wallpaper were faded from the sun. Every crack showed. Bullet holes in the ceiling and blood stains on the grass green carpet were merely the latest indignities.

The curious thing was that it didn't bother me.

Except for thoughts of Margaret, which sat like a bad meal in my stomach, I felt detached about leaving. It was as if a different person had taken up residence in my body, someone I didn't know very well. I let her do the packing.

Dr. Cookie, when she called, said it would be a while before I recovered from the demise of my childhood dream. She told me that seeing my shop physically assaulted had traumatized me. I told her that seeing my own body physically assaulted was no picnic either, but real trauma was getting kicked off the Dating Project this late in the game, with nothing to show for my twenty-seven dates but mileage reimbursement. Dr. Cookie expressed sympathy, but said that my lax screening process had compromised the scientific data.

Fredreeq said that okay, it was true that Rex Stetson and Benjamin Woo had been old flames of Joey's and Robert Quarter had gotten my number from Dave Fischgarten, and Sterling was her own husband's cousin, but this was blind dating, not stem cell research. Joey said that Dr. Cookie was miffed I'd found a man with a technically perfect List score and he turned out to be a mass murderer. Ruby said I should sell the whole story to the *National Enquirer*. But the truth was, my heart was no longer in the Dating Project. Maybe it never had been.

Uncle Theo said the pursuit of dreams is its own reward and impermanence is the nature of things and that the shop had served us well while it lasted, providing income, sanctuary, and inspiration. He did not consider my dream a failed one, merely a short one.

Fredreeq said the planet Saturn rearranges your life every seven years and there isn't a damn thing you can do about it.

THE OFFICERS WHO responded to Mr. Bundt's call had, at his insistence, taken me to the emergency room at Queen of Angels Hospital, where I was treated for a broken toe and a bruised rib and given seven stitches on my chest for gashes I wasn't aware I had. Mr. Bundt also insisted I not share an ambulance with the Weasel. Afterward, I went to the police station, where I spent the rest of Good Friday and part of Holy Saturday answering questions.

Detective Pflug was warmer this time around. He said Ruby and Mr. Bundt had given separate, glowing accounts of my actions. He assured me that Ronald "the Weasel" Ronzare was under police guard at the hospital, would soon be in jail downtown, and would not be released, on any kind of bail, any time soon. I, in turn, came clean about everything except the fifty thousand dollars from Big Eddie. As the subject didn't come up, I assumed Mr. Bundt's glowing account had left out the padded manila envelope. I wondered why.

Joey and Fredreeq and even Fredreeq's kids were waiting in the lobby when I was released, eager to take care of me. Ruby had long since been returned to her father, and while I was sorry not to see her, I couldn't say the same of him. He left messages with Pflug, at the shop, the apartment, and with my friends. I ignored them.

When I finally went to bed, I slept for fourteen hours. When I woke, it was Easter.

. . .

I WENT NEXT door to the twenty-one-hour locksmith, open even on holidays, to borrow a Phillips screwdriver. I came out to find my brother sitting in front of the shop.

"P.B., what are you doing here?" I asked.

He didn't answer. His ears were covered with foil and he rocked back and forth, a sweatshirt clutched to his stomach.

I looked around. Uncle Theo had hoped to take P.B. out on a holiday pass, if he could find them a ride. The parking lot was filled with cars, overflow from an Easter wedding at Sacred Heart, but none contained Uncle Theo. I plopped down next to my brother.

"I'm back on my meds," he said. "They take effect in a week, maybe sooner."

"So you won't be needing aluminum foil much longer."

"No." He looked up to the smog-filled sky. "They won't be listening in on me. There won't be anything to hear."

He was a study in sorrow. It struck me that with all the attendant responsibility and even pain of his interstellar communication, it gave him a sense of purpose.

A horn honked on Sunset. "No place to park!" Uncle Theo leaned out the passenger window of his friend Xavier's truck. "It's time, P.B. Wollie, I'll come tomorrow to help you move."

I waved and turned to my brother. "You've been happy on ziprasidone. You get along with almost everyone, and you feel more in control. You told me that."

"But I won't see the patterns anymore. If you can't see the patterns, you can't change the patterns. I have to go." He took the sweatshirt he'd been holding in his lap and placed it in mine. "Here."

The sweatshirt was lumpy. And warm. And moving.

From its depths emerged a large white sock that stretched, yawned, and arranged itself into Margaret. She looked up at me and blinked.

· · ·

HOW HAD SHE come to be in my brother's sweatshirt? Had Ruby and P.B., for reasons of their own, put the hospital phone number on Margaret's tag, that day in Venice, and had someone found her on the freeway and returned her to Rio Pescado? Other scenarios were even less likely, having to do with the things that happened when P.B. put his ear to the ground and listened to the dirt. I'd ask him, but chances were good I'd never get the whole story. One of life's unsolved mysteries, like the Blue Patron, who hadn't been Mr. Bundt's industrial spy, but merely, apparently, a fan.

We stood in line at Bodega Bob, Margaret and I, to buy their entire stock of raisins, three boxes. I wanted to shower her with raisins. Despite looks from my fellow patrons, I could not stop kissing the ferret's head and murmuring to her in the idiotic way people do to babies and puppies. There was a Popsicle stick tied to her back leg, like a splint, and a tear in one of her soft ears, but otherwise, she was her old self. She looked out the window, nose twitching.

I looked too, and saw Thomas Flynn, the man formerly known as Gomez, get out of a car in front of Bodega Bob.

I squatted behind a metal food rack, clutching Margaret. I'd wait it out. He'd go to my shop, I'd be gone, he'd go home. I'd call Ruby and tell her about Margaret while he wasn't there to answer the phone.

Margaret squirmed, bound for a box of Rice-A-Roni on a low shelf. I was on my knees, making a grab for her, when black shoes entered my field of vision. They were so new I could smell their leather. I worked my way visually up a dark gray suit, white shirt, and red tie, to a face. Just as I'd suspected. The new person inhabiting my body was as vulnerable to the man in front of me as the old one had been.

Thomas Flynn looked from me to Margaret and back again, his

eyes glistening. He opened his mouth to speak, then closed it. He dropped to one knee, that pristine suit on the dirty linoleum, well into my personal space.

I handed Margaret to him and stood. My own voice chilled me to the bone. "I need to pay for these raisins."

chapter thirty-nine

"It was dangerous for you to know my name. I knew early on that if things got dicey—" He stopped pacing the shop floor and came over to me. "Here, let me do that."

"No. Go away." I stood on a ladder, unwinding a string of icicle lights from the ficus tree. I would not look directly at him. Many people clean up well, but there are men truly transformed by a suit. Thomas Flynn was one, even with jacket off and shirt sleeves rolled up.

"Go away," I repeated.

He didn't go away. He stood below me, the top of his head even with my bruised rib cage. He said, "If someone questioned you, and you didn't even have my name right, they'd be less likely to pump you for information. I did it to give you credibility."

"As what, a dumb blonde? You can let go of the ladder, I won't fall, I'm three feet off the ground." He let his hand drop, but stayed where he was, so close I could smell the menthol shaving cream he used. "And when did you plan on telling me your name? Ever?"

He transferred Margaret to his other shoulder and looked up. "Before I asked you to marry me, at least. That would only be fair. Of course, now that Ruby's talking, it was just a matter of time before— whoa. Watch it there." His hand returned to the ladder.

"Marry? What is that, a proposal? Are you *kidding* me?"

"I didn't mean to make you mad. Let's back up a minute."

"You're not kidding? You're serious?" I stared openly at him now.

"You don't need to say yes or no right away. We'll date first."

"Are you on drugs?" Blood seemed to have rushed to my head. "You come in here, you tell me, in the most patronizing way, that yes, you've been lying to me since the day we—"

"If you're going to yell, I wish you'd get off the ladder, you're scaring Margaret."

She did look scared. She quivered in his arms and blinked at me. He spoke calmly. "I'm not on drugs, Mr. Gomez is. Valacyclovir. But let's do this in order." From his shirt pocket he pulled a tattered piece of paper. "For the record, I never actually lied. You made an assumption about my name that I didn't correct—a small distinction, but I thought it might matter. On that note: number one, A Good Name." He looked up. "Tommy Flynn. Not distinctive, but probably not objectionable, unless you have a problem with the Irish."

"My God. That's—where did you get that?" I reached for the List. He stepped back.

"Number two, Not a Convicted Felon. Okay, I screwed up there. I took money from my students, stuck it in a joint checking account, didn't bother getting permission slips signed, all kinds of irresponsible behavior. Did the crime, did the time, got a loan, paid everyone back with interest, apologized profusely, so I assume you'll give me credit, generous girl that you are. Next, No STDs. I'm fine, but Mr. Gomez seems to have herpes, judging by the prescription pinned to the inside of his bar mitzvah suit. But since you're just now finding this out, I'd like to know what you were thinking, having unprotected sex with me three nights ago."

"Look! Just—"

"Sorry, was that patronizing? Four, Has Car. Bought it yesterday—preowned Acura, four years, thirty thousand miles. Five, Has Job." He looked up. "Now this is interesting. High schools share your antifelon bias, so I'm now forced to work in the movie industry, a mechanical engineer for a special effects company at two and a half times my former salary. Six, Not Homeless. Modest bungalow in Los Feliz, three bedroom, we move in the first of the month, you'll like it. Seven, Five-nine or Above. No help there. Eight, Good Shoes." He displayed one black loafer. "Ferragamo."

"Look, Doc—Gomez—Flynn—"

"Call me Tommy. Nine, No Pets. Oh, well. Ten, No Smoking. I quit ninety-seven hours ago; that's probably why I've seemed stressed out lately. Eleven, No Guns. The Weasel stole it, so that takes care of that. Twelve—"

I stepped off the ladder and advanced toward him. "All right already."

"Well Hung." He backed up. "One of the few things you already—"

"*Okay!* Let's just—"

"—know about me, so we'll let you be the judge. No points on numbers seven and nine, so depending on which way you go with two and twelve, I score from sixty-six point six percent to eighty-three point three." He handed me the List, followed by Margaret. "Not a brilliant score, but let's look at yours." From his pants pocket, he produced what looked to be a grocery receipt. "I've got three items. Number one: Law-abiding. Sorry. You're harboring a ferret; they're illegal in California."

"They're what?"

"Number two: Sees her body as a temple. You drink a lot of coffee."

"So do you."

"This is my list, not yours. I also found artificial sweeteners in your cupboard. Along with a dried milklike substance—whitener, it's called. Hard to cope with one's soul mate drinking whitener. Number three: Good driver." He looked up and raised an eyebrow. "Enough said." He crumpled the piece of paper and tossed it across the room. It landed perfectly in an open trash bag. He leaned back against the counter and loosened his tie.

I caught myself folding my own list into a very small rectangle. I crossed the room and settled myself amid the pile of giveaway items, with my back to him. I pulled out a big black trash bag from an industrial-size roll, and started piling stuff in. Margaret climbed up my shoulder. "So what did you do with the suit?" I asked. "The bar mitzvah suit." That had been my stupidest moment, finding the dry-cleaning receipt in my car and not realizing poor Gomez's name had been borrowed, along with his suit.

"Returned it to the cleaners from whence it came," he said. "Ask me more."

Margaret nuzzled my neck, wrapped around it like a mink collar. "Ruby seems to think I should open another store," I said. "It's not going to happen. I loved this shop. It was the only place I ever—" I stopped, suddenly unsure what I'd been about to say.

"Wollie, you can cry over it if you want, but this place was nothing, it was a canvas. You're the artist. What you've got, you take with you. If you want to start again somewhere else, you can. If not, don't. Anything else you want to ask me?"

I couldn't look at him. I stuffed a Styrofoam Frosty the Snowman into the trash bag. Would Goodwill even want it? "You do realize you can't remarry in the Catholic Church, not until your current wife dies?"

It was a long time before he answered. "I can live without the Pope's blessing. I'm not sure I can live without you."

I turned around.

Empty of furnishings, the room echoed with the ticking of the Minnie Mouse clock, so loud she seemed in danger of a heart attack. I was able to look at Tommy Flynn now. I took him in piece by piece, as if I were going to draw him. His shirt was white, the rest of him so dark, he made me think of a fallen angel. Black Irish, it was called. I could see the altar boy he'd been some thirty years before. I wondered what he'd look like in another thirty years.

Oh, what the heck, I thought.

I decided to find out.

acknowledgments

It took me a long time to write this book, due to interesting day jobs and a dawdling nature—so long that the list of those who helped me out along the way is also . . . long. It took so long that several people actually died waiting for it and several others were born (to me). To the former, I apologize for not writing faster; to the latter, for typing while breast-feeding.

Thanks to my teachers, Claire Carmichael, Jim Krusoe, Phyllis Gebauer, Karen Joy Fowler, Michael Levin, Tony Barsha, and Robert Crais; my family, especially Ann Kozak, John Kozak, Mary Coen, Pete Kozak, Joe Kozak, Ruggero J. Aldisert, Andy Goodman, Jona Turner, Dory Goodman, Lisa Aldisert, Leah Goodman, Julia Coen, Susannah Coen, Ruth Goodman, Dianne Kozak, Andrew Kozak, Tony Kozak, Beth Karish, Agatha Aldisert, Rob and Jenny Aldisert, Batt Johnson, Sandy Brophy, and Alessandra Brophy; my partners in crime, Mike Milligan, Mike Tennesen, John Snibbe, Jamie Diamond, Abigail Jones, Sherry Halperin, Susan Jaques, Harry and Susan Squires, David B.

Carren, Bob Shayne, Jonathan Beggs, JoAnn Senger, Roger Angle, John Shepphird, Linda Burrows, Kirsten Dahl, Celia Chapman, Tori Hartman, Nathan Walpow, and Gregg Andrew Hurwitz; the home team, Julie Renick, Nelly Valladares, Catrina Boca, Susanna Crumrine, Jessica Novak, Laura Lemon, Stefanie Pinneo, Molly Haldeman, and Uli Buchta; the professionals, Neil Genda, Det. Paul Bishop, Dr. Barry Fisher, Dr. Barry Schoer, Dr. Pam Boyer, Gregory W. Avale, Ivan Eafon, the Wildlife Way Station, the Pittsburgh Coroner's Office, Steven & Co. Jewelers, Sanctuary Psychiatric Centers of Santa Barbara, and the former Camarillo State Mental Hospital; those fifty-some blind dates (you know who you are); the generous Kelly Link; my friends Sharon Samek, Dr. Tara Fields, Griffin Dunne, Gavin Polone, Tanino Privitera, Carolyn Clark Shoemaker, Tany'á Wells, Dr. Stan Passy, Kate and Paul Cirzan, Meghann Haldeman, Ed Steinbrecher, Andy Parks, Josh Young, Victoria Vanderbilt, Denise Fondo, Allyson Adams, Dan Proett, Hawk Koch, Chuck Lascheid, Cynthia Tarr, Wendy Tigerman, Gary Tigerman, Icel Dobell, Dan Reinehr, JoBeth Gutgsell, Doug Rohrer, Linda Silver, Rob Nau, Jonathan Levin, the Meano Man, Ron Fujikawa, Dylan Sellers, George and Millie Nikopoulos, Laurie Hudson, Patty Flournoy, Heike Knorz, Kim Stanwood, JJ Harris, Robin Lyn, Jackie Caine, Bo and Sita Lozoff, Elizabeth Dickey, Michael States, Emanuele Portolese, Rick Rose, Jeanne Rains, Hanna Elias, E. Mike Dobbins, Jane Gideon, Christina Panis, T. Jefferson Parker, and Monica, Angel 231; my agent, Renee Zuckerbrot; my editors, Stacy Creamer and Beth Buschman-Kelly; my attorney, Jason Baruch; my other agent, Amy Schiffman; Carol Topping; the ones who couldn't wait around, including Robert Stein, Rosalind Neroni, and Mom; the inimitable Bobby Goodman; Jinn and Fez, April, Eddie, and Rice; and the four who are my whole world: Greg, Audrey, Lorenzo, and Gianna.

Dating Is Murder

1

"**M**oth harmonica."

That's what it sounded like, the guttural, heavy-accented syllables coming through my answering machine. A piece of haiku, until the woman rattled off an almost unintelligible series of digits that went on and on, like a credit card number or the miles from earth to Jupiter. I picked up the telephone.

"Hi, this is Wollie," I said. "Who's this?"

"California? America? *Ja?*"

"Yes, California, America. Who's this?"

"Encino?"

"No, not Encino, West Hollywood. Forty minutes away, traffic permitting. Who's this?"

"*Ja, ja,* who this?" she asked.

"That's what I'm asking," I said. "Who are *you?*"

"I am Moth Harmonica."

Okay, I've heard worse. My own name, Wollstonecraft Shelley, is no picnic, especially for a girl. Or woman, as my friend Fredreeq insists I refer to myself. "Who are you trying to call, Moth?" I asked.

"Who are you?"

"No, who are—" I stopped. This could take a while, and I didn't have a while. "I think you have the wrong number," I said, and this brought forth a flurry of words that started with "*Nein! Nein!*" and ended with "Annika."

"Annika?" I said. "Wait. Not moth—you're—mother. Of Annika. You're Mrs. Glück?"

There was an excited assent, lots of *Ja! Ja!*s, and another flurry of words. I closed my eyes and took a deep breath, trying to dispel a sudden bad feeling.

"*Meine* Annika," Mrs. Glück said, "called not tomorrow—no, no, yesterday—and yesterday is Sunday, we call every week Sunday. So I leave message for host family, but called me not back. I feel for Annika *Gefahr*, um, danger, *sie ist in* big danger, as *sie* call not Sunday."

I was nodding now. My friend Annika had called her mother from my apartment the previous week. "She would freak out if I did not call each Sunday," Annika had said. "But she will call me back so it will not be on your bill." Which was why Mrs. Glück had my number.

I said, "I'd really like to help you, but I have no idea where Annika is. She's tutoring me in math, and we were supposed to meet last night"—I hesitated, not wanting to admit how I'd worried, thinking, *Annika's never even late*—"and she didn't show."

"Ah, *Gott im Himmel, sie* is dead."

"No, I'm sure she's not dead, I'm sure she's—" The doorbell rang. "Can you hold on?"

I zipped through the kitchen and living room and opened the door to Fredreeq, told her to give me two minutes, and zipped back to the kitchen. "Mrs. Glück?" I said. "I'm sure Annika will turn up, and if I hear from her first—"

"*Nein, nein,* for me you must to find her. The host family call me not back, and the agency call me not back, no one in United States of America to—"

"But if she's really missing, I'm sure her host family will contact the police—"

"*Nein,* no *Polizei,* no trouble—you are friend, *ja*? So you are to ask host family what is happen. For my daughter. *Mein Kind.*"

Fredreeq, having followed me into the kitchen, pointed to her watch and mouthed the words "Joey" and "double-parked." I nodded and waved her off. "Okay," I said. "Do you have the host family's number? All I have is Annika's line, with her machine." On which I'd already left two messages.

Minutes later I hung up and turned to Fredreeq, who was studying the contents of my refrigerator. It was early evening in late November, dark in my kitchen, but my friend was illuminated by the utility bulb. It was enough. She wore a tight, fringed jumpsuit in hot pink, low-cut with a big plastic zipper running the length of it. She had the kind of va-va-va-boom body that could pull this off, and the kind of temperament that would want to. Her hair this week was as blond as mine, not unusual in Los Angeles, but whereas I had pale skin to go with it, Fredreeq was black, a less common combination. "Where's your water?" she asked.

"In the sink."

"You don't have bottled water? What do you take on the road?"

"I don't take water on the road."

"Sister, you have got to change your ways," she said, herding me into the living room. "You have cosmetic responsibilities now. Who is this Monica person?"

"Annika, not Monica. Our Annika, from the show. Her mother in Germany says she's—disappeared." I grabbed my keys and backpack, alarmed at the word I'd just said.

"And who does the mother think you are, the FBI?"

"She doesn't know who I am, she just happened to have my phone number. She can't reach the host family—Annika's an au pair, did you know that?"

Fredreeq handed me my jean jacket. "What are you doing answering your own phone? We gotta get you thinking like a celebrity."

The word "celebrity" made me want to hide under the bed with a bag of Oreos. But Fredreeq had overstated it. I was only a celebrity to those rare people who watched a TV reality show called *Biological Clock*—too few in number, according to the Nielsen ratings, to materially affect my life. I reminded myself of this as I followed Fredreeq out of the apartment, down the stairs, and out to the street.

Rush-hour noise from Santa Monica Boulevard accosted us. There was pedestrian traffic too as we walked down Larrabee, mostly male, as befits a neighborhood known as Boystown. Fredreeq attracted her share of attention, her skintight jumpsuit an object of desire. West Hollywood is a bastion of gay and lesbian culture, which I, as a heterosexual female, found comforting in ways I didn't exactly understand.

I caught myself really looking at people, on the street, in cars. Looking, illogically, maybe, for someone considerably shorter than I, brown-haired, apple-cheeked, pretty. A girl in the last days of her teens. Annika.

"There's Joey," Fredreeq said, waving to a green Mercedes stuck in slow traffic on Santa Monica, a mass of red hair visible in the driver's seat. "What's she doing circling the block? I told her to stay put. C'mon, let's catch up." She grabbed my hand and we ran as fast as her three-inch heels allowed, click-click-clicking our way to Joey.

My friends were driving me to the night's location of *Biological Clock*. The reality show featured three women *d'un certain âge,* as Joey put it, dating in rotation three men of various ages, so the TV audience could ultimately vote on which combination of genes should produce a child, with or without romantic involvement on the part of the chosen couple. I was one of the women.

It hadn't been my idea.

Here's how it happened. I'd been—okay, still was—recovering from a broken engagement to a guy named Doc. Doc had some issues that stood between him and marriage, namely, a wife and the certainty of an ugly custody battle for their daughter, Ruby, once the wife became an ex-wife. The wife was keeping Ruby in Japan, so Doc had taken a job in Taiwan to be nearby, production work on an American film called *Mao, the Movie,* which threatened to go on as long as the Cultural Revolution. Custody would be a problem for six years, until Ruby turned eighteen, and Doc felt I shouldn't wait for him. Joey and Fredreeq agreed. I felt otherwise, but nobody seemed to care about my opinions any more than Chairman Mao had cared about the opinions of the bourgeoisie.

Joey's husband, meanwhile, had invested money in this reality show, *Biological Clock,* which had inspired Joey and Fredreeq to send my audition video to the casting director. I hadn't known I'd made an audition video. I'd thought I was being interviewed for Fredreeq's niece's sociology project. Apparently, though, me talking about my dating history was compelling stuff. Also, I was the right age and had attributes—big chest, long legs, and height, six feet of it—that made a nice visual contrast to the other two front-runner women contestants, and I'd thus beaten out several hundred hopefuls for the job. Not that I'd wanted the job. I'd turned it down flat once it was explained to me. I found the premise of the show cheesy, despite the disclaimer at the end of each episode that no couple would be required to have sex or bear children. As for fame, I'd have been happy to fork over my fifteen minutes to someone else, the way senators give away their floor time in debates to fellow senators.

But then *Biological Clock* had mentioned money. Despite the low budget, I'd be paid five hundred dollars a week for two nights' work, unusual for reality TV. And that wasn't all. The producers had invested in a number of other businesses, including a health maintenance organization offering benefits to the winning contestants and their dependents, current and future. Some people say insurance isn't sexy, but for those with dependent paranoid schizophrenic brothers on pricey antipsychotic medication, it's sexy enough.

A horn honked.

"Girl, you got some kind of bad gene that makes you change lanes every twenty seconds?" Fredreeq asked Joey.

"Yeah, it's called effective driving."

"Well, maybe they do that in Nebraska to get around the cows, but here people get shot for those maneuvers." Fredreeq and Joey had an ongoing city mouse, country mouse routine, although Joey was no more country than any other ex-model/actress who'd lived in L.A., New York, and Paris for the last fifteen years. "And can we turn down this twangy banjo stuff? You want people to think you're a hick?"

"I am a hick. Hey, Wollie," Joey threw over her shoulder, "why so quiet?"

"Cell phone." I'd dialed the number Mrs. Glück had given me for Annika's host family. In Encino, a machine answered. The voice was warm, chatty, female. "Hi there. You've reached the Quinns. Gene, Maizie, Emma, Annika, and Mr. Snuggles can't come to the phone right now. But leave us a message and we'll call you back. Bye-bye. Woof."

"Hi," I said, envisioning the people Annika had described. "I'm trying to reach Annika, your au pair. If she's not around, I'd appreciate a call from any of the Quinns. Preferably one of the humans." I spelled out my name and repeated my home and cell-phone numbers.

"Is that our Annika? From the show?" Joey asked. "How's she doing?"

"I'm not sure," I said. "She seems to be sort of . . . missing."

Joey turned to me. Traffic was at another dead stop as we neared Beverly Hills. Fredreeq had switched on the interior car light to rummage through her purse, and the glow made Joey's eyes very green and her face very white against her auburn hair. She was more than beautiful; she was intriguing, with a subtle scar running from temple to chin, white on white, a half-moon. "What do you mean, missing?" she said.

"She didn't show up for my math tutorial last night. And she didn't call her mom in Germany, which is her Sunday night ritual, so her mom is seriously upset, and she doesn't know a soul in America. Except me. And the host family, who's not returning her calls."

"Interesting."

"What is?"

Traffic moved. Joey faced forward. The Mercedes inched ahead. Our eyes met in the rearview mirror. "Annika," she said. "On the set last week, she was asking people where she could get hold of a gun."

How to claim your $5.00 rebate:

To be eligible for the $5.00 rebate, you must buy this book and Harley Jane Kozak's new novel, *Dating Is Murder*, at the same time.

Complete this entry form by hand, attach your receipt or proof of purchase, and mail to:

Harley Jane Rebate Offer, Marketing Department
Broadway Books
1745 Broadway
New York, NY 10023

Mail-in entries must be received by September 30, 2005. Broadway Books will refund your $5.00 by check, which will be mailed to the address on this entry form.

All fields marked with ★ are required:
Name★_____ M_____ F_____
Complete Address★_____ Apt. # _____
             (no P.O. Boxes)
City★_____ State★_____ ZIP★_____
Daytime Phone Number★ (____)_____ Birth Date★ ___/___/___
E-Mail Address (used for notification purposes only)_____

TERMS AND CONDITIONS:
Open to legal U.S. residents aged 21 or older at time of purchase. Void where prohibited by law. One rebate per customer. Persons in any of the following categories are not eligible to participate: (a) employees of Random House, Inc.; their parent companies, affiliates, or subsidiaries, or the service agents or contractors of any of the above organizations; (b) suppliers, distributors, and retailers of books; and (c) individuals engaged in the development of, the production or distribution of materials for, or the implementation of, this offer. All claims for the rebate must be received by 11:59 p.m. on Friday September 30, 2005. Claimants assume all risk of lost, late, misdirected, incomplete, illegible, undelivered, or postage-due entries. Rebate checks will be made payable only to the name of the person on the entry form, and will be mailed by first class U.S. mail. SPONSOR: The sponsor of this promotion is The Doubleday Broadway Publishing Group, a Division of Random House, Inc.